"Theft of primary data core components is not permitted. Return the components or your life support will be compromised. Theft of primary data core components is not permitted. . . ."

Val opened her communicator. "Williams to *Shuttlepod One*. Extraction under way. Stand by to detach the moment we're aboard."

"*Bit of a problem, Lieutenant,*" Karthikeyan replied. "*I'm reading a plasma current building in a conduit next to our breach point. It could blow any minute.*"

"Understood. Move, team! Double time!"

Once the team was clear, Williams enacted the next step in Reed's careful plan: She took aim at the central column and blew it apart. Her throat tightened at the knowledge that her action would end the lives of the remaining captives inside. It was a hard step to take, even knowing they were effectively dead already. But it might just save the team's lives, if it cut the station off from the brains that boosted its processing power.

But the announcement continued unabated. "Return the components or your life support will be compromised. Theft of primary data core components . . ." Val cursed. Either the computer had backups, or whatever process had been initiated was running on automatic. Even lobotomized, the station could still kill them.

— STAR TREK —
ENTERPRISE®

RISE OF THE FEDERATION

UNCERTAIN LOGIC

CHRISTOPHER L. BENNETT

Based upon *Star Trek*®
created by Gene Roddenberry
and
Star Trek: Enterprise
created by Rick Berman & Brannon Braga

POCKET BOOKS
New York London Toronto Sydney New Delhi

Pocket Books
A Division of Simon & Schuster, Inc.
1230 Avenue of the Americas
New York, NY 10020

This book is a work of fiction. Any references to historical events, real people, or real places are used fictitiously. Other names, characters, places, and events are products of the author's imagination, and any resemblance to actual events or places or persons, living or dead, is entirely coincidental.

First Pocket Books paperback edition April 2015

POCKET and colophon are registered trademarks of Simon & Schuster, Inc.

For information about special discounts for bulk purchases, please contact Simon & Schuster Special Sales at 1-866-506-1949 or business@simonandschuster.com.

The Simon & Schuster Speakers Bureau can bring authors to your live event. For more information or to book an event, contact the Simon & Schuster Speakers Bureau at 1-866-248-3049 or visit our website at www.simonspeakers.com.

Manufactured in the United States of America

10 9 8 7 6 5 4 3 2 1

ISBN 978-1-4767-7911-9
ISBN 978-1-4767-7912-6 (ebook)

To the memory of Mark Lenard

Logic is a means for discovering truth, not for creating it.

—Surak
Kir'Shara

2165

Prologue

January 6, 2165
TesKahr Central Hospital, Confederacy of Vulcan

T'RIN VALUED THE QUIET SOLITUDE that the data archives afforded during the nocturnal shift. It was an opportune environment for researching her dissertation, away from distractions such as the administrative requests she needed to process during daytime at the hospital or the enthusiasms of her Denobulan roommate at home. Thus, T'Rin allowed herself a moment's twinge of annoyance when a panicked, armed man burst into the otherwise empty study area, brandished his phase pistol toward her, and cried, "Don't move!"

The seemingly Vulcan male then contradicted himself by grabbing her arm and pulling her roughly from her seat, spinning her around to clutch her from behind. He held the weapon against her temple as he dragged her into the archive stacks. "You're coming with me."

She heard approaching footsteps outside the door. Her captor did not seem aware of them as yet, so she spoke to cover the sound. "Would you care to inform me of your reason for undertaking this—"

"Shut up!"

The main door opened, prompting her captor to pull her behind a tier of shelves. Through a slit in the shelving, T'Rin glimpsed the shoulders of a pair of individuals flanking the door, using the frame as cover as they peered inside. One wore the attire of Vulcan Security, while the other, who appeared human, wore a slate-gray tunic with a multicolored circular patch on the upper sleeve and at least one shoulder strap bearing two gold stripes. T'Rin was fairly sure it was a Starfleet uniform.

"Stay out!" cried the gunman. "I have a hostage! I'll kill her if you come any closer!"

"Just take it easy, Temos," the human called. "Look around you. There's nowhere you can go from here. If you harm that woman, it will only make things worse for you."

"I won't let you take me alive! Now, stay back!" It was strange to see such agitation in what looked like a Vulcan face.

"Nobody has to be hurt here, okay? I'd just like a chance to speak to the woman you're holding, if you don't mind."

"I am perfectly capable of speaking for myself," T'Rin informed the Starfleet officer.

"That's good, ma'am. My name's Lieutenant Commander Takashi Kimura. I'm with the *U.S.S. Endeavour*. What's your name?"

"T'Rin of TesKahr," she replied, recognizing the commander's attempt to get her abductor to think of her as a person. "Employee at this hospital."

"Working late tonight?"

"A private research project." She glared at Temos—if that was his real name. "Whose interruption I do not appreciate."

"Enough of this," the gunman barked. "Talk to *me*! You talk to me!"

"I'm just trying to make sure everyone's comfortable."

T'Rin raised her voice before Temos could respond. "Your concern is unnecessary, Commander. You have my leave to do what you must to resolve the situation."

"Shut up!" Temos fired through the door, forcing his

pursuers to duck. He dragged her deeper into the stacks. "Do you *want* me to shoot you?"

"No. But we are in a hospital, so my odds of survival if you do shoot me are better here than nearly anywhere else." She looked him over. "Further, since your deportment belies your Vulcan appearance, I must conclude you are an impostor. Most likely a Malurian infiltrator. Therefore I surmise your familiarity with Vulcan anatomy is limited, further reducing the probability that you could deliver an instantly lethal injury."

"Keep it up and we'll test that!" His burst of anger at her deduction merely confirmed it. The criminal class of the Malurians, known for their skills in disguise and infiltration, had been prominent in the news since they, along with other criminal organizations allied with the Orion Syndicate, had been implicated in efforts to manipulate last year's election for President of the United Federation of Planets, in favor of those factions supporting the weakening and, at the greatest extreme, the dissolution of the federal state in favor of planetary autonomy. Following that discovery, most of the Planetarist factions had voluntarily cooperated in weeding out infiltrators within their own ranks—save for Vulcan's own Anti-revisionist movement, led by Professor T'Nol, who had fervently denied even the possibility that her group had been compromised. Which, in T'Rin's view, had made it the most likely candidate for continued infiltration—a view that the current situation strongly reinforced.

"We have all the exits covered, Temos!" Kimura called. "You're not gaining anything this way."

Giving up the search for an exit, the disguised infiltrator pushed her to the floor in a short dead-end space between two tiers of shelving, then stood nervous vigil at its open end. "I'll take you all with me if I have to! I'm not afraid to die!"

The Starfleet man's response was careful, calming. "Honestly, Temos, it seems to me that what you're doing now is about trying to stay alive. Now, I'd like to help you figure out a way to do that."

"That would be agreeable for all concerned," T'Rin opined.

Temos glared back at her. "Do you never stop talking?" She merely studied him from where she sat on the floor, arms folded. "I just need time to think. Got to sort this out."

Though he seemed to be muttering to himself, his agitation made him loud enough that Kimura heard him. "That's good. Let's think this through."

"Don't tell me what to do!"

"I just want to help you figure this out for yourself, Temos. There are a couple of things you might want to consider."

He hesitated. "Like what?"

"Let me ask you something first. What reason would an agent like yourself have for sacrificing his life? It's to keep anyone from finding proof of Malurian involvement, isn't it?"

"You don't know what you're talking about!"

"I've seen how far the Raldul alignment will go to keep that secret. I once saw a Malurian leader kill dozens of his own people to try to keep us from discovering who they really were. It was ruthless. He didn't give a moment's thought to his people, didn't give them a chance to survive."

"You're lying! Garos cares about his men. He wouldn't sacrifice us unless he had to. All those men understood that." He froze, realizing he'd said too much.

But the human didn't acknowledge the slip. His goal was clearly to put Temos at ease, not make him feel more trapped. "I can understand being willing to sacrifice yourself for your cause. But what cause would be served by your death, Temos?

We already know you're Malurian. We have the evidence to prove it. You see, we knew what materials went into making Malurian masks. My ship's doctor, Phlox, figured that out. So we notified the manufacturers and vendors of those materials to be alert to certain types of orders. And when you ordered the materials for that new mask you're wearing, the one you had to make to infiltrate the hospital staff, they notified Vulcan Security. That's what led us here to you.

"And we know you're linked to the Anti-revisionists, Temos. We found the correspondence on your apartment's computer. So you see, you've got no secrets to preserve anymore. And no mission either," Kimura went on, sounding almost apologetic. "Now that we know you were trying to plant false records, there's no point in trying to hide it anymore. You'd be killing yourself, and an innocent woman, for no reason. Is that really what your alignment would want? Would that be good for Maluria?"

Temos shook his head, almost laughing. "Oh, this is insane." He sagged against the shelves to T'Rin's right. "I shouldn't even be here," he said quietly, addressing her almost as a confidant. "I should've left months ago. Garos wanted to pull me out, but the damned professor wouldn't let him."

"Professor T'Nol?" T'Rin interpreted. "The Anti-revisionist leader?"

"Oh, she assured Garos that she'd just keep me in reserve, let me lay low until the heat faded. But she couldn't wait." He made a sharp exhalation that sounded paradoxically humorous. "She made it all sound so logical, even though I knew it was a mistake to risk exposure this soon. And now look where I am!"

"If you find the professor's objective so irrational, why

endanger yourself? Why not merely surrender to the authorities?"

"I can't turn myself in! Can't risk being interrogated about my alignment."

"Temos, are you still there?" Kimura called.

"Quiet! I'm trying to think!"

"Okay, but I want to keep this conversation going, all right?"

"Commander," T'Rin spoke up, "I believe Mister Temos and I are having a productive conversation of our own. But I would like to consult you on a certain point that may be relevant."

The human paused. "Anything I can do to help."

"In your opinion as a security expert, what do you think Mister Temos's employers would do if they were concerned with the possibility of his capture? Would they rely solely on the expectation that he would self-immolate?" She held Temos's eyes as she asked this.

"No, ma'am, I don't think so. If I were in their place, I'd have long since nullified any intelligence he had. Changed access codes and procedures, relocated outposts, and so on."

"I see. Then in that case, Temos would not be protecting his alignment by committing suicide?"

"I don't think so. In fact—Temos, are you still listening?"

The gunman held T'Rin's eyes, but responded to Kimura. "I'm here."

"You said Garos cares about his men," the human said. "That he wouldn't sacrifice you for no reason. If that's true, then he wouldn't want you to do this. Now, what you need to ask yourself is: Can you say the same about Professor T'Nol? Is it worth doing this for her?"

After a long, thoughtful silence, Temos informed the

security contingent that he was coming out. He placed his weapon on the floor and allowed himself to be taken into custody. Kimura personally saw to T'Rin, thanking her for what he called her brave assistance. Unfortunately, he also insisted on taking her in for questioning and a medical examination, rather than simply letting her get back to her studies as she desired. As Kimura led her out of the archives, she contemplated that she might need to find a better refuge from all these distractions.

January 7, 2165
Administration Tower, Central ShiKahr, Vulcan

Admiral Jonathan Archer watched the news feed on First Minister Kuvak's office monitor with considerable satisfaction. On the screen, Professor T'Nol, the gaunt and severe-featured leader of the Anti-revisionist faction, was making an unconvincing attempt to explain away the testimony of the captured Malurian infiltrator. The polling figures displayed at the bottom of the screen (helpfully in both Vulcan and Terran notation, though Archer was getting better at reading the former) made it clear that support for the Anti-revisionists was crumbling with her every sentence.

"I still find it astonishing that T'Nol believed she could succeed in this plan," Kuvak said from behind his desk, clasping his hands within the shroud of his loose, flowing sleeves. The first minister of the Confederacy of Vulcan was an older man with white-gray hair framing a sour, rounded face. In the eleven years since the rediscovery of the *Kir'Shara*—the long-lost, firsthand writings of Surak, the father of Vulcan philosophy—had triggered a planetwide reformation, Kuvak had grown in serenity and self-control compared to the easily agitated High Command minister he had been when Archer had first met him. But now, Archer could hear a definite edge of irritation and contempt in Kuvak's curt, nasal voice. "Even if her operative had succeeded in planting the falsified data in my birth records, the premise that I was actually a human agent in disguise would never have been credible to the Vulcan people."

"To most of the Vulcan people, perhaps," Captain T'Pol replied from her seat alongside Archer. "But there are many who would welcome any opportunity to accuse and discredit you, First Minister, and by extension the Syrannite movement as a whole."

"On Earth," Archer said, "we used to call it 'firing up the base.'"

"It is not logical," Kuvak said, shaking his head. "If one must deliberately falsify evidence to support one's case, that should be sufficient proof that one's case is erroneous and in need of modification."

"But we have seen such behavior from Vulcans before," T'Pol reminded him.

Kuvak nodded, recalling the events that had initially brought the three of them together. "T'Nol did serve as an adviser to Administrator V'Las during his tenure," he affirmed. "It is reasonable to expect her to be similarly capable of . . . dissembling." V'Las, as Archer recalled well, had lied without hesitation or remorse in order to destroy his political enemies and agitate for an unnecessary war against Andoria—almost causing the deaths of Archer and T'Pol in the former effort and the entire crew of *Enterprise* in the latter. It had been the last gasp of the old, militaristic Vulcan before the *Kir'Shara* reforms had ushered in a new, more enlightened regime.

"Luckily, she was more inept at it than V'Las was," Archer

told him in a tone of amused satisfaction. "She really over-played her hand this time, and it's cost her the whole game."

"Quite so, if I follow your metaphor correctly." The first minister turned to T'Pol, who cut a crisp figure as always in her avocado-green command tunic (adorned with the *Endeavour* mission patch on the right sleeve and the golden arrow-head of Earth's space service on the breast) and close-fitting black trousers. "I particularly wish to commend your Lieu-tenant Commander Kimura," Kuvak told her, "for persuading the Malurian agent to surrender peacefully. Temos's testimony should discredit the Anti-revisionist movement once and for all—and without T'Nol's leadership, the remaining anti-reform factions are too small and divided to create significant difficulties."

"I shall convey your gratitude to Mister Kimura," T'Pol told him. "Although he was trained as a combat officer, I have found him to be capable of considerable wisdom and restraint." Archer chose to ignore the implied *for a human.*

"I'd say this is a good day for everyone," Archer said—then nodded toward the screen, where T'Nol had just ended her statement and was retreating from the reporters' questions. "Well, except her. From what Temos says, the Malurians, the Orions, and their allies have pulled out all their operatives in the Planetarist movement. That means we can have a proper debate about Federation law and policy without outside forces trying to sabotage the process. We can disagree honestly now—and that's what makes a democracy work."

Residential district, ShiKahr

Professor T'Nol suppressed a surge of irritation as she re-flected on the disastrous press conference just concluded.

Irritation would be an admission of vulnerability. It was not her position that was at fault, but the mentality of the masses—so blinded by the propaganda of the Syrannites and their human allies, so distracted and confused by the ambiguities of the experiential world, that they could not see the truth revealed by pure logic alone. It was unfortunate—she reflected for what was not the first time—that Surak had phrased the text of the *Kir'Shara* in a way that could be so easily misrepresented by those favoring fashionable delusions such as pacifism and the equality of non-Vulcan races. In their folly, they ignored the clarification provided by the *Analects*—the writings of Surak's disciples, who had refined and expanded upon his words and thus brought forth their true meaning.

Thus reassured of the purity of her own logic, T'Nol was able to calm herself. Of course it was not she who was at fault, for she reasoned by absolute logic, untainted by the complications of the everyday world. The cause was just as valid despite the attempt of the Malurians to subvert it to their ends. That was why she had welcomed Temos into the movement's ranks once she had become aware of him, recognizing that she could use his skills and resources to assist her in reconstructing the appearance of reality to bring out its deeper truths. That Kuvak was not, in fact, biologically human was beside the point; the purer truth was that he and the Syrannites advanced a human agenda to undermine Vulcan's strength and autonomy.

Granted, the failure and exposure of Temos was a setback. T'Nol should have known better than to place such faith in a non-Vulcan. And his superior in the Raldul alignment, Dular Garos, showed no inclination to assist T'Nol in controlling the damage Temos had caused the movement. *"I anticipated the consequences of this mistake as soon as you made it, Professor,"* the

Malurian crime lord told her during the brief communication he had allowed. *"I have already done all I could to insulate Raldul from any consequences. But the consequences to you and your party are richly deserved."* The brown eyes in his scaled gray face examined her disapprovingly before he finished: *"You are useless to Maluria now, so from this point on—if anyone asks—I do not know you."* The screen went dark.

Attempts to contact her other partners in the traditionalist movement—the High Command loyalists, the Mental Integrity Coalition, and the rest—proved similarly fruitless. Just because the surface facts now pointed a certain way, they allowed themselves to be swayed from the purity of the logic she had thought they shared with her. They all made statements couched in the language of logic, of course; but logic was always right, so how could a logically deduced position ever change? They had given in to mere politics and left her and her followers—those who had not deserted the movement— as the only true defenders of logic left on Vulcan.

Thus it encouraged T'Nol when a signal came in to her headquarters unbidden. Perhaps she still had some supporters after all. But the signal was audio only, its sender's information blocked. *"You've miscalculated badly, T'Nol,"* a deep voice intoned. For a moment she thought it was Garos again, but the new voice was sharper and rougher. *"Anyone else might be tempted to give up. But I know you—nothing will get you to change your mind."*

"Who is this?" the professor demanded.

"I'd rather not say over an open channel. But don't tell me you don't recognize my voice, old friend."

Even as he spoke, she noted the familiar timbre and cadence—but the conclusion they suggested was most illogical. "It cannot be. You—the person in question is deceased."

"Presumed deceased. A presumption I find it convenient not to correct.

But now the time has come to reveal myself to you. And eventually the time will come for the rest of Vulcan—and its Federation masters—to know it as well."

"If you are who you claim, then your assistance will be most beneficial. But why did you not come to the movement's aid before our disgrace?"

"Because your disgrace is precisely what gives us freedom to act. Now that Archer and the Federation believe they have rooted out the last of the infiltrators, they will grow complacent. And when we strike from another direction, they will not see it for what it is."

Her doubts about her caller's identity fell away. Proof was not needed; only logic revealed truth, and it was logical that he would come to her aid at her moment of greatest need, thereby ensuring her inevitable victory. "What is it you wish me to do?"

"For now, maintain a low profile. Allow the movement to appear to disperse, to fade into irrelevancy as they expect—but keep them ready to serve when they are needed. When the time is right, I will call on your aid and theirs to carry out my strategy."

"To discredit the reforms? Expose the human corruption behind them?"

"That and more, T'Nol. We shall turn the Kir'Shara itself against the Syrannites who revere it—and thereby bring down not only their government, but Jonathan Archer himself and his traitorous lackey T'Pol.

"And once they are out of the way, we will lead Vulcan back to its true martial glory."

1

"JUST LOOK AT THOSE STARS."

Lieutenant Commander Travis Mayweather sighed in satisfaction at the sheer unfamiliarity of the star patterns outside the viewports of *Pioneer*'s mess hall. "Uncharted territory," he went on. "It's been a while."

"Well, of course it's been charted," said Doctor Therese Liao from her seat across the circular table. "I mean, we can *see* it all from Federation space. We have telescopes. It's not like there are any horizons to sail over out here."

Mayweather threw the diminutive, middle-aged chief medical officer a sour look. "You know what I mean. We may know the lay of the land, but we don't know who lives out here. We haven't mapped the planets and systems in detail. And that's not even counting what we might find in the dark spaces between the stars," he went on in more dramatic tones, shifting into storytelling mode. "Rogue planets, derelict ships, subspace anomalies, you name it. Why, once on *Enterprise*, we were intercepted by this huge ship that swallowed us whole like a manta ray devouring its prey. Its crew turned out to be—"

"Non-corporeal 'wisps' who wanted to snatch your bodies. You told me that one before," Liao interposed.

He heard the disbelief in the older woman's tone. "This wasn't one of my ghost stories, Therese. It's in the logs!"

"I'll believe that when you explain to me what creatures without bodies needed a starship for."

"They couldn't live in space."

"Then how did they operate the thing?"

"I never got around to asking, okay? The *point* is," he went on with a chuckle, "we're finally out where we belong. No more experimental upgrades, no more diplomatic missions to known worlds, no more follow-ups of old pre-war surveys. Just *this*."

He spread his arms to take in the vista beyond the port. This sector of the galaxy had been inaccessible to humans and their neighbors in the past, blocked by Romulan patrol fleets and Vertian experimental raids in the intervening space. But now the Romulans were confined behind the Neutral Zone and the Vertians had agreed to cease experimentation on sapient beings, enabling safe passage to the territories beyond. The members of the expansive Rigelian trading community were already clamoring to seek out commercial opportunities in the new reaches, and since Rigel was now a brand spanking new member of the United Federation of Planets, it was up to Starfleet to serve as their vanguard. Thus, Admiral Archer had assigned *Pioneer* to live up to its name. "Going where no man has gone before," Mayweather finished.

Liao gave him a sidelong look. "Cochrane stole that line from Davida Rossi, you know." She furrowed her brows. "Or was it D. F. Black? A Boomer, anyway."

"Rossi and Black were the generation before the Boomers," he reminded her.

"But they made us possible."

"So did Cochrane."

"Until he sold out the ECS and shared his Warp Five plans with UESPA instead."

Mayweather smirked, knowing Liao wouldn't be in Starfleet if she sincerely clung to the old rivalry between the "Space Boomers," the generations of humans born and raised on Earth Cargo Services freighters, and the government-run United Earth Space Probe Agency—a rivalry that had only intensified when UESPA founded its Starfleet arm and brought stronger regulation to the spaces the Boomers had grown used to traversing freely. But these days, now that the spread of Warp 5 and Warp 7 engines was rapidly rendering the Boomers' slow-paced lifestyle obsolete, more and more freighter natives were following Mayweather into Starfleet, Liao among them. Sometimes Mayweather lamented the end of that era, but he wouldn't miss the insularity of thought that had often come with it.

"It used to be us, you know," she went on. "We were the ones who pushed out the frontiers, made the first contacts."

"We're still here, Therese. And not just you and me."

"But we're sharing it with rock jockeys," she said, using an old-fashioned Boomer term for planet-dwellers. "Earthers and Centaurians, even aliens now. It's not the same."

"It doesn't matter who makes the discoveries," he said, "as long as they get made."

She threw him a sidelong look. "That attitude is why you aren't sitting in a captain's chair yet."

Before he could formulate a response, the intercom sounded. *"Bridge to Commander Mayweather,"* came Captain Reed's crisp, English-accented voice.

The first officer excused himself to Liao and made his way to the panel by the door, pressing the intercom button. "Mayweather here."

"I want you on the bridge at once, Travis," Malcolm Reed ordered. *"We've detected an object nearby with a disturbingly familiar sensor signature."*

"Familiar how, sir?"

"I'd rather not say until we're sure. But if it's what I suspect . . . well, you'd better just get up here."

The first glimpse of the gray-hued space station on the bridge viewscreen had been enough to confirm Malcolm Reed's suspicions about its sensor signature. Its cylindrical spacedocks made of expandable latticework, like metallic versions of Chinese finger puzzles, were a dead giveaway. It was a sight he'd hoped never to see again, but had long expected that he might.

"Oh, hell," breathed Travis Mayweather as soon as he emerged from the bridge turbolift. Reed could see the same instant recognition in the eyes of his handsome, dark-featured first officer—along with a touch of dread. "I hoped we'd seen the last of these things."

Reed studied him. "So you agree it's the same technology as the automated repair station we encountered aboard *Enterprise*?"

"Believe me, I'm not about to forget that station," Mayweather replied. Reed nodded grimly. The station *Pioneer* now approached was larger than the one they remembered, with a more substantial, multilevel central body connecting to two stacked docking lattices on either side instead of one; but there was no mistaking the shared design lineage, not only of the docks but of the core module at the station's heart, a sphere bisected at its equator by a seven-sided polygonal slab. Worse, one lattice was slightly distended to accommodate a ship of an unfamiliar, spindle-shaped design. Someone was docked there.

At the science station, Lieutenant Reynaldo Sangupta looked back and forth between his superior officers with curiosity on his youthful, bronze-skinned face. "Is there something the rest of us should know, sirs?"

"It was about a year into *Enterprise*'s mission," Mayweather told him. "We'd just had our first encounter with the Romulans and taken heavy damage in a cloaked minefield. We were deep in unknown space, stuck at low warp and years away from a friendly port, but a passing Tellarite freighter gave us coordinates for an automated repair station."

"Hold on, Travis," Reed cautioned. "Right now I think it's more urgent to tell our story to whoever's aboard that ship."

"Good point," the first officer replied. "Grev, hail the alien ship."

"Aye, sir," affirmed the chubby-faced Tellarite at the communications station.

"Translation might be tricky," Sangupta advised. "That ship has—wow—a hydrogen-fluorine atmosphere at a temperature of minus twenty Celsius. That's a kind of life we've never encountered before, so who knows how their brains process language?"

"He's right," Grev said. "I'm getting a reply, but the translator's struggling with it. It may take a few minutes for our computer and their computer to hash out a translation model together."

"That makes sense," Mayweather said while Grev did what he could to assist the computer. "When we first encountered the repair station, it had . . . I think it was a helium atmosphere inside, much colder than this one. But once it scanned us, it quickly adapted to Earth-like conditions." He frowned. "All the better to bait the trap."

At the tactical station, Lieutenant Valeria Williams looked up. "Trap, sir?" asked the auburn-haired armory officer, instantly alert.

"Captain," Grev interposed, "I think we have a working translation now. I can give you the alien captain."

Reed nodded and rose to greet his counterpart. "On-screen."

The face that appeared before him was a narrow, red-hued ovoid dominated by large, faceted eyes. A small, beakish mouth was situated midway between them, and thin breathing vents fluttered softly on either side of a slender neck. The shoulders and upper portions of four long, narrow arms were visible, two in front and two behind. *"Greetings extended,"* the captain said in a piping voice. *"Know me as Rethne and my vessel as* Velelev."

"Our greetings as well, Captain Rethne. I'm Captain Malcolm Reed of the *U.S.S. Pioneer,* representing the United Federation of Planets."

The alien tilted its head. *"Unity of planets. Is this a nation's name or simply an expression of kinship?"*

Reed thought it over for a moment. "It's the first—but we like to think it conveys the second as well."

"Cleverly answered! We are pleasantly met. Though from our scans, it seems your atmosphere would not suit the conditions in the trading post."

"Trading post?" The captain frowned. "So it's not just a repair station?"

"Ah, I perceive that you have met the Ware before."

"The Ware?"

"Automated facilities such as this," Rethne clarified. *"My people, the Menaik, have only mastered the warping of space less than my lifetime ago, but we have encountered several such stations, and met others who tell us of more. It is they who name them Ware."*

Reed and Mayweather exchanged a look. "They told you about these stations—but not about the danger?" the captain asked.

Captain Rethne leaned forward. *"Danger? The Ware stations are eminently useful! Repairs, supplies, services, a haven for weary travelers, all these things they provide."*

"But at a steep price," Mayweather put in.

The Menaik turned to face him. *"Greetings extended. You also speak for* Pioneer?"

"This is my first officer, Commander Travis Mayweather," Reed explained.

"Thank you, Captain. Yes, Commander, the Ware stations drive hard bargains for their services, but they are more than worth the price."

"The price is a lot higher than you think," Mayweather said with feeling, stepping closer to the screen. "Tell me: Have you lost any members of your crew at one of these stations?"

Rethne's head lowered. *"On this visit, we have not. But six weeks ago, on our last visit here, a passenger went where she should not have been. Ground-dwellers do not understand the hazards of space, and sometimes make fatal errors. Still, the fault is mine for not tending my charge more carefully."*

Mayweather spoke urgently. "Captain . . . that passenger is probably still alive, and still on the station."

Rethne shot upright, all four arms extended in shock. *"How can this be? Her body has already been returned to TeMenaik and consecrated to the Core of Creation."*

"I'm sorry to tell you this, Captain, but that wasn't her body."

"You know that the Ware stations can create perfect replicas of any organic or inorganic matter, correct?" Reed put in.

"This is so. It is what makes them so enormously useful."

Mayweather resumed the narrative at Reed's nod. "Over a dozen years ago, Captain Reed and I served on a ship called *Enterprise*. We came across one of these stations when we needed repairs. While we were there . . . I was abducted. I was beamed aboard the station and replaced by an exact replica of my own body—exact, but dead. At first, my crewmates thought I'd been killed by an energy discharge during the repairs. But our ship's doctor had recently inoculated me with a kind of microbe that should've thrived on that kind of energy, except that all the microbes he found in the duplicate body were dead. He realized the station's replicating mechanism had created an exact double to make my crew *think* I was dead."

"Why would it do this?"

Reed picked up the tale. "We found that out when we broke into the station's control center to rescue Travis." He hesitated. "Captain . . . we found him, along with a number of other captives, hooked in to the central data core. The station was tapping into their brains to augment its memory and processing power. One or two had been there for months, others for a few years, some even longer."

"And the longer they'd been there," Mayweather added, "the more brain damage they'd sustained. Eventually they just . . . burned out. So every so often, the station must've preyed on another crew, taken one of their personnel—and made it look like an accident, complete with a body, so they'd have no idea what had happened. But I'm living proof of what these stations are really doing." He visibly suppressed a shudder. "I don't remember any of it firsthand. It kept me sedated the whole time. But I saw my . . . my 'corpse' after they rescued me. I know what would've happened to me if it hadn't been for a really attentive doctor. And I still have nightmares about it."

Rethne was stunned. *"Why? Why would the Ware extend such benevolence and then do such a thing to innocent people?"*

Innocent indeed, Reed thought. He saw in Rethne the same naïve optimism he had seen in Jonathan Archer in those glory days of pure exploration before the Xindi had attacked Earth and changed things forever. It saddened him to be the one giving Rethne her rude awakening. But better she find out this way than through more violent means. "The benevolence is the lure," Reed told her. "The stations need a steady supply of brains, so they make themselves inviting."

"But if they only use the added computing power to create the things that draw us to them . . . then where is the purpose in it?"

"We don't know what drives the people that created these things," Mayweather told Rethne. "But what we do know is that your passenger is probably on that station right now. And if she was taken as recently as you say, it's probably not too late to save her."

Reed could tell that Mayweather was already identifying with this alien stranger, based on nothing beyond their common victimization. Still, Reed wasn't about to begrudge him that sympathy. "Captain, we'd be happy to assist in a rescue operation. We've faced one of these stations before and beaten it."

"My ship is merely a commerce vessel," Rethne said. *"None of us are fighters. If there is any chance of retrieving my lost charge, then I will gratefully pay a high price for her return."*

"We ask no payment, Captain Rethne. We're explorers, new to this part of space. If we can start our relationship with the Menaik people by earning their friendship, that will be payment enough."

"Your generosity is humbling, Captain Reed. Please . . . do what you can for her."

"I will, Captain Rethne. We'll contact you when we're ready to go in. *Pioneer* out."

When the screen image reverted to the shot of the station, Mayweather turned to his captain and smiled. "You're getting pretty good at this diplomatic stuff, sir," he said.

"That's as may be," Reed replied with a faint smile. "But

this situation calls for falling back on my old skill set, don't you think?"

Mayweather nodded grimly. "Absolutely. Let's save whoever we can, then blow that damn thing out of the sky."

Ware trading post

Valeria Williams had long been impressed by Captain Reed's skill for advance planning. *Pioneer*'s armory officer was more the improvisational type herself, preferring to keep her plans loose and adapt to circumstances as her gut led her. But under Reed, she'd learned that anticipating problems and developing advance contingency plans could make things much easier for a security team in the field—or at least provide a solid foundation on which to build her improvisations. She knew her captain prided himself on the time, thought, and hard work he poured into readying himself and his crew for whatever they might face on the frontier.

But Reed's level of preparation for liberating captives from a Ware automated station exceeded his normal standards by a considerable margin. Apparently he'd been calculating strategies on and off for a dozen years since *Enterprise*'s encounter with the repair station, always expecting that there would be others. "After all," he had explained back on *Pioneer* during the briefing, "that station was designed to adapt to a wide range of environments. It had to be the work of a widely traveled interstellar civilization."

Indeed, the captain had revealed that during the Earth-Romulan War, two other Starfleet vessels had reported encounters with stations believed to be of the same origin, both in Romulan-controlled territory. Captain Shosetsu of *Yorktown*, remembering *Enterprise*'s encounter, had refused to permit his damaged task force to dock at one such station for repairs, instead ordering its total destruction to ensure the enemy could not use it. The contingencies of war had required him to forgo any attempt to rescue its captives. Later in the war, the *Eberswalde*, one of the old *Ganges*-class ships, had detected wreckage consistent with another automated station on long-range sensors, showing Romulan weapon signatures. It suggested that Shosetsu's fears were unfounded, though Williams wondered how the Romulans had caught on to the stations' predatory nature. Perhaps the number of fatal "accidents" had simply provoked their inherent paranoia.

But forewarned was forearmed, so Reed had his crew briefed and ready to act within a couple of hours following contact with *Velelev*. The first step, once Captain Rethne had retrieved her crew and undocked, was to bring *Pioneer* in on a docking trajectory and hail the trading post. As Reed predicted, the station subjected *Pioneer* to a thorough, penetrating scan and began to reconfigure itself, adjusting one of its spacedocks to fit *Pioneer*'s half-saucer hull and nacelle fins while replacing the cryogenic hydrogen-fluorine mix inside with an Earth-like atmosphere and temperature. The station transmitted no greeting, but the welcome was clear enough.

Yet *Pioneer* did not accept the invitation. The plan was to strike hard and fast, assuming the station would be at its most vulnerable during this all-too-brief period of transition. The ship veered off and opened fire with photonic torpedoes, targeting the narrow gangways that connected the docks to the main module. The original station had attacked *Enterprise* using the same robotic arms and cutting beams it had used to repair the vessel earlier, so now Reed sought to neutralize those defenses by severing the docks completely.

At the same time, Williams and her tactical team dropped

from *Pioneer*'s launch bay in a shuttlepod, following a trajectory toward the central core, letting the station's own bulk shield the pod from the shrapnel and radiation of the torpedo hits. Ensign Karthikeyan flipped the pod over, extending its dorsal docking collar—a specialized unit developed late in the Romulan War, though never successfully deployed against a Romulan ship—to seal against the upper hull of the slab surrounding the central sphere, whereupon it detonated shaped charges to breach the station's hull. Once the seal was confirmed secure, Williams led her team—oxygen-masked against any atmospheric tricks the station might deploy—into the docking collar. Karthikeyan had already turned off the gravity inside the pod, so that they didn't have to contend with a 180-degree flip.

Once Williams passed through the jagged hole, the station's gravity caught her and she dropped to the deck, rolling to come up on her feet. Clifton Detzel came close on her heels, the crewman moving as swiftly as always despite his burly frame. Sleek, ebony-dark Ensign Katrina Ndiaye followed, rolling to her feet with a dancer's grace and reaching up to aid second-class crewman Julia Guzman in her descent. Finally, Crewman Ediz Kemal lowered his lanky but solid frame to the deck.

The team held their particle rifles at the ready as they moved forward—Williams in the lead, Detzel and Ndiaye flanking the field medic Guzman, and Kemal guarding the rear—but so far the only response the station made to their forced entry was an automated announcement: "Any damage to these facilities will be charged to your vessel. Any damage to these facilities . . ."

Williams flipped open her communicator. "Williams to *Pioneer*. Entry successful. No resistance so far."

"Acknowledged," Reed replied. *"Transporter interference field engaged."*

"Understood. We are proceeding." Transporter use for live subjects had been restricted to emergencies since the discovery of the cumulative genetic and cellular damage they caused. But Captain Reed had found a novel interpretation of "emergency use": *Pioneer*'s transporter was blanketing the station with a high-gain, unfocused scanning beam in the hopes that it would interfere with the station's own internal transporters and prevent it from beaming intruders away. In *Enterprise*'s original encounter, the repair station had only beamed intruders back aboard the ship itself; but Ware programming might respond to a more aggressive intrusion by beaming the interlopers into space, or worse. Reed wasn't willing to risk that—though it was actually Williams and her team, she reflected, who were gambling on the effectiveness of the transporter interference.

Yet the team made its way through the station's clean white corridors unmolested, save by the polite hectoring of the Ware computer's mellifluous voice. Their path, based on Captain Rethne's information about the trading post's layout, took them through a sterile, white chamber adorned with circular metal tables and low-backed chairs—a place Williams never would have pegged as a recreation area if not for prior testimonials. Apparently the white circular platforms in the tables were matter replication units able to create any nonliving item on request. "Anyone want to order a quick snack?" Detzel joked as they made their way to the far door.

A chiming sound from one of the replication units heralded the materialization of a dome-shaped metal object—which fired an intense energy beam at Detzel and turned him into a glowing cloud of plasma. The heat and concussion of his sudden vaporization knocked the whole team back, and that was the least of its impact upon them.

But grief would have to wait. Williams channeled her fury into action, leaping forward just in time to dodge a second beam. With no cover beyond the flimsy tables and chairs, she turned her particle rifle onto the beam generator and blasted it mercilessly. But a second dome was already materializing on another table. Clearly the transporter interference didn't prevent the replication units from working. Were they on a different frequency, or was it because they operated over such short range? Well, that was for Rey Sangupta to sort out later. Her job was to shoot the things.

She made it to the far door, but it would not open, and the dome's emitter was swinging to bear on her. She stood boldly before the doors and leapt aside just as the emitter fired. By the time Ndiaye and Kemal's cover fire blasted the second dome, the door had been mostly vaporized, and Williams ducked through. She and Kemal covered the room from their respective entrances while Ndiaye escorted Guzman through, her own rifle blasting at the tables. In time, every table had been reduced to a smoking pile of scrap, and Kemal was able to make it through unscathed.

Well, physically unscathed. "Damn it!" he cursed, followed by *"Siktir!"* and a few other Turkish words the translator discreetly left alone. He and Detzel had been an item for a while and had remained close friends afterward. "What are these damned things? Why do they do this to people?"

"Focus, Crewman!" Williams barked. "We secure the hostage, then we blow this goddamned station out of space."

It was what Kemal needed to hear. Setting his jaw, he gave Williams a nod. The remaining team members moved forward with renewed focus and vigilance.

Soon they reached the corridor adjacent to the data core at the heart of the central sphere. According to Reed, the walls to the restricted core could be blown out by a simple phase pistol blast, so particle rifles should make short work of them—and did. Williams led the team through the breach, rifle raised against any possible threat. But as with Reed's *Enterprise* experience, the only response they met was another repeating announcement: "Incursion detected in primary data core. Vacate this section or your vessel will be compromised."

Which vessel? Williams wondered. *Pioneer* was clear of the station and there were no more robotic arms to attack the shuttle. It seemed an empty threat.

The station's public areas presented a façade of meticulously clean sophistication, but the data core looked cruder by centuries, dark and dingy with antiquated pipes along the walls. But Williams could spare little attention for the technology, as her eye was drawn inexorably to the bodies. Nearly two dozen aliens, most but not all humanoid, lay motionless on several tiers of slabs suspended from a framework of dull golden metal. Their heads and feet, where present, hung out beyond the slabs so that they almost seemed to be floating, adding to the macabre nature of the scene. Metallic devices with red and green status lights were attached to their heads—interfacing their brains with the data core, according to the *Enterprise* crew's analysis—and tangles of intravenous tubing connected their limbs to the life-support machinery in the surrounding walls as well as to the central processor, a slender, black-framed column rising to the ceiling and radiating white light from within. By itself, the column would have seemed harmless, if vaguely ominous, like an antiquated device for electrocuting insects. But those tubes linking it to the surrounding bodies gave it a vampiric quality, filling Williams with revulsion.

Julia Guzman moved efficiently through the chamber, ignoring the Ware voice's repetitive warnings as she scanned the bodies. "They're all in varying states of neurological deterioration. Most of them are all but dead, sustained only by these tubes and neurostimulators."

"Why leave them in place, then?" Ndiaye asked with an angry grimace. "Why not at least let them rest in peace?"

"This machine doesn't care about any of that," Williams said. "It's just using them as external drives."

"I know. But why wait so long to . . . to swap them out for new ones?"

"Leave the whys to Rey and the captain. Julia, where's the Menaik captive? And is there anyone else intact enough to be recoverable?"

"Over here," Guzman said to the former question. The Menaik wasn't hard to spot; due to her fluorine-based biochemistry, she was contained in a translucent polymer sac of some sort. According to Guzman's scanner, it was inflated with a Menaik-suitable atmosphere and kept chilled to minus twelve Celsius, warm for a Menaik but survivable.

"Can you detach this sac from the rest of the equipment without letting the fluorine out?" If the fluorine reacted with the moisture in the air, the resultant corrosive gas would be dangerous despite their breathing masks.

"I think so, but it'll take a minute."

"Fast as you can, Julia," she ordered. "We seem secure for now, but let's take no chances." Williams quashed the fantasy that arose in her mind: The nearly dead bodies rising from their slabs to attack the team, grisly marionettes animated by commands sent through the interface devices. She reminded herself that most of these victims' muscles and nervous systems were too atrophied to let them move at all, even if the

Ware core did have some means of controlling them. *I'll never forgive Rey for making me watch those zombie movies.*

"Lieutenant," Kemal called. He indicated another captive across from the Menaik, a diminutive biped with vaguely canine features framed by long purple fur. "This one's reading a fair amount of brain damage and muscle atrophy, but he might be able to recover."

Kemal had some field-medic training of his own, so he should know what he was talking about. Still, this species was totally unfamiliar. "Are you sure?" Williams asked him. "We have no idea—"

"We have to take the chance, sir. So all this means something."

All this—Detzel. Williams nodded. "Do it."

They found no other aliens that showed any signs of higher consciousness remaining. Reed had expected no less, which was why he hadn't sent a larger team. Still, two lives hardly seemed enough to be worth Clifton Detzel's sacrifice.

Williams chastised herself for the thought. Even a single life was invaluable. That was why losing Detzel hurt so much.

Soon, Kemal had freed the canid alien and slung it over his shoulder in a fireman's carry. Guzman completed liberating the Menaik's support sac moments later, and she and Ndiaye hefted it between them. "No telling how long this will hold," the medic said.

"Come on." The lieutenant led her team through the breached bulkhead into the corridor. Once out, she registered that the PA announcement had changed:

"Theft of primary data core components is not permitted. Return the components or your life support will be compromised. Theft of primary data core components is not permitted. . . ."

Val opened her communicator. "Williams to *Shuttlepod One*. Extraction under way. Stand by to detach the moment we're aboard."

"Bit of a problem, Lieutenant," Karthikeyan replied. *"I'm reading a plasma current building in a conduit next to our breach point. It could blow any minute."*

"Understood. Move, team! Double time!"

Once the team was clear, Williams enacted the next step in Reed's careful plan: She took aim at the central column and blew it apart. Her throat tightened at the knowledge that her action would end the lives of the remaining captives inside. It was a hard step to take, even knowing they were effectively dead already. But it might just save the team's lives, if it cut the station off from the brains that boosted its processing power.

But the announcement continued unabated. "Return the components or your life support will be compromised. Theft of primary data core components . . ." Val cursed. Either the computer had backups, or whatever process had been initiated was running on automatic. Even lobotomized, the station could still kill them.

Once they passed the shattered recreation area, that threat became real. The lights grew blindingly bright, and searingly hot gases began pouring into the corridor. The team still had their oxygen masks on, but the heat burned Williams's exposed skin and her ears popped painfully from the rapid pressure increase. "Carbon dioxide," Kemal called. "Traces of sulfur dioxide! Pressure at three atmospheres and rising fast, temperature too! This place'll be Venusian in minutes!"

"You're kidding!" Guzman called. "Don't tell me there are aliens who can live in Venusian conditions!"

"*We* can't," Williams barked. "So cut the chatter and move!"

Soon they reached the extraction point, but lifting the

rescued aliens and themselves into the pod one by one was excruciatingly slow going, even with Karthikeyan keeping both lock hatches open (and increasing the shuttlepod's internal pressure to keep the lethal gases out). And according to Karthikeyan, the plasma conduit was getting more unstable by the second. *This would be so much easier if we could use transporters,* Williams lamented privately. She would gladly take the chance of being beamed, but it would take too long to reconfigure *Pioneer*'s transporter back from interference mode.

The moment the team was back aboard and the inner hatch was closed, Williams ordered, "Jettison the collar and go, go!" Karthikeyan responded with lightning speed, but he hadn't gotten the pod more than thirty meters from the station before the conduit blew. Superhot plasma and shrapnel smashed against the polarized hull plating, knocking the pod into a tumble. The spin pushed Williams against the floor even though the internal gravity was still off, and the hull creaked ominously.

But moments later the pod recovered, its hull and all its occupants still intact, and the ensign accelerated clear of the station. Williams moved to the starboard seat behind him and opened a channel. "Williams to *Pioneer*. We're clear with the Menaik captive and one other . . . but we lost Detzel. Sir, we'd all really appreciate if you'd blow that piece of junk into atoms now."

After a respectful silence, Reed's voice returned tightly. *"Acknowledged, Val. There's nothing I'd like better."*

"Target lock holding," came the voice of Crewman Yuan, manning the bridge tactical station in Williams's absence.

"Then fire at will, Sandra. Let's end this scourge."

It brought Valeria Williams great satisfaction to watch

through the shuttlepod's side port as *Pioneer*'s torpedoes and phase cannon beams tore into the damaged Ware station and blasted it apart until nothing was left but vapor and scrap.

But it was an empty satisfaction, for one of her people was still dead.

2

Travis Mayweather made sure he was present outside the decontamination bay—now reconfigured for Menaik atmosphere and temperature—when Nimthu, the liberated Menaik female, awoke. He knew she would find her surroundings alien and confusing, even without the added disorientation from her neurological damage, and he wanted to offer her reassurance. "It's all right," he told her once he'd introduced himself and filled in the basic situation. "*Velelev* didn't have the medical facilities to treat you, so Captain Rethne agreed to let us take care of you. We've had prior experience with . . . the type of injuries you suffered."

"How was I injured?" Nimthu asked shakily, tilting her orange-complexioned head as she tried to lever herself up with her hind arms. "I do not understand."

Mayweather tried to break the news as gently as he could, but she struggled to comprehend what had been done to her. Once it sank in that her family had already attended her funeral, she panicked for a time, and Mayweather regretted that he couldn't go in to hold her hand. Doctor Liao had to pipe in a sedative gas, relying on *Velelev*'s limited medical database for composition and dosage. "I think her mental condition can be improved with therapy, but it would have to be by people who knew what they were doing," Liao told him as they watched Nimthu sleep restlessly, her four legs twisting into an intricate knot. "Her best bet is for us to reach her homeworld as quickly as possible."

They traded a knowing look. The two Boomers had experience with shipboard medical crises where the only available action was to hope a patient would survive until they reached a port with suitable treatment facilities. Mayweather was grateful that, at *Pioneer*'s speed, the wait would be days instead of months.

"Any luck identifying our other patient?" he asked.

Liao shook her head grimly. "The Menaik have never encountered his species. And whatever that station used his cerebral cortex for, it's badly eroded his memory engrams. If he ever does regain lucidity, I'm not sure even he'll be able to tell us where he's from." The diminutive doctor shook her grizzled head. "Our best bet is to keep exploring and hope we run into his people, or someone who knows them. Good thing making new contacts is what we're here to do anyway."

February 25 to 27, 2165

In time, Nimthu regained enough calm and clarity to process what had happened to her, and what had been done to save her. "I cannot express my gratitude, Mister Mayweather."

"Travis."

"Travis. That your people would risk so much for me, a stranger. Not even your own biology." She lowered her head. "I am most grateful to the one who died to rescue me. When I return, I will perform a ritual to consecrate his soul to the Core of Creation, for there is no body."

"I'm sure Clifton would've appreciated that. Thank you."

"But why would you risk so much for us?"

"Because I've been through the same thing you have."

Mayweather told her the story—embellishing it far less than he usually did, for of course her ordeal had cost her far worse than his. "I guess I had it lucky," Mayweather said. "I was only plugged into that thing for a few hours. All I lost was my immediate memory of being abducted. Well, I couldn't remember much about that week's movie either, but that was probably for the best."

Nimthu asked what a movie was, and Mayweather regaled her with descriptions of all his favorite classics, from *Casablanca* to *Godzilla* to *The Day the Earth Stood Still* to *The Planet of the Undead*. In turn, she described some of her favorite myth-plays—often struggling to remember the details and frustrated when she realized her accounts made less sense than she'd intended. But Travis told her, quite sincerely, that he found her idiosyncratic retellings more entertaining than the originals probably would have been. Menaik expressions were hard for him to read, but her laughter let him know their conversation was helping her mood. And Liao told him that prompting her to remember, even imperfectly, would help her mental recovery as well. He was very glad of that. Her fate—or that of the other, still anonymous patient in Liao's sickbay—could have easily been his.

And thus Mayweather spent as much time visiting her in decon as his duties would allow, trading stories and helping her to remember. And comforting her, as best he could through the thick door, when the nightmares came and she awoke lost and screaming. "It's all right," he assured Nimthu. "You're safe. They can't hurt you anymore. You have my word."

Eighty minutes later, the Ware battleship attacked.

February 27, 2165

Tobin Dax fidgeted in his seat opposite Captain Reed's ready room desk. The human captain was determined, intense, the trim facial hair that bracketed his mouth giving him an air that the Trill engineer had always found faintly menacing. "We need to be ready," Reed said to him and to Rey Sangupta beside him. "We don't know how many more Ware facilities we may encounter in this space. And their technology gives them a decided advantage over us. I need you two to analyze that technology and find its weaknesses."

"We did pretty well despite that advantage, didn't we?" Sangupta said. "I mean, we rescued the captive, and got one more as a bonus."

"And lost one of our own!" Reed's gaze skewered the young science officer, whose face sagged at the reminder. "I don't consider that an acceptable trade. The more we can anticipate the threat the Ware poses, the safer we'll be."

"Excuse me," Dax ventured, as much to distract himself from the urge to bite his nails as anything else. "Wouldn't the safest thing just be to, well, avoid them? If we just warn people to stay away, wouldn't that be good enough? Eventually the brains they have would just . . . lose viability . . . and the stations would break down."

"I don't like the idea of writing off the captives that are still recoverable, Doctor. And I don't think the races in this region would either. Once they learn the truth about the Ware, either from Captain Rethne or from us, many of them will probably want to mount rescue expeditions. And that means any losses they sustain will be partly due to our actions. Maybe it's not our responsibility to personally rescue them all, but I'll be damned if I don't do all I can to give any other rescuers the best chance possible to succeed and survive."

Dax shrunk in his seat. "Sorry."

"Don't apologize, Doctor. Work the problem."

Fingers absently rose toward his teeth. He grabbed them

with his other hand, kneaded them both before him. "Well, it's . . . hard to figure out. The way the stations work is pretty strange. They're clearly a trap, but the defenses are, well, oddly lacking. I know, sir, I know—they were very effective up to a point, and I'm very sorry we lost Mister Detzel. But inside the data core itself, the station seemed almost defenseless. All it could do was threaten the ships on the outside. That's a strange gap in the design, if holding the captives is so essential."

"Tobin," Sangupta said, "we need to deal with the security they *do* have. The security they don't have isn't really our problem."

"But I can't sort out the problem until I understand why the stations are designed the way they are. Why some security methods and not others? I mean, the security seems so, so makeshift. The only actual weapons we've seen the stations use are ones they replicated for the occasion. It doesn't . . . sorry, but it doesn't feel to me like the stations were *designed* to be aggressive. It's like they've been repurposed for—"

The intercom signaled from the bridge. "Reed here."

"*Sir,*" came Valeria Williams's voice, "*you're needed on the bridge right away. Two ships have just emerged from warp, closing fast, and they don't look friendly.*"

The three men hastened out the door onto *Pioneer*'s bridge. On the viewer, Tobin saw two gray-white craft, each with a polygonal core body mounted atop two boxy, pontoon-like warp nacelles. Despite their lack of central spheres, their common design lineage with the space stations struck him immediately. "They're Ware," he said.

A moment later, a glowing light passed through the bridge as the atmosphere luminesced from a powerful sensor beam. Tobin's body tingled as it passed over him. His hands reflexively went over his abdominal pouch, not that they would do any good shielding the Dax symbiont within it from harmful radiation. But he felt fine afterward.

"I'd say that confirms your appraisal, Doctor Dax," Reed said.

"Signal coming in, sir," Ensign Grev said from communications.

"Let's hear it," said Reed, taking the center seat.

Mayweather entered the bridge just as the Tellarite opened the channel. *"Your vessel is in possession of proprietary components,"* came the dulcet feminine voice of the Ware. *"Return the components or your vessel will be forfeit."*

The first officer exchanged a look with the captain. "'Components,'" he growled. "They mean people!"

"Biosigns?" Reed called.

Sangupta answered from the science station while Dax moved to take over the engineering post. "None registering, sir."

"Your vessel is in possession of proprietary components. Return the components or your vessel will be forfeit."

"Shut that off, Grev," said Reed.

"Aye, sir."

"Automated ships defending an automated station," Mayweather said.

"I know," the captain replied. "I'd hoped that if we could talk to an actual person, we might be able to reason with them."

"Sir, they're charging weapons," Williams said.

"Raise shields. Polarize the hull."

"Aye, sir. Shields raised, hull polarized."

"What kind of weapons?" Mayweather asked.

"Phased nadion pulse beams, sir." Williams threw him a

grim look. "Like the kind that took out Detzel. Much stronger than our phase cannons."

Reed threw Dax a look. "So much for not being designed for aggression."

"I know, I don't understand—"

A blow rattled the ship. "Evasive," Reed ordered Ensign Tallarico at the helm. "Val, return fire. Target critical areas." He smiled grimly. "If there's nobody aboard, there's no need to hold back."

Williams's grin was more wolfish. "Aye, sir!"

Pioneer's phase cannons barely put a dent in the Ware shields—yet each blow from the Ware cannons drained _Pioneer_'s shield generators by a fair percentage. Regina Tallarico dodged as best she could, but the small, blocky ships were faster than they looked. With no live occupants to damage, they could accelerate harder and maneuver more sharply than the Starfleet vessel. The ship was taking a pounding.

"Sir," Mayweather said after recovering from a sharp hit that had made him stumble, "our first priority is to protect Nimthu and the other survivor. I promised her that."

"Better part of valor," Reed murmured. "Regina, try to break away and go to warp. Let's see if we can outrun them that way."

But the constant barrage of energies striking the shields created too much interference to permit a stable warp field. "Trying to compensate, but one of the injectors has taken damage," Dax said. "Sir, I can do more from engineering."

Reed nodded. "Go."

Tobin ran for the lift, directing it to D deck once he was inside. Moments later, a powerful impact pealed through the ship and the lift lurched. Tobin feared for a moment that he'd be stranded in the lift, the shaft bent or crumpled by the blast damage. (Why did Starfleet think elevators were safe in an emergency?) But then the lift resumed its journey and let him out on the right level. He ran aft until he reached the heavy hatch to the main engine room, opened it, and ducked inside. "Show me the injector damage," he ordered his second-in-command, Lieutenant Prentis Morrow, as he headed down the metal steps to the lower level (not willing to trust another lift, even the small, open one here in the engine room).

But just then, another impact rocked the ship. Tobin heard the crack and sizzle of circuits blowing out in the walls even as he stumbled off the steps and slammed facedown into the deck.

"Bridge to engineering!" came Mayweather's voice. *"Our shields are fluctuating!"*

Tobin moaned in pain as Morrow helped him to his feet. He reached the intercom and punched it. "But the injector—"

"If we lose shields, we lose the survivors! Keep them up, no matter what!"

"I'm on it," Tobin said, though much of his concentration was still on maintaining his balance. "Prentis, you do what you can with the injector while I take the shields."

"Aye, sir," the lieutenant replied crisply—a habit Tobin had been singularly unsuccessful in talking him out of. The sandy-haired man jogged over to the wall panel that housed the injectors—

Just before an explosion tore through engineering and dropped half the ceiling on his head. It was the last thing Tobin saw before the other half landed on him.

Travis Mayweather awoke to find himself in a recovery bed in sickbay. The last thing he remembered was the bridge tumbling around him. Val Williams had just managed to find a vulnerable spot on one of the robot ships and blow it apart, but the other had struck before she could retarget, and then . . . he was here. "Take it easy, Commander," Doctor Liao said. "Your injuries aren't major, but even a mild concussion's no laughing matter. You just lie back."

Captain Reed came into view, his left arm in an osteogenic brace and sling beneath his loosely draped uniform tunic. "Captain," Mayweather said. "The ships . . . Nimthu . . ."

Reed's lowered gaze told him the worst. "Once our shields fell, they beamed them out almost immediately. The only mercy is that once they had what they came for, they broke off the attack and left."

Mayweather clutched his captain's uninjured arm. "I assume we're in pursuit?"

"That's not an option," Reed told him solemnly. "We took serious damage in engineering. I'll spare you the technical details, because they're past fixing."

"Doctor Dax . . . he'll find a way. He knows those engines better than anyone."

Liao and Reed exchanged a look. It was Liao who broke the news. "Doctor Dax . . . has been badly injured." She turned her head toward another recovery bed, surrounded by privacy curtains. "I managed to save him . . . all of him," she added, oddly. "But his physiology is still . . . very alien. I don't know how long it might take him to regain consciousness."

"We're going nowhere," Reed grated through clenched teeth, "until Starfleet can send a rescue ship to tow us home. The subspace radio's about the only thing still working other than life support." He held his first officer's gaze. "I'm sorry, Travis. We've lost them."

Mayweather sank back onto the bed, squeezing his eyes shut painfully hard. "I gave her my word," he said. "I promised we'd keep her safe."

Reed clasped his shoulder. "We did everything humanly possible, Travis. And we paid dearly for it."

Mayweather looked up sharply, seeing confirmation in Reed's eyes. "Who did we lose?"

Liao replied; as a doctor, delivering such news was part of her job, and she did it calmly. "Morrow and Kano died in engineering. And we lost Bergmann to an atmosphere breach in his quarters."

Travis stared up at the ceiling for a time while he absorbed it. He embraced the pain, letting it harden his resolve. "Three more people those damn machines took from us. Captain . . ."

"I know how you feel, Travis," Reed told him with determination. "I promise you—this is not over."

3

March 18, 2165
Starfleet Headquarters, Fort Baker, California

ADMIRAL ARCHER WAS pleasantly surprised at the blue-skinned face that greeted him as he and Captain T'Pol disembarked from *Endeavour*'s shuttlepod. "Shran!" Archer greeted his old friend heartily. "Good to see you."

Thy'lek Shran, chief of staff of Starfleet's Andorian Guard branch, smiled at them, his antennae high and wide like open arms. "Welcome back, Jonathan. And you, T'Pol."

The Vulcan captain nodded courteously toward the older Andorian. "Admiral. It is agreeable to see you, though I find it puzzling that the duties of a Starfleet chief of staff afford you time for such a routine greeting."

"One of these days, T'Pol, we'll convince you to lighten up. What good is having rank if you can't use it to do what you like, eh, Jonathan?"

Archer chuckled in mild amazement. If there were a secret to getting flag rank to work for you that way, he had yet to discover it. Instead, he constantly found himself at the mercy of others' demands, their insistence that only he could achieve what needed to be done. But as Shran would remind him if he raised that complaint again, that was the price of being effective.

The senior admiral led them through the spacious, echoing hangar, past bustling crowds of passengers and technicians heading to and from the numerous shuttles—not just the familiar pods, but the larger-capacity passenger shuttles that were being built now that transporters were no longer in regular use. "So I gather you didn't meet with much success at Maluria," Shran said.

But as the trio emerged onto the grassy, tree-lined grounds of Starfleet Headquarters, Archer took a moment to soak in the weather of this rare fog-free day—the clear blue sky, the lapping waves of San Francisco Bay, even a clear view of the city's shimmering towers beyond the low domes of the Headquarters complex. "It could've gone better," he conceded after savoring a deep breath. "I don't think we can expect much help from the Malurian government in containing the Raldul alignment."

Shran harrumphed. "You'd think they'd welcome our help in rounding up their own criminal class."

"The Malurian establishment," T'Pol told him, "is extremely . . . inner-directed. In their view, whatever occurs beyond their own planetary system is irrelevant to their lives. Even the mining and agricultural colonies on the other settled worlds of Epsilon Fornacis are neglected by the government on Malur itself. Despite the value of the resources they provide to the homeworld, they are considered largely a dumping ground for criminals, social outcasts, and the disaffected, providing excellent recruiting grounds for Raldul."

"So the government's neglect actually makes things worse for them," Shran interpreted. "You'd think they'd have the sense to see that they're encouraging their enemy."

"It's hard to reason with people whose minds are closed," Archer said. "The whole mission was pretty much a waste of time." He took another deep breath. "At least it was nice to get out in space again for a while. Always is."

"I know what you mean," Shran said. "Well, enjoy it while you can."

Archer stared. "Is that supposed to mean something?"

Shran's antennae tilted rakishly as he offered a knowing smile. "You know Admiral Gardner's retiring soon, right?"

"Yes." Gardner, the chief of staff of the UESPA branch of Starfleet, had successfully seen the service through the Romulan War, but had recently come to the conclusion that an "old warhorse" like himself was not the best person to shape Starfleet into the peacekeeping organization it was now becoming.

"Well, I hear you're the frontrunner to take his place."

Archer stared. "What? Hear from who?"

"Oh, various people. Including me, when I recommended you to President al-Rashid." At Archer's stunned silence, Shran smirked. "Oh, don't look so surprised, Jonathan. It's disingenuous. We all know what you've done for Earth—for all of us. Did you really imagine this wouldn't happen someday?"

Archer residence, Sausalito

"Honestly," Archer said, "I can't say I ever really thought about it."

Danica Erickson chuckled—which was pleasant for Archer, for her lanky, warm nude body was nestled against his as they lay together in his bed, propped up on the pillows. They had gone out for dinner on his first night back, discussing the Maluria mission, catching up on the latest news of their mutual friends on *Endeavour*'s crew and in the engineering firm where Dani worked, and so forth; but he had waited to broach the subject of his possible promotion until they were alone on his houseboat in Sausalito Harbor. And once privacy had been achieved, there had been other, more urgent catching up to do.

"You're cute when you're modest," she told him, her mellow alto making it musical.

"I'm serious," he told her, though he found himself laughing with her, provoked by the look in her compelling dark eyes. "I accepted flag rank because it was a chance to make a difference, and I'm satisfied with where I am. But you know me, Dani. I've never been ambitious to be anything but an explorer, a traveler."

"Are you kidding? Jonathan, your actions have changed the galaxy. No, don't give me that look. You've led whole worlds to do things they never would've considered before you came along. Big things, daring things. You're the most ambitious man I've ever known. But you're ambitious on behalf of everyone *but* yourself." She leaned against him, kissed him. "Which is why, if I hadn't taken the initiative in our relationship, you'd still be looking at me as the little girl you built toy spaceships with."

His eyes roved up and down her frame. "Believe me, I'm looking at you very differently now."

"Once you got your head out of the stars and saw what was around you in the here and now."

He studied her. "Are you trying to make a point?"

Dani caught his meaning and sat up to face him more directly, crossing her arms. "Not about us. Don't get the wrong idea. I'm not going to push you to take this job because it would keep you here with me more. I'm patient. I understand the demands on your time. And I have my own career too, my own ambitions that aren't just about you. We're both comfortable with where we are right now.

"So if I'm making a point," she went on, "it's about you,

not me. Even after all you've achieved, I don't think you've reached the limits of your potential. If Shran and T'Pol and people like them think you're right for the job, then that should tell you they have good reason. You should think about that."

Archer wrestled with the question well into the night, getting little sleep. There was certainly a lot of good he could do in such a position. He had ideas for improving Starfleet as an exploratory and diplomatic service, pushing forward new starship designs with hybrid technology from all the member worlds' fleets, encouraging more integration among the services—ideas that had met resistance from Gardner, who was too accustomed to operating from within Earth Starfleet and too slow to broaden his horizons. But then, Gardner had been stuck behind a desk here in San Francisco ever since he'd lost out to Archer for *Enterprise*'s captaincy. If Archer let himself end up behind that same desk, would he be able to retain the breadth of thought he'd gained in his travels? Or would he end up just as hidebound?

More to the point, his opportunities to satisfy his wanderlust were already diminished in his current job. He had plenty of opportunities to travel on diplomatic assignments, and he got to participate actively in Starfleet's exploratory efforts, if only vicariously through the reports of the starship crews he oversaw. But it was a more constrained, grounded existence than he found comfortable—which may be why he had chosen to buy a houseboat, a home where he could theoretically pull up anchor at any moment and sail off to parts unknown. Theoretically.

True, as chief of staff, he could still supervise exploratory efforts; the late, lamented Admiral Forrest had been very hands-on back when Archer had captained *Enterprise*. But the

Federation Starfleet was a larger, more complex organism than Earth Starfleet had been, which might make it harder for a modern chief of staff to concentrate on exploration.

On the other hand, there was Dani's warmth against him now, and the opportunity to experience it much more regularly—her own schedule permitting, of course—if he took the job. Maybe they could even move in together, or . . . perhaps more. It would be a hell of a compensation.

He hesitated to contemplate that "perhaps more," though. He had a big enough decision to make about his future as it was.

March 20, 2165
U.S.S. Pioneer

Malcolm Reed was in command of a derelict.

By the time Tobin Dax had recovered sufficiently from his injuries to examine the engines, it was already abundantly clear that even his expertise could do nothing to restore warp capacity. The Menaik could lend no assistance; their warp technology was decades behind the Federation's. The best they could do was to divert their sole armed vessel in the region toward *Pioneer* in case the crippled ship fell prey to raiders before Starfleet assistance could arrive. But the slow patrol vessel would reach *Pioneer* only a few days before Starfleet could.

Reed had tried not to contemplate the choice irony that he'd blown up the only suitable repair facility within range.

Finally, the *U.S.S. Thelasa-vei*, a *Kumari*-class vessel operated by the Andorian Guard, arrived to tow *Pioneer* back to Federation space. Reed shared the crew's embarrassment at being unable to return under their own power, though fortunately he heard little of the speciesist sentiments that some of his crew had expressed two years before, when Tobin Dax's multispecies team of engineering specialists had come aboard to upgrade the Earth ship's systems. There was still a certain rivalry between the exploration-oriented UESPA branch of Starfleet and the defense-oriented AG branch, manifesting itself as a certain smugness among *Thelasa-vei*'s crew; but it came across more as friendly taunting than something more virulent. *Pioneer*'s crew had shed blood in defense of others, and the Andorians could respect that . . . even if the crew had failed to protect those it had sacrificed for.

That was the real ignominy that ate at *Pioneer*'s crew: the fact that their sacrifice had achieved so little. They had prevented one Ware station from claiming more victims, but clearly the Ware's presence in the new sector was stronger than anticipated. And they had alerted the Menaik to the hazards of the Ware, but the fluorine-based quadrupeds had few allies as yet, so who knew whether their warnings would be heard or taken seriously?

So it came as a further blow when Reed learned his crew would sustain another loss once they arrived in the Vulcan system for repairs. He heard the news from Dax when he visited the engineer in sickbay to check on the progress of his physical therapy. "But you can't leave us, Doctor!" Reed protested. "We need you."

"Don't worry," the small, balding Trill told the captain as Doctor Liao supervised the exercises that strengthened his injured right leg. His mottled temples gleamed with sweat that, atypically, was due to exertion rather than anxiety. "I'll stay to supervise the repairs, make sure *Pioneer* is shipshape before I go." He lowered his gaze. "It's the least I can do."

"I don't just need you for repairs, Doctor. I need the best engineering advice I can get when we go after the Ware again."

Dax gave him a skeptical look. "I was there before, and it didn't help much."

"It'll be different this time."

"That's exactly the problem!" the Trill cried, then immediately shrank back. "Sir. Sorry." Embarrassed by his outburst, he refocused on his exercises.

"Go on, Doctor. You know you can speak freely here."

The engineer glanced over at Liao, who nodded encouragingly. Then he turned back to the captain. "This time you'll be going out to fight. That's not what I agreed to. Even just exploring has been . . . has been risky enough," he finished softly. "Knowingly going out against an enemy that almost killed me . . . that almost killed Dax . . . Sir, I can't be responsible for that."

Reed pondered, unsure how to respond. Tobin Dax had briefed both Liao and Reed on his true nature as a symbiotic organism, a fusion of the personalities of the host Tobin Fendus and the vermiform symbiont called Dax, the latter gaining the size, mobility, and dexterity of a humanoid body in exchange for the intellect and experience of a symbiont that could live for millennia. But he had sworn them to secrecy and shared no more details than necessary, for other races might perceive Trill symbiosis as an obscenity or a threat. So Reed's understanding of his position was limited. Still, the captain offered what he could. "I thought you told us that it was the responsibility of a Trill host to expose the symbiont to a wide range of life experience."

"Well, that's kind of the point, Captain. *Life* experience. As in the opposite of death, which would destroy all that accumulated learning." He blushed. "Maybe my own contribution won't count for much, but Lela Dax accomplished so much in her life. It's a great responsibility to carry her memories. I can't be reckless with them."

Liao punched him in the shoulder, making him wince. "I still say you're underestimating yourself, Tobin. You've accomplished a lot for Starfleet, for this ship."

"But I'm not part of Starfleet. I'm a civilian. I only agreed to help out until you could find a replacement. Somehow it's become two years."

"Years in which you've made friends among the crew."

"And helped us out of a lot of scrapes," Reed added.

"And I will cherish those memories, Doctor. Captain. Both—all of you. I hope Dax's future hosts will cherish them too. But . . . there are some more recent memories that are harder to live with. I . . . I sent Morrow over to check those injectors."

"And the Ware fired the shot that caused the ceiling to collapse. The blame is theirs."

"It's not about blame, sir. It's about . . . consequences. And things I don't want to remember. I can't go into that engine room without thinking about what happened there. I'll spend as much time there as necessary to get your ship back up to spec, sir. But then I need to move on."

Reed could offer no argument. He simply nodded in understanding. "Have you decided where you'll go?" he asked.

"I have friends on Vulcan," Dax told him. "Professor Skon and his wife T'Rama. They're expecting a baby in a few months. I always wondered how Vulcans handle pregnancy. When I was carrying my first child—I mean, when Lela was—well, never mind." He broke off, and Reed realized he'd been staring. *Infinite diversity*, he reminded himself, quoting the Vulcan maxim he'd learned from T'Pol.

"Well, we'll all be sorry to see you go, Doctor Dax," Reed told him. "Your contributions to our mission have been invaluable. And I wish you comparable success in your future endeavors."

Dax flushed, and not from the exercise. "Thank you, Captain. It's—it's been a privilege."

Reed didn't let his displeasure show on his face until he was alone in the corridor. Perhaps a civilian like Dax was better off out of this business with the Ware—but it left Reed badly wanting for engineering expertise just when he needed it the most. Where could he find someone suitable to take Dax's place?

Assuming, of course, that he could convince Starfleet to let him tackle the Ware—and give him the help he needed to do so. Reed returned to his quarters to work on the case he would present to the Starfleet brass. He knew Admiral Archer would be sympathetic . . . but Archer wasn't the only one he'd have to convince.

4

ADMIRAL ARCHER LEANED BACK in his seat, sobered by the accounts that Malcolm Reed and Valeria Williams had relayed. Of course he had gotten *Pioneer*'s report weeks ago, but it was important to hear his officers' accounts firsthand. He'd already debriefed Travis Mayweather over subspace from Vulcan, where the younger officer had remained to supervise *Pioneer*'s repairs.

"It sounds like we got lucky back on *Enterprise*," Archer finally said. "No robot ships came after us to reclaim Travis."

"It seems the station we encountered was on the far fringes of the Ware's reach," Reed replied.

Williams leaned forward, her wiry frame taut with energy. "And the intervening space was under Romulan or Vertian control at the time, sirs. If any ships were sent, they were probably intercepted."

Next to Archer, Admiral Shran gave a harumph of amusement. "Saved by the Romulans. There's a twist." Archer had asked the Andorian Guard chief to attend the debriefing because of its ramifications for border security.

"Believe me, sir, I'm not blind to the irony," Reed said. "But it demonstrates that we've underestimated the threat posed by this technology. We had an isolated encounter at the edge of its influence, but now we're expanding into territory where it holds far greater sway. And if they have trading posts and warships, who knows what else they might have?"

"Not to mention the overriding question of who 'they' are, sirs," Williams added. "We need to find out who created and propagated this technology and what their ultimate goals for it are."

Archer studied the *Pioneer* officers. "It sounds to me like you two are proposing a plan. Malcolm?"

"Yes, we are, sir," Reed replied. "We need to go back in and investigate the Ware. Discover its capabilities, its spread, its origins, and the true purpose behind it."

"Sounds like deliberately picking at an ice-bore warren," Shran said. "If you're not careful they'll swarm you and burn their way right into your heart. And no offense to your ship and its crew, Captain, but you didn't have much luck by yourself."

"That's why we need to return in greater force, Admiral. I was hoping you would assign a task force of Andorian Guard battleships to accompany *Pioneer* on a return mission to the Ware sector—with your approval, of course, sir," he added to Archer. "That would give us the strength to defend ourselves against Ware battleships until we can find who's behind this whole thing."

The human admiral tilted his head. "And stop them?"

"Or at least find a way to defend against their actions. And warn the indigenous cultures of the threat so they can take measures of their own. I know how you feel about interfering in other cultures, sir, but the peoples in that sector are the ones most immediately under threat from the Ware. I can't believe they wouldn't want to take the lead in defending themselves."

"They're also the ones most used to benefiting from the

Ware stations," Archer said. "It might be harder than you think to change their minds. Especially if you go in with a show of force."

"Believe me, Admiral," Williams said, "the last thing I want is to risk losing any more people if it can be avoided. But if a fight does start, we need to be strong enough to win this time. We need to discover the intentions behind the Ware, sir. What if the stations are just the first stage of an infiltration—gathering data about new races, getting them hooked on Ware technology to soften them up for conquest?"

Archer leaned forward, holding her intense hazel eyes. "I appreciate all those concerns, Lieutenant. But if we go in too forcefully, we could start a war rather than preventing one." His eyes darted to Reed. "Remember the Xindi. We thought they were out to annihilate us, but it turned out they were being used, tricked. We need to understand what we're up against before we decide to go in swinging."

"But, sir," Reed countered, "we also need to be strong enough to withstand the learning curve. There were times in the Expanse when *Enterprise* almost didn't make it. Times we would've been stranded or destroyed if we hadn't—taken drastic measures."

Reed lowered his gaze, embarrassed at what he'd almost brought up. But if anything, Archer was the one who still blamed himself for his act of desperation in his darkest days in the Delphic Expanse, when he'd stolen a warp coil from an Illyrian science vessel and stranded them three years from their homeworld at sublight to ensure that *Enterprise* would reach a vital rendezvous. He'd seen no other choice, and he had intended to return the coil if possible—but circumstances had forced Archer to leave the Expanse in haste to defend Earth from the final attack of the Xindi hardliners.

Later, once Archer and Starfleet had persuaded the Vulcan High Command to send a follow-up expedition to make diplomatic contact with the Xindi, Archer had requested that the Vulcan crew attempt to locate the Illyrian ship and provide aid and recompense if possible. But no sign of the vessel had ever been found. Archer could only hope that they had managed to contact a friendly warp-capable vessel and find their way home, with the worst damage being to Starfleet's reputation. But he would probably never know for sure.

Thus, he was uneasy with the anger and determination that Reed and Williams showed now. "I agree this is a threat we need to assess. But we also need to weigh our response against other concerns. The last thing we want is to provoke a war by mistake."

"Sir, I understand," the captain replied. "But . . . loath though I am to admit it . . . *Pioneer* can't handle the Ware alone. Even a *Columbia*-class ship wouldn't be powerful enough. We need a task force."

"And if you go in expecting a fight, that's usually what you get."

"A fight against machines, sir," Williams countered. "Just equipment that's gotten out of hand."

"Val, you said yourself that we don't know who's behind these things and why. The one thing we *do* know is that they're very protective of what they consider their property."

Williams lowered her head. "Yes, sir."

Archer leaned back and sighed. "I'm not saying no. Like I said, we do need to find out more. We just need to figure out the best way to go about it. And *Pioneer*'s repairs give us time to consider our options. Okay?"

Reed gave a curt nod, his ingrained discipline kicking in.

"Understood, sir." Next to him, Williams looked more frustrated. Archer had no doubt Reed felt the same inside.

"I agree with Shran, Jon. It's our first priority to keep the Federation safe."

Admiral Samuel Gardner, chief of staff of Starfleet's UESPA division, looked tired. The round-faced older man had been gray-haired since they had competed for command of *Enterprise* all those years ago, but now the rest of him seemed to be catching up, worn down by the years of tough decision-making during the Romulan War and after. Was this Archer's future if he accepted Gardner's post?

He tried not to let those thoughts show. "We all feel that way, sir. But when you're probing a hornet's nest, it's not particularly safe to poke it with a stick."

Gardner scowled, but with faint amusement. "Hm. I remember a few years back when you were the one pushing for a more active investigation of the Romulans. And you were right. If we'd taken action sooner . . ."

"Sir, that was the last war." He didn't need to say more; they both understood the expression. "And anyway, I wasn't proposing we send a squadron of warships into Romulan space."

"But you know a strong response is what the people will want when they learn about this new threat. And it's what the president will want—to deliver on the voters' mandate, show the value of a strong central state to keep the peace."

Archer grimaced. *More politics.* "There's more at stake here than popular opinion. If we should happen to trigger a war in Ware space, we don't know how many other worlds might suffer as a result. And not just in that sector. Look at what's happening on Sauria."

The admiral looked annoyed. "I know how you feel about Maltuvis, Jon. And I don't disagree. He's a tin-pot dictator and he's taking advantage of our trade deal to make himself more powerful at his people's expense." M'Tezir, the Saurian nation-state ruled by the warlord Maltuvis, had been a minor power before Federation contact, but its mountains held vast reserves of minerals vital to advanced technology, so the Federation's trade deal with Sauria had instantly made M'Tezir wealthy and powerful. Maltuvis had spent the past two years spreading his influence across Sauria, to the detriment of the civil rights of those who fell under his sway.

"But we don't have to like another government's policies to do business with them," Gardner went on. "At least the trade deal keeps lines of communications open, gives us options."

"You mean it gives us dilithium and rare earths and makes Maltuvis stronger by the day. He's already effectively conquered half the planet. If we got dragged into another war, if we needed to double or triple our shipbuilding rate, then Maltuvis could change the terms to his own advantage and we'd be helpless to refuse. And he could end up conquering his whole planet—bankrolled by us."

Gardner chuckled, making the junior admiral frown. "What?" Archer asked.

"You say you don't want my job because of the politics, Jon, but you're as political a creature as I've ever met. Now, that's not an insult," he said, holding up his hands. "We like to use it that way, but the fact is, politics is just the art of persuading people to devote their attention and resources to a common goal. Sure, sometimes that goal is just getting elected or making your in-group richer or more powerful. But convincing people to go along with a worthy goal, to do what has to be done for the greater good—that's politics too. It's not a dirty word. It's just a tool. And Jon, it's a tool you wield as well as anyone I've ever met. You have the passion and commitment it takes to persuade whole nations to your cause—even to turn enemies into allies."

Archer demurred. "I just tried to do what was best for everyone."

"And you used politics to do it. It's a means to an end, that's all. It's one thing to see a solution—the important part is convincing others to see it too." Gardner leaned back in his chair and crossed his arms. "So give me a solution, Jon. We need to poke a hornet's nest without bringing out the swarm. What's our best option?"

April 1, 2165

"You'll get your task force, Malcolm," Archer told *Pioneer*'s captain, who once again sat before the desk in Archer's office with Val Williams at his side. "But in reserve."

Reed frowned. "Reserve, sir?"

"You're right—*Pioneer* will need help if it takes on too big a threat. But what we need out there is an explorer. A ship that can go in, make contact with the locals, learn all we can about the Ware and its origins. Find a way to avoid a confrontation if possible, but gain enough intel that we're ready if a confrontation happens. More importantly, try to make friends in the region, allies you can turn to if you have to. Basically what we did on *Enterprise* in the Delphic Expanse, but with the benefit of the lessons we learned there."

"You mean, don't assume there will be a fight. Look for peaceful options."

"Yes—but also, don't go in without backup. The Andorian task force will stand by at the edge of the sector while you probe into it. They'll be ready to assist *Pioneer* if there's an imminent threat. Shran's sending a pair of fast courier ships to provide replacement parts, medical relief and transport, or other services as necessary, and to serve as subspace relays to the task force if you travel out of range or meet with comm interference."

"Sir," Williams asked, "that's all well and good, but what if we face a sudden attack?"

"I've approved your requested upgrades to *Pioneer*'s weapons and shields, Val. And now that you know what happens when you rescue Ware abductees, you'll be ready if it happens again. The courier ships could ferry any rescuees to the task force, or to their homeworlds, where they could be defended. Maybe if they get far enough fast enough, or even just transferred to a different ship, the Ware won't be able to track them down."

Williams relaxed her shoulders a bit, accepting his reasoning. "Understood, sir. I guarantee, my people *will* be ready."

"I know they will, Val."

Reed turned to her, a thoughtful look on his face. "Thank you, Lieutenant. Admiral, if there's nothing else you need from Val, there's one more matter I'd like to discuss in private."

Archer furrowed his brow. "Certainly. Val, you're dismissed." He smiled. "Go tell your dad he's free to take you to lunch."

The young lieutenant looked puzzled, but not displeased at the opportunity to spend more time with her father, Archer's aide Marcus Williams. "Aye, sir. Thank you."

"Sir," Malcolm said once they were alone, "there's one more thing we'll need. With Doctor Dax staying behind on Vulcan, *Pioneer* needs a new chief engineer. And it'll have to be the best person available if we're to take on a technological threat like the Ware. Someone who can decipher advanced alien technology by instinct and who can rebuild a crippled warp drive from spare parts if need be. Ideally, someone who's dealt with Ware technology before."

"But there's nobody else who——" Archer broke off, realizing who it was that Reed was talking about. Seeing the realization on his face, the captain nodded. "You're right," Archer went on. "He could be just the man you need."

"I trust you can arrange a meeting?"

"I'm sure he'd be happy to see you." He fidgeted. "But the rest . . . it isn't up to me. And it's been quite a while since he's done this kind of work. I'm not sure he'd be allowed to."

"You let me worry about that, sir. If necessary, I have some history of my own with his employers. I know how to make deals with them."

"I know," Archer said. "But it's the price I'm worried about."

April 2, 2165
ShiKahr, Vulcan

Tobin Dax had not expected Skon's home to be so beautiful.

From a distance, ShiKahr looked as orderly as one would expect a Vulcan city to be: a construct of perfect circles, its metropolitan area tightly corralled within the confines of a broad disk, with perfectly straight pneumatic-tube highways extending radially to the outer park ring, a dense wall of vegetation insulating the city from the vast Sas-a-shar desert beyond. But up close, it was an aesthetic feast. The streets were lined with abstract sculptures and weirdly shaped, scintillating vegetation. Great filigreed buttresses arched overhead, supporting the pneumatic tram tubes. Even many of the buildings were experiments in abstract geometry. Walking through the city was like walking through a vast art gallery—and its denizens were as orderly and soft-spoken as a gallery's patrons, allowing the tinkling of wind chimes and the ubiquitous babble of fountains to dominate the soundscape. Even the engines of the few private skimmers that hovered unhurriedly above the roadways made soft chiming sounds so as not to disrupt the serenity of the city. Skon had insisted to Tobin in the past that his people's devotion to logic and scientific precision did not impede their appreciation for aesthetics, but the Trill had never truly believed it until now.

The home that Skon shared with his wife, T'Rama, was dominated by a spacious courtyard separated from the street by a high sandstone wall. A winding path led from the front gate and around the house proper to a rear plaza dominated by a luxurious, multilimbed fountain surrounded by golden sculptures like angular trees. The glass-walled house itself was also richly appointed with sculptures, paintings, and carvings. Moreover, Skon maintained a library of antique books and calligraphic tapestries—partly for his linguistic studies, but also for sheer aesthetics, as Vulcan calligraphy was an art form in itself, inscribed in intricate geometric curves and swirls. Tobin wondered if that was why his mathematician friend had initially become interested in linguistics.

In any case, Tobin was confident that the house would be a stimulating environment for Skon and T'Rama's son. Tobin had never met T'Rama before, but he could see in her frame the taut grace and discipline of the security officer she had once been, even though that frame was now enlarged by a pregnancy in its late stages—more than ten months along, meaning the birth was less than three months away. Naturally, logically, they had already converted their guest room into a nursery well ahead of the boy's arrival, but the room was spacious enough that they could nonetheless accommodate Tobin there for a few weeks, until he could arrange lodgings of his own—or leave Vulcan, if that was what he chose. At the moment, though, he had no idea what destination he might choose once *Pioneer*'s repairs and upgrades were completed. He had given Starfleet his best effort, but it simply wasn't a job Tobin Dax was cut out for. But he was not sure what might take its place.

He had plenty to occupy him in the meantime, though. Tonight, Skon was hosting a reception in honor of another off-world visitor, a poet with whom Skon had been working on a translation project. Tobin wasn't generally comfortable with receptions or parties, but Vulcan social affairs were more sedate than most; a people who valued quiet contemplation would not look askance on a wallflower. Besides, he had absorbed enough of the *Pioneer* crew's inquisitive spirit to feel a certain curiosity about this poet, apparently the only one of his kind in the Federation. Though basically hostform (or "humanoid," as his former crewmates called it) with mammalian attributes like hair on the scalp, the lanky, aging poet had a faintly scaly quality to his greenish-gray skin—most prominently along the raised orbital and temporal ridges, which resembled those of a Denobulan but were more pronounced, bracketing a frontal ridge that widened into a spoonlike concavity at the center of the forehead. Broad, scaled ridges stretched from his ears to his shoulders, giving his neck an almost triangular shape. It was all Tobin could do not to stare as Skon introduced them. "Doctor Tobin Dax of the planet Trill, this is Master Iloja of Prim, honored guest of this home."

Skon was a tall, broad-shouldered Vulcan in his early one hundreds, just showing the barest hints of gray around his temples and in excellent physical condition despite his sedentary profession. Tobin had always found his build intimidating, tempered only by Skon's relaxed manner and the dry, subtle amusement with which he tended to observe the universe. But though Iloja was some ten centimeters shorter (though still towering over Tobin) and proportionately far more aged, the alien poet projected a bulldog toughness that made Tobin extremely nervous to get close to him.

"Uh, uh, Prim," Tobin managed to stammer out. "Is, is that your home planet?"

Iloja glowered deeply, and Tobin wondered if he had given offense somehow. "My home, yes, but only a district on my planet. Or what was once my planet. The Cardassia I knew has surely been trampled into dust by now."

Tobin cleared his throat, striving for comfortable banality. "Car—Cardassia. I can't say I've ever heard of it."

"Nor will your Starfleet likely encounter it for many years yet," the poet replied. "I was exiled from my home . . . oh, what feels like lifetimes ago. I've lived on so many worlds, with so many different ways of measuring time, that I've lost track of the years. I stay on one until the reminders that it isn't Cardassia grow too intolerable, and then I travel still farther from Cardassia, hoping to forget. I'm a living warp engine, propelled by a paradox."

"Um, well, actually, the principle behind a warp engine is mathematically very straightforward—um." He broke off under the large Cardassian's impatient glare.

But after a moment, Iloja barked a sharp laugh and slapped Tobin on the shoulder, making him drop the *pla*-berry pastry he was lifting from his plate. "I like this one, Skon. Not a hint of guile in him. A refreshingly rare quality in this universe."

"You must excuse Master Iloja's cynicism," T'Rama

interposed, handing Tobin back his pastry, which she had deftly caught well before it reached the floor. "His exile is the result of political dissidence against a regime that, according to him, is not known for its openness." She retrieved a napkin from a fold in her elegant robe and meticulously wiped her fingers clean as she spoke.

"A deeply illogical response on their part," Skon observed. "Iloja's poetry was meant to create awareness and inspire contemplation of the issues facing his people—a legitimate function for a creative work to fulfill. It also possesses considerable aesthetic merit."

"High praise coming from such an aesthetically minded culture as the Vulcans," Iloja said. "Plus it saves me the effort of saying it myself," he added with a gruff chuckle.

"Unfortunately," T'Rama said, "Skon is one of the few on Vulcan currently able to understand Master Iloja's work in the original Cardassian. But he is working with the master on a Vulcan translation."

"Really?" Tobin asked, turning to his old friend. "I thought you were working on an English translation of Surak's writings. The Kir, Kir . . ."

"*Kir'Shara*," Skon supplied. "Indeed, I have been undertaking that effort for some time, my duties at the Science Academy permitting. However, I have encountered certain difficulties interpreting Surak's concepts and expressions into as emotive a language as English. This was an issue I faced in my earlier translation of the *Analects*, but since the *Kir'Shara* represents Surak's own words rather than secondary accounts thereof, it calls for exceptional care." Tobin was familiar with Skon's earlier translation of the *Analects*, published as *The Teachings of Surak*. It would be interesting to see how different the *Kir'Shara* truly was. "It occurred to me that undertaking an unrelated task for a time might bring fresh perspectives, and Iloja's poetry presented itself."

The conversation had drawn the attention of another guest, a lanky, strong male in his youthful prime. Tobin recalled T'Rama introducing him as Surel, her successor in the post of security director to the First Minister. "Even with the most committed effort," he said, "I fear any such translation of the *Kir'Shara* will be a rough approximation at best. Useful for introducing the general population—of various worlds—to the ideas expressed in the work, perhaps. But the full power and magnificence of Surak's wisdom can only be experienced in the original Old High Vulcan."

"An overly romantic interpretation," Skon said. "It is merely a matter of understanding the historical context. The *Kir'Shara* is a product of its time and place, as is any piece of our history."

"Oh, come now, Skon," said Iloja. "This *Kir'Shara* of yours is not just any neutral historical document. It's the very work on which your civilization was founded, in your greatest prophet's own hand!" He chuckled. "For centuries, you've had only secondhand translations and apocryphal texts, and now the real thing comes along and tells you how much you've had wrong all these generations. On most worlds, that would have provoked a holy war by now."

"Vulcans are a rational, orderly people," Surel replied. "When faced with the truth, we accept it and amend our errors. There is no logic in clinging to a discredited belief."

Another voice spoke sharply from behind Tobin, making him fumble the remaining half-pastry, which fortunately fell back onto his plate this time. "Is there logic in blindly accepting the validity of alleged new evidence?" The new speaker was another male, this one middle-aged, yet with a crisp, military bearing.

"Not this again, Zadok," said Surel. "The authenticity of the *Kir'Shara* has been verified by numerous tests." Tobin scarfed down the remainder of his pastry so that he wouldn't risk dropping it again.

"All performed under the supervision of the Syrannites who profited from their findings," the man named Zadok countered.

T'Rama spoke to Tobin, perhaps in an attempt to defuse the tension between the two Vulcans. "Doctor Tobin Dax, this is Commander Zadok of the Vulcan Space Service. It was his vessel that brought Master Iloja to Vulcan."

"Uh, pleased to meet you," said Tobin, almost extending his sticky-fingered hand before he realized that would be a faux pas for at least two reasons.

But Surel and Zadok barely seemed to notice. "The three independent studies that have confirmed the *Kir'Shara*'s authentic age and provenance fall short of impartiality only in the rhetoric of Anti-revisionists and their ilk," Surel countered. "And recent events have demonstrated that the Anti-revisionists were far from impartial themselves."

"One group that was compromised by offworlders. Much as the alleged *Kir'Shara* was discovered by a human starship captain," Zadok said with some distaste. "One who even claims to have carried the disembodied spirit of Surak. It astonishes me that rational Vulcans would take such fancies seriously."

"Jonathan Archer merely assisted the Syrannites in their retrieval of the *Kir'Shara*," Surel riposted. "The Syrannites have always been dedicated to the purest form of Surak's logic. How can you call us more emotional than the aggressive, paranoid, even warlike faction that dominated the High Command prior to its dissolution?"

"Those of us who served with distinction in the High Command acted with dispassion," Zadok insisted. "To a rational mind, the use of force is often the most efficacious response to a threat. The pacifism of the Syrannites is rooted in sentiment—the emotional attachment to the sanctity of life overriding the practical need to employ violence when necessary."

"What is rational about falsifying evidence of an Andorian military buildup in order to provoke an *un*necessary war, as Administrator V'Las attempted to do?"

The commander stood his ground. "The late administrator made some . . . unwise choices toward the end. But only in the name of what he believed was the security of Vulcan and the value of our traditional ways."

"Our traditional ways were lost for centuries. Only now have they been rediscovered."

Iloja laughed. "I think I spoke too soon. Maybe *this* is what a holy war looks like among you Vulcans."

Indeed, Tobin noted that Surel and Zadok had squared off, an undercurrent of aggression faintly visible beneath their courteous veneer. But T'Rama interposed herself smoothly, her manner instantly dominating the guests' attention. Even though she was much daintier of build than her husband—and much more pregnant—stepping between two large, aggressive men to head off conflict somehow seemed a more natural move for her than for Skon. "My guests, perhaps this discussion is better suited for a more appropriate venue. We are here to pay tribute to Master Iloja, not to embarrass him with our political arguments."

"Oh, no need to stop them on my account, my lady!" Iloja crowed. "Politics is a fundamental force of the sentient universe, shaping the interactions of living beings as surely as the electromagnetic field shapes the interactions of charged particles. I've devoted most of my life, my work, to its study. And I find this debate quite . . . fascinating, to borrow a phrase. Trust a Cardassian on this; you should all be grateful you have the freedom to express such dissenting views openly without fear of reprisal."

Tobin nodded sagely, even while advising himself not to attend any more Vulcan receptions. They were just too depressing. Although the pastries were good.

5

REED TOOK CAUTIOUS STEPS into *Enterprise*'s mess hall, looking around uneasily. Not because of the setting itself, which was comfortable and nostalgic; indeed, invoking that nostalgia was how Reed had persuaded the museum staff to permit this private, after-hours tour of his old ship. The museum kept the mess hall configured as it had been on *Enterprise*'s weekly movie nights, so that visitors could watch educational presentations and docudramas about the starship's pioneering voyages into the unknown and its achievements in the Romulan War—including some simulations that Reed knew to be entirely fabricated. He had almost expected to be faced with one of those when the doors had first opened and he had heard a movie playing.

But no, the feature was an older production, one of those twentieth-century films that had been so popular among *Enterprise*'s crew. Reed was sure he recognized the heavyset, middle-aged man who was being led into an ornate penthouse by a large dog whose jaws were clamped around his wrist—hadn't he been in that movie about the arguing jurors?

Deciding that the scene represented some sort of invitation, Reed moved forward to his preferred seat in the second row. The middle-aged man had now been greeted by a younger, narrow-featured man in a dressing gown, a man he didn't seem to like much but clearly needed something from. Recognizing the visitor's discomfort with the nude artworks adorning the penthouse, the younger man activated a control that caused them to retract into the walls and be replaced by more abstract pieces. Reed was beginning to get the idea that this was a spy movie, or even a satire of the spy movies of its era. Sometimes it was hard to tell the difference.

Another man slipped into the seat beside Reed so silently that the captain almost missed it. Still, he controlled his reaction. If this was how his contact wanted it, he could play the game too. "Good evening, Mister Tucker."

The man whom Malcolm had once known as Charles Tucker III met his gaze evenly, his expression showing nothing. "Malcolm."

Reed had been hoping for a warmer reception. "It's . . . good to see you, Trip. It's been too long."

"One or two lifetimes."

"At least." Reed averted his eyes back to the screen, where the gray-suited man, evidently the chief of an intelligence agency, was struggling to persuade his reluctant former agent to accept an assignment of world-shaking importance, while a pair of beautiful women—no, now it was a trio—pampered the casually attired agent and tended to his every need.

"In case you're wondering," Tucker said, "my job isn't *quite* like that."

"More's the pity," Reed said, the feeble attempt at humor dying stillborn. "Look . . . I get the feeling you didn't come here to watch a movie with me. Perhaps we could discuss my proposal with fewer distractions?"

"All right. Let's walk." Onscreen, the chief, having grown increasingly frustrated with the agent's cavalier attitude, stormed out just as a fourth odalisque materialized.

Tucker led Reed out into the corridors, where they began walking with no apparent destination in mind. "I assume you've been briefed on the incident that damaged *Pioneer*," Reed said.

The sandy-haired man nodded. "More of those automated stations. I always figured there must be others out there."

"They're known as the Ware. And from what the locals told us, there are quite a few of them in that sector, and perhaps beyond."

"And warships too. You don't have to sell me, Malcolm—this could be a future threat to the Federation. Just the sort of thing my employers like to keep an eye on."

"Good. Because I could use you out there, Trip."

Tucker looked him over with eyes that were steelier than he remembered. "It's not as simple as that, you know. Undercover work in uncharted space isn't easy. It takes time to identify and assess local humanoids, learn enough about their culture to create a convincing cover story—"

"No," Reed said. "That's not what I'm asking for. This is a technological problem we're up against. Trip—I need an engineer."

For the first time, Tucker's control slipped. He stopped walking and stared for a moment, the initial shock on his lean face giving way to uncertainty. "I haven't exercised those skills in a long time, Malcolm."

"So you're a little rusty. It's your instincts I need, Trip. That intuition that made you the best damn engineer in Starfleet. The rest will follow. You just need to get back on the horse. Or is it the bicycle?"

Tucker almost smiled. They began walking again, Reed pacing himself to match the intelligence agent's absent, ambling stride. "Be an engineer again," Tucker drawled. "Might be nice to do something clean and simple for a while. Something constructive."

"We could help a lot of people, Trip. And not just in the Federation."

"My employers are only concerned with the Federation. Anyone else . . ." He bit off his words, and Malcolm wondered what motivated the glimpse of bitterness he caught.

"There is a complication," Tucker said after another moment. "I can disguise myself well enough to fool people who never met me. But Travis Mayweather is another matter."

"Then I'd say it's time to bring him into the circle of confidence. I can understand excluding those with no need to know, even friends and family. But now Travis has a need to know. And frankly it'll be a relief to stop lying to him at last, Won't it?"

Tucker gave him a sullen look, but after a moment he closed off again. "I'll consider it."

"There's no rush. *Pioneer* will still be in drydock a little longer, and Admirals Archer and Shran are still putting the task force together."

"Sure. And if—if I choose to accept this mission," he went on with a faint smirk, "I can think of a resource or two I'd like to corral."

"Such as?"

"I know hardware, sure, but what we're facing is artificial intelligence. Machines that *think*."

"I'm not so sure. All they do is parrot a few preprogrammed responses."

"But they're clever enough to adapt, to improvise attacks, to create elaborate deceptions. And they need to hijack all those living brains for something. I think they play dumb just to hide what's really goin' on. And if so, we need help from an expert in artificial intelligence."

"You have someone in mind?"

"There's a . . . potential resource we've been aware of. Now might be a good time to make use of him."

A door opened before them, and Malcolm realized that Tucker's meanderings had led them to *Enterprise*'s engine room. Trip seemed to be just realizing it himself as he looked around. Some of the tension left his frame as he took in the large chamber. The warp core may have been a replica, but it was a convincing one. The engine room had actually gone through considerable refitting in the years after Tucker had faked his death, but the museum had restored it to its original configuration, the one Tucker had known during the four years he'd served as *Enterprise*'s chief engineer.

Reed cleared his throat after a few moments. "*Pioneer*'s core is a little smaller," he said, "but more advanced. Doctor Dax is overseeing the latest upgrades before he stands down. I daresay we'll be leaving drydock with the most state-of-the-art engine in Starfleet."

The look Tucker gave him was . . . complicated. "Don't oversell it, Malcolm. I don't need any more persuading from you."

Reed responded warily, trying to focus on the positive. "Then you'll do it?"

Tucker faced the replica core, not Reed, as he responded. "*Pioneer* will have its engineer."

"Wonderful!" Reed wanted to clap him on the shoulder, but the forbidding aura around the man held him back. "It . . . it'll be great to have you back, Trip. I mean it."

"That's one thing," Tucker said. "You'll have to get out of the habit of calling me that."

"Of course," Reed said after a moment. "I understand."

That part was untrue. He wasn't sure how to reconcile

Tucker's attitude with his memories of the man. Had his years in the spy game changed him that much?

And if so, Reed asked himself, *whose fault is it for introducing Trip to Section 31 in the first place?*

April 6, 2165
Amsterdam, European Alliance

Willem Paul Abramson looked young for his age. Though his hair and beard were silver, his high-browed, aquiline features were those of a man in early middle age—yet as Charles Tucker watched him from a shadowed corner of the industrialist's laboratory, he imagined he could see glimpses of a world-weariness far beyond the man's apparent years. One might wonder what the founder of the Federation's most advanced cybernetics firm had to look so careworn about—if one didn't have the resources of Section 31 to divine the answer.

Abramson was currently huddled in conference with a strongly built, short-haired woman Tucker recognized as Olivia Akomo, his chief cybernetic engineer. They leaned over a slab containing the skeletal, metal-and-plastic framework of an automaton—but instead of the usual geometric shapes of Abramson Industries' maintenance drones, sensor probes, and other such devices, this one had a decidedly bipedal form. *So that's Project Aedilis*, Tucker thought. He had to wonder why Abramson was devoting so much of his wealth and resources to a project unlikely to have much commercial popularity. But then, he was known as a man of old-fashioned sensibilities.

Tucker heard the whine of a small lift rotor behind him and turned to see one of those geometrically shaped drones, a metallic sphere with a hover-drive module on the bottom and a lurid red sensor eye on the front. It closed on him slowly but menacingly, extending a phase weapon emitter. He heard another one closing from the other direction. The two of them herded him out into the light. Akomo looked up, eyes widening in her rounded, dark-hued face. "What the hell? Who are you, what are you doing here?" Her tone was one of outrage rather than alarm, her bearing assertive and sturdy.

But she still deferred to the man beside her, who studied Tucker with no sign of surprise or anxiety, though his disapproval was manifest. "You are not welcome here, sir. This is private property—though I would not expect the likes of you to respect such a concept." His eyes roved up and down Tucker's black uniform.

"Then you know who I represent?" Tucker asked.

"I know the type. Uniforms like yours, eyes like yours. Men who lurk in shadows, who spy on those they pretend to protect. Answerable to no one, obedient to nothing but their own power and secrecy."

"Well, I can see we got off on the wrong foot," Tucker said.

"What did you expect," Akomo shot back, "breaking and entering the way you did?"

"I'm afraid Mister Abramson is a hard man to get an appointment with." He took care to pronounce it the way the man preferred, with an initial "ah" sound. "But I have an urgent matter to discuss with him."

"Everything is always urgent with people like you," Abramson said. "You see only the little span of days before you and imagine that its events will change the world for all time. You fail to realize how little actually changes in the grand scheme."

Tucker met his eyes pointedly. "Well, I can see how a man such as yourself would have a different perspective on time, sir. But I assure you, what I need from you won't take up much of yours. Not when you take the long view of history, I mean."

"Willem, what is he implying?" Akomo asked.

For the first time, Tucker saw a trace of anxiety in the man's eyes. "Olivia, I suggest you let me tend to this man. I need you focused on the neural growth rate analysis."

"I don't appreciate being cut out of the loop."

"Please, Olivia. If there is anything you need to know, I will tell you. But that analysis is important to both of us."

She threw a smoldering glare toward Tucker. "Very well. But I won't be far."

As she left the lab, Tucker strolled closer to the work area, looking over the automaton with a trained eye. "Are you working on some kind of neural circuitry?"

"A revival of an old theory," Abramson replied. "My mentor in cybernetics called it 'bionic plasma,' but I prefer 'bio-neural gel.'"

"Neural computers. And in a humanoid body, too. What are you tryin' to do, build the perfect girlfriend?"

Abramson was far from amused. "Spare me your disapproval, Mister . . ."

"Call me Collier."

"Mister Collier," he echoed with skepticism, though Tucker knew the industrialist had no moral high ground where assumed names were concerned. "I have heard all the objections before. Humans have feared Frankenstein's monster for generations—though in so doing, they misunderstand what poor Mary intended by her tale."

"I think they're more afraid of autonomous drones running out of control, android assassins, all those fun things that cropped up in the twenty-first century. You remember

World War Three, right? I'm sure you read about it in history class."

Abramson turned away. "I remember," he said hollowly after a time. "But people forget the role that technology played in rebuilding *after* the war. It creates its share of problems, but it also creates their solutions." He faced Tucker again. "True, the world discovered a new humanism in the wake of those atrocities. We learned to esteem the dignity of humans as we are. To despise those augmentations that would elevate some above the rest, and those instrumentalities that would threaten us all.

"But has it occurred to you that there is something pathological about humanity's fear of being replaced? That in our celebration of the human, we have lost sight of the possibility that humanity can be improved upon? We allow technology to make human life easier and more prosperous in every way—except where it might require us to broaden our definition of humanity itself."

"And is that what Project Aedilis is about?" Tucker asked. "Creating something more than human?"

"I merely point out, Mister Collier, that our fear of such excesses makes us too wary of beneficial advances. As you can see," Abramson said, indicating the prototype with a theatrical sweep of his arm, "this robot could never be mistaken for a human. And the neural circuitry would merely improve its response time and adaptability; it would not confer a mind upon it. The project is intended merely to provide automata for menial tasks, shaped to accommodate equipment and environments designed for the human form. In Ancient Rome, the aediles were officials responsible for the maintenance of public buildings."

"Kind of an obscure reference, don't you think?"

"I am something of an antiquarian, I fear. It is also a private joke of a sort. Mister Collier," he went on without pause, striding over to a workstation, "clearly you came not to disapprove of my inventions, but to appropriate them. I have no interest in whatever use you intend for my technologies."

"That's not what I'm here for," he said. "I need help in dealing with another technology. An alien technology."

Abramson looked up sharply; that interested him. But that door quickly slammed shut again. "To do what with it?"

Tucker described *Pioneer*'s encounter with the Ware and the planned mission to discover its secrets. "You should have done your homework more carefully, Mister Collier," Abramson told him when he finished. "Abramson Industries does not take military contracts."

"I'm an engineer myself, sir—believe it or not. I'll be accompanying the expedition. But the man I used to be . . . he died a long time ago."

The older man studied him. "Really."

"What I need from you, first of all, is a cover identity. Credentials, a backstory, whatever support is necessary to make me a credible civilian expert. Although it'd certainly help matters if you could see fit to provide some diagnostic equipment, even additional personnel."

"Hm. And what makes you think I would agree to this?"

"People are dying out there, sir. Being made slaves, their minds rotting away. We don't know how far this spreads, how many species are suffering. But we do know that Federation lives will also be endangered as we spread into that space."

"People die," Abramson said with resignation. "People suffer. That is the way of things. I learned long ago that one cannot change that with ships and weapons."

"No. You change it with knowledge. The ships are just how you get to where the problem is."

"If that is so, then Starfleet is well enough equipped to handle these matters. And you can get your credentials elsewhere."

"We need to understand their interfaces between the machines and the living brain. Your people's 'bio-neural' expertise could make a big difference."

"I have tried to make big differences before," the older man told him, growing contemplative. "I have usually found it to cause more trouble than it solved."

"Don't you even care about all the lives being lost?"

"If I cared for every life . . . I would be overwhelmed. I must pick my battles, Mister Collier. And you have given me no compelling reason to pick this one."

Tucker sighed, hating what he had to do now. "I have one left, sir. You see, I did do my homework. Or my employers did. We looked through history. The history of a Mister Willem Paul Abramson, who didn't seem to exist up until twenty-six years ago. Oh, there are birth records, school transcripts—but, well, we know a thing or two about faking identities."

"Is it so wrong if a man wishes to forget his old life and begin anew?"

"Depends on the reasons for it."

"And what do you imagine those reasons are?"

"That's a question for Jacques Tarrant," Tucker replied. After giving Abramson a moment to react to the name, he went on: "Who lived a quiet life in a small town in North Africa for thirty-eight years and then disappeared when his wife died—not long before Willem Abramson first showed up. Funny thing, though, there are no records of his childhood either. And hardly any photos of the man—but our computers found one that showed enough of his face to match it to yours. And to Jerome Drexel, a man credited with helping to rebuild society after World War III. And to a twentieth-century atmospheric scientist named Wilson Evergreen.

"You're at least two hundred years old, Mister Abramson. And you don't want anyone to know it. But we do."

The look on Abramson's face had moved past resignation to a glint of wistful humor. "You know a fraction of it. I am far older than you could ever imagine."

"What are you? If it's not too personal a question. Some kind of augment? An alien? Time traveler?" He glanced at the central slab. "Android?"

"I am none of those things," replied the far older man, "though I have counted each among my onetime acquaintances." His gaze turned inward. "I was simply a fool named Akharin, whom fortune favored with the ability to recover from my most fatal errors. Through some fluke of mutation, I was granted lifetimes to learn the lessons that wiser men could master in only one."

"Now, that is one sweet deal."

"But it comes at an enormous cost. Imagine . . . finding love, over and over, only to see it wither like the petals of a flower. Holding your children in your arms, always aware that, almost before you know it, you will bury them."

Tucker was slow to answer. He understood a thing or two about giving up the life one wanted, wondering if it would ever be possible to settle down with a loved one. But the sheer scope of Abramson's grief was beyond what he could grasp. Still, it let him look at the Aedilis prototype on the slab with new understanding. "That's what you're trying for, isn't it? To create an offspring . . . or a mate . . . who'll be as timeless as you are."

"It is a hope," Abramson admitted. "The technology is still generations away . . . but I have the time."

Tucker made one more try. "The Ware technology is quite a ways beyond ours. Their stations and ships may not be self-aware, but there's a sophisticated intelligence behind them. Studying them could jump-start our computer sciences by decades, if not more."

The immortal contemplated for a long moment, as still as a statue. Finally, he said: "You will need someone who understands neural interfaces—and I will need my own best person in the field to study and reverse-engineer the Ware. For both our purposes, Olivia Akomo is the optimal choice. I will convince her. And . . . I shall arrange your credentials."

Tucker felt no sense of victory, and chose not to insult the man by extending a hand in thanks. This deal would benefit both of them, and hopefully the entire Federation. But he had made the deal through blackmail and manipulation. Faced with the most extraordinary human secret he had ever encountered, something worthy of awe and reverence, he had turned it against its holder in order to entrap him.

He was glad he would not have to live with it for more than one lifetime.

April 11, 2165
U.S.S. Pioneer, Vulcan Space Central spacedock

"There's . . . something you need to know, Travis."

Travis Mayweather couldn't recall the last time he'd seen Captain Reed look so uneasy. It was odd to see, when just moments ago the captain had sounded so proud as he reported on the progress of the task force. He and Val Williams had just arrived aboard *Vol'Rala*, a *Kumari*-class

Andorian battlecruiser whose name, auspiciously, could be translated as *Enterprise*. Mayweather suspected either Admiral Archer or Admiral Shran had arranged for that. *Vol'Rala*'s captain, Reshthenar sh'Prenni, was a former crew-member and protégée of Shran's who had earned her captaincy just as the Andorian fleet was being folded into the Federation Starfleet, and she had made quite a name for herself in the four years since—particularly in the past half-year as *Vol'Rala* had spearheaded Starfleet efforts to clean out the pirates and raiders in the Kandari Sector. Mayweather was pleased to have her along, especially on a ship of that name.

The other Andorian ships, including *Thelasa-vei*, would be arriving over the next two days, and Reed hoped to have the task force under way by the fifteenth. But *Vol'Rala* had been undergoing maintenance at Earth, putting it in position to transport the captain and Williams back swiftly, along with the civilian engineering consultants that Reed had somehow persuaded Abramson Industries to provide. Reed had been about to introduce Mayweather to the head of the team, Philip Collier, who would be serving as interim chief engineer until they could find a more permanent replacement for Tobin Dax (who, Mayweather tended to forget, had himself been a temporary fill-in when he'd begun two years prior). But for some reason, he had deemed it necessary to speak to Travis in private first, leading him into the sensor monitoring bay adjacent to the airlock anteroom.

"Something about Collier?" Mayweather asked.

"More or less." He cleared his throat, then said nothing for a long moment. "Oh, hell, I thought I'd figured out how to tell you this. But there's no way to break it gently. Might as well just get it over with."

He left the bay for a moment, then came back leading another man. "Travis . . . this is Philip Collier."

Though confused by his captain's behavior, Mayweather smiled and extended a hand to the engineer, a slim, light-complexioned man with shaggy, dark red hair and a thick beard. But then he froze when he saw the man's eyes. The color was different, but he knew those eyes, knew the face despite the subtle alterations to the features, the filling out of the nose. The knowing look on the man's face confirmed it, as did the voice in which he spoke. "Hey, Travis. Been a long time."

"T-Trip?" Surprise soon gave way to joy, and he was pulling his old *Enterprise* crewmate into his arms. "Trip! My God, you're alive!"

"Yeah, for the moment," Charles Tucker III replied, gasping for breath. Mayweather finally released him, but he kept his hands on the man's arms, patting him as if to affirm that he was real and solid. "Good to see you too, Travis."

But there was restraint in his tone, regret in his eyes. It brought Mayweather back to the ground and got him thinking about the anomaly of this situation. "How?" he asked, even as he realized it was the wrong question and amended: "Why? Why are you in disguise? Why haven't you told anyone you're alive?"

Slowly, awkwardly, Tucker and Reed took turns telling the story, starting with the events leading up to Tucker's death—apparent death—a decade earlier. When they were done, he tried to summarize the account just to get a handle on it in his own mind. "So let me get this straight. A secret intelligence branch within Starfleet recruited *you* to go undercover on Romulus to sabotage their warp seven project . . . and that meant you had to fake your death and go undercover as a Romulan?"

"That sums it up pretty well."

"It doesn't even begin to sum it up! Why you, Trip? You're not a spy. Why couldn't they send one of their own people?"

"They needed an engineer, someone already familiar with Romulan technology."

"Then you could've worked for them as a consultant. What made them think you'd be a good field agent?"

"They thought I had good empathy for aliens. A lot of the work is listening, getting to know other cultures. It's not that different from exploration."

"Intelligence agencies recruit operatives from many walks of life, Travis," Reed said. "People who travel widely and have knowledge of other cultures are ideal candidates."

"That doesn't explain why you had to make us all think you were dead!" Mayweather said to Tucker, too hurt and upset to give proper acknowledgment to his captain first. "We mourned you for months. Your brother . . . does he know? Does your family know?" Tucker shook his head slowly, silently. "Who does know?"

"Of *Enterprise's* crew," Tucker replied, "aside from Malcolm, Admiral Archer knows, because we needed his okay to arrange it. Phlox knows, because he needed to fake the death certificate."

Mayweather was going over the memory of that day in his mind. "It never did make sense. The way you sacrificed yourself . . . it never seemed like there was a good reason for it."

Reed fidgeted. "Yes, well, I always wished we'd had more time to concoct a more coherent cover story. Honestly I'm amazed anyone ever fell for such a— Sorry."

The first officer stared at both men. "So just those two?"

Tucker fidgeted. "T'Pol . . . found out later."

"Hoshi?" They shook their heads. Mayweather sighed in disbelief and paced the room. "Why? You broke her heart!

Both of you!" he added, gesturing toward his captain before turning back to Tucker. "Why couldn't you just, just go on an extended leave or something?"

Tucker shook his head. "I had to be officially dead so the Romulans couldn't identify me if they captured me. So Starfleet would have deniability."

Mayweather stared. "That doesn't even make sense! If they had any way of identifying you at all, if they had enough intel about Starfleet to find that out, then did you really think they'd only look at the records for living officers? You thought it'd never occur to them to consider that you might've faked your death?"

After a moment, Tucker just spread his hands. "It seemed like a good idea at the time. Frankly, I can't blame you for thinkin' otherwise. I've been wishin' for ten years that we'd found a better way."

"Then why didn't you come back?" Mayweather asked with prosecutorial ardor. "The war's been over for nearly five years! You didn't need to hide from the Romulans anymore, so why didn't you tell us you were alive?"

"Because I'm not!" Tucker shouted. "Okay? The Trip Tucker you know died years ago." He looked away. "The things I've seen . . . things I've done . . . I'm not the man I was."

Mayweather took a deep, slow breath. "No, I guess you aren't. The Trip Tucker I knew wouldn't have been so selfish. He wouldn't have systematically lied to his friends and cut them out of his life."

"I have obligations I can't get out of easily! The agency—"

"And what about your obligations to your friends? To the truth?"

"I do what I can to protect them. To protect the Federation. That's all I can do."

"Fine. Then I suggest you get on with it—Mister Collier."
He turned to Reed. "Captain, if there's nothing more?"

"Travis, try to understand—"

"Let him go," Tucker said.

Reed sighed. "Very well. Dismissed. But we'll talk later," he
added, trying to be kind.

But Mayweather was in no mood to accept kindness from
Reed right now. He was no longer sure he could trust it.

6

POKER NIGHT HAD BEEN a weekly tradition on *Endeavour* for more than two years—and part of that tradition was that Doctor Phlox could frequently be relied upon to provide entertaining and sometimes mildly uncomfortable surprises. Tonight, he showed up at the quarters shared by Hoshi Sato and Takashi Kimura with his arms burdened by a tray bearing four large flowerpots. Each pot contained a bulbous, yellow-green plant with aspects of both vine and cactus, emitting a pungently sweet aroma that swiftly overwhelmed even the scent of Kimura's famous wasabi chili dip. "If I could have a little help, please?" the Denobulan doctor asked, sounding winded from carrying the tray through the corridors.

As Kimura deftly relieved Phlox of the tray and less deftly searched for a place to deposit it, Sato asked, "What's the occasion, Phlox?"

"Ahh," he replied with a wide Denobulan grin, "an occasion indeed, my dear Hoshi. My younger daughter, Vaneel, has finally selected her third husband!"

Elizabeth Cutler, the honey-haired science officer, beamed in response. "That's wonderful, Phlox!" She clasped his shoulder lightly, aware that Denobulan men were not comfortable with public displays of physical affection—paradoxical though that seemed in the case of the otherwise gregarious doctor. "I know you were wondering if she'd ever complete the set."

"Yes, well, Vaneel has always been especially picky. You should have seen me trying to get her to eat her fruits when she was a child."

"Don't you mean her vegetables?" Kimura asked, finally giving up and putting the tray precariously down on the couch.

"Oh, Denobulan children love vegetables! Can't get enough of them. They usually love fruits as well, but Vaneel has always danced to her own rhythm. Sometimes I'm amazed she managed to find even two husbands who suited her eccentric preferences. Maybe that's why she went farther afield for the third."

"So are you going to keep us guessing?" Sato asked. "Who's the lucky guy?"

"That's what makes this such a special occasion—worthy of nothing less a gift than these magnificent Shendurian sting-vines."

The final member of their poker group, helmsman Pedro Ortega, looked confused. "You give out plants as wedding gifts?"

"A marriage is a living thing," Phlox propounded to the young ensign. "It requires cultivation and attention to remain healthy—yet needs to be hardy enough to survive periods of deprivation and stress. Just like these vines. Plants such as these are traditional engagement gifts for friends of the family—a bit like your old human tradition of giving out cigars at births, though without the, ah, carcinogenic aftereffects. By accepting and tending them, you demonstrate your solidarity with the couple-to-be and their commitment to cultivating the marriage."

Ortega hefted one of the bulbous plants gingerly, as if it were an unexploded bomb. "So . . . we have to keep these?"

"Oh, not indefinitely. Only until the wedding. Shouldn't be more than, oh, four months."

"Oh. Okay." The young man did not look particularly re-assured.

Sato was getting impatient to hear the rest of the good news. "So why is this particular husband-to-be so special?"

Phlox swelled with pride. "His name is Pehle Retab. He's Antaran."

Ortega looked around in confusion as the others reacted to the significance of that detail. "I don't get it."

Cutler did her job as science officer and provided the ex-position. "The Antarans and Denobulans were old enemies. They haven't had a war in three centuries, but the old resent-ments remained until about a dozen years ago."

"It was Phlox who took the first step in healing the rift," Hoshi added proudly.

"I played a small part, but not without reluctance, I con-fess," the doctor added with more modesty. "But the fact that both peoples have taken to reconciliation so swiftly just shows how ready both sides were to move on."

"But there's still some bitterness on both sides, right?" Kimura replied, holding a stingvine pot and surveying their quarters for a suitable perch. "A Denobulan actually marrying an Antaran—that's a statement a lot of people won't be ready for."

"Something Vaneel finds irresistible, I'm sure. Oh, she genu-inely loves Pehle, but the symbolic value of the marriage appeals to her sense of iconoclasm immensely. I admit I wouldn't have had the same courage, but it's something I admire in my daughter."

Hoshi moved to Phlox and put her hand on his shoulder, holding his eyes silently for a long moment. She could see that this was emotionally complicated for him, since his youngest son, Mettus—Vaneel's closest sibling in age—was estranged from his family due to his own association with anti-Antaran hate groups. Sato realized, as Phlox must, that Vaneel's choice was in part a direct repudiation of Mettus's politics, a reminder of the one great rift in Phlox's family that he might never heal.

After a moment, Phlox looked away, retreating from that complex truth. "Well, anyway, you're all invited to the wedding, of course. I've already shared the good news with Captain T'Pol, and she's confident that Admiral Archer will be willing to arrange *Endeavour*'s schedule accordingly, barring emergencies, of course."

"We wouldn't miss it," Kimura said, still unable to decide where to put the stingvine. Sato took his arm and guided him to the end table in the starboard corner, where it fit perfectly. "Frankly," the armory officer went on, "I'm still trying to get my head around Denobulan families. Each man has three wives, who have two other husbands each, who have two other wives each, and . . . how does that work?"

Phlox grinned widely. "When we Denobulans finally figure it out, we'll let you know." The group shared a hearty laugh, then sat down to play poker. "So tell me," Phlox went on to Hoshi and Takashi as the latter dealt the cards with practiced grace. "When were you two thinking of setting the date?"

The cards went flying.

April 18, 2165
Ambhat City, Delta IV (Dhei-Lta)

Caroline Paris almost felt guilty.

Captain Shumar was up in orbit at the moment, giving some of Delta IV's leaders a tour of the *U.S.S. Essex*—a stolid, dependable ship, but hardly the lap of luxury. Diplomacy demanded that the senior officer of the ship take the lead in negotiating with the planet's senior officials for diplomatic and trade ties. Which left Paris, as his first officer, with the arduous task of touring Delta's gorgeous capital city in the company of its extremely attractive mayor and his extremely attractive aides. She and her crewmates—science officer Steven Mullen and armory officer Ahn Chung-hee—had been forced to endure the sensory pleasures of its architecture, its cuisine, its street music (literally, for some of the pathways emitted melodic sounds as one strode upon them), and, most of all, its people. Extremely attractive, incredibly fit people who wore little clothing in these warm climes . . . and who had no inhibitions that the trio of humans had yet discovered.

"Now I know why the *Horizon* crew kept Delta's coordinates to themselves," Ahn murmured to Mullen as the group passed an open-air clothing bazaar where various Deltan customers were changing into and out of various graceful, scanty, and diaphanous robes, right out in the open without a trace of modesty—and leaving no doubt that their hairlessness was not limited to their heads.

"I see what you mean," Mullen replied, his dark face split by a wide, bright grin. "Who would want to share this?"

Paris, like most people in Starfleet, had heard the lurid spacer's tales of the Deltans ever since the *E.C.S. Horizon* had made first contact twenty-two years earlier: a race of bald but spectacularly beautiful humanoids with the unabashed hedonism of a Risian and the raw sexual magnetism of an Orion female. The Boomer crew had declined to reveal its location, offering implausible claims about humanity not being ready for the sheer sexual potency of the Deltans, which had only fed the suspicion that the whole thing was just another

Boomer tall tale. Yet *Essex* had recently run afoul of an un-
pleasant, warlike bunch called the Carreon, who had obtained
low-warp technology from another Boomer ship a decade ago
and had begun using it to try to build an interstellar empire
(which so far consisted only of a couple of uninhabited systems next to their homeworld). The Carreon had attempted
to commandeer *Essex* and use it to strike at a neighboring race
they declared their mortal enemies—a race whose description had matched the *Horizon* crew's claims about the Deltans.
After easily thwarting the Carreon's rather primitive takeover
attempt, Captain Shumar had decided to track the Deltans
down and see what it was that the Carreon found so objec-
tionable. Shumar's general hail had evoked a friendly reply and
an invitation for *Essex* to visit their planet, which they called
Dhei, in the V2292 Ophiuchi system, which they called Lta.
Apparently it had been *Horizon*'s Captain Mayweather who had
simplified the compound name to "Delta."

According to the Carreon, the Deltans were a race of ef-
feminate weaklings who scorned the noble arts of war, yet
whose technological superiority made them the greatest exis-
tential threat ever faced by civilization—beings repulsive to all
good Carreon, yet able to lead good Carreon astray with their
alluring ways. Digging through the oxymoronic propaganda,
it seemed the Carreon's animosity arose partly from a clash
of cultural mores and primarily from their desire for several
resource-rich star systems to which the Deltans had a prior
claim by millennia. Delta was an ancient, advanced civilization,
but its people had turned inward long ago, feeling their age
of spaceflight had brought them all the answers they needed
about the material universe. Now they led a more contemplative life, seeking higher, less tangible forms of enlightenment.
But there was nothing ascetic about them; they celebrated

passion as wholeheartedly as the Vulcans renounced it, seeing the flesh and its sensations as inseparable from the spirit.

And they made no effort to hide it from outsiders, as Paris and the others were discovering. Their tour of the verdant, open capital city now led them to one of its many lush park grounds, this one dominated by a wide, low stage on which a number of Deltans were participating in . . . Paris resisted her initial impulse to call it an orgy, for that implied something lurid and vulgar, while this was somehow more rarefied, a balletic piece of performance art. She felt intensely aroused as she watched, to be sure, but somehow it wasn't for the conventional reasons. There was surprisingly little movement from the performers, and little effort to display their more intimate anatomy to the audience or demonstrate acts of prowess. Yet there was an almost tangible aura of very powerful emotion. Paris felt it from the crowd around her as much as from the performers: a deep sense of contentment and tenderness, like being in your true love's embrace.

"Are you . . . feeling this?" she asked the other two humans tentatively, abashedly.

"The emotion?" Mullen replied, his voice quavering. "Yes. Yes, it's . . ." He shook himself, trying to focus, and turned to Mayor Serima. "This is your empathic ability, isn't it? We're feeling what you feel."

Serima's strong bronze face brightened. "So you can feel it?" he asked, the melodic lilt of his language audible even through communicator translation. "Wonderful! The Carreon could not, so we were unsure if other species could. To know you have the necessary empathy is most heartening."

"That's one word for it," Ahn chuckled, watching the show raptly.

A female aide of Serima's—her name was Kuryala, Paris

recalled—gestured toward the spectators, many of whom were joining in the festivities themselves, pairing or grouping with no evident selectivity regarding the gender, appearance, or quantity of their partners. "You are welcome to join in yourselves," she offered, stroking Mullen's arm. "Adding human voices to the chorus could generate stimulating and novel results."

Mullen flushed. "I, uh, I appreciate the, um, invitation. But . . . I have someone back on the ship, and . . ."

"They are welcome to join too, if they wish," Kuryala replied, her smile undiminished.

Paris felt the need to come to the stammering man's rescue. "It's kind of you to offer. But we humans . . . uh, we generally prefer not to be so public with our . . . choruses."

"Ah, of course," Serima said. "You prefer someplace free of distractions, so you may focus more intensely on the joining."

"Something like that."

"Well, we do have isolation chambers nearby for just such purposes." He gestured toward a row of cabana-like structures along the edge of the park. Some of the spectator-participants in the show were breaking off from the audience in groups of two or more and availing themselves of the private enclosures—although Paris was increasingly convinced that the word "private" wouldn't translate into Deltan.

The mayor took Paris's hand, his big dark eyes transfixing hers. "I would be honored, Caroline, if you would demonstrate the human way of loving to me."

Paris hadn't been this overwhelmed by a male's sexual invitation since she'd been fifteen and in the backseat of the school debate champion's skimmer. She didn't know what was coming over her. "I—I'm not sure this is wise," she managed to get out. "There's so much we don't, um, know about each other. . . . Maybe there should be, uh, medical tests, or . . ."

"My people have reviewed the medical data from your ship. They've discovered no incompatibilities or causes for concern."

"Yes, but there's a protocol . . ." Why was she still talking? She would've preferred to stop at "Yes."

"You're right," Mullen said, pulling away from Kuryala's increasingly affectionate touch. "I should, um, I should stay objective. Just observe for—in fact, maybe I should go back to the ship."

"Your loss," Ahn said as Kuryala readily transferred her attentions to him. "Come on, Commander, where's the harm? You feel it, don't you? We're safe here. We don't have to be afraid or ashamed. Just . . . welcomed. Loved."

He was right—she did feel it. What reason did she have to be afraid? "Well, it would only be polite to, uh, sample the local customs. Wouldn't want to be . . . unfriendly . . ."

She trailed off as Serima escorted her toward the isolation chambers. Ahn seemed content to enjoy the company of Kuryala and another female aide right out in the open. She could almost feel their excitement at discovering what new sensations the human body had to offer. An excitement that she shared as she laid her hands on Serima and reveled in how easily his robes came loose. . . .

April 19, 2165
U.S.S. Essex NCC-173, orbiting Delta IV

When Captain Bryce Shumar arrived in sickbay, he found Doctor Mazril and Lieutenant Commander Mullen attempting to guide Caroline Paris back to her bed along the far wall of the gleaming white room. "You don't understand," she was telling them in a serene, reasonable tone. "I have to go back."

"We discussed this, remember?" Mazril was a mature Tiburonian woman, bald with scalloped, elephantine ears and a row of small bumps running down the center of her forehead. "You need to stay here and rest."

"Yes, I overheard that conversation, but *I* need to get back." She pulled free of their grip and strode toward the exit, not even seeming to register that Shumar was in her path.

The captain caught her arm. "Commander." She ignored him. "Caroline!"

"Who? Oh, yes. She needs to stay here and rest. We should let her." She tried to pull free.

Seeing the urgency in the doctor's eyes, Shumar tightened his grip. "Commander Paris, stand down!"

But she strove harder to get away. "Let me go! No! I need to go!"

Mazril and Mullen moved in, the latter getting a firm grip on her other arm. He and Shumar held her against her worsening struggles, wincing at her shrieks, until Mazril moved in with a spray hypo and administered a mild sedative. Her struggles subsided, but by the time they'd led her back to bed, she was sobbing abjectly. After a few moments, she drifted into an uneasy sleep, and Mazril led the captain and Mullen aside.

"What happened?" Shumar asked her.

"I'm afraid the commander got the lesser dose of it," the doctor replied. She led him around the privacy curtain to the next bed, where Lieutenant Ahn lay motionless, a vacant stare on his lean face. "Ahn is in a complete dissociative state—practically catatonic. He doesn't know who or where he is, he's barely responsive . . . at this point I can't be sure if he'll ever come out of it."

Shumar absorbed the news, only his British military upbringing keeping him stoic. "And Commander Paris?"

"She seems to be experiencing a form of depersonalization—a lesser dissociative disorder. She exhibits a detachment from her sense of self, as if her experiences were happening to someone else and she were merely a spectator. Her behavior suggests that she considers herself incomplete, that she will only be whole if she returns to the planet—or that she is still there and needs to escape from the illusion of being here. Her inability to achieve that goal provokes intense anxiety or depression, as you saw."

"And will she . . . recover?"

"I would say her prognosis is good," the Tiburonian replied. "Depersonalization disorder is treatable with cognitive therapy and medication. Even comforting personal interactions and physical or sensory stimulation could help to bring her back to her sense of self. But there are other complicating factors." She moved to the main display and called up Paris's scan results. "Her hormonal balance is extremely disrupted, as is Ahn's. It resembles withdrawal from an addictive drug. This is possible to overcome as well, but it will not be easy for her."

Shumar turned to the science officer. "Mister Mullen, what happened down there?"

Mullen seemed reluctant to speak. Mazril prompted him by saying, "Commander, my examination clearly shows that both of them have been engaged in intensive and prolonged sexual activity."

The captain stared at Mullen. "Is this true?"

"Uh, yes, sir," the younger man replied. "It didn't seem . . . that is, the Deltans were just so friendly and, and open. They seem so calm and intellectual at first, but sir, they make the Risians seem inhibited. I didn't . . . join in . . . I have Melina, you know." Shumar nodded. "But . . . the temptation was incredible. It took all my willpower to say no. There was just some . . . aura about them."

"Nothing mystical," Mazril told the captain. "Both Paris and Ahn—and Mister Mullen, to a lesser extent—have the residue of extremely potent attractant and appeasement pheromones in their systems and on their skin and clothing. These pheromones are very similar to those secreted by Orion females, but in this case they clearly come in both male and female varieties, given Commander Paris's susceptibility."

Shumar had heard enough. Clenching his fists, he took a long, rueful look at his damaged—his *victimized* officers. "Then that makes the Deltans twice as great a threat."

Ambhat City, Delta IV

"Do you honestly expect me to believe this was a simple accident? You assaulted my people! Violated them! You may have damaged them for life!"

Mod'hira, prime minister of the Deltan Union, gazed up at Shumar with unwavering patience, her lovely dark eyes conveying deep sadness. "Please understand, Captain Shumar. We would never impose on an unwilling person. The fulfillment of the individual is sacrosanct to us—we would never seek to deprive another of it." With her lilting voice and bronze complexion, she reminded Shumar of how his grandmother Parvati had appeared in his youth. She emanated the same sense of gentle kindness as well.

But his anger enabled him to resist that perception. "I'd find that more credible if not for my doctor's findings about the pheromones you emit. I can feel you trying to influence me right now, so you might as well stop it."

"I apologize, Captain. Our pheromonal secretions are a reflex, not a conscious choice. For us, it is a part of everyday life, and we can choose to respond to the stimulus, or not, as we see fit. Mayor Serima and his staff were unaware that your species was more . . . vulnerable to the effect."

"But you have encountered humans before. The *Horizon* crew."

Mod'hira gave a small, sad smile. "Yes, our travelers told us of their susceptibility. But they had believed it was a consequence of the humans' long isolation aboard their freighter. And it was such a brief encounter that most of us had little knowledge of it."

Shumar crossed his arms. "According to my science officer, your people assured mine that their medical staff had found humans 'compatible' with Deltans."

The mayor sighed. "I fear that is the problem: that your people are perhaps too compatible with ours. You have the necessary empathic potential to experience the unitive effect of Dhei-ten lovemaking—the merger not only of bodies but of minds and identities, the subsumption of the self within another. But you have not yet evolved the necessary sexual or emotional maturity to be able to cope with the experience."

"So this is *our* fault?"

"No, Captain," she went on, her tone as soothing as ever. "It is a tragic mishap arising from mutual misunderstanding."

"Well, I call it a sexual assault upon my crew. Their judgment was compromised and they had no ability to give proper consent."

"With respect, Captain . . . your science officer was able to decline the invitation. I understand your anger. It is an honest and meaningful emotion and I do not dismiss it. But you should not allow it to lead you astray from understanding."

"What I understand is that my people were taken advantage of and damaged, and those who did this to them need to be held to account. I demand the arrest of the mayor and his aides."

The sadness in those eyes deepened as she shook her head. His heart leaped in his chest and he wanted to reach out and comfort her. He ruthlessly quashed the insidious urge. "I cannot allow you access to them," the prime minister said. "After what happened, they are devastated with grief. Since they were joined in love with your crewpersons when the latter . . . succumbed, they experienced much of the effect for themselves. This has been traumatic for them as well as for your people. Yours have endured worse, I freely grant, but Serima and his colleagues must bear the pain of knowing they caused that, and they are in intensive counseling to help them manage it."

"How very noble of them. And how very convenient."

"This is our way, Captain. To heal rather than punish. Our finest medical minds are at your disposal to help you treat your crew."

"The last thing they need is more exposure to Deltans."

Those bottomless eyes held his. "And the last thing you would do now is trust any Dhei-ten with their safety. I understand. But I must caution you, Captain Shumar. Though we are a peaceful people, we are not untrained in defense. Aggression is as necessary an emotion as any other, when properly managed and directed. And our encounters with the Carreon in recent years have . . . encouraged us to refresh our memory of our ancient combat skills. So if you have any thoughts of apprehending Serima and the others by force, or otherwise exacting retaliation upon us, I fear you would provoke further regrettable interactions."

Shumar bristled at her words . . . but only briefly, for

despite his outrage, he knew he lacked adequate cause for a military response. Maybe this was Paris and Ahn's own fault for being unable to keep their pants on in an alien port. He didn't want to believe that, but he couldn't prove malice on the Deltans' part either, not sufficiently to justify risking lives.

Noting his resignation, Mod'hira rose gracefully from behind her desk. "I believe the best option for us both at this point is to bring this contact to an end. I suggest you return to your Federation and advise others of your people not to come here. Perhaps, in time, we can devise protocols and guidelines that will let us prevent tragedies like this in the future. But for now, I think it best if Dhei defers further contact with the Federation until your people have further matured . . . and we both have learned greater caution."

Shumar didn't appreciate her dismissive words, but he couldn't refute her premise. "Perhaps mutual avoidance is the best option, Prime Minister," he said, giving her a stiffly courteous nod of farewell. "I will take my leave of you now—and I will hope this is the last time our two species meet."

7

SKON WAITED PATIENTLY for the security officer at the *Kir'Shara* study vault to complete his identity verification. There was no logic in irritation at a necessary and expected delay; one simply adapted to it. Skon used the time for a mental review of his research goal for today: a close, microscopic study of several ambiguous characters in the text, in hope that a determination of the precise calligraphic strokes used to etch them would clarify which phonemes had been intended. To that end, he was accompanied by Professor Semet, an aged philologist specializing in the texts of the Surakian era. Semet was an agreeably quiet and aloof man, disinclined to speak unless he had something of significance to impart. This was somewhat refreshing after several weeks with Tobin Dax as a houseguest. Dax was an intelligent individual, helpful at providing insights into the principal language of his Trill homeworld (though intensely reticent about certain aspects of his culture and biology, a reserve a Vulcan could respect), and generally introverted and quiet; but when he did choose to engage in conversation, his insecurities inclined him to speak more than was needed, and often with limited substance and coherence.

Finally Skon and Semet were cleared to enter the study vault and its heavy doors swung open. Inside was only a wide, rounded worktable supported on a thick central pillar, with control consoles and inset displays around its perimeter and a full suite of sensor apparatus mounted on the ceiling above it. The *Kir'Shara* had not yet arrived, nor would it begin its approach until after the doors had been sealed. A vault guard accompanied the two researchers into the chamber and took up a post beside the closing doors, watching them dispassionately but unwaveringly.

While irritation might be illogical, Skon still allowed himself a twinge of regret that these precautions were necessary. The security systems, installed following the Romulan terrorist strike on Mount Seleya early in the war, had been retained subsequently due to the regrettable attitudes of fringe factions such as the Anti-revisionists and certain loyalists of the defunct High Command—factions which, as Professor T'Nol's recent actions had demonstrated, were capable of excessive measures in their denial of the truths that Surak's true word had revealed. Thus, the *Kir'Shara* remained the most closely guarded historical artifact on all Vulcan, however much Skon might wish all Vulcans could observe it firsthand.

Skon dealt with this wish by reminding himself that what mattered was the philosophy and wisdom contained in the *Kir'Shara's* words, not the physical vessel that conveyed them. His own efforts to translate the text were part of the process of making its content universally accessible. Still, on these occasions when he was granted access to the artifact that Surak himself had crafted and handled, it seemed to bring him inspiration that was slow to come in other contexts.

Was this logical? Perhaps not. But the *Kir'Shara* itself acknowledged certain fundamental instincts that could not be separated from the thought process. Surak had written that the goal was not to despise or ignore these inner drives and reflexes, but to master and direct them insofar as they could be used constructively. This recognition of the power of atavism within the Vulcan psyche was why his people still practiced the traditional rituals surrounding *pon farr* and marriage, why they still undertook maturity ordeals such as the *kahs-wan*, and why they still utilized shrines to ancient deities such as the one his family maintained in Dycoon. These drives were bred into the Vulcan animal, and thus they could not be escaped, only harnessed as tools and analogies for focusing the mind. Skon's periodic visits to the study vault—however he rationalized their utility to his work—were his own form of pilgrimage.

At last Skon heard the hum of the lift machinery ascending from the storage vault deep beneath the floor. The narrow shaft rising through the base of the examination table was the only access to the transporter-shielded underground vault where the *Kir'Shara* reposed in controlled environmental conditions, mimicking those of the T'Karath Sanctuary catacombs where the artifact had been discovered. The conditions here in the study vault had been set to match as well, to minimize the stress placed on the 1800-year-old artifact when it was raised for examination.

Finally, the centimeters-thick shaft cover at the center of the worktable slid open and the *Kir'Shara* rose into view. The ark of Surak was a tetrahedral prism with a beveled base, approximately 457 millimeters in height and 220 millimeters at its widest point. (Skon had trained himself to think in human measurement units as part of his English translation efforts.) Its worn, gray metal surface was adorned with Old High Vulcan calligraphy on all three of its large isosceles faces, one of which also contained a pattern of three interlocking triangles with a small circular depression in the central, inverted one. Four similar depressions were found on another side, five on the third. These were the control keys for activating the artifact's functions. The primary activation sequence would trigger the holographic circuitry within, projecting a ring of blood-green text in the air above the artifact, with translations into other leading Vulcan languages of the time appearing in overlapping rings of other colors. There was a distasteful air of showmanship to this projection method, Skon thought, but it was believed that Surak had chosen it as a means of capturing the attention of the emotional, erratic, materialistic Vulcan populace of the era.

But the sequence Skon now carefully pressed into the artifact's controls activated its second major function, unlocking the base so that he could retrieve the actual printed texts protected within the ark. The seam between the large faces and the beveled base was so fine that they appeared to be a single piece, with only close examination revealing the hidden contents. Lifting off the upper frame with great delicacy exposed the arrayed and numbered racks holding the thirty-six thin, trapezoidal titanium sheets that bore the actual text of the *Kir'Shara* finely etched upon their erosion-resistant surfaces. The holograms had been for the masses, but these hand-sized plaques had been for posterity, ensuring that the texts would remain accessible even if the artifact's projection capability failed—since Surak had been very much aware of the risk that the wars then ravaging Vulcan might revert any survivors to a more primitive technological level.

Skon considered the plaques to be the true text of the *Kir'Shara*, the originals that the holographic projection merely replicated. This was why he sought out the original plaques themselves whenever he encountered a difficulty or uncertainty in his translation. A careful examination of the writing in its author's own hand could sometimes bring unexpected insights.

But today's unexpected discovery was far from what Skon

had hoped for. After an hour of microscopic examination, Semet finally spoke. "Odd."

"Please clarify," Skon asked.

"Certain etchings on this plate appear to have unusually rectilinear edges at micrometer resolution. I have not noted this pattern in the texts before."

Skon examined the philologist's readings. Semet's observation appeared sound. "What could account for this pattern?" he asked the older Vulcan.

"Were it a modern text, the pattern could easily be explained as the result of computer fabrication."

The amateur linguist furrowed his brow. "Computerized fabrication technologies did exist in Surak's time."

"Few remained available in the wake of the Conflagration. And all prior examinations of the *Kir'Shara* plaques have produced results consistent with hand-etching."

"Is it possible the observed pattern could be illusory? The result of some intrinsic grain in the metal?"

"You could assess the probabilities better than I, Professor," Semet observed. "It seems unlikely, but we can examine the metal for such grain."

This was promptly done, but no intrinsic pattern was found. However, the metallurgical analysis gave an unexpected reading. "These radioisotope decay levels are inconsistent with metal fabricated during the nuclear wars," Skon observed. "They are more consistent with a modern origin."

Semet frowned, contemplating the result. "This is not possible. Previous analyses have given isotope readings consistent with a Conflagration-era origin. The equipment must be miscalibrated."

This required bringing in a sensor specialist to check and calibrate the equipment, but the second reading two hours later gave the same result. Afterward, as the specialist reviewed the findings of the scan to confirm the result, Semet led Skon aside and spoke softly. "I have noted another anomaly. I almost overlooked it because we were so focused on the microscopic that I was not considering the large-scale." He showed Skon an enlargement of a certain word in the text. "Note the shape of the *halovaya*," he said, using the traditional term for the "journey" the calligrapher's pen made from start to end of a word, one in which the ideal was to lift the pen as few times as possible. "Note the diminished size of the *zh* symbol following the *dahr-trashan*, the way it connects with the *r* beneath it."

"I do not see an anomaly."

"Few today would," Semet replied. "For this has been a standard calligraphic stroke for some twelve hundred years. Yet it is a simplification of the form in use in Surak's time. The combination of characters is so rare in Old High Vulcan that I did not recognize the anomaly until I checked my notes."

Skon shared a disquieted look with Semet. "The preponderance of evidence is pointing toward an impossible conclusion: that this *Kir'Shara* is of modern provenance."

"That is certainly impossible," Semet agreed. "This museum's tests verified its authenticity years ago."

Skon gazed at the artifact, attempting to think as his wife would have done during her time as a security officer. "Which would appear to suggest that the artifact before us now is a forgery substituted for the original."

Semet, who usually absorbed all information stoically and brooded over it in silence until he was ready to offer a useful observation, now stared at the younger man in overt disbelief. "That is equally impossible! You know the security in this vault as well as I do. There is no way such a substitution could have been made."

"Yet it has," Skon said grimly. "Either all our prior tests and observations were somehow in error and the true *Kir'Shara* was never found . . . or the true *Kir'Shara* has somehow been stolen."

May 15, 2165
Federation Executive Building, Paris, European Alliance

Jonathan Archer shook his head vigorously. "There's no way, sir. The *Kir'Shara* I found could not have been a fake."

"You'd swear to that?" President Haroun ibn Ahmad ibn Suleiman Abdurrahman al-Rashid leaned across his desk, holding Archer's gaze with his dark, piercing eyes. The president of the Federation was a tall, imposingly built Sudanese man of predominantly Nubian heritage, his black hair and beard shaved close against his bronze skin and showing only a trace of gray at his temples—though from the look on the president's face now, Archer wouldn't be surprised if he sprouted a few more gray hairs in the weeks ahead. "Because you'll probably have to."

"I'm absolutely positive, Mister President. I was guided to it by . . . a very reliable source," he finished sheepishly.

Al-Rashid held his gaze. "You mean the disembodied soul of Surak."

Archer considered his words. "Call it . . . a telepathic record of his memories. It may sound strange to us, but the Vulcans understand these things."

"The Syrannites do, you mean," the president responded in his English-accented basso. "The accusation making the rounds on Vulcan since the news got out is that the whole thing was a fraud perpetrated to place them in power."

"And someone's accusing me of being part of that fraud, sir?"

"Hell, yes, they are, Jon. As part of a Starfleet plot to discredit the High Command and bring Vulcan down from its place as the dominant regional power." He gestured around him at the center of power in which the two humans sat comfortably in the gravity of their home planet. "You can see how that might appear a credible charge to some."

"Only to fringe groups and fanatics like the Anti-revisionists. This is obviously some new trick by them or the Malurians."

"Jon, your own people exposed the Anti-revisionists and their links to the Malurians. Professor T'Nol has effectively disappeared. Her followers have scattered or abandoned her. And Vulcan Security has been watching closely for any signs of Malurian infiltration. Garos and his people would be fools to try it again." Archer had to concede his point. Dular Garos would not be reckless or obvious enough to try to repeat a gambit so soon after its exposure and failure.

"These charges are coming from other groups," the president continued, rising from his seat to pace behind his desk with slow, leonine strides. Archer tried not to be intimidated by his imposing height. "Loyalists of the old High Command, Vulcans who still distrust mind-melders. . . . The Vulcans are a conservative people, Jon, long-lived and fond of their traditions. It's impressive that so many of them changed so quickly when the *Kir'Shara* was found, but that's because it was the original word of their great prophet himself, the ultimate font of tradition. Call the authenticity of that text into question and it jeopardizes all that hard-fought progress."

"Believe me, Mister President, I understand what's at stake." He shook his head. "But the charge is absurd—surely most Vulcans can see that. Their archaeologists and historians studied the *Kir'Shara* in detail years ago and verified its authenticity."

"The charge is that they were partisans of the Syrannites. The demands are for new tests by independent parties."

"Tests of the fake one, sir."

"That's the only one we have now!" Al-Rashid didn't substantially raise his voice, but he didn't have to. After an uncomfortable moment, he broke his hold on Archer's gaze and resumed pacing. "And the Council shot themselves in the foot by designing such a fail-safe security system."

"Clearly not fail-safe, sir. It must have been switched somehow."

"But no one can explain how! Vulcan logic won't allow them to believe in an impossible theft. And *logically,* if the security system is impenetrable, then the *Kir'Shara* there now must be the same one you found eleven years ago—which would mean that you and First Minister T'Pau perpetrated an enormous, I daresay blasphemous fraud against the Vulcan people."

"Sir, you know that's absurd."

"*I* know, but I'm an illogical human. I can take leaps of faith. Vulcans require proof."

Archer rose. "Then let me take *Endeavour* to Vulcan, sir. We'll figure out how the *Kir'Shara* was stolen. We'll find the real one."

Those eyes locked on his. "If it hasn't already been destroyed. That would be the logical thing for its thieves to do, wouldn't it?"

Archer's heart sank at the president's words. The loss to history would be incalculable. More, some vestige of the *katra* of Surak, the psyche and memories that Archer had briefly carried, still lingered in the depths of his soul. Some

small part of him was Vulcan now, as horrifying as that notion would have been to his younger self. But that piece of his
spirit fired him with a very human passion. "I'll find whoever
did this," he swore through clenched teeth. "And if they've destroyed it, I'll—"

"Watch yourself, Jon," the president cautioned, extending
a meaty arm to point at him. "The Vulcan protestors have already insisted that you and Captain T'Pol testify before the
Council to defend your actions. You're not storming in there
to hand down the wrath of Allah. Your job is to testify, calmly
and convincingly, of the authenticity of your find and the im-
possibility of any collusion with the Syrannites to forge it."

The admiral reined in his frustration. "It would be a
waste of time, sir. All we need to do is prove the *Kir'Shara* was
stolen."

"You proved it was real years ago and that hasn't prevented
this. In politics—even Vulcan politics—reality is what you
can sell the most convincingly. Even if it's objectively, unde-
niably true, you still need good arguments and good spin to
counter those who have a vested interest in it not being true."
Al-Rashid's expression softened a bit, and he gave Archer a
hint of a smile for the first time. "You're better at that than
you tend to realize, Jon. And I'll be sending Soval to backstop
you."

Archer controlled his frustration, accepting the reality of
the president's words. "I trust that T'Pol's crew will still be
free to investigate this mystery and find . . . what happened to
the real *Kir'Shara*?"

The president held his eyes. "I'm counting on it, Jon. Because we could lose Vulcan if they don't."

8

THE KYRAW STILL SANG great songs of the coming of the Ware.

There were older songs, sagas of the times before the Ware when the Kyraw had flown from isle to isle, roosting for a season in each before flying on to the next. Sometimes the songs told of battles waged over the best breeding grounds and highest aeries, but the islands in the migration circuit were plentiful, so those flocks crowded out of the prime grounds could still find sufficient roosts elsewhere—except maybe for the weakest who were crowded out of the archipelagoes and forced to fly across great swaths of ocean, and few of them survived to sing or be sung about.

There were songs, too, of battles over the prime fishing zones, the wealth and sustenance of the flocks. These battles had driven the great inventor heroes of legend—like Chai-hawra, who had learned to use her wing-claws to sharpen sticks that could spear rivals' wings as well as fish; or Mraak-twao, who had first persuaded the *kwieekawn* to allow the Kyraw to ride their backs and guide them in their own fishing, trading the Kyraw's aerial vantage and thoughtful strategy for the *kwieekawn*'s strength, endurance, and dexterous tentacles. These inventions made the battles fiercer, calling for more in-novation from those who elaborated upon Chai-hawra's craft.

Some even attempted to tip their spears and daggers with bits of the metal found on a few rare islands, that strange rock that could be softened by fire and shaped. But metal was too rare and precious to risk losing in a foe's body when it fell beneath the waves—especially when it could be better crafted into jewelry and art that could be traded for fish or better roosting grounds. And fish were abundant enough that it was better to retreat and settle for a less ideal fishing zone than to risk the death or crippling of your best hunter-fighters. Oh, songs were sung of deaths noble and heroic and shameful and tragic, but it was their rarity that made them worthy of verse.

But most of these songs were remembered only in fragments, for the world had changed when the Ware fell from the sky. Although the gods of sun and storms had surely sent them, the white temples had built themselves on some of the largest islands and remained there without moving. The Kyraw had given up their migrations once the bounties of the temples, the miraculous artifacts they summoned from the air itself, had made it unnecessary to wander. Those who had roosted where the temples fell refused to give up their grounds, and those flocks who had no temples had fought to claim them. And the flocks who held the temples had asked them for better weapons with which they could defeat and subjugate the rival flocks for good.

Moreover, as time passed and Kyraw supplicants sometimes disappeared from the temples or were found inexplicably dead, it came to be understood that the Ware demanded sacrifices. So captives had to be taken, slaves and outsiders whose loss would cost the growing cities nothing. And thus wars had been waged and empires built to provide tributes for the great white temples, along with the foodstuffs and rare metals that the aloof, unforgiving voice of the Goddess (for now it was known there was only one) demanded in exchange for Her bounty.

Then the empires grew beyond the archipelagoes, spreading across the vast oceans on Ware-built ships in search of new wealth to feed the temples' ever-growing demands. And so they came upon other empires and fought to claim their territories and wealth for their own temples. They had prayed to the Ware for mightier weapons to defeat their foes, and the Ware had provided. The language of the Goddess was often cryptic and beyond the ken of the Kyraw, but in time their wisest priestesses had discerned that the Goddess offered weapons more powerful than the lightning itself, weapons that could bring down the power of the sun and shatter an entire nation in one blow. The temples, they knew by now, could survive almost anything, so with such weapons they could conquer an empire in a day, claim its temple and its lands, and enslave its survivors as sacrifices. And so they summoned these weapons, and the Ware delivered, and the fury of the sun was unleashed on their enemies.

But their enemies had already sought the same boon from their temples. The fire had ravaged all the empires within half a season. Most of the Kyraw had died. The islands had been laid waste and the oceans poisoned; fish were sparse, and if any *kwieekawn* survived, it had only been by fleeing to the depths beyond where Kyraw could dive.

So now, few new songs were sung. Few were left to sing in any case, and they had little to sing of. All they had was the struggle to survive, to scrounge up what little metal they could gather and offer what few sacrifices they could capture in exchange for untainted food from the Ware. They knew now that the Goddess had cursed them, and they hated Her, yet She was all that kept them alive.

This was the history that Lieutenant Samuel Kirk had reconstructed after several days of interviewing the scraggly survivors of the Kyraw race, meter-tall corvid bipeds with blue-black feathers and semi-opposable claws on their wing-tips. They had gladly told the historian and his *Pioneer* crew-mates anything they wanted to know in exchange for food and supplies that had not come from the evil Goddess within the Ware temples. The saga of their world had been compelling and exciting for Kirk to discover, yet the concrete reality of it horrified him. Death and violence, even cultural extinction, were part of the study of history, but what had happened to the Kyraw had been shocking—perhaps because they had not brought it on themselves. A Bronze Age people at best, accustomed to only minor, limited warfare with infrequent fatalities, had been rushed into an urban, imperial age and given access to weapons of mass destruction before they were ready to understand the consequences of their use. And the result was a dying world with only a few thousand scattered survivors, scrounging and fighting over the remaining scraps while those Ware ground facilities that had survived the wars had given less and less in exchange for the more meager payments the Kyraw were able to provide. Even if Captain Reed and his team found a way to defeat the Ware, Kirk realized, this species would be unlikely to survive another century.

Now, as Kirk stood with Travis Mayweather on one of the high, rocky island crags where the Kyraw had once built their teeming breeding colonies, they could only gaze out in sorrow at the barren, fusion-blasted expanse below. "This was insidi-ous," Mayweather grated, as angry as Kirk had ever seen him. "The Romulans destroyed worlds, but at least they were open about it. This . . . the Ware got them to destroy themselves."

"*Timeo Danaos et dona ferentes,*" Kirk said.

Mayweather nodded. "'Beware Greeks bearing gifts.' Because you may just get your whole city burned down."

"The Kyraw's songs have their own versions of Laocoön or Cassandra," Kirk said. "Those who warned of the evils of giving up their migratory ways for dependence on the Ware, and who were ignored or exiled for it. But maybe those are just interpolations after the fact—a bit of foreshadowing for the moral of the story."

"I'm sure there were people who resisted change," Mayweather said. "There always are. And they're usually wrong." He shook his head. "But even they could never have imagined *this.*"

"It's something I never wanted to see," Kirk said. "The end of a world's history. Before long, there will be no more songs . . . except those I've managed to record." His voice broke. "I really need to try to capture more, preserve more—"

"We don't have time," the first officer declared. "The captain says there's nothing more we can do here."

"There are still survivors. There must be something—"

"We need to find out who's behind the Ware and stop it at the source." Mayweather clenched his fists, clearly uneasy with the orders he passed on. Kirk suspected the taller man was unaccustomed to anger this deep, unsure what to do with it.

"We still have no idea where to look," Kirk said. "Or even why this is happening. They've devastated this world . . . but nobody's come to claim it. Nobody has gained anything from this." He furrowed his brow. "How do we know what to look for when we can't even find a reason behind it?"

The taller man studied him. "Are you saying you don't believe in pure evil?"

Kirk looked at him in surprise. "I never would've thought you did, sir."

Mayweather's eyes skimmed the barren landscape, coming to rest on the one remaining structure: the gleaming industrial ziggurat of the Ware surface complex, surmounted by the trademark embedded sphere at whose heart a few Kyraw were still imprisoned, their minds too far gone for rescue even if they could be removed without condemning the rest of the Kyraw to starvation. Something very like hate and fear burned in his gaze. "I never would have—if not for the Ware."

May 21, 2165
U.S.S. Pioneer

The second Ware-infested planet *Pioneer* found had a thriving civilization built almost entirely from Ware-generated technology. When Reed and Mayweather tried to alert its natives to the predatory nature of the automated facilities, they ran up against the elaborate system of ritual and dependence the locals had built around the Ware, in which it was considered an honor to be selected for sacrifice so that one's family and neighbors might thrive. Reed's warnings had been heresy to them, and they had unleashed the automated orbital drones that the Ware had given them to defend their planet from raiders. *Pioneer* had been forced to retreat, and there had been no point in calling in *Vol'Rala* or any of the other Andorian cruisers for backup; even a fleet of eight ships couldn't overthrow an entire government, and there seemed to be no one on the planet who wanted them to. For the second time running, Travis Mayweather left a strange new world feeling only bitterness and frustration. So far their mission was getting them practically nowhere. A few starship crews they'd contacted had taken their warnings to heart and promised to spread the word through the region, but others had dismissed their concerns or, like this planet's natives, deemed the price in lives minor enough to be worth paying. And when entire pre-warp civilizations were under the thrall of a technology beyond their ability to grasp, their cultures and religions shaped in response to its relentless demands, the problem seemed almost intractable.

The third Ware-infested planet they found was at an earlier stage of occupation. Its humanoid natives were far enough along in their industrial era that Ensign Grev was able to monitor their radio transmissions, revealing a culture that reminded Mayweather of the Earth seen in the classic mid-twentieth-century movies he had watched so often back on *Enterprise*.

"Except," the soft-spoken young Tellarite reported to the others around the situation table, "it seems they've had a spate of amazing technological breakthroughs in the past few years. A corporation in the dominant nation, Worldwide Automatics, has taken credit for inventing these pioneering new technologies, in concert with their government."

"Yeah," put in Rey Sangupta, "but the Ware satellites orbiting the planet pretty much argue otherwise." *Pioneer* was currently holding station behind one of the planet's two small asteroidal moons to avoid detection by whoever might be monitoring those satellites' sensor feeds.

"I think we're going in the wrong direction." The comment came from "Phil Collier," as Charles Tucker insisted on being called now. The bearded, red-haired engineer went on: "Each planet we're finding is at an earlier stage of infestation. We may be going on a tangent past the Ware's sphere of influence."

"Not necessarily," Mayweather riposted, his voice cold. "Expansion into space isn't a perfect sphere. The Boomers reached Sauria and Delta long before Starfleet even got as far as Andoria. Ware infestation could easily have jumped to distant worlds and then expanded out from them in all directions, filling in the gaps."

"Possibly. But we should try heading on a different course to see if the pattern holds."

"And just forget about these people?"

"Travis, we've talked about this," Captain Reed put in. "We can help them best by going to the source."

"Captain, you've seen the reports. The Ware's only starting to get a foothold down there. It's early enough that we could stop it before it's too late. I could lead a team down—"

"The captain's right, Commander," Tucker said. "We have to look at the big picture."

"And just let the little guys suffer? That's how it is for you, isn't it? You talk about big, lofty goals and don't notice how much you're hurting individuals along the way. Well, there *is* no big picture without the pieces that make it up! Somebody has to pay attention to them, or have you forgotten that?"

"Travis!" Reed barked. Mayweather caught himself, realizing that the others were staring, unused to such anger from their first officer. "In my ready room," Reed went on, moving past Mayweather and drawing him in his wake.

"I'm sorry, Captain," Mayweather said once the ready room door had closed behind them. "You know this is personal for me."

"I know that, Travis. But how much is what the Ware did to you and how much is what Trip did to you? Or what I did?"

Mayweather fidgeted. "I'm not angry at you, sir . . . not anymore. I know how seriously you take your obligations, both professional and personal. You wouldn't reveal a secret that you didn't think was yours to tell." He sighed. "But

Trip . . . Honestly, sir, I don't know who Trip is anymore. The Charles Tucker I knew would be champing at the bit to go down and help those people. Sir, if they find out what the Ware is really doing to them, I know we could save them." At Reed's skepticism, he went on, "And maybe we could learn something that could help us deal with the Ware out here too. If it's still new down there, below full strength, then maybe we can get through its security and learn something about what makes it tick."

Reed considered his words for several moments. "That is possible," he granted. "But you know how risky it can be to make contact with a pre-warp civilization."

"Sir, that civilization's already been contacted by something that doesn't have its best interests at heart. They're already being damaged. We have a chance to stop it."

"Are you sure that's what this is about, Travis? That it's really about them, and not some personal vendetta against the Ware?"

Mayweather sighed. "You know me, Captain. I'm not the vengeful type. And really . . ." He gave a rough chuckle. "Whatever I might feel about whoever's behind the Ware . . . the stuff itself is just machinery. I outgrew getting mad at machines when I was twelve and doing my engineering rotation aboard the *Horizon*. Sir, I'm just worried about the people down there. The people who are getting abducted and turned into living data drives. The people mourning lost loved ones that might still be alive to save. They shouldn't have to go through that, and I'd like the chance to help them."

"All right," Reed conceded after a moment, "but what about the other elephant in the room?"

"Sir?"

"Our friend Mister Collier. You can't forgive Trip for what

you feel he's done to you, to Hoshi, and you can't stand being on the same ship with him."

"That's not why I want to go to the planet, sir."

"Are you sure, Travis? I seem to recall another time when you chose to deal with a conflict aboard ship by leaving."

Mayweather winced. His decision to transfer off *Enterprise* following the destruction of his parents' ship was not one of his fonder memories. "Sir—all due respect, that's kind of a low blow. I'd just lost my family."

"And you blamed Admiral Archer for abandoning them."

"At the time. But that was a long time ago."

Reed held his gaze. "So was Trip's decision to fake his death. A decision I helped talk him into, let me remind you."

Mayweather wanted to be angry at Reed's line of questioning, but he couldn't. Whatever limited supply of anger he possessed was already in use elsewhere. And he couldn't escape the recognition that Reed might be on to something. So he was silent for a long while as he thought it over. "You're right, Captain," he finally said. "I do have . . . issues . . . with Commander—with Trip that I inappropriately brought into the briefing, and I'm sorry about that." Reed nodded in acceptance. "But there's a lot more going on here than him and me. I'm not a strategic thinker like you, Malcolm. I can't look at the Ware and see patterns of expansion or technological challenges or sociopolitical transformations. All I see are the people who are suffering as a result of it. People like Nimthu, who I promised to help but couldn't. I don't want to fail anyone else I might be in a position to save."

After another moment, Reed nodded. "Very well. I'll authorize a small fact-finding mission. Lead a team of your choosing down to the planet. But: Get Doctor Liao to disguise you as natives. They're humanoid enough that it shouldn't be difficult."

"You're sending us in undercover? We can't tell them what we know?"

"I want you to get a feel for the situation down there, learn about the culture and attitudes, before you decide whether to reveal yourselves openly. And I advise caution on that front. You know we can't stay to back you up."

"I didn't expect you could."

The captain let out a breath. "I can assign one of the Andorian couriers to monitor your party from space while *Pioneer* continues the mission. But with those Ware satellites in orbit, they'll have to keep their distance unless you really need them. So choose your team—and your actions—wisely, Commander."

"I appreciate it, Captain. I won't let you down."

Reed clasped his arm and told him the thing he most wanted to hear. "Don't let *them* down, Travis."

9

KUVAK WAS LOOKING NERVOUS AGAIN. Although the first minister greeted Archer, Captain T'Pol, and Commissioner Soval politely enough, expressing his confidence in the admiral's ability to fend off the questions of the reactionary factions in the Vulcan Council, Archer still sensed a touch of irritation that it had been this human who'd had the poor taste to discover the *Kir'Shara*, when leaving it to the Vulcans would have made things so much easier.

So it was fortunate that there were friendlier faces to greet him—or at least more neutral ones. Kuvak's predecessor, First Minister T'Pau, was present, for she had also been called to testify about her involvement in the *Kir'Shara*'s recovery. The diminutive Syrannite leader acknowledged Archer and T'Pol's greetings placidly while a younger Vulcan male approached Archer and held up his hand in the split-fingered Vulcan salute. "I am Surel, security director to the First Minister. It is a privilege to work with you, Admiral," he went on with thinly veiled intensity. "Your discovery of the *Kir'Shara* was a profound service to all of Vulcan, and I trust that together we can stymie those who would undermine that achievement."

"I . . . appreciate your vote of confidence," Archer replied, wondering if this face was a little too friendly. He was uneasy with true believers, even ones on his own side.

But the very pregnant woman accompanying T'Pau was a more welcome sight. "T'Rama," Archer greeted her with pleasure, offering his carefully practiced approximation of the salute. "It's a pleasure to see you again." Indeed, his acquaintance with the serene former security officer was one of his few pleasant memories of the turbulent Babel Conference they had attended nearly a year before.

"It is agreeable that circumstances have permitted us to renew our acquaintance, Admiral," T'Rama acknowledged, "even though the circumstances themselves are disagreeable."

"And . . . you look lovely," he said, gesturing toward her belly and not knowing what to do with his hands. He was sure Vulcan women would be uncomfortable with humans gushing over their pregnancies.

"I look considerably more rotund, Admiral," was her dry reply.

"Well . . . yes. But that's . . . because you're bringing new life into the world. We humans find that beautiful."

"Ah. I understand. So it is not merely a polite fiction to reassure females who are insecure about their appearance. This is gratifying to know." Archer could swear she was teasing him, but he wouldn't embarrass her by saying so in a room full of Vulcans.

Luckily, T'Pol changed the subject. "What is the nature of your participation here, if I may ask, Lady T'Rama?"

It was T'Pau who answered (and not for the first time, Archer found himself wishing Vulcan feminine names were easier to tell apart). "I have asked the Lady T'Rama to consult with Director Surel on the investigation. As his predecessor, she oversaw the design and installation of the *Kir'Shara* study vault at the Academy Museum."

"And he who is my husband, Professor Skon, was one of

those who discovered the theft and substitution of the artifact," T'Rama went on. "I believe his expertise in the textual study of the *Kir'Shara* could be of further value in this investigation."

"In that case," T'Pol said, "I would suggest that you coordinate with Lieutenant Commander Kimura, who will be leading our own investigation. Our communications officer, Lieutenant Commander Sato, is also an accomplished linguist and cryptographer whose skills could complement those of your mate."

"I would value their insights, Captain."

"Perhaps, then," Kuvak suggested to T'Rama, "you should adjourn to *Endeavour* with the captain while the admiral remains to discuss matters with us." T'Pol glanced to Archer, who nodded his consent. "As for the rest of us," Kuvak continued once the two women had made their farewells and left, "there is much we must discuss to prepare you for the questions you will face in the upcoming hearings."

"I'd appreciate that, First Minister," Archer said as they took seats around an antique oval conference table, its edges and legs inscribed in intricate calligraphy. "Because, to be honest, I'm surprised at the intensity of the backlash this . . . incident has provoked. I knew about the Anti-revisionists, of course, but it seemed to me that they were a minority, that most Vulcans welcomed the Syrannite reforms. How else would they have spread so quickly?"

"This is very true, Admiral," Surel told him. "Those of us in the younger generation proved particularly receptive to the new, more spiritual and peaceful interpretation of *cthia* to which the *Kir'Shara* exposed us." Archer nodded, recognizing the Vulcan word for the complex philosophy that humans translated as "logic." "Our interaction with humans,

Lorillians, Trill, and others had made us more tolerant, more receptive to new ideas and perspectives. And many of us thus became uneasy with the practices of the High Command and the harm they had inflicted upon races such as Andorians, humans, and Agarons."

T'Pau looked at him sidelong. "But our primary concern was for the Vulcan spirit itself. The High Command's disruptive treatment of other societies undermined our own integrity and dignity—much as the consuming of animals for meat would do. It threatened to reawaken the violence that Surak taught us to restrain for our own salvation."

"Surak also taught us to revere diversity," Surel reminded her. "The High Command sought to suppress those views it did not share—including your own Syrannite philosophies, my lady." Archer was impressed to see T'Pau concede the point to the director. The admiral was well acquainted with T'Pau's considerable ego and her benign contempt for offworlders. Anyone who could get her to back down was worth getting to know.

"But you must remember," Commissioner Soval added, "that Vulcans are a long-lived people. There remains an entrenched clique of older individuals who hold positions of prominence and authority and thus have much invested in the status quo." The gray-haired commissioner hesitated. "I admit to having been one of these individuals myself, until my convictions compelled me to rethink my stance—with no small assistance from the wisdom of the late Admiral Forrest." Archer accepted his words with a grateful nod. Soval had once been one of the most entrenched Vulcans of all, parroting the will of the High Command in its efforts to restrict humanity's spread into space. But after Maxwell Forrest had died saving Soval's life in the opening salvo of the civil war provoked by

V'Las, Soval had faced a crisis of conscience and gone on to take several incredibly brave actions that had cemented him as a trusted ally in Archer's mind. "These entrenched interests are the audience to which the Anti-revisionists and other traditionalist factions have pandered."

"And while they are small in number," Kuvak added, "they hold disproportionate influence in society, for they include the heads of many influential clans, leaders of industry, respected elder scholars and philosophers like Professor T'Nol, and the like. This is why they are able to exert such influence on policy." Kuvak wrung his hands before him. "They hope to capitalize on this crisis to win support for a vote of no confidence in the Syrannite government, enabling their return to power."

"But T'Nol was discredited, humiliated," Archer replied. "This whole thing sounds like just the sort of trick she'd pull to try to rehabilitate her image."

"That was the first angle I investigated, Admiral," Surel replied. "But to my surprise, I found no evidence that the Anti-revisionists are involved, or even that they still exist as an organized group."

T'Pau elaborated. "T'Nol's faction was merely the most prominent of a coalition of traditionalist groups. They went dormant once she was shamed and marginalized, but the new charges concerning the *Kir'Shara* have provoked many of them to renewed activity."

"One of the leading protest factions," Surel said, "is a clique of High Command loyalists, former military personnel led by a man named Zadok—who, under V'Las's regime, commanded one of the lead ships in the Battle of Andoria. There was never any evidence of his direct involvement in V'Las's criminal actions, but he and many of his fellow officers were dismissed from service when T'Pau dissolved our combat fleet."

"Provisions were made, of course, to provide them with new training and career opportunities," T'Pau added. "No Vulcan wishes to let the mind sit idle. But Zadok and others like him have found difficulty adjusting to non-military pursuits—in part because they do not agree with my decision to disband the fleet. They are still convinced that the old ways were correct."

"Don't tell me they think V'Las was in the right!" Archer replied, startled.

Soval took up the thread. "Most of the loyalists acknowledge V'Las's corruption, but consider it an aberration in an otherwise necessary system that should have been reformed rather than dissolved."

Surel set his jaw. "Most, but not all. I have had occasion to debate with Zadok, and I am convinced that he and his associates not only consider V'Las to have been in the right, but that the charges against him were—forgive me, Admiral—a political ploy instigated by you and Starfleet Command."

Archer shook his head and gave a curt laugh. "I hope you'll all forgive *me* for the observation, but isn't all this exactly the sort of thing that Vulcan logic is supposed to raise you above?"

"The very nature and practice of logic have been called into question by the *Kir'Shara*," T'Pau replied. "All of Vulcan has been reexamining the meaning and methodology of *cthia*. Much of what we have always believed to be Surak's true wisdom has been supplanted by a new text that reinterprets and even contradicts many deeply held convictions. In particular, the *Kir'Shara*'s revelations about the essential role that the melding of minds plays in the Vulcan psyche were extremely disruptive to that majority who had been raised to believe that melding was an aberrant practice of a small fringe community."

"One of the principal protest factions," Kuvak put in, "is the Mental Integrity Coalition, a group that has continued to denounce melding despite the words of the *Kir'Shara*. They are one of the groups most receptive to the idea that the text is a Syrannite fraud."

"But surely the majority of the Vulcan people have seen that the new, more peaceful system works," Archer said. "The Syrannites haven't torn down the social order. The planet hasn't been conquered by aliens. Vulcans are even *less* emotional and more logical than they were fifteen years ago—or so it seems to me."

"Why, thank you," Soval said, with Kuvak not far behind.

"As for the majority of the Vulcan people," Director Surel told the admiral, "they strive simply to live up to Surak's teachings as they understand them. If they can be persuaded that the *Kir'Shara* is fraudulent, they would likely switch their allegiance back to the traditional interpretations of Surak's word. In which case the Syrannite government would be shamed and removed from power, just as V'Las was."

"And that," said Soval, "could lead to the restoration of a High Command willing to withdraw Vulcan from the Federation—or at least to attempt to dominate it politically and culturally."

"Which would be sure to drive the Andorians out," Archer said. "And I doubt the human worlds would be very happy about it either."

"This is why you must present a convincing case before the Council, Admiral," Kuvak said. "There is more at stake than Vulcan's future. For as Vulcan goes, so goes the Federation."

After the meeting, Soval told Archer, "You did well. I believe you will be able to bring a number of convincing arguments to bear against the protest factions—so long as you remember to restrain your tendency toward emotional expressiveness."

"I'll do my best, Commissioner," Archer replied with an irritated glare. At Soval's raised eyebrow, he sighed. "Sorry. It's just . . . All this political maneuvering and debating feels like a waste of time to me. Personally I put more trust in T'Pol and her people to find the *Kir'Shara* thieves and expose this fraud—the *real* fraud."

"I would have thought you understood Vulcans better by now, Admiral. We thrive on debate and discussion." He paused. "True, rhetoric has not always been your strongest suit. I seem to recall a rather clumsy metaphor involving an ungulate called a gazelle."

Archer glared at the reminder. "It got the point across, didn't it?"

"It did," Soval conceded. "Barely. But since then you have gained much experience in persuasive rhetoric—and in debating with Vulcans. You have long practice dealing with us as both adversaries and allies, and your time carrying Surak's *katra* brought you insights into our people that no other human has ever shared. President al-Rashid chose wisely, Admiral: There is no one better suited to this task than you."

Archer found Soval's compliment damning, for it merely trapped him further in the political arena that was increasingly starting to look like his destiny. But maybe, he began to realize, it was time to accept that reality and start working to make the best of it. If this was what everyone expected of him, maybe there was a way he could use that for positive ends.

After all, the future of the Federation was what really mattered. If swallowing his pride and becoming a politician was what the Federation needed of him, then so help him, he would become the best politician he could.

May 23, 2165
U.S.S. Endeavour

Takashi Kimura listened patiently as Professor Skon summarized the imperfections he had found in the replica *Kir'Shara*. His presentation, delivered to Captain T'Pol, Hoshi Sato, and Kimura as they stood around the bridge situation table with Lady T'Rama, was methodical and meticulous, supplemented by a comprehensive set of image files projected on the table's surface and the surrounding wall screens. But once Skon completed his exhaustive—and slightly exhausting—review, it was left to his wife to sum up the whole thing far more elegantly. "The cleverness of this forgery lies in its very imperfection," T'Rama said. "The errors are subtle enough to elude routine observation, so that the artifact appears as though it were meant to be convincing; yet they are noticeable enough to make it inevitable that the forgery would be discovered."

"What is more," Skon added, "the errors are of a sort that would tend to elude offworlders yet be evident to Vulcan experts—for instance, the use of a calligraphic stroke that only a lifelong student of ancient Vulcan texts would know to be anachronistic. Thus, they create the impression that the forgery was created by offworlders."

"And it will be difficult to prove otherwise," T'Rama said. "The deviousness of this fraud is that the discovery of its fraudulent nature actually works in the plotters' favor. The question then becomes one of the identity and purpose of the forgers, and it is difficult to win a case based on motive when the evidence is not in dispute."

"Our best option," Captain T'Pol said, "would be to recover the real *Kir'Shara*."

"I can see no logical reason why its thieves would have kept it intact," T'Rama told her grimly. "In all likelihood, it has already been destroyed."

Kimura knew his captain well enough to recognize the barely contained anguish in her eyes—but it seemed to him that the other two Vulcans had almost the same reaction. "First Surak's *katra*," T'Pol said, "now his words. So much of him has been taken from us."

Sato frowned. "But the words have been copied into every database on Vulcan and throughout the Federation. Even the forgery has the correct text, just with a few subtle errors in the reproduction."

"But the authenticity of those words has been called into question, Hoshi," T'Pol told her. "Unless we can prove the *Kir'Shara* was real, then its wisdom is as good as lost. And if the original is gone, we may never be able to prove it existed."

"Then we have to prove it was stolen," Kimura said, leaning resolutely forward on the situation table. "Lady T'Rama, you know the security on that vault inside and out. Have you got any idea how the artifact could've been switched?"

She shook her head, looking weary. "I have been unable to formulate a rational hypothesis. The doors to the study vault could not have been opened without the entry being recorded electronically and witnessed by live guards. The storage vault is inaccessible save by its lift. The doors and the top of the lift shaft are under constant visual surveillance, and the feed is embedded with a time code to defeat attempts to loop the image. The chamber is equipped with sonic, thermal, pressure, motion, and chemical sensors. The lift shaft is too narrow for most any humanoid to enter and too sheer to allow them to climb out again. The entire complex is transporter-shielded, and any transporter beam powerful enough to overwhelm the shielding would have triggered numerous sensors across the Science Academy grounds."

"What about a Suliban Augment?" Kimura suggested. "There might still be a few out there who haven't been arrested or killed off. And they were engineered to resist detection by most kinds of sensors. One of them could've camouflaged himself and snuck in behind a study team, then contorted enough to fit down the shaft."

"I considered that possibility, Commander," T'Rama told him without impatience. "There would still have been biological and fiber traces left within the shaft, and there were none. Moreover, we have thorough security recordings of every study session, and at no point is the *Kir'Shara* unseen or unattended. There were no opportunities to switch it while it was under study, and no evidence of any unauthorized openings of the shaft cover."

Kimura couldn't resist smiling and chuckling a little, drawing scandalized looks from the three Vulcans. "I'm sorry. I don't mean to trivialize this in any way—it's just that this is one of the most perfect locked-room mysteries I've ever come across. It's really kind of exciting."

T'Rama's gaze softened, as did Skon's after the couple traded a look. "I understand completely, Commander Kimura," she said. "The intellectual challenge is fascinating. And it has been a long time since Skon and I encountered a puzzle we could not solve between the two of us. It is indeed . . . stimulating."

"Good," T'Pol said. "Because you will need to devote your full attention to this problem until you do find a solution. I recommend you review all the security data once again, in depth, and see if it brings any new insights. I will report our . . . status to the admiral." She nodded at the Vulcan couple before moving forward into the bridge proper.

Kimura and Sato exchanged a look. "So. Hours of tedious staring at security footage," he said.

"Sounds like a lovely evening," Hoshi answered with that wry twist to her dainty lips that always drove him wild.

"As long as I'm with you," he murmured, winking.

Sato cleared her throat, turning back to the Vulcan couple. "So! Um, we could adjourn to the briefing room. It's quieter there."

Skon and T'Rama traded a look. "Let me instead invite you both to our home," Skon told them. "My own study is equipped with high-resolution displays sufficient for the security review, yet the surroundings are more comfortable. Also, should we wish to visit the museum vault itself, it is reasonably proximate."

"Additionally," T'Rama said, "we could all benefit from a meal before we undertake such an intensive effort. And Skon is an excellent cook. Provided you are both satisfied with vegetarian fare."

Now the human couple traded a look, and Sato spoke for them both. "That sounds lovely. We're honored by your welcome."

"Okay, then," Kimura said. "I'll clear it with the captain and arrange for a shuttlepod."

As he moved toward the captain's chair, he couldn't help reflecting on how effortlessly Skon and T'Rama seemed to function as a team—husband and wife freely speaking for one another because they were so much in sync. It pleased him to think that he and Hoshi had a very similar rapport . . . even without being married.

Even without . . .

He quashed the thought instantly. Despite Phlox's playful query the previous month, Kimura knew that marriage between two members of the same Starfleet crew, let alone the same command crew, was out of the question. Hoshi knew that as well as he did.

But he wondered if she regretted it as much.

10

URWEN ZEHERI PULLED GANLER NIBAR under a storm awning just in time to avoid the gaze of the Worldwide Automatics mechanical sentry that whirred overhead. "Jumping *jilazi*, that was—" Zeheri hushed the boy, who went on in a whisper. "That was close, Urwen. I keep forgetting to watch out for those crazy contraptions."

"I've learned to expect surveillance by now," Zeheri told the lanky youth. "WWA didn't stop watching me once they got me fired."

Ganler gave a cocky smirk. "That's because they know it just made you more determined. You'll tear down this beast yet." He chanced a peek beyond the heavy metal awning. "Especially if they keep doing crazy things like watching people from the air. Who doesn't know how to hide from things out of the sky?"

"That's one more reason I'm convinced Vabion didn't invent these things himself. They're not designed for our world."

Ganler rolled his orange-pupiled eyes. "Not your Underlanders again, Ur!"

"Watch your tone, pal. A good inquisitor follows the evidence, not preconceptions. A good news scribe, too," she reminded the young apprentice.

"Ohh, storms. I get enough lectures on newsgathering from Najola. I don't need two mentors."

Zeheri peered out. "It's gone now. I think we can make the wall if we're quick. Come on!"

Luckily, Ganler's legs were as quick as his tongue, so he darted out promptly alongside her and kept pace easily as she ran. Still, they were taking a gamble that WWA didn't have more mechanical eyes watching them from somewhere. Five years ago, she would have only had to worry about living guards who could be fooled or bribed to look away. Of course, five years ago, she would have had her inquisitor's badge and a warrant from the magistrate. But Daskel Vabion owned most of the magistrates now.

Thank goodness for Ganler Nibar, then. His mentor, Najola Rehen, may have grown up with Zeheri, but the news scribe found Zeheri's theories about WWA as implausible as the chief inquisitor had. Like so many others, she couldn't understand why Zeheri cared so much about the disappearances of a few homeless mendicants and mental patients. Yes, custom said every member of society was a precious contributor in generations like these when the climate worsened and all had to pitch in for mutual survival; but modern sentiments said that those who contributed nothing, those who were drains on society's precious resources, could not be as worthy of attention. Zeheri found that view hypocritical. Didn't Vabion, his fellow corporate cronies, and their puppets in the government all insist that Vanot was entering a time of plenty when modern technology would conquer the climate once and for all and scarcity would be a thing of the past? Why, then, should anyone be considered a drain on society? And why were the numbers of jobless, homeless Vanotli swelling while only those who were already rich saw the benefits from the revolutionary technologies and medical treatments WWA rolled out several times a year? And why were those who protested the growing inequality so often silenced or stripped of their professions, and why were there more and more mechanical eyes watching them all the time lest they speak out of turn again?

Perhaps Ganler did not share her passion on these points, Zeheri reflected, but he was eager and curious; and despite his protests he was fascinated by Zeheri's wilder theories about the source of WWA's recent surge of spectacular scientific breakthroughs. So he was willing to assist her investigations when Najola Rehen would not, and Najola was willing to tolerate it as part of his training. So at least Zeheri wasn't in this alone. Having someone so enthusiastic in her corner, even if he doubted some of her conjectures, helped keep Zeheri going.

Plus she needed his skills as a sport climber to help her scale the wall they now approached, the least protected of the walls surrounding WWA's manufacturing center in this district of Stone Valley Hold. It was the newest factory WWA had built, its security not yet fully in place, so it was her best chance of getting inside one of the highly secured facilities and learning the secret of how Vabion made the technological miracles that had elevated him to the top of the corporate mountain—and maybe, just maybe, how that secret connected to the mysterious disappearances.

But just before they rounded the last corner to their access point, Zeheri heard voices. She caught Ganler's shoulder and pulled him short of the corner. "Quiet," she hissed. "Listen."

His eyes widened as he caught the voices as well. Zeheri listened closely, finding the cadence of the voices odd, their speech unrecognizable at this distance. She peered around the corner and saw two men and a woman, all adults—and all unusually tall and strong of build. The bigger man and the woman had tightly curled hair and fairly typical complexions, while the slightly smaller, younger man was a bit paler with straight hair. The woman, for some reason, wore no hat.

"Look," Ganler hissed. "The second man is holding some kind of machine."

Zeheri pulled out a pocket telescope and looked closer. "You're right. A flat rectangular box . . . There's a picture on it!"

"You mean a logo?"

"No, a moving picture! Like a movie screen, but smaller."

"*Glisp!*" Ganler breathed, another of those corny euphemisms he'd picked up from the radio serials. One consequence of the reduced birth rates during harsh climate periods was that young folk had fewer peers to corrupt them. "I've heard some of the rich folk have little movie boxes in their parlors now. Movies sent right to their homes like radio shows."

"But not this small."

"So what are they watching? *Raiders from the Underland*?"

She punched his shoulder lightly. "I warned you, brat. No, it's like a blueprint of the factory, but it moves."

"They must be WWA security. Using some new toy to look for us."

"No . . . they look as furtive as we are." The big man gave a whispered instruction to the woman, who nodded. The woman took several steps away from the wall while the big man knelt and cupped his hands. A moment later, the woman ran toward him. He caught her foot in his hands and heaved her upward—all the way to the top of the wall!

"Jumping *jilazi*—and I mean jumping!" gasped Ganler. His cooling fins, which had just begun to relax as his pulse slowed after exertion, now stiffened again. "Did you see that? He tossed her clear to the top of the wall!"

She hissed for silence from the lad, afraid he'd give them

away. But the three big strangers seemed intent on their gymnastics routine. The big one lifted the other man up to where the woman could take his hands and pull him to the top of the high wall. Then he jogged back—close enough for Zeheri to get a good look at his very impressive rear—and took a running leap halfway up the wall, making Zeheri gasp in amazement. He let the others catch his hands and then walked up the wall as they pulled him to the top. She wondered how they could possibly get down, but then they simply hopped from the top of the wall one by one, unconcerned with the drop. From the sound of it, they all landed safely on the other side.

"Have you ever seen anyone that strong?" Ganler asked. "Who are those people?"

Zeheri didn't dare voice the possibility that came into her head. Even she found it too incredible. But that didn't stop her from being curious. "Come on. We may be onto a bigger story than we knew."

If nothing else, the strangers had proven this was a safe place to scale the wall, although they had to do it the slower, more conventional way, with the fine silken line Ganler had concealed under his cloak. But soon enough, Zeheri had her feet safely on the ground inside the wall. She'd rolled up her hat inside her sash for the climb, wondering if that was why the female stranger had doffed hers, and now she smoothed out its gray felt and returned it to her head while Ganler completed his descent. "Any sign of them?" the boy asked as she straightened the brim, making sure it wasn't brushing against her cooling fins.

She pointed toward one of the interior buildings of the factory complex. "I caught a glimpse of them rounding that corner. Come on!"

They jogged forward, using the building for cover. But no sooner did Zeheri peek around the aforementioned corner than a hand grabbed her, dragged her forward with amazing strength, and slammed her against the wall. "Who are you? Why are you following us?" It was the strange woman, still bareheaded.

"Leave her alone!" Ganler leapt out in her defense, but the woman whirled, pointing some kind of strange gun at him—a gun Zeheri belatedly realized had been jammed into her own sternum a moment before.

But the leaner man intervened. "Easy, Katrina! He's just a kid."

Ganler bristled at the characterization. Zeheri was more puzzled. Anyone could see that Ganler had an apprentice's torc around his neck, and thus that he was old enough to be treated as a full member of society. True, most people would not feel entitled to shoot an apprentice as a result—but then, most people were not WWA security goons. The fact that these people showed concern for the lad suggested they were something else altogether.

Zeheri addressed the leader. "We're not after you," she told him, holding his vivid gold eyes. "In fact, something tells me we're both after the same thing. Answers about Worldwide Automatics and how it makes those fancy little toys." She glanced over at the movie box in the smaller man's hands, the weird gun in the woman's. "Though it seems you've got some fancy toys of your own. Competitors, maybe?"

The leader pondered. "In a manner of speaking. You don't seem to think too highly of Worldwide's 'toys,' Miss . . ."

"Zeheri. Urwen Zeheri."

He smiled, and her heart skipped a beat. *Lousy heart. Get a hold of yourself.* "Pleased to meet you. I'm Travis."

She played it cool. "This isn't the best time for a social gathering, Travis. We've been lucky avoiding the mechanical sentries so far, but the longer we stand around—"

The second man waved his box. "We can tell where the, uh, sentries are. It's okay."

"What is that?" Ganler asked, stepping forward to take a closer look at the box. "Can I see how it works? I bet a machine like that could be pretty useful for a news scribe."

"Uh, maybe when you're older," the man said. Then he muttered, "Like about two hundred years . . ."

"The lady's right, Rey," said the one called Travis. "We need to find the primary data core."

"Aye, sir." He waved the box around, and Zeheri could see the picture on it changing, as though it were some kind of camera that could see through walls. "It should be this way."

"All right. Miss Zeheri—"

"We're coming with you," she said. Before he could protest, she went on: "Unless you want us to make enough of a fuss to bring down the sentries. And before you get any ideas, Miss Katrina," she added with a sidelong glance to the woman, "I don't care what kind of gun that is, shooting us will probably get their attention too."

Travis looked impressed. "Okay. Follow us." They set off, the one called Rey leading the way. "And we weren't going to shoot you," he told her after a moment. "We're here to help."

"Help." She gave a wry smile. "It used to be we all helped one another when the climate turned hostile. We couldn't afford not to."

He furrowed his brow, and she noticed that the bright spots adorning his forehead and temples were oddly sharp-edged. His cooling fins were odd too—they just sat stiffly behind his ears, showing no changes with his mood or activity.

And there was something strange about the way he talked, as though his mouth movements didn't quite match his words. "So what changed?"

She frowned back at him. "Don't you know?" No one could forget the War of All Holds, the madness when the dictator Fetul had waged a war of conquest well into the beginning of a storm cycle, abandoning all the ancient codes of cooperation between holds during times when the climate became the common enemy of all. No one could be unaware of the hardships all free and decent Vanotli had needed to endure in order to break Fetul's tyranny, the waste of lives and resources that should have been preserved to weather the impending generations of storms. That was what had enabled the corporations to rise to power in the first place, for their technologies and wealth had enabled the Vanotli to recover and reunite in the wake of the terrible war. Yet now they forgot the lessons of unity they themselves had embraced in the years of rebuilding. Where could Travis, Rey, and Katrina be from if they did not know of the events that had reshaped the entire world in a single generation?

But before Travis could answer, Rey interrupted. "Sir, over there." He gestured toward a central building. "I'm picking up life signs inside. Low level, as if they're . . . you know."

Travis nodded, his features grim. "Are they Vanotli?"

"Hard to tell without getting closer, but I think so."

Zeheri stared. "They have people alive in there? Prisoners?" Had she found the missing victims?

"Not exactly," Travis told her. "But there's no time to explain. Rey, can we get them out?"

Before he could answer, an alarm sounded. A female voice emerged from a loudspeaker somewhere. *"Unauthorized sensor activity detected,"* the woman intoned with unnatural calm. *"This area is restricted. Vacate these premises or your life functions will be compromised.*"

Rey made an odd sound: "Uh-oh." He then elaborated, "Drones coming in."

"I hate that voice," Travis grated. "Come on, let's get out of here."

They ran for the wall. Zeheri and Ganler had to struggle to keep up, for the strangers were startlingly fast despite their bulk. But Travis took her hand—his own was surprisingly cool—and pulled her after him, while Rey took Ganler's upper arm and helped him forward. The strangers used their exceptional strength to help Zeheri and Ganler over the wall first—another thing that convinced her of their benevolence—and quickly pulled themselves up Ganler's rope to follow. But Zeheri saw two of the angular, gray mechanical sentries come into view around the warehouses and called a warning. Katrina raised her odd pistol and fired at the nearer of the two. Instead of a bullet, it fired a bright beam of some kind, like a searchlight only tighter, brighter, almost like lightning. And it had the effect of lightning, causing an explosion where it struck the sentry. The machine, hovering by means no one outside WWA understood, faltered and fell, and a moment later the second one succumbed to Katrina's lightning gun the same way. "*Glisp,*" Ganler sighed as he stared at the spectacle, before Zeheri urged him down the rope. After all, there must be more than two mechanical sentries.

The strangers jumped down from atop the wall as easily as before, while Zeheri made her way more slowly down Ganler's line. Impatiently, she let go of the rope, dropped, and rolled to her feet. Refusing to be upstaged by the strangers despite their superior strength, she called "Come on!" and ran forward, ignoring the pain in the ankle she'd twisted slightly when she landed.

The others followed her lead through the winding, narrow streets of the ancient fortress city, and a few moments later she noticed Travis jogging beside her, holding something out for her. "You dropped this."

It was her hat. Grinning at him warmly, she took it from his hand and planted it firmly atop her head once more.

"I was an inquisitor," Urwen Zeheri told Travis and his colleagues as they and Ganler basked in Najola Rehen's hotroom, drying their clothes and hair. The expected storm had finally opened up, its fierce wind and rain sufficient to stymie WWA's sentry machines in their pursuit, its lightning interfering with the radio signals they used to communicate. Zeheri could be reasonably sure they had not been tracked to Rehen's home, and that they were now safe from surveillance within its thick walls and storm-shuttered viewslits. The government's mechanical spies—be honest, WWA's mechanical spies—grew more pervasive by the day, but as far as Zeheri knew, they had not yet devised one small enough to sneak inside a home like a *snel* bug.

"I'd been investigating a series of mysterious deaths and disappearances in the outer zones," she went on. She was aware that Travis had deftly deflected her questions about his own group by asking about her; but she'd found that recalcitrant witnesses could often be encouraged to open up by a little give and take. Besides, it was nice just to be listened to for a change. "Nobody else saw a pattern, or wanted to; the victims were just vagrants or bottom-income laborers, the kind of people who vanish all the time and have no one to miss them. At least, that's the way people think now," she added with a grimace. "With all the new industries and machines to shelter us and tame the climate, they feel we no longer need every hand working together to survive the harsh times. So the industries and their government cronies hoard their gains and encourage us not to care about those left out in the elements."

"But you still care," Travis said, eyeing her appreciatively.

She flushed. "At first, I didn't. I thought the cases were a waste of my time, let them gather dust on my desk while I pursued more glamorous homicides and assaults. Finally my chief inquisitor pressured me to clear my caseload, and when I looked at the files together, I noted a pattern. Most of the victims had last been seen at or near one of the charity fabricators WWA had installed in the outer zones the year before."

"I thought you said the corporations didn't care about the poor," Rey put in.

Rehen had just come in from the kitchen, bearing mugs of hot cider for her guests. "They care about their image," the diminutive journalist told him. "WWA hoped a conspicuous act of charity would distract the press from some of our burning questions about their sudden, inexplicable burst of innovation over the past four years."

"Makes sense." Rey took a sip of his cider, visibly suppressed a grimace, and forced a smile toward Rehen. "Wonderful." The journalist rolled her eyes and moved on, trading a smirk with Zeheri. The young stranger had been flirting steadily and unsuccessfully with Rehen since the moment he'd laid eyes on her, seemingly unaware that, as mistress to an apprentice, the journalist was committed to chastity. His ignorance was another sign that these strangers were from someplace very far indeed.

Travis's eyes fell upon Zeheri, and she found herself glad

she had no apprentice. "So you suspected WWA in the disappearances?"

She cleared her throat. "Not at first. Who was I to doubt our great benefactors? But it was the only lead I had, so I looked into it. And I began to meet resistance, the kind you get when people have something to hide. At first I thought it was just about avoiding bad press, but then I started to get hints of something more going on. There were questions about how Vabion had made all these amazing breakthroughs. He and his assistants couldn't have achieved such enormous advances in so many fields of science all at once. There must have been others working on them too, but there were no signs that he'd recruited other scientists, no papers in the literature that would point toward any of these inventions. If anything, Vabion seemed to be turning away scientists and engineers who wanted to learn more about his factories and fabricators."

"They *are* automated," Rehen reminded her with long-suffering patience.

"But someone had to design and build the automation. That's where I ran into a stone wall."

She turned back to Travis. "Then a source within WWA contacted me and told me that there had been a few mysterious deaths among the wealthy buyers of WWA's new fabricators and other machines, and that they'd stopped since Vabion started the charity program in the outer zones. He said that people within the company suspected a connection."

"Right," Ganler said. "And that's when they found his body outside the walls after a level six cyclone."

"I couldn't accept that it was suicide," Zeheri went on. "But the chief didn't want to hear the case I was starting to put together. She'd just wanted me to close some unimportant cases to improve the department's record. Once it became clear I wasn't going to let go, I found myself fired—supposedly for wasting department resources on frivolous investigations, but, well, the chief owns stock in WWA. So do most of her superiors. Nobody wanted answers to the questions I was asking."

Rey smiled at Rehen. "Except for you and Ganler?"

Rehen sighed, at both the question and the ulterior interest behind it. "She got Ganler interested in her crazy ideas. Me, I think she's just looking for some big conspiracy that she can prove to get her job back. But, well, we go back a long way, and Ganler needs the practice."

Zeheri resisted the urge to needle her old friend about her willful blindness. It wouldn't be fitting in front of guests. Besides, Rehen was really putting herself on the line by sheltering and assisting Zeheri, even if she didn't buy Zeheri's theories about what was going on inside WWA. Taking on the corporation that practically ran the government was not a particularly safe undertaking from a career standpoint, as Zeheri had learned. And she couldn't blame the levelheaded Rehen for looking askance on where Zeheri's conjectures had led recently. There were times when Zeheri herself feared she was going mad. That was why it was so heartening to meet these strangers whose technology was as inexplicably advanced as WWA's, and whose innate abilities were so extraordinary.

No more patient indulgence, then. "And now you're here, Travis. And you obviously know a lot more about what's going on in WWA than I do. So it's your turn to answer some questions."

Travis exchanged uneasy glances with Rey and Katrina. "There's not that much we can tell you about Worldwide Automatics," the big man replied slowly.

"Don't try to snow me with what you don't know," she insisted. "I'm concerned with what you *do* know. You knew there were prisoners inside that factory, and you were expecting to find them. You have machines as advanced as WWA's, but who else on the surface could possibly have that kind of science?"

"Here we go," Rehen muttered before removing herself from the hotroom.

After a moment's thought, Travis replied, "The important thing right now is that, yes, there are people alive in there. Most are probably too far gone to save, but we might be able to help a few."

"'Too far gone'?" Ganler asked in dismay. "What are they doing to them in there? Some kind of scientific experiments? Turning them into robot-people? A mindless army controlled by an electronic brain?"

"Quiet, Ganler," said Zeheri. "This isn't one of your movie serials."

"Actually, the kid's not far wrong," Rey said. "But there's no army."

Travis hesitated, but then met her eyes and spoke plainly. "That automation WWA uses . . . you must have wondered how it's so intelligent, so versatile." She nodded. "Well, there is an electronic brain involved—but it needs living brains too. The machines are called the Ware. They seem benevolent, giving people everything they want, but at a high price."

"Sure," Ganler said. "Only the rich and the government get to live in luxury. The rest of us are lucky to get handouts."

"But you're talking about a higher price," Zeheri said. "In lives."

"They need living brains to boost their computing power. So they take people. They do it in secret—fabricate fake corpses the same way they manufacture food or machines."

"*Glisp,*" Ganler breathed.

"Although," Rey put in, "it sounds like they aren't bothering anymore with your homeless people. Maybe the Ware only expends the effort with people who'll be missed if they just disappear."

Zeheri frowned. "You talk about the Ware like it's alive. Like it's actually running things."

"It is," Travis told her, and she could see in his eyes that there was something very personal about his anger. "This Vabion didn't invent it. It's using him to spread itself, to get the Vanotli dependent on it so it can prey on your minds." He rose and began to pace. "Maybe if we can talk to him, explain what's going on—"

She stood to face him. "Don't underestimate Daskel Vabion. He was a genius even before this Ware came along. And there's nothing that happens in Worldwide Automatics that he doesn't approve and control. If his machines are taking people and wiring up their brains, you can bet he knows it and approves of it."

"Then we need to prove this to your friend Najola. If she can publicize this—"

"She'd be out of a job faster than Urwen was," Ganler interrupted.

"Why can't you fight them?" Zeheri challenged. "Your people. You have science as good as theirs, and you're incredibly strong."

"It's not that simple," Travis replied, though he clearly regretted it. "Right now, the three of us are all we've got. We can't defeat the Ware by ourselves."

"But there are more of you. You had to come from somewhere. Who are you, Travis? Where are you from?"

"Oh, stop avoiding it, Urwen," Ganler said, then turned to Travis. "You're Underlanders, aren't you?"

"Underlanders?" asked Rey. "What the hell are Underlanders?"

"Like you don't know."

"It would almost make sense," Zeheri said. "I used to think they were just an old legend, a cliché from the radio adventures. Ancient peoples who discovered or carved out gigantic underground holds, got heat and light from Vanot's fiery core. So they never had to spend half their generations struggling against ice or drought or storm, but were free to advance far beyond the surface world, to breed themselves to physical and mental perfection." She scoffed. "Nonsense, right? But now we've been invaded by machines that think, machines that can't be from the Vanot we know—and here you are, people with extraordinary machines and incredible strength and no clue about Vanotli customs and culture. If you're not from the Underlands, where else is left?"

Rey chuckled. "Oh, I don't know. How about outer space?"

She frowned. "Outer space? What does that mean?"

"You know—up there. Other worlds, other stars in the sky."

"Don't give me fantasy tales!"

Rey laughed again. "You're the one believing in mole people from the center of the planet!"

"But that makes more sense than, than flying through vacuum! I'm not naïve. I know the other planets are barren rocks or balls of ice, and other stars are too far away to reach."

At a look from Travis, Rey broke off. "If you say so."

"So enough nonsense," Zeheri told Travis. "Are you going to tell me who you are, where the Ware comes from, or not? Are you . . . Did your people make it?"

"No," Travis told her. "We're still learning about it ourselves. But it's a danger to all of us, and we can help each other find ways to fight it. That's all that matters right now." He fidgeted. "I wish I could answer all your questions, Urwen, but

I don't think it's a good idea." He took her hand, and she was struck again by how pleasantly cool his was. "All I can tell you is that we're here to help. Can you trust us?"

She looked into his eyes for a long while. There was still something off about the golden hue of his pupils, about his cooling fins and spots, but she didn't think she'd ever seen so much sincerity in anyone's face. She wanted to believe him. She wasn't sure she should trust that feeling—maybe it was just a side effect of the other things she wanted to do with him. But somehow she trusted it—trusted *him*—in spite of her better judgment. Maybe it was just that he was too strange to be unreal, if that made any sense.

"I trust you," she said. "And I'll help you if I can."

"Good," Travis replied. "I think we should get some sleep now . . . but in the morning we'll begin working on a plan."

As they filed out of the hotroom, Ganler sidled up to Zeheri. "No doubt about it—they're Underlanders," he whispered.

She wanted to argue, to insist that they must be with some secret research group in a foreign hold. Maybe the Ware had been some project of Fetul's mad war machine, and Travis was part of some secret government group still uncorrupted by WWA's money. Surely that would be a sane explanation.

But as she lay awake in the deepest hours of the night, she could no longer deny that she hoped Ganler was right.

11

". . . AND HOW LONG, ADMIRAL, had you been acquainted with then-Minister Kuvak?"

Jonathan Archer tried his best not to lose his patience at the questioner, an overweight, elderly Vulcan named Stom who continued his obtuse interrogation with blithe, methodical slowness. "As I already told you, Councillor, I never *met* First Minister Kuvak until the moment T'Pau and I entered the High Command chamber with the *Kir'Shara*."

"And yet your entry was timed to coincide perfectly with Minister Kuvak's deployment of a *to'tsu'k'hy* neuropressure hold against Sublieutenant Torac, his acquisition of Sublieutenant Torac's firearm, and his use of said firearm to hold Administrator V'Las hostage."

"I had no knowledge he intended to do that. We arrived at a critical moment, and we just happened to give Kuvak the distraction he needed to act on his own."

"Then you acknowledge that Minister Kuvak had the premeditated intention to stage a coup against Administrator V'Las."

Archer took a deep breath. It was entirely possible that Stom was deliberately trying to get him to lose his temper. He'd heard a lot of rhetoric already about the dangerously aggressive nature of humans and their Andorian allies, scare tactics from High Command loyalists hoping to convince Vulcan to re-arm itself. He refused to play their game. "As we all know, Councillor, Administrator V'Las had just committed mass murder against the Syrannite enclave in the T'Karath Sanctuary, had ordered his orbital defenses to fire on an allied Earth vessel, and was attempting to launch a preemptive war against Andoria based on fabricated claims that they'd developed a Xindi planetbuster weapon. Even though the Andorians had been warned of the attack and had readied their defenses, V'Las ordered the invasion to proceed anyway, with reckless disregard for the Vulcan lives that would be lost for no reason. It seems to me that V'Las forced Kuvak's hand."

"Yes, you mention that the Andorians were warned of the High Command's classified operations plans. That warning was delivered by then-Ambassador Soval, was it not? With assistance from the crew of the Earth vessel *Enterprise,* which you yourself commanded at the time, did you not?"

Archer glanced at Soval beside him. The commissioner showed no reaction to the insinuation of treason, and Archer strove to follow his example. "None of these facts are in dispute, Councillor, and I see nothing to be gained in rehashing them. The Vulcan people are well aware of the events that transpired eleven years ago and the reasons why they were necessary."

"The reasons as presented by the Syrannites and Starfleet after the fact." The interruption came from Councillor T'Sess, a thin-faced older woman who, according to Archer's briefing material, was as deep in the pocket of the Mental Integrity Coalition and its anti-melding prudes as Stom was in the pocket of Zadok and his High Command loyalists. "The only reason these claims were accepted was because they bore the weight of the mythical *Kir'Shara* behind them. Yet now we know that the *Kir'Shara* was a fabrication."

On Archer's right flank, opposite Soval, Captain T'Pol leaned forward. "All that is now known is that the artifact currently in the museum is a forgery. This does not erase the abundant evidence confirming that the artifact found eleven years ago was authentic."

"But it does call the integrity of its sources into question."

"The professors who discovered the current fraud have been affiliated with the Academy Museum for years. One of them is the bondmate of the security officer who oversaw the vault's design. What reason would they have had to lie before, yet tell the truth now?"

"Professor Semet has only infrequently had opportunities to study the alleged *Kir'Shara*. It is possible that he never discovered the flaws in the forgery until his recent session— whereupon Professor Skon was obligated to cooperate lest his own complicity in the forgery be exposed."

Archer seethed at the accusation, but kept it inward— mostly. "With respect, Councillor . . . it's hardly fair to make such charges without evidence."

"The evidence of the artifact's falsehood is indisputable, Admiral. What is without evidence is your own assertion that an impenetrable security system was somehow undetectably penetrated by thieves who stole this hypothetical original in order to replace it with an identical copy." T'Sess tilted her head back and peered at him down her long, thin nose. "Or do you suggest that the undetectable translocation of matter is one of the mystical psionic abilities alleged by the artifact's text to be the birthright of all Vulcans?"

Archer didn't take the bait. The maddening fact was that, until he and his allies could determine how the real *Kir'Shara* had been substituted, logic favored those who insisted the fake *Kir'Shara* must be the same one found eleven years ago.

There had certainly been no shortage of witnesses willing to testify in support of that notion. Prominent archaeologists had been brought in to discuss the total lack of reliable evidence for the *Kir'Shara*'s existence prior to its discovery at T'Karath in 2154. Unfortunately, the archaeological evidence from the time of Surak was muddled enough due to the wars raging in that era that the rival experts called in on Kuvak's behalf were unable to provide a single, clear explanation for how the ark was lost in the first place or how it ended up in the sanctuary. The suggestions made by some that the High Command had deliberately expunged evidence to ensure the *Kir'Shara* was never found came off sounding more paranoid than persuasive. That was the problem with V'Las's legacy: His crimes had been so extreme that an honest accounting of them sounded like a delusional rant. No wonder so many Vulcans were now receptive to the idea that his misdeeds had been exaggerated by his foes. Even to those who knew the truth about V'Las's crimes, the motivation behind them remained elusive to this day. According to T'Pau, there had been some intimations that he had been colluding with Romulan agents as part of their efforts to soften up the sector for invasion. The former First Minister had suggested that V'Las's unexplained disappearance during the Earth-Romulan War may have actually been a defection.

But even if that were so, V'Las was long gone, quite possibly dead, and the Romulans had been soundly beaten. The monitor outposts along the Neutral Zone had been in place for nearly five years and had detected no traffic of any kind, and intelligence reports of ship movements and intercepted communications within the Star Empire indicated they were shifting their resources and attention to rebuilding their own worlds rather than preparing a new invasion force. What was happening on Vulcan now seemed to arise within the Vulcan people themselves. No surprise there, really; movements like Terra Prime on Earth and the rabid Alrondian separatists in the Andorian system, even those that had been stirred up by the efforts of the Malurians and the Orion Syndicate, had still originated from the grass roots of their respective cultures, from the old guards resistant to change. Archer had hoped that purging those groups of Malurian and Orion influence would break their power. But instead it seemed to have made the surviving factions more entrenched.

Could it be, Archer wondered, *that the Federation's worst enemies come from within?*

ShiKahr Residential District

"Do you mind if I ask you a personal question?" Hoshi Sato inquired of T'Rama as they set the table for the meal that Skon and Kimura were preparing in the kitchen. Apparently they'd missed the couple's other houseguests, *Pioneer's* former engineer Tobin Dax and a poet from a distant alien race, as the poet had persuaded Dax to accompany him to a recital. Sato had been sorry to hear that; the chance to hear poetry in an entirely new language was very enticing. She hoped she would have the chance to meet this Iloja of Prim before *Endeavour* left Vulcan.

"I permit the asking," T'Rama replied, "though that in no way obligates me to answer."

The human woman gave a small smile at the reply. "I know that Vulcans are usually betrothed in childhood," she said. "Which means that spouses tend to be close to each other in age. But you're much younger than Skon, aren't you?"

"I am approximately fifty-five Earth years of age," T'Rama confirmed, "while Skon is a hundred and seven. I was bonded to another in childhood, but on reaching sexual maturity, my intended bondmate determined that he had a clear and exclusive preference for males. Since Vulcan's population is stable and there was no compelling societal obligation to procreate, the logical response was to release him from his commitment to me and allow him to seek a more compatible mate."

"Very gracious of you."

"Not at all. I did wish to have children, and thus it was logical to choose a partner with compatible interests."

"So how did you meet Skon?"

"Our bonding was arranged by his clan's matriarch. We were both in need of new bondmates, and our psychological profiles were deemed compatible." She was quiet for a moment, projecting a cool Vulcan reserve that Sato had never sensed in T'Rama until now. "As for Skon's eligibility, I ask you to understand that some matters are far more private."

Skon was bringing a bowl of what looked like chopped peppers out to the table. "It is all right, my wife," he said. "I do not mind discussing the fate of T'Melis. It is . . . relevant to our pursuits here." Sato noted that Kimura had moved to stand in the doorway, listening in on the conversation.

"My first wife was an officer in the High Command," Skon elaborated. "We deferred childbearing due to the demands of her career. She was then killed in an avoidable skirmish with the Andorians."

"I'm so sorry," Sato told him.

"The time for grieving is long past, but the respect you show her memory is appreciated, Commander. And it is true that her death was a lamentable waste, for it served no legitimate purpose. The High Command, principally in the person of then-Minister V'Las, needlessly provoked the Andorian conflict, choosing aggressive responses that seemed—and, in retrospect, most likely were—intentionally designed to antagonize the Andorians further. I frequently debated with T'Melis, exhorting her to see reason. But at the time, advocacy for peace was painted by the High Command as Syrannite propaganda bordering on sedition. T'Melis would not hear my words and threatened to dissolve our marriage and have me investigated for subversive allegiances if I continued. Soon thereafter, her squadron was deployed to Gliese 229, where their confrontational response to a perceived Andorian incursion provoked retaliation. The incident gave V'Las and his hardliners the cause they had sought to advocate for a more aggressive response . . . at the cost of two hundred seventy-six Vulcan lives, including my wife's."

Sato had no words. Merely repeating her expression of sorrow would seem hollow. But Skon filled the silence himself after a moment. "This is why I am committed to the study and propagation of the *Kir'Shara*'s wisdom—and why I am strongly motivated to succeed in our mission to expose the fraud and prevent the resurgence of the High Command."

Things were quiet for a few minutes after that, but once the four of them were seated at dinner, Kimura broke the ice. "Well, if you ask me, whoever arranged your betrothal picked well. You two are very different on the surface, but you mesh well."

"Indeed," Skon said. "I have found my marriage with T'Rama to be more harmonious than that with my previous mate. T'Melis was a combat specialist with whom I had little common ground. While T'Rama's training is in security, her skills are more oriented toward detection and deduction. We share a fascination with the solving of conundrums."

"In our own distinct ways, of course," T'Rama added. "There is more pure logic and structure involved in his work than mine, a fact which I often find cause for envy."

"Yet I," Skon continued, "have often found it difficult to deal with the more chaotic business of sapient beings and their motivations. It was T'Rama who encouraged me to take up linguistics as a way of gaining new insights into the workings of the mind. Indeed, it even improved my abilities in software engineering, once I began to think of programming code in terms of language as well as mathematics."

"Do not understate the benefits you have brought to my work, husband," T'Rama said with what Sato dared to label privately as affection. "Your mathematical insights have assisted me in a number of investigations over the years."

Hoshi chuckled. "You can use math to solve crimes?"

"Certainly," Skon told her. "The principles of mathematical forensics were formulated over a thousand years ago by T'Kea of Mond—frankly, an underappreciated genius."

"I advise you not to query further," T'Rama said, "or we will be distracted from our investigation for most of the night. T'Kea is a favorite subject of his."

"I had no intention of diverting our guests from their responsibilities," Skon replied primly.

"You never *intend* to, my husband."

"Well, anyway," Sato said, hoping to head them off, "you do have a lovely home. It feels so welcoming. Peaceful. On Kreetassa, they say a harmonious home reflects a harmonious marriage."

"We thank you for the respect you show our home," Skon replied.

Kimura smiled. "Yeah, I think you two will provide your son with a good home," he told them, nodding toward T'Rama's ample belly. "Won't be long now, will it?"

"We expect the birth in approximately four weeks," Skon replied, "with a margin of error of approximately five days in either direction."

"I would not mind," T'Rama observed, "if the margin favors an earlier arrival. The fact that human gestation takes only nine months is a trait I have come to admire about your species."

Hoshi chuckled. "Thanks—I think."

May 24, 2165
Orion transport *Rimula-Bero*, on approach to Delta IV

Devna came to the bridge as ordered, along with Ziraine and Rilas, once the ship came into communication range with the planet the humans called Delta IV. The reports that a low-level intelligence asset in the Federation had relayed to the Orion Syndicate had spoken of the Deltans' hedonistic ways, and thus Parrec-Sut had wanted to put the maximum amount of beauty on display for the eyes of whoever answered his hail.

That hail had drawn only a "stand by" response for several minutes, long enough for Devna and her slave-sisters to begin trading nervous looks. Finally, an elegant, hairless woman with bronze skin and vast dark eyes, her beauty undiminished by her age, appeared on the screen, instantly captivating Devna's attention. *"I am Mod'hira, Prime Minister of the Dhei Union. I bid you welcome to our star system, traveler."*

At the conn, Parrec-Sut gave his most charming smile in response. "My thanks to you, Madam Prime Minister. It is an unexpected honor to be greeted by one of your stature."

"Visitors from other worlds are an uncommon occurrence for us— significant enough to warrant the highest attention. Your race is new to us. You said you are . . . Orion?"

"That name will do." It was another human coinage, Devna knew, assigned decades ago by the first human freighter crews to encounter her people; apparently the humans placed her home sun in an arbitrary grouping of stars symbolizing a mythical giant, one whose name bore some resemblance to her race's name in one of its major language families. The leaders of the Syndicate had appreciated the association with a figure of such predatory power, and had thus embraced the label for its intimidation value. Devna often wondered why they had done so, since few besides humans would understand the import; but she had long ago learned the folly of questioning the whims of her masters and mistresses. Sometimes, for those who relished wielding power over others, being arbitrary was the entire point.

The motives driving Parrec-Sut's mission to Delta IV were much more straightforward, however. His own mistresses, the Three Sisters who ran the Syndicate, derived their power over other Orions from the exceptional potency of their sexual pheromones, just as most Orions could influence and manipulate other humanoids through their own more moderate pheromonal allure. The Sisters' relative monopoly on that power was precious to them, so much so that Navaar, the senior of the Three, was still raging over the recent theft of an Orion hormone supplement by a narcotics syndicate that was now marketing it as a sexual enhancement drug in the human colonies. So Navaar had naturally been disturbed upon learning of a race whose pheromones rivaled the Sisters' own in—potency—not merely in the females of certain elite lineages, but among the entire population. Even more disquieting was the Starfleet report that at least one human had been driven nearly insane and another placed in a coma from the sheer intensity of their sexual encounters with the Deltans. From any other source, these tales could be dismissed as lurid exaggerations; but Starfleet was known for its humorless rectitude. Thus, Navaar had been genuinely concerned that the Deltans might be able to compete with the Orion elites at their own game.

Fortunately, the damage inflicted upon the Starfleet officers had led the Federation to break off contact with Delta, leaving the world unprotected. Parrec-Sut's mission, and that of his slaves, was to assess the Deltan race's potential as a threat—and their potential for enslavement. The Sisters would not tolerate such a powerful competitor, but if they could break such a power to their will, it would be a major triumph.

Parrec-Sut continued. "We are traders, come from far away in search of new customers for our wares and services. I would be pleased to meet with you and discuss what we have to offer."

Mod'hira gave an apologetic smile. *"Ordinarily, I would be delighted. Sadly, a recent incident has forced us to adopt caution in our dealings with outsiders. Our people . . . emit pheromones that can compromise the judgment of other species. We have no wish to risk imposition upon the free choice or well-being of others."*

Devna wished she could take the beautiful prime minister's sincerity at face value. Freedom was a fantasy she had let herself indulge at times in the past. But the lure of that fantasy had once led her into an error of judgment that had nearly ruined her career as an intelligence operative, and she had endured months of humiliation as the lowliest of sex slaves to atone for her failure. She now knew better than ever that no one who held power truly believed in the freedom of others.

Parrec-Sut himself had to struggle to keep the disbelief out of his voice as he said, "How commendable." He gestured to the three slave women, who moved closer to the pickup in compliance. "But I can assure you, Madam Prime Minister . . .

my people are accustomed to intense pheromones and the desires they can create. We've had our own problems dealing with more . . . susceptible races. Perhaps we could even give you some advice on how to manage your encounters with them."

"*Stand by.*" Mod'hira turned to confer with her advisers for several moments. "*Your offer is intriguing, but we are still wary from our previous encounter. Perhaps it is best if we ease into contact. I recommend you dock with the station orbiting the fifth planet, Iatu. It is a popular tourist site; the rings of Iatu iridesce magnificently under the periodic x-ray surges from our sun. The next maximum is just over a day from now. If you dock there, you can behold that wonder and meet many of our people.*"

Parrec-Sut nodded. "While still limiting our mutual exposure. I understand. It's a fair compromise. But I look forward to . . . establishing a closer relationship between our peoples," he finished with an open leer.

"*That is my hope as well,*" the prime minister replied, without reciprocating his subtext. "*Mod'hira out.*"

Once the screen went dark, Parrec-Sut twisted his lip and made a snide grunt. "Pathetic. They should be easy marks."

Devna hoped her master was right, for she was determined to prove her value to the Sisters once again. She owed a particular debt to the youngest Sister, Maras, who had taken pity on her and given her the means to redeem herself by exposing the traitor who had enabled the theft of the hormone supplement. Devna was still unclear on why Maras had helped her. She had always believed, along with everyone else, that Maras was quite stupid, surviving only through her exceptional sexual magnetism and the indulgent affection of Navaar. But Maras had allowed Devna to glimpse the sharper mind beneath the moronic façade. It was a secret Devna knew she must keep on pain of death, but would have been glad to keep in any case, for there were definite benefits to a Sister's patronage, even—perhaps especially—a secret one. If nothing else, the sex was incredible, as one would expect from the Three Sisters' most ravenous member. Devna had no illusions that she was anything but Maras's slave, at best a pampered pet of whom she might one day grow weary. But few Orions could aspire to anything better in life, so Devna was grateful for what she had. And thus she was committed to earning the second chance Maras had arranged for her. If there were a way to bring the Deltan race under the yoke of slavery, she would move the very stars to find it. She knew the Deltans would surely suffer under Orion enslavement—but it would be preferable to the fate the Sisters would arrange for them if they should prove unsuitable for the whip.

May 24, 2165
U.S.S. Endeavour

"Much has been said about the crimes Administrator V'Las is said to have committed," said the stern, middle-aged man on T'Pol's desk monitor. *"Allegations that the administrator is no longer present to defend himself against. But too little is said these days about the wise decisions V'Las made during his decades as a minister and administrator within the High Command."*

The speaker was Commander Zadok, the leader of the High Command loyalists, whose partisans within the Vulcan Council had called him to testify and essentially handed him the floor as a platform for his militaristic rhetoric. As one of the witnesses, T'Pol should optimally have been present in the Council chamber, as Admiral Archer and Commissioner Soval were. But she had duties as *Endeavour*'s captain that were not being fulfilled while she sat idly in the Council gallery, so she had disdained protocol and shuttled back to the ship. After all, factions like Zadok's were already long since convinced that she was undisciplined, mercurial, and overly contaminated by her long association with humans, so she need not fear doing any further harm to her reputation in their eyes, even if their opinion had mattered to her in the slightest.

Still, she kept the hearings playing in the background while she studied the reports that her first officer, Aranthanien ch'Revash, had brought to her ready room for her review. The veteran Andorian officer now sat in the corner seat, watching Zadok's speech on her desk monitor. *"From the start, V'Las recognized the potential danger that humanity's Warp Five Program created for the galaxy. It was through his urging that the High Command acted to put a check on the humans' rapid technological advancement, delaying their expansion into space long enough to cool their aggressive fervor to expand. It was at his insistence that a Vulcan monitor was placed aboard the first human Warp Five vessel,* Enterprise—*although he could not have known that the assigned monitor, Subcommander T'Pol, would prove so susceptible to human influence. Let us note that it was then-Ambassador Soval who selected the monitor."*

"Coward," Thanien growled softly. "Doesn't have the courtesy to insult you to your face."

T'Pol didn't bother to look up from her reports. "I have yet to register an insulting statement."

"Hm, yes, point taken."

Zadok had continued under their exchange. *". . . Soval should have known better, given his own respectable experience on the Andorian front. Many living Vulcans still remember how the Andorians first swarmed across space two centuries ago, their aggression driving an expansionistic haste, exacerbated by the technologies they had stolen from the first Vulcan emissaries to their world decades earlier."*

"Hardly 'stolen,'" Thanien said. "Those initial Vulcan missionaries were happy to let us study their science. Part of their effort to condition us to logic. Though it simply enhanced our existing theories." He smirked, antennae twisting wryly. "I imagine your people were quite surprised to meet us in space less than a century after we . . . advised them to leave our world."

"Mistakes were made," T'Pol acknowledged, "on both sides."

"*. . . And it should come as no surprise that Earth and Andoria, such similarly aggressive cultures, fell so readily into alliance. It should come as no surprise that Jonathan Archer's first action upon establishing contact with the Imperial Guard was to assist it in exposing our listening post at P'Jem—the first in a string of events that undermined Vulcan security and intelligence along the Andorian border and escalated affairs to the brink of war.*"

"Well, at least he didn't blame you this time," said Thanien.

"I take it as implicit."

But Zadok did not dwell on that point, so as not to give rival councillors a chance to challenge the logical flaws in his thesis. "*In the years that followed, Earth and Andoria often colluded to undermine the peacekeeping efforts of the High Command. In nearly every such case, Jonathan Archer was at the heart of events. And who was it that happened to 'discover' the alleged Kir'Shara and enable the Syrannites to depose V'Las just in time to allow the Andorians victory against our pacification fleet? None other than Jonathan Archer. To the logical mind, does that not appear exceedingly . . . contrived?*"

"*Do you propose, then,*" asked one of the councillors, "*that the Kir'Shara is part of a plot by Earth and Andoria to undermine Vulcan power?*"

"*Consider the events that have occurred since. The High Command was dissolved. The Syrannite government hobbled Vulcan's fleet and ultimately dismantled most of it. And Vulcan was absorbed into an alliance whose military consists overwhelmingly of Earth and Andorian starships. I submit,*"

Councillor, that Vulcan has already been conquered, a bloodless occupation made possible by collaborators within the government."

"There has been no subjugation. No attempt to undermine the Vulcan way of life."

"There have been abundant such attempts, rooted in the propaganda of the mythical Kir'Shara. The normalization of melding, an invasive and neurologically harmful practice that undermines Vulcan logic and discipline and violates the personal privacy we hold so dear. The new pacifist teachings, undermining the Vulcan people's ability to defend themselves from threats the Syrannite government leaves unchecked."

Thanien's antennae perked up. "Captain . . . did Commander Zadok just imply that his followers should engage in armed rebellion against the Federation?"

T'Pol had looked up at that as well, and now she met her first officer's gaze. "He is sensible enough to avoid saying it outright. But he is evidently seeking to plant the idea."

"Is there any chance that enough Vulcans are convinced by his lies to act on that idea? We both know your people are more than capable of violence if they believe it is logically justified."

The captain was slow to answer. "I expect that most Vulcans will consider the evidence fairly. But there are always those who begin with what they wish to be true and selectively interpret the evidence to fit it. Zadok is such a one, and he would not have become the leader of the loyalists were there not a fair number of others—fellow soldiers with combat training—who agreed with that mentality."

T'Pol rose from her seat. "I will contact Commanders Sato and Kimura and advise them to redouble their efforts. The urgency of discovering the true *Kir'Shara's* fate may be greater than we have realized."

12

"I GOTTA ADMIT," Charles Tucker said as he studied the product menu of the trading post's matter replication system, "I can see the appeal of these stations."

Next to him, reflected in the glossy surface of the display screen, he saw Olivia Akomo's saturnine features shifting into a sour expression. "If you ignore the cost, of course."

"I meant to people who don't know better. It's a hell of a lure these folks have set up. I mean, just look at all these gadgets." In hopes of gathering intelligence on the Ware, Reed had decided to dock at one of their trading posts and pretend that *Pioneer*'s personnel were normal customers. Captain Rethne had told them that upon the completion of a routine visit, the stations would broadcast advertisements for additional Ware trading, repair, and recreation facilities in the region; Reed hoped that such information would help them assemble a map of Ware territory and help them track the technology's origins. Fortunately the stations in this region were evidently not in communication with more distant ones, for this trading post had not recognized *Pioneer* or its crew, allowing them to carry out the deception. Still, even with all of Reed's precautions to prevent any of his crew from being taken—declining any offer of shipboard repairs, requiring that all personnel remain in groups of two or more at all times—it made even Tucker nervous to stand here in the lion's den and pretend to be unaware of the danger.

Fortunately, the Ware technology provided a compelling distraction. "There are technologies here that could advance the Federation by centuries," he continued. "Never mind the items offered for sale, the matter replicator alone would be a revolution. Imagine how much longer starships could stay in deep space without having to resupply at a starbase or a friendly planet. As long as they had asteroids for raw materials and starlight for energy, they could replace any expended supplies or damaged components, even rebuild shuttlepods or the ship itself if they needed to."

"That's why you're really here, isn't it?" Akomo asked. "It's not a rescue mission to you, it's about acquiring this technology."

He winked. "Hey, I'm an Abramson consultant, just like you, remember? We're both hoping we can discover something useful here."

She grimaced at the reminder of his deception. "And I suppose you and Captain Reed just happened to hit it off well enough to seem like you've been friends for decades."

"Looks that way."

After a pause, she went on. "Working with Willem Abramson for five years, I've learned a thing or two about people pretending to be someone they're not."

He studied her rounded features. "How much do you know about him?" He asked partly as a Section 31 agent, hoping to learn more about the anomalous immortal, but partly just as a man wondering how much someone who led a life of false identities could truly share with another person.

"Enough to know it isolates him. Keeping up the walls all the time. Knowing that, eventually, he'll have to run away again. I don't know specifics, but I've gathered enough to be quite certain that Willem has several contingency plans for faking his death."

"I daresay he's got some practice at that," Tucker mused, drawing an odd look.

After a moment, Akomo went on. "But I trust Willem, Mister Collier. I grew to trust him before I knew he wasn't who he claimed, so I was able to go on trusting him after I learned.

"You, on the other hand, have yet to earn my trust. So no, Mister Collier, I'm not about to concede that we want the same things." She shook her close-shorn head. "For one thing, the Ware is so dependent on living brains that I doubt we'll find the kind of artificial intelligence breakthroughs Mister Abramson is hoping for."

Tucker thought it over. "On the other hand, if we could learn more about how the Ware interfaces with organic brains, it could improve your ability to interface the brain with bionic limbs. Maybe even prolong life with cybernetic bodies."

She thought over his words, her silence indicating that she could not easily refute the suggestion. Eventually, she said, "You have a point. It does align with some of the projects Willem and I have been pursuing."

"The bio-neural circuitry?"

"For one." Her eyes darted. "Consider the 'lock-in' syndrome associated with certain victims of delta radiation, for example—their neural tissues so degraded that normal prosthetics and brain scanners can't get through to whatever consciousness remains within. If we could devise a more sophisticated interface, it might allow some degree of communication, at least." She shook her head. "What am I saying? For all we know, these stations might have the means to repair such damage directly. I read in the logs how that first repair station healed Captain Reed's injuries. Imagine what other breakthroughs they could offer." She caught herself. "At least . . . those that don't depend on a living brain's processing power."

Tucker's gaze went unfocused as her words sparked a thought. Maybe there was a tangible benefit they could gain right now.

U.S.S. Pioneer

"No, Trip!" Malcolm Reed's fingers gripped the edge of his ready-room desk. "It's out of the question."

"But, Malcolm, this could be the answer! You remember the way that first repair station fixed your leg. It saved you weeks of healing and therapy! And I've seen the medical scans the station made of our whole crew." He fidgeted. "Granted, the Ware aren't big on privacy. But they've diagnosed your genetic damage and offered to fix it!"

"It's not a question of their ability. You're asking me to profit from the enslaving of sentient minds."

"I'm asking you to think about your future. Malcolm, I know how much you've always wanted to have children. I was devastated when Phlox told me about the transporter damage." It had been the good doctor's analysis of the subtle genetic damage to Reed's reproductive system, along with the mild neurological deterioration that had left Admiral Archer desk-bound, that had led to the discovery of the cumulative harm inflicted by Earth's transporter technology. Both men had been among the heaviest users of the transporter, and Tucker, who was right up there with them, had been relieved but a bit guilty when Phlox had determined that, by the luck of the draw, he had avoided any lasting damage. On top of that survivor's guilt was the added guilt that he, as *Enterprise*'s chief engineer for four years, had failed to discover the flaw in the technology in time to spare his friends from its lasting consequences. "You shouldn't have to give that up forever. This is your chance to fix it once and for all!"

"I'm not out here for my own self-interest, Trip!"

"Of course not, but there's a tactical reason for it too. The more we play along, the more we lull the enemy into a false sense of security."

"You're talking about these machines as if they were sentient."

"I'm just considering that someone could be monitoring the machines."

"If that were so, we would've been recognized from last time."

"Maybe you destroyed that station before it could transmit its information. We just don't know. That's why we're here: to learn everything we can. And you know as well as I do that sometimes you have to cozy up to an enemy, do things you don't want to do, in order to get the intelligence you need."

"And while I'm at it," Reed replied, "I conveniently manage to indulge my own personal needs, is that it?"

"If it serves everyone, why not?"

"Because 'everyone' includes those poor people this station is currently exploiting and slowly killing. People I have every intention of liberating when we're done here. Who knows how much we might accelerate their mental deterioration with every additional demand we make of the station?"

Tucker was sobered, surprised by the question. Reed caught his reaction. "That didn't even occur to you, did it,

Trip? Nor did the way I'd feel about it. I'd rather have no children at all than have them owe their existence to that kind of moral compromise."

"Oh, I get it," Tucker said, raising his own voice to match Reed's level. "This is you claimin' the moral high ground, lookin' down on me for the compromises I have to make to do my job. I can understand that from Travis. He's entitled. But let me just remind you, *Captain*, that you were doing this job before I was. You were the one who got me into Section Thirty-One in the first damn place, remember?"

"I can never forget that!" Reed cried. "That's exactly the problem. Yes, I've made compromises in the past, but I've seen how high the cost is, to myself and to others. Working with the section in the Klingon Augment affair almost cost me my freedom and the respect of my captain. And what I did to you . . ." He trailed off.

Tucker frowned, studying him. "What you did to me?"

"Just look at yourself, Trip. I can't even *call* you 'Trip' outside this room. You had to give up your whole life, hide from your friends and family . . ." He shook his head. "It was one thing during the war. I could convince myself that the hell you went through was no worse than the hell most of Starfleet went through, that it was worth it for the greater good it served. But the war's been over for five years and you're still trapped. They'll never let you go as long as you live, will they? And it's my fault for getting you into it in the first place!" He turned away, tamping down his anger. "So I've had my fill of making choices that come at the expense of others. I've seen where that leads. And it's not pretty."

Tucker could think of nothing to say in response. But the conversation stayed on his mind long after Reed dismissed him.

Great Ancient Hold, Vanot

Prime Minister Pevrat Hemracine leaned forward over her desk, her fleshy arms supporting her considerable weight, as she skewered Daskel Vabion with a watery gaze. "This break-in should never have been allowed to happen. Why are your mechanical sentries so blasted useless in a storm?"

"You know why, Pevrat," Vabion replied. In contrast to her agitation, he sat as calmly as ever in his chair, his lean, dark fingers folded before him. But his tone conveyed a warning that Hemracine took to heart. There were certain answers he could not give in the presence of her other advisers. "Rest assured my engineers are working on the . . . development of designs better suited to Vanot's environmental conditions.

"As for the break-in itself, while there were certain . . . anomalies about the infiltrators, they were unable to do any harm. The system is designed to defend itself, and it did so, forcing them to flee before they could gather any useful information."

"What do you think they were looking for?" That was finance minister Hatior Daus, a small man whose finger kept compulsively going to his nose as if to push up a pair of spectacles. It had been two years since he had undergone treatment at WWA to correct his vision (and restore his hairline), yet the atavistic habit persisted, an indicator of the man's inflexibility. "You say they had some kind of sophisticated measuring implements. Are they rivals seeking to steal your secrets?"

"You trouble yourself over nothing, Mister Daus," Vabion replied.

"Nothing? That's not the word you used to describe your stocks when you encouraged us all to invest in them so heavily. If you were to lose your monopoly on instant fabrication or, or propellerless flight—"

"I think he means that there are deeper concerns here than our portfolios." Bantik Weroz, Hemracine's chief political adviser, turned her thin face toward Daus with a calculating expression. That face had been middle-aged a few years ago, but thanks to her WWA treatments, she now looked fifteen years younger. "Like what would happen to us if Miss Zeheri succeeded in her investigations into the disappearances. Even Mister Vabion hasn't yet bought *all* the magistrates."

"Zeheri," the prime minister cursed. "Why can't we just make her disappear?"

Vabion tilted his clean-shaven head toward her. "That would be too conspicuous, given her known and highly public pursuit of this investigation and her close association with journalists. We are better served by discrediting her."

"Maybe," Hemracine said. "But I can't help feeling it's a stopgap. Your machines have quite an appetite, Daskel. The more of them you sell, the more brainpower they need to provide their services. Eventually more people will begin to wonder about the disappearances. And what if the brains of the poor and the damaged aren't enough for them? What if they decide they need to acquire a higher class of brain?"

"I assure you, Pevrat, the system has no volition of its own. It follows a complex set of programmed instructions—no different from the calculating engines WWA developed for codebreaking in the War, just immensely more miniaturized, allowing them to be far faster and more elaborate."

"It is different," Weroz pointed out, "in that those calculating engines did not incorporate living brains. Can you be so sure your 'system' doesn't think?"

"My dear Weroz, I am firmly convinced that most *people* do not actually think," Vabion said, making a point to keep his gaze upon her. "We ourselves are elaborate calculating engines following prewired programs and conditioned responses. Only a few of us ever develop sufficient introspection and flexibility of thought to reach the point of true sentience."

"If that charming sentiment was meant to reassure me, Daskel, it didn't work," Hemracine said. "The mindless outrage of the mob is exactly what I'm afraid of. All of us here see the value of taking people who were drains on society and putting them to work for the benefit of the economy. But the traditional ideals still hold sway, and we are well into another storm cycle."

"A cycle that Worldwide Automatics is well on the way to taming," Vabion reminded her. "There will no longer be any need for austerity or population control, and thus the old sermons teaching us to cherish every person's contribution, no matter how meager, need no longer sway the people."

"In time, perhaps," Weroz said. "But there's still a lot of idealistic sentiment in the wake of the War. The generation that stood against Fetul won't die off anytime soon. In fact, many of them are among the poor and damaged, and their comrades would not appreciate their . . . involuntary contribution to the economy the way we do."

Vabion smiled. "My friends. You speak as though the mood of the populace were like the weather, a force of nature outside your control. We are beginning to master the weather, in fact, but directing the minds of the public is a far easier proposition. If there is a risk of disclosure, we must simply get ahead of the story. Reveal the system's use of living brains ourselves, and present it as a positive."

The others stared, several steps behind him as always. "How in the storms do you suggest we do that?" Hemracine demanded.

"We present it as an innovation of our own design to increase the power of the system. Decree that inmates sentenced to execution will have their sentences commuted if they volunteer for a new program whereby their brains will be tapped to increase the efficiency of WWA technology. It will appear to be a humane alternative, allowing them to contribute usefully to society for the remainder of their lives. And however brief those lives are, it will be an improvement on what they were slated for."

Hemracine stared for a long moment. "You are one cold son of an Undertroll," she said, albeit with admiration.

"And what happens," Weroz asked, "when we run out of condemned inmates and the system still demands more?"

"Hmm," Daus muttered. "Well, I suppose if it goes over well, the penalty could be extended to lesser offenses. As needed, of course."

Hemracine grimaced. "Wonderful. And in time we'll have to invent new crimes to keep up the supply."

Daus shrugged. "Well, Vabion did say we can relax the population laws. There will always be plenty of poor people."

The prime minister threw him a disgusted glare, but said nothing, aware that she was in no position to claim a moral high ground. "All right," she said. "I'll take the measure under consideration. We're adjourned." But once the advisers and Vabion had risen and headed for the door, Hemracine spoke softly. "Daskel, stay a moment."

Once they were alone, she sidled closer and spoke. "No matter how cleverly you dress it up, you know this is only a stopgap."

"Of course."

"Can you give me any idea how close you are to taming the beast?"

"As you know, Pevrat, I and my best cyberneticists have been working steadily on the problem ever since we recovered the first landing craft. But whatever world created this technology must be enormously beyond us. Its defenses against deconstructing or modifying its programming code are . . . robust. You know we have lost a number of experts in the attempt."

She grimaced, remembering tales of specialists miraculously translocated into walls or high into the open sky, or simply disappearing. "You're not telling me anything new."

"Because I have nothing new. The problem persists."

Hemracine strode back to her desk and slammed a meaty fist against the wood. "We were fools, you know. Machines falling out of the sky and offering us endless riches and power . . . and we just embraced it. I ask you, Daskel, who's really in control? Are we managing this problem, or just finding new ways to bend over and give it what it wants?"

"Control *will* be mine," he assured her. "No problem is intractable to a sufficiently imaginative and dedicated mind. It's simply a matter of gaining enough information. The more I study the system, the more my understanding grows. And in time, I will master it."

Her only response was, "You'd better." He recognized it as dismissal and left—though it was a polite fiction that she had any real authority to dismiss him. He could impoverish her with one signature, or bring down her government with one endorsement of a rival. For that matter, she probably would not be alive today had Vabion's technology not cleared her arteries and repaired her heart. Everything the prime minister had, she owed to him, and he could take it from her again with ease. Daskel Vabion allowed nothing to be out of his control.

Except for one thing. Once alone in the lift—an automated one driven by a WWA processor, so there was no attendant to witness it—he allowed himself a grimace of frustration, for

Hemracine's words had been an aggravating reminder of his one failure of control. He was the greatest mind on the planet, but someone out there from somewhere else had outsmarted him, building a machine that even he could not comprehend.

No, it simply could not stand. He would break the system somehow. He would understand its code, tear down its defenses, and make it truly serve his will. Or, failing that, he would find a way to travel to its source. He knew, as no one outside of WWA besides Hemracine knew, that Vanot was circled by orbital drones that delivered the fabrication units to the ground and that occasionally demanded cargoes of captured Vanotli for delivery elsewhere. He knew the system must be merely one portion in a larger technological ecology that spread across the stars. If he could just alter its programming enough to make a lander come for him and deliver him conscious and uncompromised to its source, then he could do business with its creators and enter into a true partnership.

But first he had to penetrate its defenses and alter its programming, and the effort to circumvent its security had already taken lives. He knew he might die himself before he mastered this problem.

But if Daskel Vabion could not conquer a mindless machine, then he had no business living.

13

"WE HAVE BECOME PREOCCUPIED of late with the question of whether the lessons brought to us by the *Kir'Shara* truly originated with Surak. I submit that this is the wrong question."

The speaker, T'Zhae, was a whip-thin Vulcan female whose cocoa-dark hair fell halfway to her waist. She was also startlingly young; in Phlox's medical judgment, she was less than two Earth decades of age, younger even than Hoshi Sato had been when she had first joined *Enterprise*'s crew. But she was as welcome in this forum as anyone. That was the egalitarianism Phlox so admired in the Vulcans, and he was glad he had happened to track down his old acquaintance Tobin Dax in time to get invited on an excursion to this debate house—a combination coffee shop and public forum where ordinary Vulcan citizens gathered to debate logic, philosophy, politics, poetry, art, and whatever other issues took their fancy. It was the Vulcan equivalent of Denobulan social gatherings like *gueaa-dancing* and Stump the Philosopher, or human customs like poetry jams and karaoke. Phlox was quite enjoying it, just as he was enjoying the opportunity to get acquainted with Dax's new friend Iloja of Prim, whose orbital ridges Phlox found most formidable and whose neck structure was anatomically fascinating. Oh, and his poetry was charmingly vicious as well.

There was no viciousness in T'Zhae's presentation, but

there was a cool, intellectual passion beneath her words. "Surak would not have tolerated becoming the object of a personality cult," she went on. "He insisted he was an ordinary Vulcan—a teacher, not a prophet. The insights that came to him, he insisted, were equally available to all who chose to meditate upon them. The wisdom lies in the words themselves, not their scribe.

"Thus, if the lessons inscribed in the *Kir'Shara* are sound, if meditating upon them brings us greater *cthia* and serenity, if it heals the rifts that had arisen between communities in recent generations, then does it matter when and by whom those words were written? Surak, revered though he is, is a memory. We are the Vulcans who live today, and who shape the future. Thus, it is we, through our own choices and actions, who give legitimacy to a philosophy. The wisdom is ours to discover and to enact in our lives. Even if the document imparting the lessons is a lie, that does not matter if the lessons themselves are true."

"Marvelous!" Iloja murmured to his tablemates, barely managing to keep his voice low enough to avoid irritated glances from the adjacent tables. "I thought these Vulcans were a cold people at first, but do you see the passion in her eyes? There's true idealism there, true dedication." He sighed and shook his head. "On Cardassia, the Obsidian Order would be hauling her away for reconditioning right now, if not arranging for her suicide following a lovers' quarrel."

"I see what you mean," Phlox replied, trying to keep the mood cheery. "She reminds me of my own daughter, Vaneel. Always passionate in her convictions, always eager to question and challenge the precious assumptions of society." He chuckled. "Vaneel forced me to rethink a thing or two over the years, and I'm eternally in her debt for it. I hope this young lady's parents are just as proud of her."

Tobin Dax was watching her distractedly as she completed her speech and stepped aside for the rebuttal speaker. "I like her hair," he finally murmured.

Iloja let out a bark of laughter, this time succeeding in drawing glares. "She's a little young for you, isn't she, my friend?"

Dax flushed. "You have no idea," he replied sheepishly. "But . . . well, she seems older. Really smart."

"This is Vulcan," Phlox told him. "They're all really smart."

"Although sometimes in monumentally stupid ways," Iloja added.

The rebuttal speaker was a more mature male—a few years below T'Pol's age, Phlox estimated. He was tall and lean, but his fitness and bearing suggested a military background. Indeed, the man declared, "I am Soreth, formerly a subaltern in the High Command." Many in the audience made subtle sounds or gestures of disapproval.

"My . . . learned opponent," he continued with respect so measured as to be clearly sarcastic, "has attempted to suggest that the source of a philosophy is irrelevant so long as we are swayed by it. I submit that the intentions behind the philosophy and its propagation are entirely relevant. For these teachings are those of the Syrannites—a long-standing radical group that originated within the melder community."

"Uh-oh," Tobin murmured. "He's one of those." Soreth was not the first partisan of the Mental Integrity Coalition to have spoken tonight, though he was the youngest.

"Our history clearly shows the dangers of melding. Before Surak, the powers of the mind were wielded as weapons, trapping our ancestors in a constant state of warfare and tyranny where no individual's mind was safe from violation. Surak himself condemned these practices and taught us to respect the sanctity of the Vulcan mind. Only when our minds were safe from external assault were we free to master them.

"Thus, the renewed embrace of melding threatens to erode the barriers that keep us sane and safe within ourselves— between logic and emotion, between self and other, between private and public. Melders thus often have difficulty respecting the barriers that must exist between Vulcans and more emotional species if we wish to preserve our integrity. We have seen how melders such as Soval and T'Pol have been swayed by human emotion and human agendas. This led inexorably to a melder-led Syrannite government that has allowed even more alien intrusion into Vulcan life. Thus, these teachings contained in the alleged *Kir'Shara* serve to undermine everything that makes us Vulcan.

"Now, I do not agree with Commander Zadok's conclusion that Vulcan has already been conquered," he insisted to the skeptical crowd. "That would imply that it is already too late, and this I do not consider true. I do support the reconstitution of the High Command, but as a precaution, a deterrent against outside forces that would seek to undermine what we are. We must restore the barriers that preserve our Vulcanness."

Once Soreth stepped back, T'Zhae was quick to rebut him. "Even in the *Analects*, Surak's constraints on melding referred only to invasive and non-consensual melds. Yes, throughout history there have been cultures that read this as a condemnation of melding itself, but they were few. Most simply adopted the policy that melding should be attempted only by trained adepts, or through their mediation—but those adepts were respected by most Vulcan societies until the High Command came to power and propagated what are now known to be myths about the medical hazards of melding.

"We now understand that the melding of minds is the

essence of what makes us Vulcan. It does not erode our identity—it reveals it. By sharing our minds with others, we discover ourselves through their eyes. And only then do we truly know ourselves."

"I concede," Soreth replied, "that the potential for telepathic contact exists within any Vulcan brain. But so does the potential for hallucination or psychosis. So does the potential for rage and violence. In the normal Vulcan brain, the telepathic potential is unexpressed. It must be activated through the telepathic intervention of a melder—a member of that minority of the population in which the potential is spontaneously active."

"This is a proven falsehood. The ability is present in every Vulcan brain from birth, as demonstrated through the mating bond—which is unquestionably psionic, despite the belief propagated in recent generations that it was merely hormonal in nature. But we must learn to exercise the skill, just as we learn to walk or to operate a keyboard or to play a lyre. It only lay dormant in most modern Vulcans because we were conditioned to deny it. But that denial is pathological. Have you not seen the thesis of T'Rin of TesKahr, demonstrating the steady rise of mental illness during the generations when the melding ban was in place and the substantial decline since the ban was lifted?"

"A thesis which has not yet been peer-reviewed," Soreth countered. "Nor has there been enough time to verify that the reputed decrease is anything but a temporary fluctuation."

"You ignore the preponderance of cases in which melding itself provided the cure to mental illness. Pa'nar Syndrome has been effectively eradicated in less than a decade. It only took that long because so many sufferers were slow to accept the simple cure."

Soreth continued to ply his case gamely, even though the bulk of the crowd seemed to side with T'Zhae. "There," Iloja opined, "is a man who will never change his mind if he lives to be two hundred. So young for a Vulcan, yet so very old already."

"I don't know about that," Dax said. "Nobody can live a long life without changing."

Phlox chuckled to himself. *Not on Trill, perhaps*, he thought.

"But change can mean losing what flexibility you once had," Iloja responded. "A mind—or a nation—that starts out free and open can become so ossified in its fears and prejudices that it leaves less and less room for innovation. Eventually it must die and give way to something new. It's only a question of how long and how viciously it fights against the inevitable."

Dax stared at the cranky old poet. "You don't think that'll happen here, do you? I mean, these are logical people, whatever side they're on. The old guard must see they're fighting a losing battle." He gestured around them at the mostly young audience, at the vibrant debater who was barely out of girlhood. "Demographics alone will make them irrelevant sooner or later."

"There are none more desperate than those who see their way of life dying around them," Iloja intoned. "The more inevitable their fate seems, the more violently they resist it."

Tobin leaned closer, whispering, "You don't seriously mean to suggest that Vulcans would resort to armed insurrection?"

"For all their veneer of logic, Vulcans have the same drives and passions as any other species—maybe even more so than most. And you've heard from that Zadok how easy it is to concoct logical justifications for violence.

"Indeed," Iloja went on grimly, "the thieves of the *Kir'Shara* have already committed violence of a sort. Naturally they must have destroyed the original as soon as they obtained it, to ensure that its reality could never be proven. That is a profound act of violence against history and the soul of a people."

"History, perhaps," Phlox conceded. "But I agree with the young lady up on stage: The ideas of the *Kir'Shara* will remain with or without the artifact. I believe that good ideas triumph in the end. It's evolution: Adaptive ideas, those that help a society thrive and grow, win out over harmful ones. Peace, tolerance, openness to exchange with other species: These ideas create more opportunities, allow individuals more chances to survive and more options to succeed. Therefore, they have an evolutionary advantage over violence, intolerance, oppression—ideas that tend to destroy lives or restrain their opportunities.

"Why, look at Denobula. In just a dozen years, we've mostly moved beyond our old enmities toward the Antarans—and now my Vaneel is taking an Antaran as a husband! So you see? Peace only increases our opportunities, reproductive and otherwise, and thus has a selective edge."

Iloja grinned. "Politics as evolutionary biology! I'm intrigued, Doctor Phlox. I'd love to discuss it more."

"I'd be happy to oblige!"

"But tell me, Doctor: Do all Denobulans share your rosy view? Have they all embraced their former foes so readily?"

Phlox grew somber, thinking of Mettus, his estranged son. "I must admit, the answer is no. In fact . . . some have only grown more entrenched in their old hatreds. More determined to resist the inevitable change."

"And so it is here on Vulcan," Iloja concluded. "Mark my words: There will be violence before this is resolved."

Phlox hoped he was wrong about Vulcan—and feared even

to contemplate how his words might apply to an upcoming Denobulan wedding.

ShiKahr Residential District

Hoshi Sato felt Takashi Kimura's eyes on her as she stood at the glass wall of their guest room in Skon and T'Rama's home, gazing through the vertical green slats of the open blinds at the ornate fountain in the courtyard beyond. It was a warm night, as most nights were on Vulcan, and she was sweaty from her earlier exertions with Takashi; so she found it comfortable to stand here nude before an open pane, letting the faint night breeze anoint her skin with the delicate, cooling moisture it wafted in from the fountain.

Yet as Takashi rose from the bed and padded toward her on feet as bare as the rest of him, she could tell from the corner of her eye that his gaze was not lustful or acquisitive. After eight years, being nude together was a routine intimacy, the touch of his skin against hers simply a reminder of their closeness and trust. Although, she reflected absently as she turned to watch his approach, the view was still spectacular. Being the lover of an armory officer who kept himself at the peak of physical conditioning had considerable benefits.

Still, they had sated those emotions at length a little while ago, though Hoshi had been a little inhibited considering Vulcan hearing. Now, her thoughts were elsewhere, and Takashi, attuned to her as always, made no effort to draw them onto other subjects. He just put his left hand on her shoulder, brushed his flank against hers—lightly, for they were both warm enough in this air.

"We never talk about it," he said after a while. "The long term. But I saw you watching T'Rama." He let the fountain's monologue fill the air for a while. "You want a family some-day," he said, not as a question.

Her right hand on his left was her only answer for a few moments. "I always used to think," she said at last, "that I'd lead a nice, quiet life as a professor on Earth, or maybe Alpha Centauri."

He nodded. "They have one hell of a university there."

"That I'd have plenty of time for a career and a family," she went on. "Get married by thirty, have a kid by thirty-five . . ." She trailed off. They both knew her thirty-sixth birthday was less than two months away.

She shrugged, leaning against him. "But then Admiral Archer roped me into joining *Enterprise*. And I always thought it'd just be for a few months, or a few years, and then I'd go back home and get my life back on its intended course, with the bonus of some really wild experiences in space.

"But now I've been doing this for fourteen years . . . and I can't see myself giving it up. This is the most important thing I've ever done. I've helped . . . bring worlds together. Prevent wars. Build alliances. These are such critical years for the Federation . . . we're still fighting for its survival all the time, it seems. We're needed where we are, Takashi. There's still so much good we can do."

He nodded sagely, silently, going into the inscrutable *sensei* mode that she found such an adorable affectation. She leaned her head on his shoulder and appreciated it for a time. "All this is true," he finally said. "But look at T'Rama and Skon. Can you watch them and doubt that bringing a child into the world, and raising it well, is also a very good thing to do?"

He squeezed her shoulder and strode back to bed, and that was the last thing he said on the subject that night. But Hoshi stayed up, staring out at the fountain, for a long time thereafter—because she couldn't shake the feeling that she'd very, very nearly been proposed to.

May 25, 2165
Vulcan Science Academy Museum

It had been Tobin Dax who finally put the investigators on the right track. "We're looking at this wrong," the Trill engineer had said after hours of helping his hosts and fellow houseguests search through the security footage from the *Kir'Shara* study vault. "We're treating it as a theft. I mean, we're looking for breaches to the entries we know about, and at the times we know about. But this . . . well, this is a magic trick. Invisibly switching one thing for another. And magic is about, well, making the switch where people aren't looking." He'd done a trick with some antique Vulcan coins he'd picked up somewhere, demonstrating the principle. It took two run-throughs before Takashi Kimura had caught on to when the Trill had actually palmed the coin in his left hand, much earlier than it had seemed.

Thinking about this had crystallized something nagging at the back of Kimura's mind. He had called up the feed from the day the switch had been discovered, showing it to Skon and the others. "Do you notice anything unusual here?" Skon had been uncertain until Kimura ran feeds from several earlier study sessions.

Though it had been T'Rama who spotted the discrepancy. "The *Kir'Shara* arrives sooner. From the moment the lift is activated to the moment the ark emerges is some seven seconds shorter than the average."

Skon had done some calculations in his head. "The standard deviation on the lift speed is zero-point-four seconds. A seven-second discrepancy is well outside expectations."

"Moreover," T'Rama had said, "the time it takes the artifact to emerge fully, from tip to base, is well within the expected range seen in other instances—approximately six-point-four seconds."

"That's too close to be a coincidence," Sato had remarked. "But what does it mean?"

Kimura had grinned as the epiphany came to him. "It means we've been looking at every access point except the right one! Come on, we've got to get to the museum!"

Now, in the study vault, it didn't take long for Kimura to find what he was looking for. "We've been focusing on the shaft cover on top of the table as if it were the only access point," he told the others as he knelt below the mushroom-shaped study platform.

"But it is," Skon replied.

"No, it's just meant to be. But what about the table itself? The shaft comes up through this base here. And it's just high enough . . ." His scan of the table's support column gave him the result he was expecting. "Yes. There's a removable panel here, and it looks like it's been unsealed and resealed within the past month. We'll need to get a forensic team in here for a full analysis."

"I think I get where you're going," Doctor Dax said. "It's like palming a coin or a card. It's already there before you reveal it."

"Exactly."

"What are you two talking about?" Sato demanded, taut with anticipation.

"The perfect way to switch the *Kir'Sharas*," Kimura said. "In plain sight, when everybody was looking." He rose and faced the group to explain. "Sometime before Skon and Semet discovered the swap, someone came in here, removed that panel on the base, and inserted the fake *Kir'Shara* on top of a duplicate lift platform. It was already there *inside the table*, just waiting to be found. Then, when Skon and Semet called the lift to raise up the artifact—"

"I see!" Skon declared, satisfaction in his eyes. "The real *Kir'Shara* was still in the vault below. But as it ascended in the shaft, it pushed the replica into view above it. That is why the replica emerged several seconds early—because it was above the actual *Kir'Shara*, which had not yet cleared the shaft."

"And never did," T'Rama added. "The real one was still hidden within the base of the table even while you and Professor Semet were discovering the forgery. Where it awaited an opportunity for the thieves to remove it while no one was looking, for we thought it had already been removed!" Kimura grinned to himself at their excitement. Intellectual satisfaction was one emotion Vulcans didn't seem to mind expressing.

"But wait, that doesn't make sense," Sato said. "This whole vault is under constant visual surveillance. Anyone bringing the fake in or taking the real one out would've been seen."

Tobin thought it over. "Skon, what did you and Semet do after you discovered the forgery?"

"We summoned a team of archaeological specialists to confirm our observations."

"Did they bring equipment?"

"Yes, they did."

"I want to see that footage, if you don't mind."

They went to the security room nearby and scanned through the footage for a while. Indeed, the analysis team had brought in a number of scanning devices, which a museum assistant had carefully rolled in on a cart. "Here," Tobin said, scanning at high speed through the footage. "The cart is placed right next to the study table for nearly two hours. Very close to the central column."

"But the base is open," Skon said. "No one could be concealed within it."

"Um, sorry, Skon, but even an Earth magician from centuries ago could've used mirrors to hide someone inside a cart and make it look empty."

"Mirrors would not work in this case," T'Rama said. "The cart was scanned from too many angles, and with so many people moving around it, reflections of their limbs would have been noted." She leaned forward. "However, I take your point. There are more advanced forms of concealment now available. Commander Kimura, if your hypothesis is correct, then there must have been an earlier instance when a cart was placed against the study platform long enough to allow the initial substitution to have been made."

A scan of the security footage soon turned up just such an instance—and, moreover, the cart bore the same ID number and was pushed by the same assistant, rather more slowly than seemed necessary given its ostensibly light burden. "We need to find that assistant," Kimura said.

"I have already checked the museum records," T'Rama told him. "Her name is given as T'Salan, and she left the museum's employ four days after the forgery was discovered, yet before it was made public. Supposedly she had taken a position off-world, and she moved out of her dwelling the following day." She checked the databases further. "There is no subsequent record of her."

"She's got to be the thief," Sato said.

"The accomplice, that is," Kimura replied. "The thief was the one hiding inside that cart. A cart we need to find right away."

*   *   *

U.S.S. Endeavour

The cart had disappeared as thoroughly as T'Salan had, but Sato had transferred the high-resolution security files to *Endeavour* so that she and Cutler could run a full image analysis. The museum's equipment was at least as good as *Endeavour*'s Vulcan-designed sensors and analytical tools, but Starfleet records contained scans of more than one form of stealth technology against which the security footage could be compared.

And indeed, it wasn't long until she and Cutler reported their findings to Captain T'Pol and Commander Kimura. "There's no doubt about it, Captain," Cutler said. "There's a holographic signature around the base of the cart . . . and it matches the technology used in the Romulan holoship we encountered back on *Enterprise* eleven years ago."

The captain was visibly troubled by the news. "Is it possible there could be Romulan infiltrators on Vulcan?" T'Pol asked.

"They've been quiet since the war ended," Kimura said. "As far as we know. But we still don't even know what they look like. They could be anywhere."

Cutler shrugged. "If they look enough like us to pass for us. We have some reports suggesting they're humanoid, but we can't even be certain of that."

T'Pol paused in thought for a few moments. "The possibility that there are Romulan infiltrators on Vulcan cannot be dismissed," she said. "At the very least, it should be investigated seriously. Commander Kimura," she went on, turning to the armory officer, "your priority must be to track down the woman calling herself T'Salan. We must discover her true identity . . . and affiliations. There may be even more at stake here than we have realized."

14

May 26, 2165
Iatu Vista Station, orbiting Delta V

FOR SOME REASON, none of Devna's tricks worked on the Deltans. No matter how studiously she played the innocent and strove to make herself alluringly vulnerable, she received nothing but apologetic rebuffs from the men and women she approached. The paradox was bewildering. The Deltans were anything but a sexually reserved people; she'd come across numerous duos and groups availing themselves of the romantic lighting from the shimmering rings and auroras, blithely permitting her to watch their playful yet intricate lovemaking. Yet when she offered to join in, she was politely but firmly turned down.

It had been that way since Parrec-Sut had first brought her, Ziraine, and Rilas aboard the station, extoling the sensual wonders his women had to offer, a sample of which they would happily provide by demonstrating the galactically famous dances of Orion. The women had had their work cut out for them trying to draw the Deltan tourists' attention away from the glorious dancing colors of the rings of Iatu—not to mention the vast, swirling auroras that adorned Iatu's poles with shining red crowns. Indeed, even drawing the tourists' attention away from one another had been a challenge, for they were a stunningly beautiful race, and the men and women alike were attired in loose, scanty, or diaphanous garments in many lively hues.

Still, she had given it her all, and not just for the sake of the mission. Dancing was Devna's favorite part of the seduction game. It was a chance to express herself, to wield the potentials of her body entirely on her own rather than at the whims of a master or client. True, it was a tool, an advertisement of herself as a commodity; yet it was the one small part of her life where she was allowed, even encouraged, to be creative. Since she did not have the curves or the raw animal frenzy of Ziraine and Rilas, she had learned to emphasize her grace, her suppleness, her sensitivity. Although she wore as little as her slave-sisters, she was demure, restrained, and teasing in comparison; yet what she held back compared to her dance partners often made her audiences crave her even more intensely. When something was not given freely, after all, it was generally presumed to be more valuable.

Of course, she and her dance partners had the added weapon of their pheromones, which the stimulation and sexual display of the dance prompted their bodies to secrete in abundance, and which their movements were carefully designed to distribute through the air. Although Devna could see the effects of the Deltans' own pheromones on one another just by watching the casual intimacy of their interactions. She could feel the allure they radiated, a sensory aura as stimulating as that which she felt from more pheromonally potent Orion women—when they were in a friendly mood toward her—yet not as overpowering. That was strange: The Deltans had the means to wield influence, but it remained unfocused, unutilized.

Moreover, watching the Deltans' interactions had given her no sense of their hierarchy. Did the males dominate? Did the females? Did the pheromonally strong dominate the weak as on Orion? Discerning the power dynamic between a race's genders was an essential step in learning how to manipulate them sexually, yet Devna could not even begin to see a pattern.

And even her most sensual dances, and those of her slave-sisters, had failed to get them into any Deltan beds so they could gather more intelligence. The Deltan spectators had responded mainly with polite, restrained applause. Some of them seemed more amused than anything else. When Parrec-Sut had made it clear that all three women's companionship was available as a gift to any interested party, as "a gesture of friendship between two peoples with much in common," every one of the Deltans had courteously declined. When pressed, a chubby-faced but fit older male named Tanla had said it would not be appropriate. "We have learned the dangers of taking advantage of—forgive me—sexually juvenile peoples." All of Sut's protests about his women's extensive experience in the arts of pleasure would not change their minds, to the slaver's utter bewilderment.

Still, a few of the Deltans had praised the grace of Devna's dancing, so Sut had decided that maybe her subtler approach would work better with these ethereal people than the raw animal passion of Rilas and Ziraine. So he had sent her back in to ply her demure wiles and determine, on her own, the viability of enslaving the Deltans.

With the entire mission now riding on her, Devna was well aware that another failure could mean her death. So she had proceeded with her greatest care and delicacy, wielding all her skills as both seductress and spy to win over the Deltans. Yet still she got nowhere. The Deltans continued to perceive her as unready to play in their league, although they seemed to hope she might learn something from observing their frequent sex play. But the more she watched, the more confused she became.

Now, she sat alone in a deserted observation gallery, gazing out at the scintillating Iatu, which glared down on her like a divine, condemning eye as the station's polar orbit took it above the planet's southern extreme. That eye blurred with tears—her own, as she despaired of ever solving the paradox and proving herself worthy of the second chance Maras had given her. The prospect of her death if she failed troubled her less, for she had always known that her existence was merely an indulgence extended by her masters until such time as they chose to withdraw it.

"You're trying too hard."

Startled, Devna gathered herself, wiped her eyes, and turned. Standing behind her was a young, brown-skinned Deltan woman named Pelia, whom she recalled from the first day—the hairless beauty had complimented her dancing, yet had expressed puzzlement at the bits of fabric and metal she wore, which only obstructed the view and dug into the skin. Devna had made it clear that Pelia was welcome to remove the offending garments from her, but the Deltan woman had suddenly pulled away, making polite apologies.

Now, it seemed, Devna had a second chance. "What do you mean?" she asked, pitching her breathy voice for maximum innocence.

"What you just did," Pelia replied. "Everything you do, everything you say, is calculated for effect. Even your sincerity is a pretense." She sighed. "I've been trying to be polite like everyone else, let you down gently, but I've realized that's no less a pretense. Someone should be blunt with you."

"I would welcome that." She said it as a ploy, yet realized she was completely sincere.

Pelia responded mainly to the former, her huge dark eyes holding Devna's with impatience. "You Orions don't seem to understand that what you do is in very poor taste."

"What we do?"

"Attempting to use sexuality for . . . for manipulation, deception. Gaining influence over others." She grimaced in distaste. "Is this how you always relate to one another? Is it all about trickery and games, jockeying for advantage?"

Devna's uncertainty this time was completely unaffected. "How else would it be? What would any person do but try to serve their own ends?"

Pelia sat next to her and lightly stroked her shoulder. "Rely on others to aid them, perhaps? None of us are alone, friend."

Devna's green fingers brushed against Pelia's brown ones, gently and enticingly. Pelia pulled her hand away just as gently. "You don't have to do that."

"I know you want me to," she challenged.

"I do," Pelia affirmed in relaxed tones. "But what concerns me—what concerns all of us—is what *you* want."

Laughing, she purred, "Isn't it obvious?"

"I'm afraid it is," Pelia said. "What's clear is that what you're doing . . . it *isn't* what you want. It's what your companion Parrec-Sut wants *of* you. It isn't about your wishes or feelings at all."

"Oh, it is," Devna asserted, allowing more strength into her soft voice. "I want nothing more than to attain what I seek."

"But not for your own sake. You seek to prove yourself to someone else. Maybe Sut, maybe another. Why can these others not come to us and assert their desire freely? Why do they use deception, send you in their stead?"

Devna stared at her. "How do you know these things?"

Pelia smiled. "We are like you in the strength of our pheromones, our libidos. But we are also empathic. We share our emotions, our sensations, not only our bodies. So we can tell that what you feel is not from you and is not toward us.

And we can tell that what Parrec-Sut feels . . ." She shuddered. "There is something predatory in him."

"He is a male. Have you no predators among your own?"

"Aggression has its place," Pelia granted. "But not as part of sex."

Devna scoffed. "Now you use deception. Sex is pursuit. Sex is conquest."

Pelia shook her smooth, elegant head. "There was a time, long ago, when some of my people believed that. When they made it into that. We've seen the same in other species, like the Carreon. But that's a corruption, a misunderstanding of sex."

"My people understand sex extremely well."

"You understand how to use it as a weapon. You don't understand what it's *for*."

After a moment's hesitation, Pelia took Devna's hands in hers and closed her eyes. What came over Devna a moment later was . . . beyond her capacity to describe. It was powerful, profound. It was passionate, yet not venal. It made her feel like . . . no, that wasn't right, because there had been no *her*. It was like she had no longer been herself, but had been part of something greater. She had never felt so whole. "What was that?" she gasped.

"A taste of how we make love. Of what making love is truly for." Pelia continued holding her hands as she went on, smiling. "Sex didn't evolve for power or control. It creates life. It builds bonds within social species like ours—creates trust, relieves stress, eases sadness. It's meant to be an act of giving, of sharing. Using it to take, to control—that isn't what the universe intended it for."

Moments ago, Devna would have dismissed that as superstition. But after what she had just been through, the universe seemed somehow more tangible to her. "I . . . I would like to learn more," she said.

Beaming, Pelia leaned in and kissed her deeply. Devna stared at her afterward. "I thought . . . you didn't want to."

"I was waiting for you to express a true desire of your own. Now you have." She kissed Devna again. "And now . . . you're finally ready to learn."

May 26, 2165
U.S.S. Pioneer

"Forward shields are at forty-nine percent!" Valeria Williams cried even as *Pioneer* shuddered under another barrage from the Ware battleships. "But they're holding for now."

"They've held this long," Malcolm Reed replied. "We just have to hold out a little while longer." It had only taken a day this time for the drones to arrive in retaliation after Williams's security team had raided the trading post and liberated four survivors: three humanoids from Vanot, who were very confused and asking if they were someplace called the Underland, and a large, vulpine biped who called himself a Balduk and would have likely gone on quite the rampage if he'd been in any condition to move before translation could be established.

"Doing my best, sir." Spears of phased nadion energy lashed out from *Pioneer*'s flank and tore into the nearer cruiser as Ensign Tallarico swung the ship around in an evasive arc. A moment later, a photonic torpedo flew with surgical precision to pierce the resultant weak spot in the robot ship's shields, blowing it to scrap.

Or so it seemed. "That drone is twenty-seven percent intact," Ensign Achrati reported from the science station. "It may still be able to self-repair."

"Acknowledged," Williams said, chastising herself for her

premature sense of victory. "But right now there's a higher priority."

A hammer blow rang against the hull, nearly knocking Reed and several others from their seats. "I suggest you attend to that priority with alacrity, Val," the captain grated out. It sounded like he'd bitten his tongue.

"Working on it, sir," she said, wincing in sympathy. "Dorsal shields now at thirty-seven percent."

"Redirect power to dorsal plating."

Her hand had already moved to the appropriate controls. "Redirecting, aye."

"Sickbay to bridge." It was Liao's voice. *"Starfleet may have upgraded the ship to take this kind of knocking around, but the crew are as fragile as ever. We're running out of beds down here. Any idea how much longer we have to keep this up?"*

"Until they stop coming or we find out what we need!"

"You realize you're gambling with the lives of your crew."

"I am keenly aware of what's at stake, Doctor!" he grated. "And I'm trusting you to see that that doesn't happen again. So trust me to do the same."

After a moment, the doctor's chastened voice came back. *"It's a deal, Captain. Sickbay out."*

Williams redoubled her focus on the battle, aware of the corollary to Reed's words: He was trusting *her* to carry out his tactics and ensure the crew remained protected. But at the same time, Liao's words were a reminder that Williams was partly responsible for putting them in harm's way in the first place. She'd agitated for this mission with Admiral Archer, determined to repay the Ware for killing Detzel and the other three—but what if her zeal to avenge them only got more of her crewmates killed?

She knew she didn't dare second-guess herself in battle.

But her decisions seemed to keep endangering her crew. Last year in the Rigel system, her decision to save an innocent Rigelian girl from assault had delayed her delivery of vital intelligence to *Pioneer* and gotten the ship's historian, Samuel Kirk, tortured and almost killed as a result. She'd grown rather fond of the gentle, thoughtful historian, yet he'd barely spoken to her since then—or perhaps she'd simply been avoiding him. It took time to get over something like that, and she didn't want to force any reminders on him.

Instead, she'd thrown herself into her work, determined to do better in the future—only to fail to save four of her crew from Ware attacks. That was unacceptable. This time, with so much more practice and preparation, with so much more at stake, she *had* to get it right.

As if to mock her, a new contact appeared on her tactical board. "Sir," she reported heavily. "Two more Ware battleships closing at one-twenty-eight mark thirty. ETA nine minutes."

"They're getting closer together," Reed said. Once they'd taken out the first two ships, they'd been given a good six hours to make repairs before this battle began. Even if Williams did succeed in taking out the second drone ship before its reinforcements arrived, the shields might not be able to withstand much more. And this time, there'd be no chance of the drone ships battering down the shields and beaming off the liberated "components," for the four rescuees had already been transferred to the courier *Tashmaji* and spirited swiftly away. If they didn't gain the necessary information soon, they might have to abort this stratagem—a better failure than losing lives, but a failure nonetheless. But Williams prayed that the arrival of this newest pair of ships would give them what they needed.

Five minutes later, she managed to cripple the second ship,

but only after the torpedo tubes had been compromised. But Achrati shook her head grimly. "It's already self-repairing, sir," she said. "And the other one's showing signs of life too. In a few minutes we could be under attack from four directions."

"Mister Collier, estimate on torpedo tube repairs?" Reed asked.

"Twenty minutes at least, Captain."

Setting his jaw, Reed turned to Grev at communications. "Ensign, signal Captain sh'Prenni."

But Grev's gentle eyes widened as he stared at his console. "Sir, Captain sh'Prenni is hailing us!"

Reed and Williams traded a look of tentative triumph. "Put her on."

Reshthenar sh'Prenni's strong-jawed, striking blue face appeared on the viewscreen. *"We have a result, Malcolm! Those last two filled in the gap quite neatly."*

"Not a moment too soon, Thenar," Reed told her. "How long until you can reach us?"

"Just watch."

Less than a minute later, the *U.S.S. Vol'Rala* surged out of warp behind and beneath the two approaching drone ships and strafed them fiercely with its wing cannons as it swept by, the kinetic energy of its high-sublight flight adding an extra kick to its particle beams. The *Kumari*-class cruiser then spun in its path and fired backward at the drones as it thrust to decelerate, letting them close with it. Before long, two *Sevaijen*-class light cruisers, which Val recognized as *sh'Lavan* and *Flabbjellah*, followed their flagship out of warp and caught the Ware drones in a pincer. The robot ships broke and ran in opposite directions; *Vol'Rala* altered course to pursue one while the two smaller battleships harried the other.

But *Pioneer* was taking a renewed pounding from the two

drones Williams had damaged, and without torpedoes, her phase-cannon fire had limited effect. "Dorsal shields are out!" she barked, wishing there were a way to channel her sheer fury into the phase cannons.

"Regina, keep our belly to them," Reed ordered. But the more intact, mobile drone was maneuvering to trap *Pioneer* between the two robot craft.

But then it rocked under a barrage from the third *Sevaijen*-class ship, *Kinaph*. The lithe, maneuverable cruiser, still fresh and unwinded by battle, handily dodged the drone's erratic fire and finished it off. Moments later, the bulbous-browed, pointed-eared visage of *Kinaph*'s captain appeared onscreen. *"Do you think you can handle the last one on your own?"* asked Kulef nd'Orelag. *"I don't want to place you under too much debt to me."*

After a nod from Williams, Reed told him, "We can handle it, Captain. And rest assured, I won't forget that debt." Nd'Orelag was the first Arkenite captain in Starfleet, his ship commissioned to commemorate the former Andorian subject world's recent admission as the Federation's ninth member. Arkenites had a very strict and clear-cut set of beliefs about the payment of personal or communal debts, and Williams hoped Reed wasn't getting himself in trouble by accepting the obligation.

With no more need to divide her attention, Williams took satisfaction in blowing apart the surviving drone fragment with phase cannons alone. By now, though, the two remaining drones were doing their best to circle around toward *Pioneer* and fulfill their relentless quest. She could hear over *Vol'Rala*'s comms that the drones were attempting to broadcast their ultimatum about the "theft of primary data core components"; Reed had long since ordered Grev not to bother airing the predictable hails, but apparently sh'Prenni hadn't grown sick of them yet. Indeed, the tall, lively captain seemed quite amused by the drones' mindless insistence on the return of their so-called property and the relentlessly pleasant voice in which the threats were delivered. For a while, it almost seemed like she was toying with her drone, for it continued to function even after *Flabbjellah* and *sh'Lavan* had finished off theirs. But before the drone could draw too near the damaged *Pioneer*, sh'Prenni grew serious, her antennae angling forward decisively, and she ordered a series of maneuvers that swiftly reduced the last drone to dust.

"*That should do it, Malcolm*," the Andorian captain reported, smiling over the viewscreen. "*Sorry* Thelasa-vei *couldn't join the party, but it needed to be far enough out to confirm the triangulation. Thanks to Captain th'Zaigrel's data, we've successfully calculated the probable origin point for these drones. And it's consistent with both the map you got from the trading post and the dispersal pattern your Mister Collier proposed for the planetary Ware components. We may have just found their source.*"

Williams pumped her fist in triumph. There had been a point to this after all. She sent the shipwide signal to stand down from tactical alert and transmit final damage reports to the bridge, and she was relieved to pass along sickbay's notification: "No fatalities or critical injuries, sir."

"Excellent." Reed turned to the screen and gave *Vol'Rala*'s captain an appreciative smile. "Thank you, Thenar. I never doubted that a ship named *Enterprise* would come through for us."

"*It's a storied name in both languages, true; but let's give a little credit to the* shen *in the center seat, shall we?*"

"Absolutely. We couldn't have done it without you."

"*Damn right. You almost didn't do it with us. You said you could hold out long enough. That was cutting things very close.*"

"But we *did* hold out."

"*I'm simply saying that next time, you should let us be the bait. We're bigger than you are.*"

"Hopefully there won't be a next time," Reed said. "If we finally find the Ware's makers and can actually *talk* to somebody, maybe we can get them to listen."

Sh'Prenni looked skeptical. "*Malcolm, these people have no problem with enslaving and devastating primitive worlds to feed their chambers of horrors. Trust me: There will be a next time.*"

Williams took her warning to heart. One success was not enough. No matter what came next, she could not let herself fail again.

May 26 to 27, 2165
Stone Valley Hold, Vanot

The strangers had been quick to shoot down Urwen Zeheri's plan for getting the goods on the homeless abductions. She had been convinced that if she, Ganler, and their mysterious new allies staked out the so-called charity centers the WWA had installed in the outer zones, in time they would witness an abduction and be able to follow the captive back to wherever they were held or experimented on, gathering photographic proof that would convince Rehen and allow her to convince the media and the inquisitors of the crimes WWA and the Hemracine government were committing. But the tall, muscular man called Travis had let her down gently, telling her that the captives weren't transferred by any method she would be able to track. "What do you mean?" she'd demanded. "Do they suck them underground and use some secret tunnels?"

"Something like that," he had replied after the hesitation he showed whenever he chose to hide something from her. She'd wanted to bring all her interrogation skills to bear and break his reserve, but she needed his cooperation and was reluctant to alienate him.

In time, they devised another stratagem. Though few WWA employees were allowed within the automated factories, Vabion frequently sent in his top engineers and computational encoders, presumably to maintain the equipment. "That's not likely," Rey said when she offered that conclusion.

"That's right," Zeheri realized. "You've said the equipment isn't theirs. It's beyond anything we've ever known—are you saying it's beyond even Vabion's best people?"

Rey traded another secretive look with Travis. "Let's just say I'd be surprised if they knew more about the Ware than we do."

Travis leaned forward. "What matters is, they can get past security. How are they cleared?"

"That's the tricky part," Zeheri told him. "They use identification cards that the machinery can recognize somehow. It's not just the writing or the picture—I've seen people arrested trying to get in with forged credentials. There's something more that the machines are sensing."

"Some kind of radio-frequency tag or molecular encoding," Rey suggested to Travis.

"Probably. Can you find out if we get close enough to scan one of those cards?"

"Sure—but we'd need to contact, uh, our friends to do the fabrication. We don't have the equipment in our . . . vehicle."

Zeheri had tolerated their careful avoidance until the next day, when Ganler had come to her in a state of wild excitement. "I followed Rey when he went to pick up the cards. He just went to a spot outside the walls and spoke into that tiny radio of his . . . and then there was a sound like a strange wind and a sparkle of light, and the cards just *appeared* out of nowhere at his feet!"

She had striven to calm him, suggesting that perhaps he had seen the light from some kind of underground lift, illuminating dust motes in the air. True, she'd heard rumors from former WWA employees that whatever Ware machinery was hidden behind the fabrication centers' façades seemed to summon things out of thin air like magic. But she couldn't be sure how much of that was exaggeration or drink, and even if there were truth to it, it required large mechanisms. She could, at this point, allow herself to believe that Underlanders were assisting her new friends, but believing they had the power to create matter out of nothing was just too much.

Still, it was enough to crystallize certain doubts she'd been having, doubts that forced her to confront Travis that night. She took him into her guest room, closed the door, and spoke. "I accept that you have secrets to keep. I've tried not to push you. But if we're going into danger together, I need to know I can trust you implicitly. I need to know you aren't hiding anything that could hurt me or Ganler if we follow where you lead."

Travis reacted uneasily at the latter name. "I'd feel a lot better if we left Ganler behind."

"What have you got against his youth? He's bright, he's quick, he's responsible."

"I've got nothing against him. I just don't want him hurt any more than you do. Where I . . . come from, we wouldn't let someone so young go into danger."

"Life is danger, Travis. Children can fall down the stairs or drown in the bath or poison themselves with the wrong pills. Teaching them how to *cope* with danger, to develop judgment and skill, makes them safer."

"Not this kind of danger, Urwen. None of us will be safe. What could happen to us if our security passes don't work . . ." His eyes were haunted. "I wouldn't wish that on anyone. I wouldn't face it myself in a million years if there were any other choice."

She placed a hand on the side of his face. "Then tell us, so we can face that danger with our eyes open. *Trust* us, so that we know we can trust you."

He took her hand and lowered it to clasp it in both of his. "I want to. Believe me, Urwen, I hate keeping secrets from you. But I promise you, we haven't *lied* to you about anything. And we haven't kept anything from you that could hurt you. If we've kept secrets, they're only ones that might hurt you—or your people—if you *did* know them."

"I don't understand that."

"I'm not sure I do either." He sighed. "Honestly, I don't know what I should or shouldn't tell you. You think we're so advanced, but the truth is, we're still pretty new at all this. There's a lot we don't have rules for yet. And I've seen that lead to some pretty bad mistakes. I'm just trying to protect you."

It was the first time she'd seen such vulnerability and doubt in him. But it didn't burst her illusions, didn't destroy the romance of this exotic, strong, mysterious stranger with superior wisdom. It only made him more real to her, more accessible. She pulled him closer. "You can protect me best by letting me take care of myself, Travis. I'm not a child—or even an apprentice."

He looked her over. "No . . . you're definitely not a child."

She underlined her point by kissing him. After that, they rather swiftly lost the thread of the discussion.

15

May 27, 2165
Irinthar Mountains, Vulcan

AS A MOSTLY PEACEFUL SOCIETY, the Vulcans had little need for security cameras in their cities. But the keen memories of the Vulcan citizens were the next best thing. Generally, Vulcans respected one another's privacy, but when the officers of the ShiKahr reasoning force (as the local police were charmingly known on Vulcan) showed its citizens the image of the former museum assistant calling herself T'Salan and explained the importance of tracking her whereabouts, most citizens were willing to search their memories for matching faces. A few even acknowledged an acquaintance with her, though could reveal little about her as a person; to a one, they reported that she had been reticent about herself even by Vulcan standards.

Still, Director Surel was able to track T'Salan's movements to the safe house she had used to prepare for the *Kir'Shara*'s theft. She had left little evidence behind, but, as she had not expected the safe house to be discovered, she had overlooked enough of a DNA trace to allow Surel to discover T'Salan's true identity, a former High Command administrative aide named L'Resen, who had worked under the supervisor of Commander Zadok's fleet. Further tracking of L'Resen's movements revealed that she had left ShiKahr for Kel Province in the far north of Vulcan, but had disappeared shortly after her arrival there. However, the

Kel reasoning force was able to determine that she had gone to a recreational goods fabrication facility and ordered gear for mountain climbing and survival in what passed for cold weather by Vulcan standards. This had suggested that her goal was in the Irinthar Mountains, the northernmost range on the planet. Surel's search of declassified High Command records had turned up a reference to a secret military supply depot in those mountains—overseen by a division to which Zadok had once belonged.

Thus it was that Takashi Kimura and an *Endeavour* security team, along with a government security squad led by Surel, were now perched on the slope just above the depot, a bunker well camouflaged in a notch in the low, scrub-covered mountain. The all-human team was weathering the polar conditions much better than Surel's squad; to Kimura, the chill here was no worse than on an autumn morning in Hokkaido.

Still, other aspects of the setup made him uneasy. "Are you sure you don't want to bring in a larger team?" Kimura asked Surel.

"Based on our tracking of Zadok's associates, this team should be adequate to confront the maximum number of partisans likely to be within the bunker," Surel replied. "After all, we do not wish to provoke a violent reaction if it can be avoided."

"All due respect, Surel, but we're talking about a man who's been actively advocating violence."

"As a logically, if ruthlessly, applied tool. If possible, we must persuade him that his most logical option is surrender. I shall request a parley."

Kimura stared at the young security officer. "You think you can talk these fanatics out of their convictions?"

"No. But I can demonstrate that they are tactically

outmatched and persuade them of the futility of forcible resistance."

"And how do you plan to do that?"

Surel quirked his brows in what Kimura, after years of serving under Captain T'Pol, had come to recognize as the Vulcan equivalent of a smile. "Do you recall our game of chess, Takashi?"

Kimura remembered. On the flight up to the polar regions, Kimura had accepted Surel's challenge to play a game of chess entirely in their minds, keeping mental track of the pieces on an imaginary board. After only a few moves, Surel had declared that Kimura would be mated within another ten, then proceeded to explain exactly how his defeat would occur. When Kimura had protested that he'd been hoping for a longer game, Surel apologized, saying that this was a fairly typical way for Vulcans to play chess among themselves. Once they had modeled the entire game to a decisive outcome, where was the point in acting it out step by step? "Once a conflict is resolved in the mind," Surel reminded him now, "the actual action is secondary."

Kimura smiled back. "Remind me to talk to you about a man named Sun Tzu," he replied. "Still—I'm coming with you to this parley."

The director pondered. "It is expected that the parleyers will have armed backup as a deterrent. But why do you feel it necessary to come yourself?"

"Because the difference between chess and real life is that it's hard to cheat at chess."

Surel brandished his comm device and transmitted a message toward the bunker. "Attention within. This is Vulcan Planetary Security. As you can no doubt detect, we have your facility surrounded. You have no option for withdrawal. I invite your representative to attend a parley so we may determine a logical resolution to this confrontation."

After a few moments, a reply came over Surel's device. *"Parley is accepted, per the standard forms."*

Surel signaled two of his officers, Tozek and T'Syra, to back him up. Kimura did the same with Crewmen Money and Alonzo. The four men and two women descended the slope toward the bunker entrance, weapons at ready, while their respective teams covered them from the crest. As they neared the bunker, its heavy door opened to admit four Vulcans while another two flanked the entrance. Kimura recognized the male as Commander Zadok, and was fairly certain the female was L'Resen. *Logical,* he thought. *They don't want to show us too many faces we don't already know.*

Surel's gaze went to L'Resen as well, then back toward her superior. "Commander Zadok," he said. "You have chosen wisely if your intent is to turn over L'Resen, alias T'Salan, for arrest. She is wanted in connection with the theft and forgery of the *Kir'Shara*."

"You have no proof any such crime has occurred," Zadok countered.

"Proof is for the courts to determine, Commander. We do, however, have compelling evidence that L'Resen obtained employment with the Science Academy Museum under forged credentials, and that she operated an equipment cart employing holographic camouflage technology of suspected Romulan origin."

"You cannot prove," L'Resen said, "that I had any knowledge of the cart's modifications."

"You could not have overlooked its increased weight, ma'am. In any case, this is not the appropriate forum for this debate. If you accompany us back to the capital, you will of course be granted legal representation and the opportunity to present a defense."

"We do not recognize your authority," Zadok told him.

"I am the duly authorized representative of the Vulcan High Council, Commander."

"You are an agent of the Syrannite puppet government, a regime put in place through an armed coup on behalf of the Earth Starfleet. Even now, you can do nothing without Starfleet at your side, directing your actions." His gaze shifted to Kimura. "What authorization do you have to intervene in a domestic matter between Vulcans? Your very presence here is illegal."

Kimura made no effort to respond; this was Surel's operation, after all. "This is a military facility," the Council security officer replied, "occupied by individuals who have advocated armed insurrection. If you truly wish to advocate the rule of civil law, then your logical option is to accompany my forces peaceably and allow the legal system to do its work. It is contradictory to condemn military intrusion into civil affairs while mounting an armed resistance to civil authority."

"It is not contradictory for Vulcans to reject the interference of offworlders in their affairs. Let this dispute be between Vulcans; otherwise, you merely prove you are the pawn of these aliens."

Kimura grew increasingly uneasy as the debate went on in circles. *Zadok's stalling,* he realized. *But for what?* Directing Sascha Money to take his place flanking Surel, Kimura stepped back a few paces and flipped open his communicator. "Kimura to *Endeavour.*"

"Endeavour. T'Pol here."

"Captain, do you detect any unusual activity at our location? I think Zadok is trying to distract us from something."

"Stand by."

A few moments later, Elizabeth Cutler's voice came over the channel. *"You were right, Takashi. I had to widen the scan, but I'm picking up transporter activity from the other side of the mountain."*

"Are they beaming more troops in?"

"No, something is beaming out."

"I don't get it. The bunker doesn't go all the way through the mountain. And it's too deep to beam out from."

"They may have a transporter wave guide running to the surface as an emergency egress," T'Pol advised.

Kimura had heard enough. "Surel!" he called. "They're beaming out! This is a decoy!"

But Zadok, L'Resen, and the other loyalists were already raising their weapons. Money and Alonzo were quick to open fire, and Tozek and T'Syra flanked Surel as he retreated. The rest of the combined team was storming down from the crest within moments. The loyalists carried on their cover fire as they fell back into the bunker.

"We must reach the entrance before they seal it!" Surel called. The team continued to return fire. Zadok and L'Resen vanished inside the bunker, and Kimura spotted one of his guards reaching for what was most likely a door control. Kimura drew a bead on him with his particle rifle's sights and dropped him unconscious to the floor.

Within moments, the team was in the entryway. "Too easy," Kimura said. "This may be a trap."

"A logical assessment," Surel replied. "But we must secure what evidence we can to prove the theft occurred. And we must preempt any efforts to destroy such evidence."

"Agreed. Just be careful."

"There is a time for care and a time for risk, Takashi. We must hurry!" Determined, the young security chief led his team into the bunker. It seemed reckless to Kimura, but then he realized what Surel had probably already deduced: Given the estimated size of Zadok's group and the amount of time they had been stalling, it was likely that only a skeleton force remained to destroy the evidence and guard their retreat. Thus, the risk of haste was warranted in order to preserve whatever evidence might remain. So Kimura wasted no more time in ordering his own team to back up the Vulcan force. He advanced into the bunker with Money and Alonzo at his flanks, with Ensign Bragen and Crewmen Valmar and Janley following behind.

Surel's team moved briskly ahead of them, clearing the first few rooms they checked, and at first it looked like smooth sailing. They split in two directions at a fork, and Kimura sent Bragen, Money, and Janley to back up T'Syra's quintet while he, Benedetta Alonzo, and Bayani Valmar stuck with Surel, Tozek, and the remaining three Vulcans.

Once they were some distance away from the other half of the team, Surel raised a hand to order stillness, then listened. "I hear a transporter in use," he reported. "Mister Kimura, we will go ahead and attempt to halt their escape. Take your team to search for evidence."

Kimura didn't like splitting up further, but it was necessary and efficient. His team began a room-by-room search with scanners in one hand, particle rifles in the other.

In the third room they checked, they detected two biosigns. He and Alonzo flanked the door while Valmar, their resident countermeasures expert, hacked the door panel and overrode the lock. The tall Filipino ducked aside just as the door slid open, and a bolt of phased energy barely missed his shoulder. Alonzo tossed a stun grenade through the open door, and she, Kimura, and Valmar burst into the room. The two loyalists inside were dazed but still conscious, a testament to Vulcan re-siliency. Kimura brought his rifle to bear and relieved the nearer target of consciousness while Alonzo did the same with the other—whom Kimura realized was L'Resen. The small, viva-cious Italian stood guard at the door while Kimura and Valmar moved into the room to study the tables of equipment within.

"I think we've hit paydirt, sir," Valmar said after scanning the equipment. "These look like antique tools for metalwork-ing and etching . . . This chamber here could be used to artifi-cially age the metal."

Kimura directed him to the console at the end of one of the tables. "Did they leave any intact files?"

Valmar worked on the computer for a few moments. "Mmm, the data's wiped, but hold on . . . yes, there's a direc-tory fragment remaining. Translating the filenames . . . Sir, I think these were museum scans of the original *Kir'Shara*."

Jackpot! "Record everything, then secure it and get it—".

"Sir!" Alonzo cried from the doorway, just before an en-ergy bolt took her in the shoulder.

Kimura and Valmar rushed to flank the door, checking their scanners. There were at least ten Vulcan biosignatures in the corridor outside—coming from *both* directions. "How'd they flank us?" Valmar demanded as he dragged the moaning Alonzo out of the line of fire and reached for the first aid kit on his belt.

"The transporter sounds," Kimura realized. "We assumed they were evacuating. Perfect cover for beaming a team in be-hind us!"

"But *Endeavour* detected them beaming out!"

"I think there are a lot more people here than we realized," Kimura said. "Other factions backing the loyalists. This was always a trap."

Firing from the doorway in both directions, they managed to stun several of their assailants, but there were plenty of others to keep them trapped. It was only when Surel's team came up from behind one of the two groups, setting up a crossfire that Kimura and Valmar both joined in to neutralize the whole lot, that the other group fell back. "Keep pushing them back," Surel ordered. "We must get to the exit with all due haste."

Kimura fell in beside him, while Valmar picked up Alonzo. "But the evidence—"

"I trust you scanned it?" Kimura nodded, and Surel continued: "That must suffice. I have discovered something urgent that we must report without delay."

Kimura was about to protest that at least L'Resen should be brought in to testify, but the shooting started again and he was forced to drop the issue and focus on the fight. They managed to drive the loyalists (or whoever else had been waiting in reserve) up the corridor toward the fork, while Surel ordered the other half of his team—already battling their own opponents—to do the same, trapping their adversaries in the middle. Kimura contacted Money to give the same order. *"We lost Bragen,"* Sascha Money reported back, her voice tight. Kimura squeezed his eyes shut and let the pain pass through him swiftly, intensely. *"But we'll make it back, sir."*

Kimura realized that Tozek was not one of the wounded Surel's people were carrying; he must have fallen as well. But if they wished to avoid more casualties, they needed to focus on the battle. Coordinating over comms, the two Starfleet-Vulcan teams closed the pincer on their enemies. But that only drove the loyalists to fight back more fiercely.

But then he heard a voice speaking to the loyalists over

their comm channel, ordering their retreat. The deep, harsh masculine voice sounded familiar, but he couldn't place it. Identifying it wasn't as important as the question of why they were breaking for the exit.

He and Surel exchanged a look. "We have to move *now*," Kimura said, and he could tell the director already knew it.

Both team leaders ordered an evacuation and pushed forward. But even though the loyalists were also in retreat, they were determined not to make it easy for their foes, raining fire down the corridor. Kimura tried not to think about what he was risking as he pushed forward, for the risk if he didn't was far more absolute.

Or so he thought until a bolt of blinding light flashed in his right eye and . . .

And nothing was clear after that. He was on his back and couldn't move or think clearly, and Surel was over him, calling, but he couldn't make out the words. He felt himself being picked up, carried like a child, until another flash struck close and Surel tumbled and dropped him. Kimura faded out again for a moment, then heard Surel's voice. He recognized the words *"emergency beam-out,"* and it refreshed his memory enough to let him realize that the blurry sight before him was Surel sprawled on the floor, holding a communicator in his hand. Surel's chest and arm were covered in bright green, and there was green liquid on the floor.

Kimura felt himself fading again, but then he felt the pressure of warm fingers on his face, and there was a presence inside his mind that brought his thoughts into focus. The presence spoke to him: *You must tell them what I saw, Takashi. They must know!* A memory flooded into him, a memory that wasn't his: a Vulcan speaking on a monitor, giving orders to Zadok. An older, gray-haired Vulcan whose face he'd seen before. Suddenly he knew whose voice he had heard in the corridor.

But then he heard the explosions starting, and then his body began to tingle and burn. He didn't know whether the blast wave or the transporter beam had gotten to him first.

16

May 28, 2165
U.S.S. Endeavour

DOCTOR PHLOX SPENT HOURS operating on Takashi Kimura, even summoning the assistance of a pair of surgeons who shuttled aboard from Vulcan's spacedock. Benedetta Alonzo and Pamela Janley had both needed their injuries treated as well, but Phlox had reported them both in recovery hours before Hoshi Sato heard any further word about her lover. The procedure took long enough that T'Pol was able to compose letters to the families of both Bernard Bragen and Bayani Valmar, informing them that they would never see those loved ones again. Both had given their lives heroically: Bragen in defense of his teammates, both human and Vulcan, and Valmar in acquiring and protecting the scans of the forging equipment in the bunker, scans that had been found on his body when it had materialized along with the others—although his scanner had been damaged in the explosion and Cutler was unsure how much data she would be able to recover, a serious problem given that L'Resen had evidently died as well, leaving the scans as their only real evidence of the forgery's origins. But transmitting the letters had done nothing to distract Sato from her fears, only reinforcing her dread that she might soon have to send a third letter to Hideto and Emiko Kimura about their son. *And who would write a comforting letter to me?* she wondered at one point in the long vigil.

At another point, she wondered how the Vulcans handled such matters. The families of Surel and his subalterns Tozek and Semorn would now have occasion to find out—as, presumably, would the families of the estimated eleven unconscious loyalists left behind to die in the explosion, once their remains had been identified. Even the Vulcan newscasters, commentators, and private journal authors whose chatter Sato monitored seemed stunned by the magnitude of this act of violence. What had been a political debate about alien fraud and manipulation had now escalated to open violence by Vulcans against their own. Although the chatter from the planet below was much more subdued than it would have been on Earth, for most of the populace were patiently waiting for more information before they formed conclusions—the reverse of how too many humans tended to operate, even in this comparatively enlightened age.

In time, Phlox reported that Kimura was stable and out of surgery, and Captain T'Pol permitted Sato to accompany her to sickbay. But Hoshi was dismayed to see no sign of Phlox's normally irrepressible cheer and optimism; instead he wore the stern but empathetic countenance with which he delivered bad news. "I've done all I can for him," he said in slow, heavy tones, "with the commendable assistance of Doctors T'Ruun and Venast. But I must ask you to prepare yourself, Hoshi."

She took a deep breath, striving for her discipline as an officer. She had been through many terrible things before. "Go ahead, Phlox."

"Takashi sustained extensive primary and secondary blast injuries to the left side of his body, in addition to serious flash burns. I've had to remove a portion of his left lung, and his left kidney was a total loss. I've implanted a Tumodian lamprey to perform hemodialysis for the moment; it's a similar principle to how my osmotic eel cleanses wounds." Sato nodded. "I'm sorry, but his left arm also had to be amputated. And I'm afraid at this point I can't assess his viability for a biograft or prosthetic arm, for there's extensive nerve damage to the shoulder." He looked to T'Pol. "I'm afraid his physical recovery would take months at best, and he's unlikely to regain sufficient mobility and strength to resume his duties as a starship armory officer."

"Understood, Doctor," T'Pol said, subdued. Her gaze remained on Sato.

Phlox took a deep breath. There was worse news? "There is . . . also significant brain damage." Hoshi gasped. Phlox maintained his calm, clinical tone, spelling it out with a detached relentlessness that was almost a comfort. "He's sustained injury to his right frontal and parietal lobes, evidently due to thermal and radiation trauma from a particle beam. It's too early to assess the extent of his impairment, but judging from the areas of the damage, Takashi could well have issues with motor skills, language, sensory perception and integration, visual memory, advance planning and problem-solving . . ."

Hoshi realized T'Pol had caught her; she had momentarily lost her balance. The warmth of her captain's hands— her friend's hands—on her shoulders helped her regain her strength. "I'm all right, Phlox. Go on."

"Keep in mind, Hoshi, I'm only listing possible effects. Not all of them will necessarily apply. In fact, I'm fairly certain the commander's brain damage could have been far worse."

"What do you mean, Doctor?" asked T'Pol.

"Crewman Alonzo reported seeing Director Surel place his hand on the commander's face just before the explosion.

I detected neurochemical residues of a type I've seen before, specifically in Admiral Archer and Corporal Askwith following their telepathic contacts with Vulcans in the original *Kir'Shara* affair. It would appear that Surel, with his dying breath, initiated a mind meld with Commander Kimura. It seems to have had a stabilizing effect on Takashi's neurological functions; a rough analogy might be the effect of the medications delivered to stroke victims to ameliorate ischemic damage. There are even signs that Takashi's brain has already begun to reroute some of its functions around the damaged areas, perhaps under Surel's guidance."

T'Pol took a step toward him. "Doctor . . . is there any sign that Surel . . ."

Phlox anticipated her and shook his head. "I'm sorry, Captain. Doctor Venast raised the question of a *katra* transfer as soon as we learned of the meld, but even with his expertise guiding us, we could find no evidence of any foreign engrammatic pattern in the commander's brain."

Sato barely registered their words, which were almost gibberish to her. She remembered something about *katra*s from the original *Kir'Shara* incident, something to do with how Admiral Archer had discovered the ark. But it was of little interest to her now. Takashi would live . . . but would he still be the man she loved? Even if he were, he could no longer be a starship officer . . . and what would happen to them then?

But T'Pol was still speaking, concern evident on her face. "That means that Surel had the opportunity to preserve his *katra* in his final moments, yet he chose to sacrifice that opportunity—to consign his essence to oblivion. What could have been important enough to require such a sacrifice?"

Phlox pondered. "He was a dedicated Syrannite. Perhaps he considered the preservation of Commander Kimura's life and sanity to be of sufficient importance. We know from Admiral Archer's experience that a katric transfer can be quite stressful on a human. The director may have been unwilling to risk further damage to the commander for his own personal gain."

"Logical," T'Pol conceded. "But it is also possible that Surel discovered something of importance, and upon his imminent death, transferred the knowledge to Commander Kimura to ensure it would reach us."

Phlox pursed his lips, tilting his head in a shrug. "It's possible."

"Then I need you to revive Commander Kimura at the earliest possible opportunity. It may be imperative that we speak to him."

The doctor was about to protest, but he paused on seeing the resolute look in T'Pol's eyes. "Theoretically, I could revive him briefly right now. But I would emphatically advise against it. It would delay his recovery and possibly impair it to some degree."

"I'm afraid I must insist, Doctor. He may hold vital information."

"And he may be in no condition to communicate it."

"Do it, Phlox." The words grated out of Hoshi's throat, emerging with almost physical pain. "It's what he'd want you to do if there were any chance it could make a difference."

Phlox grudgingly conceded and led them inside. Sato tried to control her shock at the sight of her lover's bruised and battered form on the scanner table, the stump where his left arm had been, the shaved, swollen, and bandaged right side of his head. That beautiful face, that strong, sleek body, now broken and vandalized. And who knew what might be left of the sweet, magnificent warrior-philosopher inside, the man who could field-strip and reassemble a particle rifle in under thirty seconds but would walk fifty kilometers to rescue a wounded bird?

The doctor injected Kimura with a stimulant, insisting that he could not allow them to speak to him for more than two minutes. What seemed like ages later, Kimura's eyes began to open and he moaned softly. "Takashi?" she prompted softly. "It's okay. It's me."

"Ho . . . Hoshi?" he murmured after a moment, filling her with relief. His eyes brushed across her—but did not stop, did not focus on her. "*Doko ni* . . . I hear . . . where you?"

Hoshi gasped. Phlox stood comfortingly near, though touching was not his way. "Sensory and linguistic impairment. But they may not be permanent. It's actually a good sign that he's responding so well already."

She took his hand . . . his surviving hand . . . and it seemed to help him focus on her, though his eyes would still not fully lock on. "I'm right here, Takashi."

"Hoshi-*chan* . . . *Samishi katta desu* . . . Thought . . . never see you again."

"*Yamero, baka*," she snapped in a quavery voice, telling him to stop such foolish talk. "We're both here," she assured him, trying to keep him focused on English. "You're safe aboard *Endeavour*."

"Endeboru . . . *uchūsen* . . ."

"Starship. That's right." She patted his hand. "You're back home." She ignored the fact that it wouldn't be his home for much longer.

"Commander Kimura," T'Pol said. "Do you recognize me?"

The sound of his commanding officer's voice seemed to trigger some reflex to strive for greater alertness. "*Senchō* . . . Captain. Captain T'Pol. Yes. Yes, ma'am."

"I am grateful that you have returned alive, Takashi. You have done us a great service. But if you can, I need you to perform one more service. I need you to concentrate. I need you to remember the events in the bunker."

"The bunker . . ." Suddenly his gaze sharpened. "Surel! They shot him . . . *yurusenai!*"

"Stay calm," Sato urged. "It's okay, don't strain yourself."

"No. Hoshi . . . important, have to . . . Captain . . . Surel showed me. What he saw. Who he saw. Who . . . who's doing all this." He trailed off, confused.

Phlox moved closer, watching Kimura's vitals on the monitor uneasily. "Captain, he's been agitated enough. He has to rest now."

"*Ie!* No, Doctor!" Kimura grated out. "Have to . . . report. Can't . . . remember . . ." His gaze locked on T'Pol. "Meld. Surel gave me . . . I give you."

Taking his meaning, the captain looked to Phlox. "Would there be any risk involved with a meld in his condition?"

"There's a risk involved with being awake in his condition, Captain. Any further cerebral activity . . ."

"The contact would be brief. The information is prominent in his mind, so it should be simple to retrieve it with a light mind touch. A full meld should not be necessary." Her gaze softened. "And perhaps there is some way I can . . . ease his distress, as Surel did."

Phlox held her gaze. "Very well. But use great delicacy, Captain."

"Of course." T'Pol glanced to Sato, as though seeking permission. Hoshi nodded, and T'Pol carefully placed her fingers on Kimura's temple and cheek, as gently as if his skin were loose-packed snow.

Moments later, her eyes widened and she staggered back

in shock. Hoshi moved to catch her, but she recovered. "Captain?" Phlox asked.

"I'm all right, Doctor." She turned to Kimura. "Thank you, Commander. You may rest now." She nodded to Phlox, who administered a sedative. Sato held his hand as he went under.

T'Pol made her way over to the console near the sickbay door and contacted the bridge, requesting a communications channel to Admiral Archer. It was some moments, however, before the admiral's voice came over the channel. *"Archer here. This isn't a good time, T'Pol."*

"Sir. Commander Kimura has just relayed vital intelligence about the identity of the individual behind the dissident plot."

Archer paused. *"I'm glad to hear the commander pulled through. But I'm afraid his intelligence came a little late. We've been beaten to that particular punch."*

Vulcan Council Chamber, ShiKahr

"Your disbelief is logical, my fellow Vulcans," said the man whose planetwide address was being carried on the Council chamber's monitors—a stern-featured older Vulcan with steel-gray hair and intense blue eyes, unusual for his species. *"My Syrannite enemies, and their Andorian and human backers, have spent years spreading propaganda that I had died or defected to the Romulans. Indeed, their agents have made more than one attempt to bring about the former fate, which is why it has been necessary for me to remain in hiding. But I am prepared to provide proof, as soon as it can be delivered in a way that will not jeopardize my safety, that what you see before you now is true:*

"I am V'Las."

The subdued murmurs among the councillors were an uproar by Vulcan standards, Archer knew. But then, tensions had been high ever since the bombing. Such a blatant act of violence had provoked an upwelling of fear and outrage— logically, unemotionally expressed, of course—toward the High Command loyalists and their traditionalist allies. It was no wonder, Archer realized, that their true mastermind had found it necessary to step out of the shadows. The resurrection of V'Las was the one thing dramatic enough to draw the public's attention from the bombing and give the disgraced former administrator a chance to take control of the narrative.

And that was exactly what he was doing. *"I know my return will not sit well with all of you. There have been many false charges leveled at me . . . and some true ones,"* he conceded with a tilt of his head. *"I have made errors in judgment, which my foes have exploited to paint me as a tyrant, a violent madman, even a Romulan collaborator. I acted in good faith on military intelligence that I am now convinced was engineered by the Andorians to embarrass the High Command. I acted too forcefully against the Syrannites, provoking them to extreme actions in response. I was blind to the Syrannite sympathizers within my own government, for I could not believe that such a longtime associate as Kuvak was capable of betrayal, or that such an esteemed diplomat as Soval could be concealing the perversions of a melder."*

"Oh, give me a break," Archer muttered to himself. Next to him, T'Pau glared, having no patience for his human irreverence. On his other side, though, Soval's gaze conveyed sympathy with the sentiment.

"And perhaps I have made a mistake in remaining hidden for so long, allowing matters to escalate to this extreme. In their determination to conceal their falsification of the mythical Kir'Shara, the Syrannites and the Federation have first slandered and then persecuted those of us who never lost faith in the true Vulcan way—a way of discipline and strength, purity and authority. And now that persecution has culminated in an attempt to plant false evidence that these loyal Vulcans were responsible for their forgery—an attempt that Starfleet aggression swiftly escalated to the point of tragic violence."

V'Las paused as though he could hear the disapproving murmur of the councillors. He might well be watching monitors showing the reactions of Vulcans in public assembly areas all over the planet, Vulcans aware of the same thing that weighed on the councillors now. And he was smart enough to preempt their criticism. *"Do not misunderstand me, citizens of Vulcan. I do not attempt to deny that Commander Zadok chose to activate the self-destruct device in the Irinthar facility himself—despite being forced to leave behind eleven of his own people, most of whom had probably already been killed by the human intruders. This was not an easy choice for the commander to make. But logic dictates that force is often the only option to repel* force.

"Consider what has occurred, citizens. A Starfleet team—a human military unit—undertook an armed raid on sovereign Vulcan soil. Is this what membership in the supposedly 'United' Federation of Planets means? That our worlds no longer have the right to police our own affairs, or to protect ourselves against armed intrusion by an alien military? Yes, Starfleet claims its team was acting with the invitation of the Syrannite government. But is this logical? Recall that the first action of the Syrannite government was to dissolve the High Command, the organization that had kept Vulcan safe from alien invaders for centuries. Oh, they retained its name and some semblance of its organizational framework, but the defense fleet that had kept Vulcan strong and safe for centuries, that had enabled us to bring peace and order to our neighbors, was withdrawn and kept in abeyance—even after *it became clear that the Romulans posed an active and growing threat to the security of our region. The Syrannites left the defense of the sector in the hands of humans—a backward, aggressive species that seized the opportunity to build the largest military fleet in the region and then allied with our historic foes, the Andorians, to create an even larger combined fleet. And at the same time, even though the actions of the Romulans had proven the danger Vulcan faces from offworld aggressors, First Minister T'Pau chose to* dismantle *our defense force altogether and eradicate the last vestiges of the High Command."* V'Las shook his head.

"And we are expected to believe that the Starfleet force at Irinthar was subordinate to the Syrannite contingent? Is it not more consistent with the facts to conclude that Starfleet initiated the aggression?"

V'Las leaned forward, his gaze hardening. "My fellow Vulcans, the troubling reality is that we are now faced with the first step in an outright military occupation of our planet by alien forces. Now that their use of a fraudulent Kir'Shara has been exposed as a lie, they have begun to escalate to open force. And it will not end here.

"In the face of this prospective invasion, it is a logical necessity to take up arms in the defense of our community, our home. It is necessary to strike against aspiring occupiers, and their collaborators within our own society, to make it clear that the cost to them will be dear if they make the attempt. When dealing with violent, irrational species like those that dominate the Federation Starfleet, this is the most effective way—the only way—to deter their aggression. Commander Zadok understands this, which is why he acted as he did.

"And I assure all of you who are loyal to the true Vulcan way that he does not stand alone. To those of you who choose to align with Zadok and myself, to take a stand against offworld occupation even if it requires employing the same violent methods our occupiers use . . . I promise you, we have the numbers to do what is necessary, and we have the means. We can take Vulcan back from those who have corrupted our logic, hobbled our strength, and subordinated our proud people to the violent whims of far younger races."

He grasped the folds of his robe and lifted his chin. "And I, V'Las of Vulcan, stand ready to lead you in the defense of our world, as I did before. Together, we can restore Vulcan to its former height—and to its proper standing in the galaxy."

The address ended, and the councillors promptly began chattering among themselves. Archer turned to Soval with some dismay. "Did he just imply that his loyalists have the military strength to mount a coup?"

"I believe he did more than imply it, Admiral," the commissioner answered grimly. "V'Las has never been one for making empty threats. On the contrary, his preference—as you well know—is for overkill."

"But do you think anyone's going to believe the lies he spun?"

T'Pau answered. "The incident in the Irinthar base demonstrates that V'Las already possesses a larger, more militant cadre of supporters than we had believed, Admiral. We have seen that they are willing to employ great violence, even to sacrifice their own people. If we cannot discredit him soon, there may be civil war."

Archer set his jaw. "I'll get my people on *Endeavour* working on cleaning up those scans from the bunker."

"Even they may not be sufficient, Admiral," the youthful Syrannite told him with cool solemnity. "Without physical proof or a live prisoner, they will be able to claim that the sensor evidence of forgery was itself forged. The computer interpolation of degraded data is similar enough to computer simulation that its probative value is questionable."

"You can't be trying to tell me he's already won!" Archer insisted.

T'Pau met his gaze. "I am not, Admiral. But even if we do prevail . . . the fight is likely to be a long and costly one."

17

VABION WATCHED WITH SATISFACTION as the intruders materialized in the holding chamber of his security headquarters. He
took pride in having trained the system to deliver the intruders it ejected to this location. It was a small step toward assert-
ing control over the mechanism, but it was something, even if
it was more a matter of convincing it to choose to cooperate.

And if these intruders were what he thought they were, he
might be on the verge of gaining far more control.

He had the ex-inquisitor Zeheri and the apprentice assisting her separated from the other three, whom he kept confined long enough to make them sweat and then had brought
before him in his local office, a space carefully designed to
direct the eye toward his desk and leave no doubt who was
dominant here. "Welcome," he told his esteemed visitors. "I,
as you know, am Daskel Vabion. You need not introduce yourselves; you are called Travis, Rey, and Katrina, are you not?
Although in your private communications with your cohorts,
you used other names: Mayweather, Sangupta, Ndiaye."
He hoped his pronunciations were not too outrageous.

The biggest of the three, Mayweather, took a step forward.
"You're awfully well informed, Mister Vabion."

"Worldwide Automatics does not advertise how pervasive our surveillance truly is," Vabion replied. "However, it

surprises me that you were unable to deduce its presence, given your own obvious level of advancement." He held up a pair of the devices that had been confiscated from them: a rectangular tablet containing sophisticated measurement instruments and a powerful, compact two-way radio with miniaturized computational circuitry built into it, somehow instantly translating their language into Stone Valley dialect. His engineers had advised that the confiscated weapons remain contained and untouched until they could be analyzed. "Why you did not take more care to conceal your conspiracy with Miss Zeheri, or your jaunts outside the walls to visit your lander craft and communicate with your associates in orbit, is a mystery to me."

The paler one, Sangupta, spoke up. "Well, maybe we're advanced enough to know better than to use our technology for invading people's privacy."

"Yes," Vabion went on with a sigh. "I had initially allowed myself to hope that you were the creators of the automated system, arriving at last to follow up on your initial gifts to our world." He turned their devices in his hands. "But a cursory examination reveals that while your equipment shares certain common principles with the system, it is based on a different and somewhat less sophisticated technology."

He put the devices down and leaned forward, facing Mayweather. "But you are not industrial spies, I think. You come from other stars, as the system did, so surely you could access it more directly than by coming to Vanot. Competitors, then? Do you hope to sabotage my systems and offer your own, clearly inferior models to one of my rivals?"

"No," Mayweather told him. "We're people who've seen the harm this technology does. The lives it preys on." The alien's large eyes searched his. "You can't be unaware of all the disappearances. Do you know—really know—the price your 'system' demands in exchange for its gifts?"

"I am not without compassion, Mister Mayweather, but I am a practical man. Every new breakthrough carries a cost. The burning of coal poisoned the air and created new diseases. The invention of the electric car led to fatal collisions and battery explosions. Air travel provided a more efficient way to wage war. The cost in lives of my system is small compared to these—particularly since few of those individuals chosen to serve have actually died."

"Their brains are being eaten away every day!" Mayweather cried in anguish. "Most of them are past saving already. I know. I've tried."

"Many more people out there on the streets would be past saving if not for the food, clothing, and medicines Worldwide provides. I do not call it an ideal arrangement, but I strive to ensure the balance remains positive."

Sangupta grimaced. "Leaving aside the utter hypocrisy of that, have you thought about the long term? The more you spread the Ware—the more dependent on it you become—the more lives it's going to demand."

"And the more impossible it'll become to wean yourselves from it," Mayweather added. "I've seen it happen. Your greed could doom your entire world."

Vabion scoffed at their hypocrisy. "Except for the one thing you possess that could liberate our people for all time: the power to travel between the stars. The Vanotli could never be destroyed if we could spread to other worlds. Indeed, why stay on this storm-tossed wreck of a planet at all? Our climatologists tell us that at times in the past, Vanot has maintained a stable, temperate climate for tens of millennia at a time. Surely there must be other worlds out there that are already in such stable cycles."

"If that's what you want," Mayweather asked, "why haven't you just ordered up a spaceship or two from the Ware? I know they have them for sale."

That evoked genuine surprise, and Mayweather caught it before he could suppress the response. "It hasn't offered them to you, has it? Whoever sent it to you, they want you hooked. They want to make sure you're good and dependent on them before they offer you any more benefits." He leaned forward in his seat. "Or maybe they'll never bother to offer you space-flight. Why go to the trouble, when they've already got you nicely corralled and can harvest bodies from you whenever they want?"

He'd struck a nerve—Vabion had to grant that much. The Vanotli took a moment to gather himself. "I think you underestimate my resolve, Mister Mayweather. I have already made progress in understanding the—the Ware, you call it? It is only a matter of time before I break its encoding and learn how to turn it to the Vanotli's benefit."

Mayweather laughed. "You? You're over two centuries be-hind my people. And, like you said, the Ware is even ahead of us. You wouldn't have a chance."

"Before today, perhaps not. But today I have you. And you have a ship that can travel between stars. You can take me to the source—help me decipher and re-encode it."

"And why would we help you?"

Vabion sighed. He loathed resorting to petty thuggery. But as he'd said, he was a pragmatist. He activated a buzzer on his desk, and a moment later, two of his security personnel led Urwen Zeheri into the office. "Travis!" she called, and Va-bion noted that her attention was only on the leader. "Are you okay? Where's Ganler?"

"Isn't he with you?"

"Apprentice Nibar is safe in our custody," Vabion told them both, "but I am content to leave him where he is for now."

"You're really low, Vabion!" Sangupta cried. "Taking a child prisoner!"

"He, and you, forged WWA credentials and trespassed on our facilities. I am entirely within my legal rights to detain you. However, I am offering your group an alternative to incarceration."

"If we take you to the source of the Ware," Mayweather replied.

"Exactly. I direct your attention to the collar affixed around Miss Zeheri's neck." The offworlder's eyes went to the gray metal-and-plastic device. "As you can see, it is an instrument of Ware design, intended for penal use. As is the matching implement I wear around my wrist." He slid up his left cuff to let them see it. "Which will allow me to do this." With a grimace of distaste, he depressed the contact on the bracelet. Zeheri convulsed in pain and fell to the floor. Vabion promptly released the contact as Mayweather ran to her side. "My apologies, Miss Zeheri, but I had to demonstrate the sincerity of my threat. Be assured, all of you, that the collar is quite capable of delivering a lethal shock if I so choose. Or if anyone should attempt to tamper with it," he cautioned Mayweather, whose hands jerked away from the collar—then clenched into trembling fists as the big man turned a smoldering gaze on Vabion. "The same will occur should my own heart stop, in case you have any ideas." Mayweather took a deep breath and controlled his rage.

"Excellent," Vabion continued. "Now that we've established our parameters, we can keep this civilized. I should add that Apprentice Nibar is equipped with an identical device. I gather from my surveillance recordings that you have a particular aversion to endangering those of apprentice age. I trust this will sufficiently motivate you to cooperate."

Mayweather stared at him through lowered brows for a long moment. "We don't know the source of the Ware," he finally said. "We're searching for it, but we haven't found it yet. I can't guarantee anything."

Vabion smiled. "I'm actually glad to hear you say that, Mister Mayweather. I trust it more than glib assurances that you'll give me everything I demand. Believe it or not, while I insist on having the upper hand in any business deal"—he flourished the control bracelet to make his point—"I hope that this can be the beginning of a more equal partnership."

"You are out of your mind."

"I'm simply forced to extreme measures by my circumstances. Look at it from my point of view. I'm attempting to master a technology sent to me from another star, by beings with abilities and motivations I cannot grasp. Now I'm faced with more beings from still another star, again with powers and knowledge well beyond my own. If I'm to have any hope of dealing with either on an even footing, I need some form of leverage. It's simply a matter of self-defense."

"You'll use any excuse to seize control, Vabion," snarled Zeheri.

"And you should be grateful for it, my dear, for I am safeguarding Vanot's interests in the face of an alien community we are all but powerless against. I hope you'll learn in time to appreciate that." He fingered his collar idly as he went on: "Although I can't blame you for not being in the mood to see it just now."

"You know what?" Mayweather asked. "I find that the

longer people spend trying to rationalize their actions, the more it proves how indefensible they are."

Vabion took it in stride. "Well, then, in that spirit, I suggest we get on with this. Since you came down in a landing craft, I assume you prefer not to send living beings by dematerialization. I'll defer to your experience on that point, so I suggest you escort me to your lander at once."

"All right," Mayweather replied after a pause. "But Urwen stays here."

"Certainly not. I won't let her out of range of my control bracelet. Apprentice Nibar will remain here as an additional safeguard—as will Miss Ndiaye. I gather she is your security officer, so I can best control you out there if she remains here. But I trust Miss Zeheri's ongoing presence by our side will serve to remind you of what's at stake if you don't cooperate."

"You son of an Undertroll," Zeheri cursed.

Chuckling, he lifted her exquisite chin with his finger. "Don't be so ungrateful, my dear. Thanks to me, you're about to go on a journey to where no Vanotli has ever dreamed of going before."

U.S.S. *Zabathu* AGC-11-09

Zeheri had barely registered Vabion's words about landing craft and beings from other stars, dismissing them as more of his empty excuses. She'd let herself hope, as Travis led the group out past the hold wall and into the stormbreak forest beyond, that he was just playing along with the industrialist's delusions, leading him into some kind of trap.

But then they had come upon the strange, stubby-winged, propellerless aircraft in a clearing too small for any plane to use. And then she had seen a pilot whom Travis called

Karthikeyan, as pale as Rey and with unnaturally black eyes. And then they had somehow lifted into the sky and she had seen the ground falling swiftly away. Then the craft had effortlessly pierced the dense, turbulent clouds overhead, and before she knew it she was gazing down on the curve of Vanot with only starry black space around the craft. She had been too stunned to speak. But she had noticed the look of triumphant wonder on Vabion's face, as though he'd expected this all along.

And then a larger flying craft (was that even the word for this?) loomed over them and took them inside, and the people Travis spoke to were like nothing she'd ever seen, tall blue-skinned creatures with silver hair, their heads sporting strange, moving stalks that writhed and pointed toward her as if they could see her. She was terrified and bewildered and only wanted to go home and let Najola reassure her that it had all been a bad dream. But she was still an investigator, so she watched and listened as Travis ordered the blue people to set a course to intercept a pioneer at distortion six, whatever that meant. The blue people accepted his commands and spoke to him as a fellow officer, and she knew this was where he belonged. And she realized that the strangely rigid fins that Travis and Rey and Katrina had behind their ears were false, that their eyes must look the same as Karthikeyan's—that they weren't even Vanotli!

Once the blue people had moved on, Travis came over to her, albeit under Vabion's watchful eye. "You lied to me!" she cried before he could speak. "You manipulated me!"

"I was only trying to protect you. Your people weren't ready for this."

But she could see in his eyes that he didn't find his own words convincing. "You protect people by *giving* them the knowledge to cope with what they may face. Hiding the truth endangers them." She pointed at the lethal collar around her neck. "Or hadn't you noticed?"

"I promise—I will get you out of this. Ganler, too."

"Don't promise me anything! I don't even know what you are anymore! You didn't even trust me with that!"

He looked at her helplessly. After all, there was nothing he could possibly say to her now.

June 3, 2165
U.S.S. Pioneer

The Ware hub was not what Malcolm Reed had been hoping to find. Once it had been confirmed that the origin point for the drone ships had been a K-type star system, Reed had hoped they had found the homeworld of the Ware's creators. Instead, they had simply found the mother of all Ware automated stations, drawing on the star's light for power and its dense planetesimal cloud as a source of raw replication material.

But once *Pioneer* had completed a quick flyby to take long-range scans and then reunited with *Vol'Rala* and the other ships, analysis had suggested that "mother" might have been an accurate metaphor. The hub was a honeycomb assemblage of dozens of the familiar polyhedral modules and expandable Chinese-puzzle docks, yet with the docks extending straight outward from the interconnected modules rather than athwart them, the better to fit within the dense framework. Many of the docks contained drone ships of various types undergoing construction or maintenance. Smaller drones flitted between the hub and nearby asteroids, shuttling raw materials for the warp ships' construction. Tucker suspected that it must receive occasional shipments from the other stations, delivering the rarer supplies that alien ships traded for the Ware's services—antimatter, dilithium, plasma injectors, and the like. Was that the reason for the Ware's activities as much as the demand for living brains? And if so, Reed wondered, what was the ultimate purpose of it all, beyond mindless self-propagation?

Fortunately, Charles Tucker's reaction was more pragmatic. "This could be our way in," he told Reed and Captain sh'Prenni as they met in *Pioneer*'s briefing room with Olivia Akomo and sh'Prenni's chief engineer, Silash ch'Gesrit. "We've had no luck with hacking our way into the Ware's coding, finding some way to reprogram it or shut it down. Judging from the warnings we keep getting from that *lovely* voice we all know so well," he went on, evoking wry and weary grins from the others, "its builders were crazy paranoid about industrial espionage. They didn't want anyone deciphering their software secrets."

"So what makes this hub our 'way in'?" Reed asked.

Akomo picked up the account. "We're seeing not only battleships in the hub's docks, but seeder ships as well—ships that deliver Ware to planets like Vanot and bring back captives. It stands to reason that it also manufactures its own mining drones. So since this facility produces ships with a range of different programmed functions, it follows that its system must contain the root code that underlies them all. If we can break through to that level, it might finally give us the means to modify the Ware's programming, get it to shut down its defenses."

"Just here?" sh'Prenni asked. "Or could we shut down the lot of it at once?"

Tucker looked skeptical. "It doesn't seem like they're all networked that way. And they have pretty robust defenses.

This won't be a silver bullet if it works. But it'll give us a weapon."

"Or an inoculation," Akomo added. "A means of managing the Ware. I'm not sure we should be so quick to just take it all down. The more I study this technology, the more undeniable its potential becomes. The medical breakthroughs, the advances in transporter and fabrication technology, cybernetics . . . Just imagine what we could do if we could harness it. If we could protect living beings against capture, make the system truly safe—"

"Would it even work?" sh'Prenni challenged. "Would it have enough brainpower to be functional at more than a basic level?" She shook her head. "And what about the consideration of the species it's been preying on for generations? Would you want to profit from a discovery that emerged from the suffering and violation of thousands?"

"For the majority of both our histories, Captain, there were few that didn't. But what we learned helped us move toward a better world."

"A world where we no longer tolerate such moral compromises."

Akomo looked startled as she realized what she'd been saying. "I didn't mean—I wasn't saying we should just let them continue. I just meant . . . Just because knowledge came from a moral compromise, that's no reason to blind ourselves to it. Refusing to use it for the greater good just makes things worse."

"In any case," Reed interposed, "we first need to obtain the solution before we can decide how to deploy it. And for that, we need to get aboard that station."

"You should be old hands at that by now, Malcolm," said sh'Prenni.

"Yes, and that's our advantage. But this will be an exceptional challenge given its size and complexity."

"And given," Tucker added, "that we need to occupy it, not just raid it and blow it to pieces. Not easy when the things can repair their own damage."

"Fortunately," sh'Prenni went on, "you now have a whole fleet to assist you."

Reed smiled at her, telling her what he knew she wanted to hear. "And I intend to make considerable use of your services."

June 4, 2165
Ware hub complex

The first service was provided, ironically, by the only two ships that weren't with the rest of the fleet. *Thelasa-vei* and *Tashmaji* rendezvoused some parsecs away and arranged their own raid on another, relatively close repair station—with the assistance of three low-warp Balduk defense ships that had been patrolling the region, the crews of which had been outraged to learn of the Ware's true nature and grateful to the Andorians for returning their liberated officer. Not long after they reported freeing two more Balduk and a Tyrellian (whatever that was) and destroying the repair station, the hub complex launched four of its boxy-nacelled battleships to chase them down. The *Ilthirin*-class courier sped clear with the rescuees while the *Kumari*-class warship and its Balduk escorts stood ready to lead the battleships on a merry chase, keeping them distracted while *Pioneer*, *Vol'Rala*, *Kinaph*, *Flabbjellah*, and *sh'Lavan* tackled the complex.

With a heavy battlecruiser and four light cruisers, it was not difficult to take out the complex's numerous repair docks, and in some cases the ships within them. One battleship got clear before its dock was reduced to scrap, making things complicated for *Pioneer* until *Kinaph* came to its rescue and joined it in finishing off the robot ship—adding one more debt that Reed now owed to nd'Orelag.

The three *Sevaijen*-class cruisers bracketed the complex with transporter interference while *Vol'Rala* sent boarding teams in three of its shuttles. Lieutenant Williams's tactical team and Tucker's engineering team were part of the assault, but the Andorian shuttles were better armed and armored than their Earth counterparts, and thus safer against the complex's retaliations. Once aboard, the tactical teams used their accumulated knowledge of Ware systems to trace the complex's transporter/replicator circuits and destroy them systematically, neutralizing the complex's ability to replicate weapons and replacement parts or to transport the boarders into space. But it was a race to take out all the transporter systems before the surviving ones could restore the damaged ones. At one point, a swarm of mining drones attempted to ram *sh'Lavan* and forced it to raise its shields, cutting off its transporter beam; the gap in the interference pattern enabled the complex to beam two Andorian security troops into space. Fortunately, the entire team was in full EVA gear, and *Kinaph* was able to deploy a shuttlepod to retrieve the two guards.

Once the teams reached the complex's data cores (it had six), the grim business of triage began, the determination of who could be saved and who was too far gone. But Charles Tucker was grateful to leave that task in the hands of Williams and her team. His job, along with Olivia Akomo and Commander ch'Gesrit, was to analyze the complex's data network and locate the data core containing the root code, or at least determine the minimum amount of the complex's computer network that needed to be preserved in order to reverse-engineer the programming. With that determined, the starships could destroy the complex's other modules and reduce the amount of potentially self-repairing systems they needed to watch out for.

In time, the grungy data core had been cleared of captives, corpses, and those in between, leaving it a slightly less macabre place for the engineers to work. Only Commander ch'Gesrit dared to broach the question that had already been on Tucker's mind: "How do we know there aren't important parts of the program encoded in the captives' brains? What might we be missing by disconnecting them?"

"They have to swap out . . . the captives so often," Tucker replied, careful not to call them components, "that any basic programming must be backed up in the cores."

"Right," Akomo said. "The . . . the brains are probably used for random-access memory. Sensor data, temporary pattern storage, real-time processing, and the like."

"I hope so," the Andorian replied. "Just so I don't have to listen to you squeamish civilians stammering every time we bring them up."

Civilians, Tucker thought. *If only he knew.*

Though their main objective was to reach the root code, the immediate priority was to locate the control circuits for the transporter and self-repair systems and ensure they were deactivated. As they tapped the data core and studied its activity patterns, Akomo shook her head. "A pity to treat technology this elegant as something to be shut down or destroyed. Imagine if we could incorporate these self-healing systems into our own ships. Not to mention the technologies for healing living tissue."

"Technologies they don't care to apply to their own captives," ch'Gesrit sneered.

"That's just what I'm saying. Maybe if we could take control of the medical systems, they could help us repair the brains of the captives who are otherwise past saving."

"Watch out for temptation, Doctor. That's the trap of the Ware. Our job is simply to find a way to shut it down. Those are our orders, and civilians or not, you're pledged to follow them."

Akomo conceded the point with a sour, silent look. Satisfied, ch'Gesrit moved to examine another part of the chamber. Once he was out of earshot, Akomo leaned closer to Tucker. "Okay, so we need to find a way to shut it down. But I trust you're still keeping an eye out for useful knowledge along the way."

He studied her, recalling her earlier words in the briefing. "Sounds like you changed your mind about my priorities."

She shook her head. "It was just the initial shock of it. As I said before, every advance has come at a cost. We just have to focus on turning it into something positive." Her dark eyes roved uneasily. "It's for the good of the Federation, right? The most good in the long run. So let's get to work."

Tucker had thought he would be pleased to hear Akomo finally agreeing with him. So why did it give him a sense of loss?

18

May 30, 2165
ShiKahr Business District

TOBIN DAX WAS ALMOST feeling sorry for Soreth. The lanky Vulcan had returned to the debate house this evening with the intent of resuming his argument against melding, but the reemergence of V'Las had forced him into a debate over the prospect of armed rebellion. "Is this how you would preserve the integrity of the Vulcan mind?" young T'Zhae demanded of him in her rebuttal. "By condoning acts of terrorism and advocating armed insurrection against the Federation?"

Soreth floundered, aware of how many eyes were upon him. The room was packed tightly tonight; the bombshell had the whole planet talking, and Tobin was sure that they were streaming to debate houses like this all over Vulcan to sort through their reactions to the news. "I do not . . . I do not find the prospect of violence desirable," he finally managed. "But the High Command, which I take pride in having served, played a valuable role in defending Vulcan and its allies against invasion and internal strife."

"By 'internal strife' you mean the liberty of our allies to make their own choices."

"Freedom of choice requires responsibility—the maturity to judge wisely." He paused for a moment, then spoke more resolutely. "We can respect the independence of younger civilizations while still recognizing their need for guidance, for protection against the cost of their own folly and aggression."

"Good recovery," Iloja of Prim murmured to Tobin and Phlox, who again shared the same table. "The sentiment is dangerously condescending, of course, but his delivery is improving. The lad has a future in politics."

Tobin declined to respond, for the Cardassian poet's words drew more glares from adjoining tables than they had last week. It seemed tonight's patrons were less inclined to hide their disdain for aliens in their midst.

"Should we not protect ourselves first from our own folly and aggression?" T'Zhae riposted. "We assume we have the superior wisdom, the greater maturity, and that this entitles us to dictate the correct direction for other races. But we cannot even recognize truth when we hear it. V'Las is a traitor and a terrorist whose lies nearly brought Vulcan to ruin, yet now that he returns with more lies and attempts to lead us back to the ways of violence that Surak gave his life to save us from, Vulcans across the planet declare their open allegiance to him. How can we have so completely forgotten what we are?"

A new voice spoke from the crowd. "We cannot preserve what we are if we allow aliens to destroy it!" A burly Vulcan male of about Soreth's age rose from his table and strode forward to the debate stage. This was Vokas, who had spoken earlier in favor of V'Las's faction but apparently had now decided that the polite conventions of the debate house no longer applied to him. "V'Las saw the threat that offworld intrusion posed to Vulcan purity of thought and culture. He attempted to resist the erosion of our influence abroad, the influx of alien ideas and individuals onto our planet."

"The Vulcan way is to celebrate infinite diversity in infinite combinations," T'Zhae countered.

"An idea corrupted by the Syrannites to excuse the contamination of our world with foreign influences."

"How can it be interpreted in a way consistent with the exclusion of diverse influences?"

"How can you claim to respect diversity," sneered Vokas, "yet reject the right of those who stand with V'Las to defend our beliefs in Vulcan integrity?"

"The rights of the one do not include the license to disregard the rights and dignity of others. Those who speak of 'rights' to defend their own self-interest at others' expense have no understanding of what the word means."

"*Brava,*" Phlox cheered under his breath.

But Vulcan hearing was keen, and it drew the attention of Vokas regardless. "Look," he said, pointing to the three offworlders' table. "Look how much alien influence is among us everywhere we go. The constant influx of new species, bringing their emotion and their chaos, confusing our youth with ideas that run counter to what Vulcan is. This is a quiet invasion, an occupation so insidious we have not seen it until it was too late. We have a right to take action against it!"

The support from the others at Vokas's table, and more than a few of the patrons elsewhere in the crowded establishment, was vocal. Many eyes now locked on Tobin, Phlox, and Iloja with open hostility—in a cool, controlled Vulcan way, of course, yet Tobin had seen predatory animals stalking their prey with the same dispassionate intensity.

"Maybe we should leave," Dax suggested to the others. "I-I've lost my appetite."

"Nonsense," Iloja countered. "This is just starting to get interesting!"

"I've been in situations like this before, on Earth," Phlox

told the Cardassian exile. "I feel that discretion would be the better part of valor, as the humans say."

"I was forced to flee from a fight once," Iloja told him. "Given the choice, I never would have left." His steely eyes darted back and forth. "Look around, my friends. We are not alone here."

Indeed, not all the heated debate came from the V'Las loyalists. The mostly younger Vulcans who stood with T'Zhae and the Syrannites were well represented here, too, and several now subtly interposed themselves between the loyalists and the offworlder trio, wordlessly offering their protection and support. After a few moments, the proprietor of the debate house, a dark-skinned older female, stepped to the stage. "All are welcome here," she intoned firmly, "to speak and to listen. So it has always been. And so it shall remain." She gestured toward the two uniformed members of the city reasoning force who flanked the establishment's entrance. The message was clear: Disruption would not be tolerated.

But Vokas was determined to save face. "Then I do not choose to stay where those who threaten the true Vulcan way are welcome." He stormed out, most of his supporters joining him. Soreth looked undecided about whether to join them. Eventually he chose to retreat to a corner near the exit, studiously averting his gaze from the trio of offworlders. Yet many of the reformists nodded approvingly toward them or raised their hands in the Vulcan salute. Tobin made a feeble effort to wave back, while Phlox nodded graciously in acknowledgment.

"There, you see?" Iloja said. "Stand your ground and others will stand with you. If only . . . some I knew back home had possessed a fraction of this courage. Excuse me." He wandered off to speak with the reformists, basking in their fervor.

Even with the tension broken, the loss of one of their

party made Dax feel exposed, and he shrank into his seat, looking around nervously. "You can relax, Tobin," Phlox said with restored cheer. "We're welcome here."

"Here, maybe, for the moment. But on Vulcan?" He shook his head. "I came here because I wanted to come someplace peaceful. Someplace safe. Instead I show up just in time for a revolution."

"Admiral Archer and Captain T'Pol may still find a way to prevent that."

"Even so . . . Oh, maybe I should just go home to Trill. Maybe it's a bad idea for any . . . any Trill like me . . . to leave the homeworld at all. There's just too much danger."

With an understanding look on his face, Phlox leaned closer, speaking softly. "I understand, Tobin. Being joined is a great responsibility."

Dax stared, flushing with panic. "You . . . you know?"

"Don't look so surprised. I'm an expert in xenomedicine and I've been around the quadrant once or twice. And as a medical man," he reassured the Trill, "I'm well-practiced at confidentiality."

Dax sighed, shoulders sagging, and spoke even more softly in response, aware of the Vulcan ears around them—though it seemed most of the crowd had congregated around Iloja, whose raucous storytelling would drown out anything Dax said. "Then you understand what I'm afraid of," he told Phlox.

"I understand a host's obligation to protect his symbiont. But my understanding," the doctor went on gently, "is that a host also has an obligation to provide the symbiont with a wide range of experiences that it can pass on to future hosts. It seems to me it's not easy to do that without facing a little danger now and then."

"Then maybe I'm just not a very good host," Tobin sighed. "It's all right—maybe the next one will be braver or better."

"Physical bravery isn't the only source of worth," Phlox assured him. "You can do great things as an engineer, as a scholar, as—who knows? Returning to Trill may indeed be the right path for you, Tobin—so long as it leads you to new challenges. If you go home only to retreat from further challenges . . . well, not only will that not serve Dax, but I don't think it will serve Tobin very well either."

Kel Province, Vulcan

"Our numbers are still small," Commander Zadok reported with dissatisfaction. "For every loyal Vulcan who speaks out in our favor, several more remain in the thrall of the Federation. Even now, we have not done enough to win support."

V'Las kept his hands folded serenely before him, admitting no weakness. "It does not take large numbers to win a world, my friend," he said. "A small group can triumph with sufficient dedication—and sufficient strength. You have served us well in that regard, Zadok. If not for the ships and weapons your loyalists managed to rescue from T'Pau's purge, we would have no chance now."

Zadok acknowledged V'Las's praise with a nod. "Yes, Administrator. We stand ready to strike as soon as you give the order."

"Employing violence at this stage would be reckless," Professor T'Nol protested. The thin-faced academician sat at the monitor bank along one wall of the austere command bunker, surveying the broadcast and data channels to assess the state of the public mind. "Granted, we have the numbers and weaponry to succeed in a coup of Vulcan itself. But what of the Federation? Al-Rashid will not tolerate a loss of federal control over one of his member worlds."

"Let Starfleet come," Zadok said. "Their weapons are inferior, for T'Pau did not share our best armaments with Earth. And their sensors and computers are largely of Vulcan design, meaning we know how to subvert them. This is what we have spent the past decade preparing for." Indeed, Zadok had acted cleverly on his own initiative over the years, working with fellow loyalists to falsify the dismantling or destruction of warships, fighters, and weaponry and to stow them in secret High Command depots on outposts throughout the Nevasa system. V'Las was grateful for that, for he himself had been in no position to lead the resistance.

In fact, he had originally had no intention of doing any such thing. After his mission to foment war with Andoria had failed, he had feared that if he remained on Vulcan, the investigations into his actions as a High Command minister and administrator might expose his years of collusion with the Romulans—and perhaps even his parents' true identity as Romulan sleeper agents embedded on Vulcan more than two centuries ago.

The Rihannsu had declared war on their ancient enemies as soon as the first Vulcan ships had intruded on their territory, for they had feared what the Vulcans might do upon learning their true origins as the Sundered, they who had marched beneath the sigil of the raptor's wing before their voluntary exile. They had hidden their identity behind a new name for their empire—*Rom'ielln*—and defended their borders fiercely, rebuffing all contact. In time they had learned that the Vulcans had embraced a philosophy of nonviolence and sickly intellectualism, but their disgust at what a once-proud warrior race had degenerated into had made them even more determined to repel the Vulcans, and so the war had dragged on for a hundred years, mostly cold but with periodic bursts of violence to remind the Vulcans that the *Rom'ielln* meant business.

But then—so V'Las's parents had explained to him—Praetor Sartorix had come to power and argued that, by provoking the rising influence and militancy of the High Command, the Rihannsu were pushing the Vulcans to become more Rihannsu-like themselves. Thus, in a fit of optimism, Sartorix had conceived a subtle plan for reunification. The empire already had sleeper agents working to undermine Vulcan from within, but now Sartorix ended the war to get the Vulcans off their guard, then gave the sleepers a new mandate: guide the Vulcans back toward their true nature so that the Sundered could be rejoined once more. The aggressive Andorians had made a perfect enemy to rally the Vulcans against in the ensuing decades, and V'Las had continued his parents' efforts to exacerbate tensions with Andoria until Vulcan was drawn into a great conflict that would surely reawaken its people's warrior spirit.

But then the *Kir'Shara* had been rediscovered despite the sleepers' decades of effort to efface all archaeological evidence of its existence, and its words had discredited the selective reinterpretations of the *Analects* they had used to guide Vulcan in a more militant direction. Defeated at the cusp of his ultimate triumph, his spirit broken, V'Las had sought to leave the planet with his Romulan contact, Major Talok. Even knowing he might face torture or execution for his disgrace, he would rather have died with the dignity of his Romulan birthright than endure the insipid kindness of Vulcan rehabilitation—or risk betraying the secret he had been trained his entire life to preserve. But Talok had implied that V'Las would still be needed to further the Romulans' efforts on Vulcan, that his failure was only a delay in their plans. Reassured that he was still of value, V'Las had remained on Vulcan and submitted to their mockery of a justice system—pretending to concede his errors and accept rehabilitative counseling in order to preclude too deep an investigation into his past.

The following year, however, the Romulans had launched their conquest of what had hitherto been Vulcan-controlled space, and V'Las understood that he had been used. The war he had been instructed to foment against Andoria had been meant not to awaken Vulcan's warrior spirit as he had been taught, but to distract and weaken the High Command sufficiently to negate it as an obstacle to Romulan expansion. Indeed, the dissolution of the High Command upon V'Las's failure had served them even better, leaving the region wide open for invasion. Reunification with Vulcan had never been their goal . . . unless it was through the forcible reabsorption of a broken, conquered Vulcan people as subjects of the empire.

Still, V'Las had struggled to convince himself that his ancestral people were worthy of his loyalty—that their deceit about the true objective behind his rise to power had been necessary to ensure he could not reveal the truth under interrogation. With that in mind, he had chosen to flee Vulcan; now that the government was sufficiently preoccupied with the war, his disappearance should draw little attention. He had done what he could to sow suspicion of his assassination by Romulan or Andorian agents, then clandestinely made his way off Vulcan and eventually to Romulus, hoping to prove himself to his true people by bringing valuable intelligence about the state of affairs on Vulcan and what it would take to ensure they remained out of the war.

"What we must do," T'Nol was now saying, "is act to

subvert the Federation from within. Archer is the one they follow, and we have already done much to discredit him for his role in the *Kir'Shara* fraud." V'Las suppressed a scoff. T'Nol was so committed to her lies that it seemed she'd even persuaded herself of their truth. That was why it had been so easy to convince her that the Anti-revisionist volunteers that Zadok had sacrificed in the bunker raid had actually been murdered by the Starfleet force. "If they lose faith in him, then they will lose faith in his favored followers such as al-Rashid. Then we can work over the next several years to build support for a candidate of our own to challenge and defeat al-Rashid in the next election. You, perhaps, Administrator." She tilted her head. "Although I understand if you consider it more important to retain your power base on Vulcan. Perhaps another candidate could be chosen, one with experience in the Federation electoral process."

"You mean yourself," Zadok scoffed.

"If the administrator deems it the more logical choice," the professor replied primly.

"Our goal is to stand against the Federation, not sell out to it."

"I thought you were a strategist, Commander. With one of our own in place at the heart of the Federation, we could enact policies that would weaken federal power and allow the maneuvering of Vulcan into a central role. Why rebuild Vulcan astropolitical dominance through force when we can do it through politics?"

"Your plan would take too long, T'Nol," Zadok insisted. "More offworlders come to Vulcan every year. More young Vulcans, detached from our traditions and subject to alien influence, are born every year, and more of our esteemed elders and defenders of tradition die every year. If we wait too long to take back control of how our youth are educated, we may lose our chance forever."

"Three years is not an undue interval to wait, Commander. If we wish our recovery of Vulcan to succeed, we must first remove the Federation's ability to retaliate. Strike now and it is a certainty that Starfleet will come in force to reconquer Vulcan for the Syrannites."

V'Las laughed, drawing a scandalized look from T'Nol. "And would that be such a bad thing, Professor? You know your history. When has the military occupation of an unpacified populace done anything but create even more intense resentment for the occupiers? If you want to discredit the Federation, what better way than to make them the face of oppression?"

Zadok was nodding. "I see. It is logical. The more we compel Starfleet to crack down upon the populace, the more Vulcans we convert to the cause of armed resistance."

"Precisely, my friend."

T'Nol looked between them with disbelief, then fixed her eyes on V'Las. "This is what you have intended all along. The entire purpose of our coup is to *invite* Starfleet occupation. Have you considered the cost to the Vulcan people?"

It was all he could do to restrain his rage at the insinuation. The last time he had attempted to undermine the Vulcan people, the Romulans had thanked him for the intelligence and advice he had offered . . . then interrogated him with an invasive mind probe, a brute-force technological substitute for the telepathic skills the Romulans had lost through some quirk of mutation, environment, or history. They had scanned his brain with sufficient brutality to reduce him to permanent catatonia or death—if he had allowed it. But sleeper agent or no, V'Las had spent his entire life mastering the mental disciplines of a Vulcan—not the telepathic ones, of course, but the skills for knowing and regulating one's own mental state. V'Las had retreated within his own mind to save his sanity, allowing the Romulans—his people, his nation, his betrayers twice over— to believe he was a mere vegetable until he had lulled them into sufficient complacency to permit his escape.

V'Las had wandered the fringes of the empire after that, a man adrift without a homeworld. His Romulan loyalties had been a lie, nothing but a trick to manipulate him. But he had begun to realize that by birth, and by a far more ancient and fundamental ancestry, he was Vulcan. It had been his Vulcan strength that had allowed him to endure the treachery of the Romulans, to survive and triumph even as the Star Empire buckled under its own undisciplined aggression and fell to defeat. Ironically, the lie he had been trained to propagate against the Vulcan people had proven to be the deeper truth: Vulcan was superior, powerful, unbeatable. Vulcan was his salvation and his true home.

And so he had realized he must return to save Vulcan— from itself and from the aliens who profited from its pacifism. He would return to complete the mission he had started long before, but now with conviction: to bring Vulcan back to its martial destiny, to make it strong enough to crush any who challenged its superiority, whether Andorian, human, or Romulan.

Yet it had not been until after the war's end, in that window before the completion of the Earth outposts guarding the newly created neutral zone, that V'Las had finally been able to escape Romulan space. The swift emergence of the Federation soon thereafter had given him pause, forcing him to keep his distance from Vulcan until the conditions were right. But on reaching out to the world of his birth, V'Las had found he still had dedicated supporters such as Zadok, loyal warriors who had served as his agents on the ground and laid the foundations for his eventual return. Plus fools like T'Nol who could be easily manipulated.

Reminding himself of that, V'Las moved closer, facing the professor and holding her gaze sympathetically. "Have you not spoken eloquently, Professor, of the cost to the Vulcan people if we do not resist the Federation and their Syrannite puppets? Of the cost to the Vulcan soul if we allow the words of the *Kir'Shara* to enfeeble us and lead us into mental perversion?" She fell silent, considering his words. "As you yourself just said, there is value in playing a long game, a strategy that will take years to play out. My strategy may well take decades, and yes, individual Vulcans will suffer in its execution. But that hardship will be a crucible that will burn away the disease of pacifism and reforge the Vulcan race into the mighty weapons we once were."

His words made her uneasy. "Before Surak, you mean. Before logic saved us."

"Yes, logic saved us, but pacifism may doom us! Vulcans survive, not by denying the aggression within us, but by disciplining it, directing it logically and wisely. This is what Surak truly taught. Not Syrannite sentiment, not the emotions of empathy and grief, but the cold, pure discipline of reason. Imagine what we could achieve as logical warriors, our power controlled and mastered and *used* more effectively than ever before. The galaxy could not stand against us!"

T'Nol contemplated this for a long moment. "A long game," she finally said. "I begin to understand. This is the reason for the contingency plan you assigned me."

"Exactly. It will not be easy to repel Federation occupation. But we will be ready to create a new scandal that will thoroughly discredit the occupiers and the Syrannites once and for all, and then Vulcan will be ours!"

"It is, again, reckless to rely so heavily on an untested contingency," she hectored. "You are aware that the specialists I employed have not yet determined a means to achieve your desired results."

V'Las kept his smile constrained so as not to offend her too badly. "But that, my dear professor, is the beauty of the long game. It will be years before the time comes to put that particular piece into play—abundant time to determine how to perfect it."

"Perhaps. But in the meantime, the risk of its discovery remains considerable. I still say it would be wiser to—"

Zadok interrupted, his patience lost. "All your 'wisdom' is timidity. Nothing but excuses to defer action, to make only safe moves, to protect yourself. No wonder all your movement ever achieved was subordination to others."

T'Nol's gaze in return was scathing. "Administrator V'Las could not have begun to orchestrate his return to power without the foundations my organization laid."

"Indeed not," V'Las assured her. "Let us not fall into conflict among ourselves, Professor, Commander. We must be unified, and work to divide our enemies."

That succeeded in quashing their dispute for now. But privately, V'Las agreed with Zadok. T'Nol's cowardice was disgusting. If he did not need the resources and personnel she provided, he would gladly strangle her with his own hands.

But in time, he would no longer need her. And then she could be sacrificed . . . along with the many Vulcans who must fall in the years ahead so that Vulcan itself could thrive once more.

Now, though, V'Las turned his thoughts to more

immediate priorities. There were other, specific Vulcans who needed to be dealt with in the short term . . . and one particular human as well. Killing Jonathan Archer was another pleasure he would have to defer . . . but the fate he had in store for Archer before then might be even crueler.

19

May 30, 2165
Orion transport *Rimula-Bero*, orbiting Delta V

FOR DAYS NOW, Devna had been reeling under the impact of what Pelia and her friends had shown her. But it was nothing like the marathon sexual training she had expected, not rooted in technique or physical stamina. Those aspects of it had been extraordinary, yes, but mainly in their honesty, their purity. All her life, Devna had known sex only as a power stratagem, a means to manipulate or be manipulated. Now she understood that she had always had it wrong. Not just sex, but *life*. There was more to existence than jockeying for power or control. People could give without expecting something in return. They could be allies—friends—without the need to defend against common foes. And there was so much more she had no words for.

Which was a problem, since she had to find the words to convince Parrec-Sut to leave the Deltans alone. "They're no threat," she assured her master. "They have no desire to use their seductive arts to gain power over other worlds. Otherwise they would have mastered the Carreon and the humans long ago."

"Then they're weak," Sut interpreted. "They should be easy to enslave."

"No," she gasped, and only her soft voice kept it from sounding like a challenge and bringing down instant punishment. Still, her master glared, and she strove for the right way to continue. "They . . . they are too unaccustomed to authority. They would take orders poorly."

"We'll beat that out of them quickly enough."

"They're too delicate, Master. They would not survive."

His massive hand seized her chin, reminding her how easily he could crush her jaw. "I have some experience with delicate slaves," he reminded her. "If I have to sacrifice a few to calibrate my technique, that's fine; there are plenty on the station. We have room aboard for most of them."

Devna wanted to argue further, question whether the life support could sustain that many, but she knew it would only bring punishment—and perhaps betray her wavering allegiances. She reminded herself that susceptibility to alien kindness had led to her previous mistake and the punishment that had followed. And she couldn't let Maras down. Maras was kind to her. Or was she truly? Devna had learned a whole new meaning for kindness these past few days, something very different from Maras's indulgences.

Still, that did not matter. Maras and her sisters held Devna's life in their hands, even as Parrec-Sut did. They were entitled to command her, and she was obligated to obey them without question, regardless of her personal wishes or remorse.

She reminded herself of that as she obeyed Sut's instructions to take advantage of the Deltans' trust in order to access Iatu Vista's communications array and radiation shielding, sabotaging both so that Sut could beam a full load of Deltan tourists aboard the slave transport. She reminded herself as she watched Sut snap the neck of the elderly, kindly Tanla to make a point to the others, as the guards ruthlessly shot down the few Deltans who tried to fight back. She reminded herself as she saw the look of betrayal and bewilderment in Pelia's beautiful eyes as the elegant Deltan woman was thrown into the slave hold along with her surviving friends—most in various states of undress, and not always from having been beamed aboard that way. She kept on reminding herself as *Rimula-Bero* fled the system, easily eluding or shooting down what limited system defenses the Deltans had.

But the more she reminded herself, the less she believed it. The idea that any thinking, feeling mind could be owned was irreconcilable with the lessons she had learned from Pelia and her friends—with her new understanding of herself as a part of something transcendent, united with all other beings. What hurt them hurt her; what demeaned her demeaned them.

Pelia had spoken to her of the differences among the non-Deltan races they had encountered—how humans' capacity for empathy and unity had been close enough to the Deltans' own that it had overwhelmed their minds and identities, but how other, more ruthless peoples like the Carreon had been less susceptible, at least by cultural conditioning if not by genetics. Pelia told Devna that her own capacity for empathy was strong for her kind, which was why the Deltans had been drawn to her; yet while she had felt a tantalizing sense of unity in her lovemaking with Pelia and the others, she had still been able to recover her sense of self afterward. Did that mean she had less empathy than a human?

She remembered Tucker, the human spy she had met two years ago, and his compassion, his belief in freedom. He had told her that, even though he was as imprisoned by his agency as she was by her master and mistresses, he still considered himself free because of the bond he shared with the one he loved. And that had given him the empathy to offer her freedom as well. The temptation of that dream had swayed her enough to help him, earning her punishment. But she hadn't truly understood it until now. Maybe that love he shared was the same kind of oneness she had known with the Deltans. Maybe that was why the human had found it so impossible to accept that another sapient being could be a mere piece of property.

And maybe that was why it was so hard for Devna, now, to accept that Pelia and the others were property. She struggled to remind herself that she had to accept it, that it would be their lot for however long they lived, and she was powerless to change that. Just as powerless as she had been to refuse Parrec-Sut's orders to trap them in the first place.

Why, then, was she so convinced that the Deltans' fate was entirely her fault?

May 31, 2165
Starbase 8

Caroline Paris had just about convinced Captain Shumar that she was ready to return to duty. Doctor Mazril's course of neuroleptics, antidepressants, and parietal stimulation had pulled her back from the brink, and two weeks of intensive counseling at the starbase had helped her come the rest of the way. It had been fifteen days since her last fugue state, five days since her last uncontrollable crying jag, eight days since her last inappropriate sexual advance toward a fellow officer. If anything, she now doubted that sex with a mere human would ever satisfy her again—hence a couple of the crying jags. And she still dealt with some survivor's guilt over the fact that she'd recovered fully (or nearly so) while Ahn Chung-hee had been shipped back home to Vega Colony with little hope that he would ever emerge from his total dissociative state. But she insisted to Shumar that her screwed-up personal life would have no effect on her performance as a Starfleet officer.

Shumar had been very sweet and solicitous about the whole thing, but she was starting to find him a little overprotective, and did not hesitate to tell him as much. No, she did not need an extended vacation. No, he did not have to accept Admiral Narsu's invitation to transfer *Essex* to his fleet operating out of Starbase 12, on the opposite side of the Federation from Delta—at least, not on her account. She wasn't going to run away from a sector of space just because of one experience on one planet. Given how events on Delta IV had played out, the odds were that she'd never need to deal with the Deltans again.

At least the Deltans waited two days after she told him that before they sent their distress call.

When the call came in, Shumar and Paris were in Commodore Chang's office at the heart of the carved-out asteroid that was Starbase 8, conducting a performance review for Ahn's replacement as armory officer, Lieutenant Morgan Kelly. On learning of the distress signal's origin, Shumar glanced at Paris. "Commander, perhaps you should——"

"I'm not going anywhere, sir," she replied, steeling herself. Then, to Ensign Avila on the office monitor: "Put it through, Miguel."

Paris's heart skipped a beat as the regal face of Prime Minister Mod'hira appeared on the screen. *"To the Federation Starfleet, this is an urgent plea for assistance. I understand that you have little reason to think well of us after our recent mistakes, but we are in desperate need."* In her warm, lilting voice, Mod'hira went on to describe how thirty-three of her people had been abducted by Orion slavers who had come to them offering friendship. *"While we have the means to defend our home system, the* Rimula-Bero's *crew took us by surprise and eluded capture, killing six of our defense personnel in their escape. Now they are gaining distance from Lta more swiftly than we can pursue. We can only imagine the fate they have in store for our loved ones. Since we have no conflict with their government and they have made no demands, the abducted ones are unlikely to be hostages for some concession or payment. So we must conclude they intend to keep our people, or kill them. Either fate would be intolerable."*

Mod'hira sighed. *"We have no right to the protection of Starfleet, no relationship by which you owe us anything. But only you have the vessels capable of locating and rescuing our loved ones in time. And despite the negative outcome of our prior meeting, I believe you of Starfleet to be of benevolent intentions. I know your species possesses empathy in considerable measure. I pray to the Infinite Oneness that you will heed that empathy and choose to aid those we have lost. If you do this, then you will have the deepest gratitude of the people of Dhei."*

"The nerve of these people!" Shumar cried moments after the screen went dark. "After what they did to us, now they expect us to do their policing for them?"

Paris saw the concern for her in his eyes and would have none of it. Rising to intercept him as he paced, she held his gaze firmly. "So what are you saying, we should let the Orions get away with enslaving a bunch of innocent people?"

He stared. "Innocent? Caroline, that you of all people could say that! Why——" He broke off, realizing the delicate ground he was treading on, and stammered. "I, I mean . . . I see the way you react when the Deltans are even mentioned. The thought of what they did to you . . ."

"Bryce." She didn't use his given name often, even off duty. It got his attention. She took a deep breath and finally dared to voice the thoughts she'd been afraid to admit. "The reason I don't want to think about them isn't because the memories are painful. It's . . . it's because they're too wonderful, too amazing. What they showed me . . . the feelings, the connection . . . it made the most devoted love I've ever shared with anyone feel like a passing infatuation. It was a, a *unity* with another person like I've never known. It was the most profound joy I've ever felt." She sighed. "The unbearable part is having to live without it."

"An addiction."

"Maybe—but only because we're not strong enough to handle it." She laughed. "Doc Mazril tells me love is neurochemically similar to addiction anyway. Yet we encourage it in our own species. We want to get swept away by it, to feel like we're part of another person. This is just that, but more intense. More . . . highly evolved." She felt tears in her eyes. "It's not evil. It's just . . . not something we're ready for."

Paris clasped her captain's arm. "And it was our own fault, Ahn's and mine, for not being careful enough. For not knowing our limit."

"The Deltans could've stood to be more careful themselves," Shumar answered stiffly.

"Maybe. But it was an honest mistake. They don't deserve to be sold into slavery for it."

He studied her for a moment. "Do you think Ahn would feel the same way?"

His subdued anger rolled off of her. "Captain . . . wherever Chung-hee is right now . . . he's probably too happy to want to come back. He probably feels like he's one with all things. All *people*."

Taking her point, Shumar gave an uneasy nod. He stepped away and paced before the window, beyond which Paris could see the endearingly clunky sphere-and-cylinders shape of *Essex* as it orbited the station. "I'm still not entirely convinced of their benevolence," the captain said. "But just imagine if the Orions managed to persuade or coerce the Deltans to use their . . . wiles on the Syndicate's behalf."

"They wouldn't do that willingly, Captain."

"If they're so empathic, they might find themselves empathizing with their captors. That's a chance I don't want to take."

She saw he was firm in his position. "Well. Just as long as you rescue them, I guess the reasons don't matter."

After a moment, he softened fractionally. "Well, of course the reasons matter. Both reasons. After all . . ." He adjusted the hem of his tunic. "No one deserves to be sold into slavery, do they?"

Paris smiled. "Couldn't have said it better myself." She hesitated. "Could you . . . use a first officer?"

He examined her. "As long as you don't intend to go to their rescue personally . . ."

She thought about it—very briefly. "No . . . No, I don't suppose that would be a great idea." She smirked. "I mean, Lieutenant Kelly deserves a chance to show what she can do, right?"

Shumar smiled. "That's the spirit. Well, come on, then, Commander. We've got a slave ship to hunt down."

She waited until he'd turned away before she pumped her fist in the air and gave a very soft *"Yes!"* Then she gathered herself and followed him out into the corridor that had been roughly carved through the asteroidal rock. "But how?" she asked once she caught up. "We don't know their course, and if we went all the way back to Delta to try to pick up their trail, it'd give them a huge headstart."

"That's right. Our best bet is to intercept them from ahead."

"But that's a hell of a lot of space to search. And Orion ships are pretty good at stealth."

Shumar stiffened his upper lip. "Then we'll just have to be better at looking."

20

June 2, 2165
ShiKahr

WHATEVER RESPECTFUL HUSH might have fallen over the High Council following the death of Surel and so many others had quickly passed. Archer and T'Pol had spent the past two days facing renewed grilling from Councillors Stom, T'Sess, and their fellow partisans about the rationale for, and the legality of, the *Endeavour* team's inclusion on the raid, with many infuriating insinuations about how human recklessness might have provoked avoidable violence. Archer had struggled mightily to keep his temper in check, but then T'Pol had delivered a coolly scathing dissertation on how it had been the remorseless Vulcan logic of Commander Zadok that had led him not only to lure his adversaries into a death trap, but to murder nearly a dozen of his own personnel and allies, individuals that Commander Kimura's team had taken pains to incapacitate without lethal force.

Once the session was finally over, Archer was eager to shuttle back to *Endeavour*. The broadcast of tonight's water polo quarterfinals should surely have come in from Earth by now, and he hoped that watching the recording would help cleanse his mental palate of the foul taste the hearings had left. Before he and T'Pol could even get outside the Council building, though, the latter received a transmission from Commander Thanien. *"There's been an explosion in the residential district, Captain,"*

Endeavour's first officer reported. *"The location is the home of Professor Skon and the Lady T'Rama."*

Archer and T'Pol exchanged a horrified look, one thought foremost in both their minds: *The baby!*

T'Pau insisted on postponing her own testimony to accompany Archer and T'Pol to the site. The intensity in her eyes reminded Archer that T'Rama was not only her former security director, but a member of her clan through marriage.

They arrived to find the front gate in the red sandstone wall blown inward, the mathematically precise arcs of its ironwork twisted and torn. Within, Archer could see that the glass front wall of the house was shattered, the room within a smoldering, blackened wreck. Once T'Syra, the interim security director, showed him and the two Vulcan women through the gateway, Archer was relieved to see T'Rama alive and well outside the house—though his relief faded when he realized she was leaning over her husband, who lay on the ground with paramedics tending to him.

T'Pau strode through the rubble and chaos as if it weren't there, and Archer and T'Pol hastened to follow in her wake. "T'Rama," T'Pau said firmly, aware that she would be competing for the woman's attention.

T'Rama straightened. "My lady."

"What is Skon's condition?"

"Serious, my lady. They are readying him for transport to the hospital now. It is too early to say more."

"And yourself?" Archer asked. "The baby?"

"I was meditating by the rear fountain when the missile struck, Admiral. I sustained some minor lacerations and surface burns . . ." She broke off, coughing a few times. "And perhaps some smoke inhalation in the effort to bring Skon outside to safety. Fortunately, our house guests were away at a poetry recital."

T'Pol surveyed the scene warily, as if expecting a further strike. "Director T'Syra. Have the perpetrators been identified?"

"Not as yet, Captain," the tall woman replied. "This district is open and sparsely populated. There were no witnesses nearby."

"But it would be logical to surmise," said T'Pau, "that this is another strike by V'Las's partisans."

"But why?" Archer asked. "Why strike them now? They're not involved in trying to reconstruct the data from the raid."

"The attackers may not have known that," T'Pol suggested.

"Or," said T'Pau, "this may have been retaliation for their previous efforts. We are dealing with irrational minds."

"This may be the first in a series of planned terrorist strikes," T'Syra advised. "My forces are deploying citywide, and we have alerted the reasoning force. Perhaps, First Minister, it would be advisable for you to withdraw to a secure location. And you, Admiral, Captain, should consider returning to your vessel."

The paramedics were lifting Skon into an ambulance skimmer now. "I shall stay with my husband," T'Rama told them, "and notify you of any change in his condition."

"I'm not going to run and hide from terrorists," Archer said. "That's what they want."

"Director!" One of T'Syra's subalterns approached the group as the ambulance hovered away.

T'Syra turned toward the older male. "Yes, Somnel?"

"We have found a glove outside the wall. It may have been left by one of the assailants."

Trading a look, Archer and T'Pol hurried after T'Syra as Somnel led them out the gate and around the curve of the courtyard wall. But as they came into view of the ornate archway over the adjacent road, Archer dimly glimpsed a moving shape through its thick stained glass. "Over there!" he called.

But it was too late. Particle fire blazed from the archway's edge, and only T'Pol's quick reflexes saved Archer as she bowled him to the ground. The admiral looked to T'Syra for support—only to see Somnel calmly driving a knife into her side, where he knew the Vulcan heart was located. "No!" Archer cried as the interim director fell to the ground with an offended expression on her face.

T'Pol and Archer scrambled for cover; having come directly from the High Council chamber, neither officer was armed. But T'Pol was struck and fell limp. Desperately, Archer clambered over to her and felt her wrist. Vulcan blood pressure was so low that he couldn't tell whether she had a pulse or not—until he felt the faintest exhalation of warm breath against his cheek as he leaned over her face. *They're shooting to stun*, he realized. *So why kill T'Syra?*

Return fire finally erupted from around the courtyard wall, but more raiders were arriving, pinning the Council forces in a crossfire. Just as Archer realized the answer to his question— that someone wanted to take him and T'Pol alive—a skimmer rocketed into view and jerked to a stop between Archer and the Council forces. A middle-aged, tough-looking Vulcan male opened the door and held him at gunpoint. "Get in. Bring the female."

Archer pretended to comply—but if these thugs wanted him, they'd have to work for it. He whirled on the gunman and grabbed at his particle rifle—

And then there was pain, and he knew no more.

ShiKahr Central Hospital

"Have they been tracked?" Thanien ch'Revash demanded.

Though T'Pau was far smaller and younger than the

Andorian commander, the former First Minister stared him down effortlessly, her stern poise humbling him for his rudeness. "The vehicle was found abandoned in the park ring," she told him once he had calmed down. "Unfortunately, our pursuit was delayed by the need to attend to Director T'Syra's injuries." The director was in heart surgery now; it seemed likely that her attacker had calibrated her injury to leave her alive but critical, so as to achieve just such a delay. "They were transferred to a faster craft, which was tracked as far as the Forge. Unfortunately, the electromagnetic storms in that region interfered with further tracking, no doubt as the abductors intended."

"These extremists become more emboldened by the day," Thanien observed.

"No doubt the reemergence of V'Las has inspired them to greater aggression."

"That comes as no surprise," the veteran officer answered. "The Andorians owe much spilled blood to V'Las's policies."

"The Syrannites as well," T'Pau reminded him. "And very nearly my kinfolk this night."

Thanien met her gaze, acknowledging silently that they shared grief and an incentive for action. "How do they fare?"

"Let us see."

T'Pau led him to the observation window of the recovery ward, where Tobin Dax stood vigil along with an alien of an unfamiliar species, whom Tobin introduced as Iloja of Prim. "Looks like Skon's gonna be okay," Dax told them. "And the baby's fine."

"I would like to keep it that way," Thanien said. He noted that T'Rama had spotted their arrival; she heaved her gravid frame upward with surprising grace and moved toward the door. Thanien waited until she arrived to continue. "I am gratified you are well, Lady T'Rama. But as I was about to say, I am concerned for your continued safety. As we've seen, V'Las's loyalists have infiltrated even the Council security force. They may well have agents within this hospital as well. For your safety, and that of your child, I recommend you accompany me to *Endeavour*. Our doctor will be more than capable of caring for Skon."

Dax nodded. "Phlox is a good man. I agree, you'll be in good hands with him." He shrugged. "Quite a conversationalist, too."

"Lady T'Pau," Thanien went on, "you may be a target as well. I recommend you also return to the ship with me, at least for the time being."

"I am still needed to address the Council. With Archer and T'Pol gone, Soval and I must carry the burden of the argument."

"I have already insisted on Soval's return to *Endeavour*, for he is a key Federation official. If you accompany us, you may consult with him aboard the ship. We will then provide transportation and escort for further testimony, once it's scheduled."

T'Pau looked impressed. "We were once taught that Andorians were incapable of logic. One more of V'Las's lies."

Thanien bowed. "You are most gracious."

"Um, I'd like to come with you too, if it's okay," Dax said. He scoffed. "I thought I'd be safer on a planet than a starship, but right now, well . . ."

"As my human colleagues say, the more, the merrier, Doctor." Thanien turned to the poet, Iloja. "And you, sir?"

"Thank you, but no," the wide-necked alien said. "I've grown rather tired of running."

Thanien found the man's comment somewhat rude. After years of dealing with humans and Vulcans, it was refreshing.

June 3, 2165
Kel Province, Vulcan

After some minutes of silence, Jonathan Archer spoke up. "Seems like old times, doesn't it?"

T'Pol reviewed their situation. She had awoken some seventy-eight minutes ago to find herself and the admiral in an unfamiliar facility, stripped to their Starfleet-issue black undershirts and shorts and held in quite secure restraints on hard platforms angled at some thirty-five degrees off the vertical. Said platforms were equipped with what appeared to be medical sensors and monitors, and tubes suitable for intravenous injection were connected to their wrist restraints. Whoever had secured her restraints had taken the slenderness of her wrists and hands into account. When she had attempted to force a hand free, she had felt something sharp pressing against her wrist: the intravenous injectors, no doubt, but angled and reinforced so as to tear into her flesh should she persist in the attempt. Archer, upon finally awakening some twenty-four minutes ago, had been no more able to free himself than she had been; his strength was only human, after all, and his hands bulkier. All told, it was not an agreeable situation.

But over the years, she had learned to appreciate the human practice of "whistling in the dark," as they called it. "Indeed," she affirmed. "I do seem to spend significantly more time in bondage when in your company."

There was a long pause. "I'm . . . not gonna go near that one."

"That would probably be wise."

Archer's wrists jerked against his restraints—a token expression of frustration, for he had already tested them thoroughly. "You know," he said, "maybe getting promoted to Gardner's job wouldn't be so bad. A nice quiet desk job back home sounds pretty good right about now."

"A desk job would not have precluded the Council from bringing you here to testify," T'Pol replied. "Besides . . . it was not that many years ago that a fanatically xenophobic faction in *your* home system abducted me. Your world has no intrinsic edge in security over mine."

The admiral met her eyes, looking apologetic. "Point taken, T'Pol. I want you to know . . . I haven't forgotten that this is your home we're fighting to protect."

She returned his gaze absolvingly. "I never imagined that you had."

"'Protect'?"

The harsh, scornful voice was unmistakable. T'Pol and Archer turned to see V'Las striding into the chamber, Commander Zadok close behind on his flank. The presence of Professor T'Nol further to the rear was unexpected, but—upon reflection—not at all anomalous. It was logical that the Anti-revisionists had remained a part of the traditionalist coalition despite their purported dissolution.

V'Las shook his head as his gaze shifted between them. "Admiral Jonathan Archer. The man who discovered the true word of Surak and brought down Vulcan's only means of defense." He moved closer to T'Pol's pallet. "And *Captain* T'Pol, in your Federation livery. You have betrayed Vulcan time and time again, from P'Jem to today. And you dare to pretend the two of you are protecting Vulcan from those of us who wish to make it strong once more?"

"There is no strength in lies," T'Pol shot back. "I never

understood the true strength within me until I studied the *Kir'Shara*'s wisdom. Now you would take that wisdom from the Vulcan people once again. To serve whom, V'Las?"

"I serve Vulcan. The true Vulcan, as it was in our days of glory."

"Then how is it that your operatives concealed their theft using Romulan holographic technology? Perhaps the rumors of your defection during the war were true. Or perhaps you were their agent all along, deliberately starting a war to weaken the fleet and permit their conquest."

The hesitation in the traitor's blue eyes all but confirmed her accusation. But a moment later, he pulled himself up with pride and conviction. "Everything I have done, then and now, has been with the intention of turning the Vulcans back into the warriors we were meant to be. Whatever . . . errors in judgment I may have made in the past, my commitment to Vulcan is stronger than ever."

Archer peered at V'Las in bewilderment. "It's insane . . . but I think I believe you. You've convinced yourself of this jingoistic bullshit along with your followers."

"We follow V'Las because we see the logic in his words," Commander Zadok countered. "Vulcan was strong under the High Command, a power that sheltered and regulated dozens of worlds. We were leaders—not passive followers in a Federation run by erratic primitives."

"True leadership comes from ideas," T'Pol told him, "not the barrel of a gun. There is more lasting power in convincing others to follow you by choice than in forcing them to submit against their will."

"When the masses are given a choice," V'Las told her bitterly, "they often make the wrong one. The past eleven years have proven that."

"Wrong for you," Archer said, "and your corrupt elite. Drop the rhetoric, V'Las—you just want to seize power again."

T'Nol finally spoke. "We want to restore things to the way they were. Before the influence of offworlders like you. Before all these . . . changes."

"You think guerrilla warfare will let you put things back nice and neat the way they were, Professor? You should study more Earth history. Nothing ever goes back to the way it was after something like that. It leaves permanent scars."

Zadok scoffed. "Your facts are in error. We are no mere guerrilla force. We are an army, ready to strike en masse and take back our planet from your occupation. And within hours, it will be too late for your Starfleet to prevent it."

"You are mad," T'Pol told him. "A violent coup will not only provoke Starfleet retaliation, but will invalidate your cause in the eyes of the Vulcan people. There may be disputes over the correct interpretation of Surak's teachings, but few would dispute that he opposed Vulcans killing other Vulcans."

V'Las was gloating again. "Our cause, my dear captain, will seem entirely valid to the Vulcan people—once you and your human master publicly invalidate yours."

She met his eyes evenly. "I fail to see how our martyrdom could achieve anything of the sort."

"Had I meant to kill you, I would have done so already." He furrowed his brow. "Did you think I had you brought here for some sort of retributive torture, or merely to boast of my victory?"

"I wouldn't put it past you," Archer spat. "You're one of the most clichéd, melodramatic bad guys I've ever met."

"You humans have the strangest habit of conflating reality with fiction, Admiral. But perhaps that will serve my purposes here . . . for I seek to convince you that a fiction is reality."

"Speaking in riddles doesn't exactly disprove my point."

"Then I will speak plainly," V'Las declared. "Once the coup is under way, the two of you will make a public statement confessing that you forged the *Kir'Shara* in order to discredit the High Command and install the Syrannites as a puppet government for Earth and Andoria. This will legitimize our seizure of power in the public's eyes. Even if Starfleet does come to retake the planet, they will have lost the people."

"And what in the hell makes you think we would ever do a thing like that?"

"Because," V'Las told him, "you will both believe it to be absolutely true."

Archer remained puzzled, but a wave of dread rushed through T'Pol as she realized what V'Las intended. "No," she gasped. "You of all people . . . you would not use a mind-melder against us."

"Why not?" he countered, looking amused. "I'm a practical man, Captain. I can change with the times."

"You mean you're a hypocrite," Archer grated. "You persecuted melders when it served your agenda, and now you'll use one to violate our minds just to get what you want. You've got no loyalty to anything but your own power."

V'Las's voice grew cooler, softer, yet that made him seem even more dangerous. "You're very wrong, Admiral. I have more loyalty to Vulcan now than I ever had before. And that is why I will do anything—*anything*—to ensure its strength."

With that, he led the others out of the room. "V'Las!" Archer cried. "I won't let you do this! I'll find a way to stop you!"

T'Pol was touched by the intensity in her friend's voice. She remembered the first time he had spoken in such tones on her behalf—thirteen and a half years ago in *Enterprise*'s sickbay, once she had told him how Tolaris, a dissident Vulcan who had renounced logic and the stigma against melders, had abused his own telepathic skills in order to force a meld on her. She had initially consented to the meld out of curiosity, but he had pressured her to go farther than she was comfortable with, continuing to force the meld even after she had explicitly demanded that he stop. The violence of the coercive meld had triggered the progressive neurological damage known as Pa'nar Syndrome, which she had believed to be terminal for two years until T'Pau had revealed and administered the cure.

At the time, her relationship with Archer had still been uneasy, sometimes hostile; and although she had not approved of emotionalism on general principles, his protective outrage upon learning of Tolaris's assault had affected her deeply, for it had shown that he had come to see her as a member of his crew. In retrospect, she saw it as one of the key formative events in their friendship. But that did nothing to ameliorate the trauma of the experience itself, or the distress she still felt when she recalled the assault. The prospect of being put through such an ordeal a second time was unconscionable.

But this time, she feared, neither Archer nor she would be in any position to prevent it.

"A melder?" T'Nol demanded once the door to V'Las's office sealed behind her, leaving them alone as she'd requested. "You would employ such corruptions in service to our cause?"

V'Las seemed untroubled by her concerns as he circled behind his desk, resting a hand on the back of his chair. "Why should you care? T'Pol is a melder herself. Archer is a human. This is the most efficient way of reconditioning their minds."

"I am not concerned for them, Administrator, but for ourselves. How can we restore Vulcan to its proper values if we compromise those very values in pursuit of our goals? You yourself were one of the staunchest defenders against melder corruption."

"Because it served my goals at the time. Now, using a melder serves my goals."

"And where will you find a cooperative melder?"

V'Las gave her a knowing look. "Come now, Professor. We both know the potential exists in all Vulcans. The stigma did nothing to reduce the number of melders—it just minimized the practice, or at least kept it hidden from public view. Naturally there were those within the High Command with the training or natural inclination for melding. I even employed melder operatives on occasion for . . . special missions. To gather intelligence, to reprogram a mind, to kill undetectably. Some of those operatives are still among Zadok's loyalists."

T'Nol was dismayed by what she was hearing. "Our goal is to restore Vulcan's intellectual purity and strength."

"Use your reason, T'Nol! How can the power to enter and influence others' minds be anything but a strength?"

Bewildered by the question, she fell back on the certainties she had been raised with. "Melding is too intimate, too emotional. It risks neurological imbalance and damage, loss of identity, even physical debilitation."

V'Las considered her. "I think it's time you learned the truth about something, T'Nol. When did medical science reveal these neurological hazards?"

"Approximately two hundred and sixty years ago."

"About midway through Vulcan's war with the Romulans."

"Yes . . . but what is the relevance of that?"

"The relevance, my dear professor, is that the Romulans had begun infiltrating Vulcan with undercover operatives by that time."

T'Nol stared. "Not to doubt your word, Administrator—but how could such alien infiltrators pass undetected?"

"Because they were not aliens. Their forebears had evolved on this world like the rest of us."

It took her a moment to realize what he was telling her. "You mean the Romulans . . . are the Sundered? Those who marched beneath the raptor's wing?"

"Why else do you think they were so implacably hostile to a Vulcan ruled by Surak's ways?" V'Las circled around his desk, nearing her. "Or so threatened by a Vulcan that retained the mental abilities they had somehow lost?"

The implication was staggering. "No."

"Yes, T'Nol. Those 'medical findings' on the hazards of melding were the work of Romulan sleepers, seeking to undermine the Vulcans' telepathic advantage."

T'Nol could not accept what he was saying. "If you knew this, then why would you have promoted the stigma?"

"Because at the time, I was working with the Romulans." The revelation stunned T'Nol, but he gave her no pause to absorb it. "I believed that their warrior strength combined with Vulcan rationality could make both races stronger. And discouraging melding reduced the chances of anyone discovering the . . . actions and goals that I and those like me preferred to keep private."

He paced before her, and when he spoke again, it was more to himself. "But I was a fool to believe the Romulans had Vulcan's interests in heart. I have learned from that mistake. Now, my only priority is to make Vulcan strong. And that means encouraging all our strengths, telepathy included."

T'Nol studied him in disbelief. "I thought you supported a return to our old ways."

"Haven't you been listening, T'Nol? The melder prejudice was an imposition on our old ways, one that never should have been there. It was a *revision*, my friend, exactly the kind of off-world contamination that you so rightly abhor. You should welcome its abandonment. So long as it is in service to the true Vulcan path, rather than the pacifism and weak-willed tolerance of the Syrannites."

T'Nol's mind reeled at the paradox she was faced with. Accepting the change in doctrine V'Las proposed would mean acknowledging that she had been . . . had been . . . *wrong*. But she had arrived at her conclusions through pure logic, and logic was infallible. Yet that would mean that V'Las was wrong, and how could that be? She had concluded decades ago that V'Las and his supporters stood for the purest, most correct interpretation of *cthia*, which was why she had aligned herself with them. That had also been the logical decision, so it could not have been wrong.

Perhaps . . . perhaps this was a test of her purity of logic. He presented her with an untenable premise to make her doubt her convictions. The response must be to present a decisive logical counterargument for why she had been right all along on every count. She simply needed to meditate on the question until clarity came.

The door signal chimed, and V'Las called, "Enter!" The panel slid aside and Zadok stepped in. "Yes, Commander?"

"Sokanis is here, Administrator. He will require two *V'hral* in meditation to prepare, and then the meld can begin."

"Excellent. Tell him to begin with Archer. His mind should be the simpler one to subvert."

"Yes, Administrator. Also, our operative in spacedock has

confirmed that T'Pau, Soval, Skon, and T'Rama are all aboard *Endeavour*. Skon lives, but his condition is serious. It is unlikely that his clanmates will leave his side. And the Andorian now commanding the ship has Soval aboard for his safety."

V'Las nodded in satisfaction. "Excellent. Let us prove him wrong. Do your forces stand ready?"

"Yes, Administrator," Zadok answered with martial pride. "As soon as the signal is received, they will advance on the target cities and Space Central."

"Excellent. Order our operative to proceed with the sabotage at once. The target time is four *V'hral* hence. Sokanis should be done by then."

"Yes, Administrator." Zadok saluted and left.

T'Nol turned to V'Las. "Sabotage?"

"Of *Endeavour*," he explained. "An efficient way to dispose of my remaining enemies, now that the two I need alive are in my control."

"You will destroy the ship?"

"Earther warp drives are powerful but fairly primitive. Susceptible to catastrophic failure if the right safeguards are disabled. To the public, it will look like a tragic accident, a failure of human technology costing countless Vulcan lives. At which point I will step forward to restore order and hold Kuvak's government accountable for allowing such a tragedy to occur."

The eagerness in his voice, on his face, gave T'Nol pause. "Many innocent Vulcans will die."

"You knew that would happen in any case. Logic, Professor. The needs of the many outweigh the needs of the few."

"Yes, of course," she murmured. It was a simple calculation, so it must be correct. And V'Las's plan to shape the circumstances in his favor was intricately reasoned.

Or was it? Intricate, yes, but to what goal? Was it truly

necessary to abduct and mentally violate Archer and T'Pol, to kill T'Pau and her clanmates—including an unborn child—in order to set the coup in motion? Would not the brainwashing of their two captives achieve the legitimization he sought without the destruction of *Endeavour* and Space Central? Was the brainwashing even necessary given the longer-term legitimization stratagem he had assigned to her experts? It seemed as though V'Las was more concerned with personal vengeance on individuals who had wronged him than he was with the logical needs of Vulcan.

And what of his commitment to his own allies? The Mental Integrity Coalition had served V'Las with equal dedication to her own Anti-revisionists. They believed he would stand with them and restore the melding ban once more. But even now, an actual melder was in this compound, readying to employ his perversion in V'Las's service. What if the administrator were sincere about his plan to embrace melding wholesale? Would he really cast aside a staunch ally so casually?

And if so, what was to prevent him from casting T'Nol aside when it suited him?

No, logic could not be wrong. T'Nol was still sure of that. But other *people* certainly could be.

21

June 7, 2165
U.S.S. Zabathu

URWEN ZEHERI HAD NEVER been prone to unreasoning fear. Few Vanotli who grew up during a storm generation could last long if they didn't develop strong backbones. But these past few days aboard a ship of the stars had been a terrifying ordeal for her. The vacuum and radiation outside *Zabathu*'s thin hull weighed constantly on her mind. She'd grown up within walls protecting her from the elements, but somehow the very intangibility of these new dangers made them more unnerving than the wind and rain and lightning. Worse, the gravity aboard this ship pulled oppressively, making her heavier and more sluggish than she was accustomed to. If Travis and his friends had evolved in gravity like this, it would explain their supernormal strength and durability. But it just made her feel fragile and helpless by contrast.

And the company inside offered no comfort. The blue creatures—Andorians—who made up most of the crew were more alien than any Underlander she had ever imagined. And Travis and the other humans, now restored to their natural appearance, were even more off-putting for how closely they resembled the Vanotli she'd believed them to be—and for how they'd lied to her the whole time. True, Travis and the others had made no secret of being from another place; Rey had even hinted at coming from the stars. But then they had simply played along with her ignorance, as if patting her on the head and laughing behind her back.

Though in her more honest moments, during the long hours she spent huddled in her cabin trying not to look out the portal at the terrifying void beyond, she admitted that perhaps she was angrier at herself. Some inquisitor she had been, letting her prejudices blind her to the evidence. But she still felt Travis had taken advantage of her. In fairness, he'd been completely honest with her since their abduction. He'd come to her that first day and told her everything: about his distant homeworld Earth and their own, surprisingly tentative probing into space, about his first encounter with the Ware and how he himself had fallen victim to it, about the Federation of Planets and its mission to save worlds like Vanot from being overrun by the Ware. She could sympathize with his reaction to having been personally violated by the Ware, his determination to protect others from it; but she had reminded him once again that keeping people ignorant did nothing to protect them. The Vanotli may not have mastered starflight yet, but they had aerial flight and industry and radio, they had a scientific outlook that had demolished the superstitions of the past (all right, except maybe the Underlanders), and they had unified as a people to stand against the atrocities of Fetul. Surely they had at least earned the status of an apprentice, the right to be educated rather than coddled like infants.

How frustrating, though, to know that the one person on *Zabathu* who most agreed with her outlook was Daskel Vabion, her abductor. He was the only other aboard of her own race and heritage, yet he was the most alien mind on the ship, the last one she could turn to for sympathy or support—particularly given the bracelet he wore and the collar she wore, ever-present reminders that he could kill her, or Ganler or

Katrina back home, on a whim. She didn't understand how the bracelet's signal could be received back on Vanot, now that they had traveled so far, but apparently Ware science, like Federation science, could surmount such obstacles.

So Zeheri had spent most of the past few days by herself in her cabin. Not that she'd been curled up in a ball, panicking; she'd made full use of the cabin's access to the ship's electronic brain, studying its records and learning all she could about their situation, and particularly about the Ware. She was still an inquisitor at heart, determined to fight for justice no matter how far removed she was, professionally and physically, from the Vanotli justice system. So she did what she was good at and gathered information. Unfortunately, her study of the electronic records only revealed how little understanding the Federation had of its automaton enemies. And though Vabion had been cagey in response to her interrogation attempts, she had sensed from his veiled frustration that he was as much in the dark as the Federation was.

Zeheri was just beginning to persuade herself that she needed to leave her cabin to gain more information when the decision was made for her. An alarm klaxon pealed over the ship's loudspeakers mere moments before *Zabathu* began to tremble like a hut in a fierce lightning storm. Determined to find out what was going on, Zeheri rushed from her cabin and tried to remember the way to the ship's bridge. No doubt Travis would be there.

Before she reached the bridge, though, a forceful blow to the ship knocked her off her feet and caused the lights to flicker. She hit the deck hard in the high gravity, and at first she thought the swirl of lights in her eyes was from a blow to her head. But then her entire body tingled alarmingly, and when her vision cleared, she was not where she had been. Travis had told her of the teleportation abilities of the Federation and the Ware, but experiencing it firsthand was deeply unnerving. It took all her discipline to avoid panicking as she pulled herself erect and looked around.

She, Vabion, Travis's party, and the ten Andorians who made up *Zabathu*'s crew all stood in a spare white room whose aesthetics she immediately recognized as Worldwide Automatics design—meaning it was actually Ware design. The ship must have been overpowered, its energy shields (like something out of Ganler's adventure serials) knocked out to enable their transportation. They were all in enemy hands now—Vabion no less than the rest, she thought with some satisfaction.

But the industrialist recovered more swiftly than the others. "Administrative request, operator Vabion, code V-V-zero-four-six. Acknowledge."

"Your inquiry was not recognized." Vabion was taken aback by the mechanism's response.

"We're not on Vanot," Travis told him. "It wouldn't recognize your codes." Still, Zeheri caught Rey's intrigued reaction to the revelation that Vabion even had an access code. From what they'd told Zeheri, they'd made no progress determining how to access the Ware's control systems.

"The Ware on Vanot is but one part of a larger infrastructure," Vabion replied, unperturbed. "It stood to reason that data would be shared across the system. Evidently it's more partitioned than I'd hoped."

"Who are you?"

It was not the chillingly polite feminine voice of the Ware. This one was rougher, more emotive; Zeheri would call it masculine if not for a certain animal quality. Or perhaps "alien" was the word. In any case, it sounded like a living entity.

Zabathu's shipmaster stepped forward. "I am Commander Finirath ch'Mezret of the Federation courier *Zabathu*," the stocky Andorian declared. "And I demand that you return us to our ship immediately!"

"You will identify and explain yourselves! You are with the alien force that has been assaulting our facilities and disrupting our commerce, are you not?"

Travis held a hand up to ch'Mezret. "I'm Commander Travis Mayweather of the *U.S.S. Pioneer.* Are you the beings responsible for the technology called the Ware?"

"Do not evade! Yes, the facilities are ours. Do you acknowledge your guilt in the ongoing acts of vandalism and sabotage against the commercial infrastructure of this sector?"

"If you mean, have we been liberating sentient beings from the slavery you subject them to for the sake of powering your 'infrastructure,' then hell, yes," Travis fired back, and Zeheri suddenly felt a twinge of the attraction and admiration that she thought she had left behind her. "You have no right to prey on other species like that!"

"All customer groups are richly compensated for the resources they provide," the voice insisted.

"Compensated? I've seen worlds devastated by the Ware, societies enslaved, all to feed your hunger for living minds."

"We are not responsible for how consumers may abuse our products."

"It's the products that are abusing the consumers!"

Suddenly intense pain surged through Zeheri and she fell hard once more; the gravity in here was not much better than aboard *Zabathu.* When she recovered and pushed herself back to her knees, Vabion was saying, "Just a reminder, Mister Mayweather, of who has the authority to speak here." As Travis moved to Zeheri's side to help her up, Vabion looked up at the unseen source of the voice. "As you can see, these others are my prisoners. I am Daskel Vabion, founder and chief executive of Worldwide Automatics, the distributors of the Ware on the planet Vanot. I captured these saboteurs and compelled them to bring me here in search of you, so that I could learn how better to use your technology and improve its distribution across Vanot.

"So you see, we share a common interest. Like you, I am a businessman seeking to preserve commerce and increase profit. If we work together, I can help you deal with the others who are disrupting your operations. As I have demonstrated, I have this group under my control."

After a deliberative pause, a second, similar alien voice spoke. *"You are a primitive. What could you offer that could benefit us?"*

"I am the most advanced intellect on my world. I have spent years analyzing your technology, learning from it. Test me and I will show you what I can do."

"There is nothing you can know that we do not."

"There is at least one thing." Vabion pointed to Travis. "I know that this man here is stolen property. Years ago, he was appropriated as an adjunct processor for a Ware repair station. His people vandalized that station in order to recover him."

Zeheri traded a shocked look with Travis as they both belatedly remembered how fond Vabion was of surveillance. Her collar must have included a microphone that Vabion had monitored through his bracelet controller.

"Impossible," came the first voice. *"A stolen component would have been recovered soon thereafter."*

"The facility in question was on the outskirts of your territory, evidently too far for a recovery vessel to reach. But if you examine him, you will no doubt be able to confirm that he has been an adjunct processor before. And that means," Vabion went on with weight, "that his neurological configuration is suitable for your needs. I will return him to you as a gesture of my friendship."

The horror in Travis's eyes was heartbreaking. He had told Zeheri of his ordeal, but she hadn't realized how much it haunted him until now, as he reacted to the prospect of being returned to that existence. "No," he breathed. "Vabion, even you wouldn't do that."

"My apologies, Mister Mayweather, but as I have told you before, I am a pragmatist. This is simply a means to an end."

"We have no shortage of processor candidates," the second voice came, *"thanks largely to the donations you have provided us."* Vabion bowed as if accepting thanks. *"Why should this particular processor be of value to us now?"*

"Because, as you said, his fellows are attacking and destroying your facilities." He tilted his cadaverous, shaven head. "Do you suppose they would be so quick to destroy a Ware vessel . . . if they knew it had one of their own people hooked into its data core?"

Travis stood in stunned silence, while Rey's eyes raced as if in desperate search of a solution to this plight. Zeheri found her hand brushing against Travis's, closing around it.

"Very well," came the first voice. *"We will reinstall the processor."*

"The processor is in my possession and I am prepared to *exchange* him."

"What is your price?"

"Merely that you allow me to accompany him so that I can personally supervise his reinstallation. I've developed some refinements of my own for your control interface, and I would welcome the opportunity to demonstrate them to you."

The voice was skeptical. *"You may supervise. Stand beside the processor."*

Vabion complied, holding up his bracelet as a wordless command to Zeheri to release Travis's hand. The look of desperation and fear in the human's eyes as they were beamed away stayed with Zeheri for some time thereafter. Despite his strange features, she realized, Travis was not so alien after all.

June 10, 2165
U.S.S. Pioneer

"This is the biggest one yet," Valeria Williams reported as she scanned the incoming Ware fleet. "Six standard battleship drones . . . and one larger vessel, type unknown."

"Mister Collier," Reed asked over the communications channel, "I don't suppose you're getting any closer to deciphering the Ware control systems?"

"*If we were, I would've told you,*" Tucker's voice replied, though the time was past when Reed would automatically trust that statement from him. "*We've learned plenty about how the software works, but it was designed to resist reprogramming.*"

"*I'm not convinced it is entirely design,*" came Olivia Akomo's voice. "*I'm tempted to say it's more of a defense mechanism—like the Ware has evolved to resist threats to its survival.*"

"*More likely that someone programmed it with an evolutionary model in mind,*" Tucker added. "*Either way, it's putting up a good fight.*"

"Which means we'll have to deal with these drones the old-fashioned way," Reed said.

On the viewscreen, Captain sh'Prenni smiled as she leaned back in *Vol'Rala's* command chair. "*Good. It's been days since we've gotten any further target practice. Now that* Thelasa-vei's *rejoined us, we should be in for some good sport.*"

"Sirs," Williams interposed from tactical, "you may want to hold off on that. I'm reading life signs on the drone ships."

Reed stared at her, then looked to sh'Prenni. "Is it possible we've finally attracted the attention of the builders?"

"No, sir," Williams went on. "I'm reading Andorian life

signs . . . human . . . and two readings consistent with the Vanotli on the larger ship." She paused. "But there are two unidentified biosigns on that ship as well."

The mix of species was disturbing, considering that they hadn't received a report from *Zabathu* or Mayweather's team on Vanot in days. Reed turned to Grev. "Try hailing the largest vessel."

The face that appeared on the viewscreen was unexpected: a tall, thin man with a dark complexion, a shaved head, light spots across his brow and temples, yellow-orange eyes, and small fanlike fins behind his ears. *"Attention Federation task force. My name is Daskel Vabion, founder and chairman of Worldwide Automatics on the planet Vanot. I speak to you on behalf of the owners of the facility you have illegally occupied and sabotaged. Evacuate the station and withdraw or we will reclaim it by force."*

Reed was nonplussed. How did this man from one of the Ware's tributary worlds, a planet whose technology was more than two centuries behind Earth's, come to represent the Ware's builders? "This is Captain Malcolm Reed of *Pioneer*," he replied. "Mister Vabion, I'm not certain you entirely appreciate the situation you've found yourself in. The technology these . . . owners have brought to your world is predatory and destructive, whatever promise it offers."

"I beg you not to condescend to me, Captain Reed. I appreciate the situation well enough to have captured your Mister Mayweather and his party, to compel the ship Zabathu *to bring us into contact with the Ware's owners, and to arrange for Starfleet personnel to be placed aboard the ships now closing on your position. Not only do we outnumber you by one,"* Vabion went on, *"but we have a tactical advantage. We have nothing to lose by destroying your ships—but you will kill your own people if you destroy ours. So if you now appreciate the whole situation, Captain Reed, I again recommend that you withdraw your personnel and vessels from the station immediately."*

"Starfleet doesn't submit to the demands of hostage-takers, Mister Vabion. Release our personnel or we will recover them by force. You should be warned that we have plenty of experience liberating captives from Ware control."

"From stations, perhaps. From battleships? I doubt it. Our ships will be in firing range in moments; I advise you to reconsider while you still can."

Vabion's face vanished from the screen, replaced by the image of the seven ships closing in. The largest one—easily distinguishable by the control sphere embedded in its main body—seemed to be holding back now while the others spread out into an attack formation. Reed ordered Grev to signal the Andorian fleet. "Attention all vessels. Assume defensive formation around the hub facility. Be aware that there are Starfleet hostages aboard all attacking ships. We will engage to disable, not destroy."

A moment later, Captain sh'Prenni's face came on the viewer. *"That's what they want of us, Malcolm. To make us hold back."*

"Then their mistake is to confuse precision for weakness," he told her. "Surely your armory officers are skilled enough to take out their weapons, defenses, and propulsion without endangering the hostages aboard. I know mine is."

Sh'Prenni grinned. *"So it's a challenge to our pride, is it? You're on. We'll get them back safely and defend the complex."*

"I know you will. Good luck, Captain."

Once the viewer reverted to the shot of the battle formation—now with several of the Andorian cruisers moving into view as they took up positions around the hub complex—Williams reported, "Forty seconds to firing range, sir."

He held her gaze. "I trust you won't make a liar of me with regard to your targeting skills, Val."

Determination burned in her eyes. "I won't let our people down, sir."

22

T'POL STRAINED AGAINST HER BONDS once more, accepting the pain as the needles jabbed into her wrist. She only subsided when she heard the warning hiss of the mechanism preparing to inject sedative into her veins. She considered whether she might be able to rip her arm free rapidly enough to avoid the injection, and whether the resultant blood loss could be stanched before she lost consciousness through that means instead. The injectors were, naturally enough, positioned directly over the major veins in her wrist, and venous bleeding was slow. However, as she strained, she felt additional barbs digging into her skin above the radial and ulnar arteries. The bleeding from them would most likely be severe.

"We're not going to get out that way," Archer observed grimly.

"No." She considered the options for a time, taking a deep breath before speaking. "Admiral . . . when V'Las's melder arrives, we must persuade V'Las to let him meld with me first."

Archer stared in shock. "What? T'Pol, there's no way."

"It is logical," she said, drawing strength from the words. "I have . . . more experience with invasive melds. I have mental disciplines that would enable me to fight back. I may be able to overpower the melder."

"No, T'Pol. I'm not going to let you go through that again." He gave a brave smile. "Besides, I'm the one who taught you how to meld, remember? I got a lot from Surak's *katra*. Tell me your techniques and *I'll* fight him off."

"They would be difficult to convey with words. And with respect, Admiral, it is my mind and my decision."

Archer held her gaze. "I respect that, T'Pol. But I'm still your commanding officer. We both want to sacrifice for each other, but I have the extra stripe, so I win." He sighed. "Besides, I'm the one V'Las really wants to punish. I'm the one who found the *Kir'Shara* and set all this in motion."

"With the guidance of the Syrannites, and of Surak himself. You are not solely responsible. Nor can you be blamed for how V'Las and his followers have responded to that event."

"Being in command means I *am* responsible. For my actions and for their impact on other people. There's an old saying among Earth's mariners . . . that a captain is responsible for his own ship's wake."

"V'Las is responsible for his crimes."

"But I'm responsible for trying to stop him! This is on me, T'Pol."

"You are being illogical, Jonathan. If you fail to overpower him, he will still meld with me."

"Then at least I can soften him up so you can finish him off."

"The effort will likely damage you."

He gave her a solemn look. "T'Pol . . . would you rather damage yourself for a member of your crew, or let them damage themselves for you?"

She looked away. Logically, it was a subordinate's duty to put one's physical or mental well-being at stake for one's superior. But it was also a captain's duty to take care of her crew above all else. It was a difficult equation to balance. "I understand your wishes, Admiral. But I still protest."

"Duly noted." He smirked. "If it makes you feel better, you can take the hit for me next time."

She threw him a look of skeptical amusement. "You realize that we may not be able to influence V'Las's choice one way or the other."

"Like I said, I'm the one he's really after. I just have to irritate his ego enough to make sure he picks me first."

"Then it is fortunate," T'Pol replied with a raised brow, "that you have such abundant experience at irritating Vulcans."

U.S.S. Endeavour

Tobin Dax had nowhere he wanted to go.

Sickbay was too depressing. Skon was still in a coma, or what the Vulcan doctors called a "healing trance;" according to them and even to Phlox, they'd done all they could for him medically and the rest was a matter of his own physical and mental resiliency. That was not encouraging, for athleticism was more T'Rama's purview. And Dax was hesitant to face her as well, since it was too depressing to ponder the prospect that the baby might have to grow up without his father. Let alone grow up on a Vulcan ruled by V'Las, or under Starfleet occupation.

That concern kept Dax away from the public areas of *Endeavour*, for the off-duty personnel—those who weren't working overtime in the search for their abducted captain and admiral—were all monitoring the news and discussion feeds from the surface. Tobin had tried that for a while, but it had grown too distasteful as the voices speaking in favor of peace, tolerance, and loyalty to the Federation were increasingly drowned out by the fervor of the voices backing V'Las and Zadok. He knew that most ordinary Vulcans did not share those radicals' intensity of belief, but he was afraid that if the loudest few argued long enough and persuasively enough, if they were able to obscure the truth enough with their on-slaught of propaganda, then the rank and file might simply accede to their control. That was the handicap of populism; it depended on the investment and participation of the masses, while oligarchy and authoritarianism thrived on their passivity.

Then why don't you get more active? he asked himself. *Hypo-crite.* He would have once imagined that it was the voice of Lela, the Dax symbiont's original host. But over the years, that illusion had faded as the memories and thought pat-terns of Lela Dax had grown more integrated into his own personality. Or had they? Lela had been brave, ambitious, iconoclastic—one of the first women in the Trill legislature, one of the pioneers of diplomatic relations with Vulcan, one of the first Trill to leave her homeworld. Tobin had inherited her wanderlust, at least, so what had become of her courage, her outspokenness?

Courage led you to Pioneer, he told himself, *and look where that got you.* Lela's legacy may have been within him, but the Tobin half was dominant, providing his volition. She could offer ad-vice and goad him forward, but how he acted on those drives was his own choice, and that was the problem. He couldn't wield ambition or courage with the same deftness and good judgment that Lela had possessed, so it just got him—and more importantly, Dax—into trouble when he tried. The memory of his brush with death on *Pioneer* was still so strong that he couldn't bring himself to volunteer in *Endeavour*'s en-gine room, couldn't face the memories it would evoke. And so he was left with nothing to do but languish in his guest quarters and hope that others with more competence and fortitude could save the day.

So he was surprised when his door chime signaled and he found T'Rama standing in the corridor. Once he'd invited her in and shown her to a seat, he said, "I thought you'd be with Skon."

"My physical presence or absence can have little impact on his recovery at this stage," T'Rama replied. "The telepathic bond we share will notify me should my . . . presence be required." Her hands unconsciously folded over her womb. "In any case, even though we have been temporarily expelled from our home, you are still a guest of our family, and my duties as host remain."

Dax shook his head. "You don't owe me anything."

"We all owe one another something. That is what V'Las would have us forget. And a host's obligation to her guests is something she owes to herself as well." She rose and moved to the console. "To that end, there is something I wished to show you. Our other guest is making an address over the public network. I thought you might find it worth hearing. He began several minutes ago, but I shall replay it from near the beginning."

Tobin moved alongside her to view the console screen. Once T'Rama had Iloja's address cued to what she deemed a suitable moment, she let it replay. *"My world is not known to you,"* the poet-in-exile told them, *"and may not be for generations. I am an outsider—someone that many of you are saying should not be heeded, should not even be permitted on your world. Well, the regime that rules my own world said the same thing about me, even though I was a native and once a citizen in good standing. I was an astronomer and theoretical physicist. I studied planets in distant star systems, seeking other civilizations that Cardassia might one day trade with and learn from. But I found my* work co-opted by those who used it to assess potential threats and targets for plunder. And when I protested, when I spoke to the people of how my work should more rightly be used, I was branded a dissident, stripped of my position and good standing. When that only made me more vocal . . . well, I was eventually driven from Cardassia, forced to seek out the worlds I had once charted, no longer as scientific curiosities, but as refuge and shelter.

"Ultimately that quest brought me to Vulcan, where I found myself welcomed by a people who valued science and philosophy as highly as I did. A people who embraced diversity of thought and the new insights it could bring—into the universe and into the self. Here, I thought, might be a place where I could finally rest."

Iloja's gaze grew harder, more hooded. "Yet recently I have seen a familiar pattern emerging here on this world so far from my home. Politicians tell the people they must be strong. They must be pure. They must fear and expel those who come from outside, who think differently, who believe differently.

"True, on Cardassia, the causes were different. Our people were impoverished, our resources depleted and our ecosystem damaged by the excesses of our ancestors. Disease preyed upon millions, forcing the survivors to adopt lives of discipline, austerity, and caution to avoid infection. Powerful families hoarded and squandered our scant resources, bringing Cardassia near to ruin, until the military seized power and redistributed what little remained.

"In time, we found a new balance: a joint government of the military, the elite families, and a council to represent the masses. It kept our world alive, fed and protected our people. But in time, after generations of struggle, sacrifice, and courage, the great threats to our existence subsided—but the three branches of the state had grown too accustomed to the taste of power to wean themselves from it. Politics obeys its own physics, and power abhors a vacuum. So when the state lost the dangers it existed to fight, it sought new dangers within—and made certain that it found them. The danger of those who questioned the continued need for austerity and military rule. The danger of those who still found meaning in the religion of our Hebitian forebears. The danger of those who did not think in the approved way. Most of all, the danger of those who questioned whether the powerful few currently in charge should remain in charge. Those people threatened only the state— but the state was Cardassia, or so it always told us. What threatened them threatened us all . . . or so it suited them to make us believe."

The refugee philosopher paused for a moment. "It is true that the issues facing you now on Vulcan are not the same. I need not restate the countless words that have been spilled over the merits of peace and the logical need for aggression, over the sanctity of the mind and the benefits of melding, over the purity of Vulcan thought and the ferment of alien ideas, over the right to stand alone and the need to stand with the Federation. You all know these debates, and most of you know where you stand within them.

"But I submit that none of those are the debate you should be having. None of those are the right question. They are the questions that certain parties want you to dwell upon . . . so that you do not see the issue that truly matters.

"Those who urge you to preoccupy yourself with the outsiders who threaten your world, or the others of your own kind whose practices endanger your way of life, direct your focus to the other in order to keep you from looking at yourselves—from seeing what you become when you turn against your fellow beings and live lives defined by fear and exclusion. They do not want you to notice how your own horizons grow more constrained as you agree to impose more limits on others. They do not want you to notice how much of your own freedom you are surrendering to those who promise to protect your way of life from the intolerable other.

"This I have seen," Iloja went on, his voice growing more quiet, but more angry. "When my government branded me a threat for saying that science should be free of military objectives, I was forced to go into hiding—though I did not remain passive. I loved my world and I was determined to fight for it. Aware that the state might threaten my family to force my surrender, I arranged for my wife and daughter to be safely hidden as well. But in time, I learned that my wife was a prisoner of the Obsidian Order, convicted of treason before her trial and condemned to death unless I surrendered. I did not understand how they had found her—until I learned that our own daughter had turned her in. Because she believed she must be a good and loyal Cardassian and betray her own parents, condemn her own mother to torture, for the good of the state." He hissed the last word through clenched teeth.

"Do not think this means Cardassians do not value family as Vulcans do. Family is everything to us. Family was all that kept us alive through the dark generations before the three-part state arose—though it was family that nearly ruined us as well. As I said, it is everything, and not all things are good. But the state had created a world in which it had become normal, even expected, for citizens to turn against one another. To define their righteousness by whom and what they stood against, rather than what they stood for. And so, in the name of protecting our people and our traditions, they had shaped a generation who thought nothing of condemning their own mothers to torture in order to punish their fathers. All our best efforts to raise our daughter to be good and righteous . . . were unable to prevent it. Because the state convinced her that it was good and righteous to betray those dearest to her. To devalue anyone who disagreed with her beliefs and judge them unworthy of love, of loyalty, even of acknowledgment as people."

Iloja needed some moments to gather himself. Dax was weeping openly by now, and T'Rama watched him do so without judgment. "This was why I did not resist when the Central Command offered me exile as an alternative to execution. Because I had already lost everything I had been fighting for. The state had proved stronger than even my love for my own child, my guidance and example as her father. I could not bear even to die on Cardassia after that. I accepted passage on one of the few alien ships that bothered to trade with our impoverished world. I began to run, and never looked back."

He gathered himself, eyes meeting the viewer again. "Now

I find myself on Vulcan, and though I do not love it as deeply as I loved Cardassia, that is exactly why I can remain—why it does not hurt unbearably to see what your world threatens to become. But I love Vulcan enough—I respect Vulcan enough, if that means more to you—that I cannot simply retreat and leave it to its peril. I must take a stand once again.

"And so I have told you what I have seen. I have told you what a world becomes under a military state that justifies its existence through the exclusion of the outsider, the denial of the different within itself. I have shown you how even the most reasonable of justifications can lead to tyranny and brutality—if you build a society based on how you judge others rather than how you judge yourselves.

"I ask you, people of Vulcan: Do not choose your path because of the Federation; because of Starfleet; because of Romulans or Andorians; because of melders or liars; or even because of me. Look at yourselves. Decide who you wish to be, and what you will and will not do. That is the question that the tyrants do not want you to ask. But it is the only question that truly matters.

"Think long on this question, my Vulcan friends. It is my hope that you will all live long and prosper. But only you can ensure that you do."

Dax was silent for quite a while after the speech ended, and T'Rama respected it. Finally he asked, "Do you think it'll make a difference? What he said?"

"I doubt it will change the minds of those who are already committed to V'Las's cause," she said. "What matters, though, is that it made a difference to Master Iloja. He acted to serve his conscience—as must we all."

She nodded deeply to him and left him to his thoughts.

Vokas had to admire the elegance of V'Las's plan for the destruction of *Endeavour.* The administrator's engineers had found an easily overlooked flaw in the backward, overcomplicated design of the human-made warp reaction system, one that exploited human psychological shortcomings as well as their engineering shortcomings.

The burly young Vulcan had been gratified when V'Las's agents had approached him shortly after his expulsion from the debate house some nights ago. He had made his interest in the traditionalist movement known to a member of his acquaintance some time before, and he had made his public condemnation of offworlders in the hope that it would demonstrate his sincere desire to play some role in the impending revolution. Little had he expected that he would be called upon to strike the very first blow, to initiate the action that would set the entire uprising into motion. Certainly he was aware it was because he was expendable—because he had no provable affiliation with the revolutionaries and could be disavowed as a lone operator if he were discovered. Two of the offworlders he had denounced in the debate house were aboard the vessel now, giving him a plausible motive.

But Vokas also had the benefit of being a legitimate employee of Vulcan Space Central, and he had been able to persuade a colleague assigned to *Endeavour*'s spacedock berth to swap assignments with him off the record, so that the colleague could attend to an ailing relative. With the access and clearances his colleague had innocently granted him, Vokas had been able to board the Federation starship without suspicion and make his way here to the command processor bay for the deuterium conditioning and injector assembly. It had been quite simple to penetrate the security on the system, for who would expect a saboteur seeking to destroy a warp reactor to target the *matter* side of the reaction rather than the antimatter? Or that it would be as simple as bypassing a few low-level safeguards and substituting a few control chips dedicated to thermal regulation?

It only took Vokas a few minutes to complete his work and ensure that the sabotage would go undetected. He then made his way off the ship quite casually, assured in the certainty of its inevitable annihilation.

23

DASKEL VABION WAS SURPRISED by the limited performance of the Ware battleships. Given that their technology was generations beyond that of Starfleet, and that the Starfleet personnel were inhibited in their attacks by the presence of the hostages aboard the drones, he had expected it to be easy to retake the hub facility. But the automated ships had revealed limitations Vabion had not expected. For one thing, he had failed to consider the enormous accelerations required for travel across the great distances of space—or at least had overestimated the tolerance of humans and Andorians for such accelerations, on the assumption that their more robust bodies could withstand them better than a Vanotli frame. In retrospect, given that he and Zeheri had been able to withstand travel aboard *Zabathu*, he should have surmised that the vessel employed some kind of inertial cancellation field, perhaps as an aspect of its gravity generation system. Since Ware battleships were not designed to accommodate living occupants (for any live adjunct processors were kept aboard control ships like the one he now rode aboard), they were not equipped with the necessary acceleration dampers. Thus, they had to limit their accelerations to avoid killing the hostages, which put severe restraints on their maneuverability.

Which meant, logically, that they should have compensated

by pursuing an aggressive strategy to neutralize the Starfleet vessels. However, they only seemed to fire on enemy ships that fired on them first or that came between them and the hub they were attempting to retake. It was as if they were programmed only for the defense of their territory or property, unable to adopt a fully aggressive stance.

"Can you do nothing to alter their engagement patterns?" Vabion demanded of his escorts.

The two aliens who flanked him were far stranger than either humans or Andorians. They were stout, rotund creatures with teardrop-shaped bodies tapering to smallish, tubular heads with elongated snouts; their shape suggested a parasitic insect, although their cream-colored fur and warm breath marked them as mammalian in origin. They each crouched on a single pair of thick, bent legs, and their arms and torsos were encased in sophisticated armor of Ware design. At the ends of their forearms were intricate manipulative digits that appeared fully mechanical. They called themselves Pebru, but they had told him little else as yet—at least, not intentionally.

"The Ware operates as it is designed," said the larger of the two Pebru, Govar by name. "It is sufficient; we have already neutralized two of the smaller battleships." Indeed, two Andorian craft had been crippled and forced to fall back, but an equal number of drones had sustained significant damage thanks to the precision fire from the Starfleet vessels, particularly the one with the half-disk forward hull and the two rear tubes, evidently the lead ship *Pioneer*. Vabion was impressed at their ability to neutralize the battleships' propulsion and weapons without costing the lives of the hostages; however, both automated ships were already in the process of self-repair.

"But you could modify its operations to achieve more. Your inflexibility is compromising our advantage."

"The Ware has suited us for generations," Govar insisted. "Should these drones fail, we shall simply summon more."

"We now have an opening," said Zixin, the second Pebru. "We do not need reinforcements. We can push through into teleport range of the hub and remove the infestation."

"But surely they'll be in the data core, which is shielded against teleport rays," Vabion replied.

"Why?" asked Zixin.

Vabion stared. "Because their goal is to decipher your programming code and gain control over the Ware. Didn't you review the data from the scan of Travis Mayweather's brain?" It had been necessary to sedate the powerful human before he could be placed back into interface with the command ship's data core, for he had fought quite ferociously, managing to break Vabion's left arm in the process—a minor inconvenience that the Ware had swiftly repaired. But once the neural interface had been installed, Mayweather's knowledge could be scanned without the need for him to be conscious. Vabion had reviewed the data pertaining to the Starfleet engineering team and the equipment they had brought aboard *Pioneer* at the start of the mission, giving him an idea—filtered through Mayweather's non-expert perspective—of the equipment's potentials.

"No one has ever gained the ability to reprogram the Ware," Govar said.

"No one?" Vabion challenged.

"There is no danger of it."

"Still, you can't teleport them away so long as they remain in the core." He considered. "I suggest you teleport me aboard the hub."

"Why?" Zixin challenged.

"To examine their work and determine whether they have made any progress. I know, no one has ever reprogrammed the Ware, but these are aliens from far away. Who knows what new abilities they may have? If they have gained any ground at sabotaging your technology, we need to know so we can repair it."

Govar considered. "How would you protect yourself from harm?"

"Let me take the hostages who are aboard this ship. Leave Mayweather in place, of course, but I will need the Starfleet man Sangupta as hostage for his crewmates' behavior—and Miss Zeheri as a hostage for Sangupta's behavior." He held up his bracelet. "As you know, I have her firmly under my control."

Govar stared. "You have an inordinate fondness for hostages, Vabion."

"I'm a businessman. I value leverage."

"The Starfleet ships are regrouping," Zixin said. "Our access to the hub will not last long."

Govar fidgeted. "All right. We will send you. But this had better work."

It was the most amateurish threat Vabion had received from a business partner since his apprenticeship. But, like so much else, it told him volumes about the Pebru.

U.S.S. Pioneer

"Taking heavy damage, sir!" Valeria Williams called over the crack and thunder of weapon impacts against the hull. "Thruster arrays one and four are down. We're down to hull plating on ventral starboard, and the ventral phase cannons are out."

The hull shook again. "Target that ship with dorsal cannons and fire at will."

A few moments later, the drone ship was spinning and adrift on the viewer. "Hostage's life signs holding," Williams reported with relief. "But, sir, that ship's just going to regenerate again. Either we need a way to free the hostages . . . or we need to consider what they'd want us to do."

Reed caught her subtext. "You mean sacrifice them."

It was the last thing Williams wanted to suggest. Her determination throughout this mission had been to ensure that no more Starfleet personnel lost their lives. But as the battle raged and the casualty reports came in from sickbay and the other ships, it was becoming increasingly clear that there would be no way to prevent fatalities unless drastic measures were taken. She would have readily given her own life to protect the rest of her crew and comrades. But with that certainty came the realization that every one of the hostages aboard those ships would want the same.

Sh'Prenni made her opinion known over the open channel to *Vol'Rala*. *"We're taking heavy damage too, Malcolm. It may be the only way to turn the tide. And they're all trained soldiers."*

"That's a last resort, Thenar."

"And we're close to needing it."

"We don't need to sacrifice all of them, sir," Williams said. "That seventh ship, the one holding back—it's clearly controlling the others." She hesitated, aware that the control ship was the only one with human biosigns aboard—no doubt two of their missing personnel from Vanot, including at least one of her good friends and possibly one of the captain's oldest friends. But duty compelled her to go on. "It . . . it's the only one we'd have to take out."

"Sir!" called Achrati from the science station. "A transporter signal has just been relayed from the control ship through one of the drones . . . terminating on the hub. They've boarded it."

"Life signs?"

"One human, two Vanotli."

Only one human. Meaning one was still aboard. So much for fate sparing her from the awful choice.

But that one remaining reading was faint, detectable only because Collier had devised a way to scan through the Ware data core shielding. Meaning that whoever was in there—whether it was Commander Mayweather or Rey or Katrina—had been plugged into the machine, used to help kill their own crewmates.

She knew none of them could tolerate that burden any more than she could. "Sir," she said, "the ship's vulnerable if we target it now."

"Wait, Val," Reed told her. "Let's find out what's going on first."

Ware hub complex

The security team had come instantly alert when the newcomers had beamed into the corridor adjacent to the data core. But at the prompting of the lean, shaven-headed man from Vanot, Rey Sangupta filled them in on the situation: That man, Vabion, would kill the Vanotli woman with him if he found himself threatened or disobeyed. Charles Tucker's intelligence training told him that the woman could be sacrificed for the sake of the mission; but whatever part of him survived from before Section 31 argued otherwise. He instructed the security team to escort Vabion and his hostages into the data core.

"Don't cooperate with him," Sangupta protested. "He sold

Commander Mayweather out to the Ware's builders! Helped them plug him back into the data core, even showed them some improvements on the interface! They're using the commander's brain to coordinate the attack!"

Tucker stared at Vabion, filled with fury. "Do you have any idea what you've done to him?"

"Rather better than you do, I imagine, sir," said Vabion. "Indeed, I'm rather better informed than you about a number of things, which is why I have the upper hand here. Now, if you please."

Grudgingly, Tucker permitted the Vanotli man to study the team's equipment and quiz him and Akomo for a time on their findings. "I see," he finally said. "You have made excellent progress. Although you're headed for a dead end I encountered myself in my first year of analysis. The code has numerous such traps built into it. It took me another year to learn how to circumvent it. You've come remarkably far in mere days, no doubt from being closer to the root code and, well, having an equipment advantage. But I doubt you'll be able to escape the trap without my assistance."

Tucker stared. "Your assistance? Haven't you already cozied up to the Ware's creators?"

"As I said, I have information you lack. For instance: There is no way the beings aboard that ship are the Ware's creators."

Tucker found himself staring along with everyone else. "What?" he finally mustered.

"Oh, they are the ones distributing it to Vanot and other worlds. I had hoped that by contacting them, I could learn the secrets of the Ware and gain true control, rather than being at the mercy of its procedures and its . . . appetites. But I see now that the Pebru are merely one more set of customers. They aren't nearly intelligent enough to have created the Ware and have no idea how to reprogram it. I assume they simply managed to institute the planetary seeding program to give it a source of living brains so they themselves would be spared." He sneered. "Or maybe it simply demanded a better class of brain than they could provide."

He turned to examine the equipment. "You, on the other hand, are on the right track. If we cooperate, pooling your technology and my experience with the code, we may be able to gain root access and take control of the Ware at last."

A disbelieving Tucker asked, "Why the hell should we believe you're on our side when you put Travis back into hell, when you come here with hostages?"

"As for Mister Mayweather, the procedure was quite painless. As for Mister Sangupta and Miss Zeheri . . . Well, why do you suppose I convinced them to let me bring two hostages?" He touched a control on his bracelet, and Zeheri's collar popped open. "I knew you would require a show of good faith. Miss Zeheri, thank you for your cooperation, and I apologize for the inconvenience."

Zeheri gingerly dropped the collar to the floor and let Sangupta pull her away toward the others. Rubbing her slim neck, she asked, "What are you up to now, Vabion? You can't expect us to believe you're suddenly an altruist, not after it was your idea to put Travis and those Andorians into those machines in the first place."

"Altruist?" Vabion gave a dry chuckle. "No, Miss Zeheri, my motives are exactly what they've always been. I want to understand this technology, to gain control over it rather than being controlled by it. If the Pebru had been able to provide me with that, I would surely still be with them. But instead, you are the ones who offer me the best chance of gaining control. And since you cannot do it without my knowledge and experience, that puts us on an even footing." He turned to Tucker. "We need each other, Mister Collier. And time is of the essence if you wish to rescue Mayweather and the others. I suggest you think quickly."

"You know what I'm thinking?" Tucker told him. "That you overestimate yourself. Maybe you've spent a lot of time studying these systems, maybe you're a genius by Vanot standards, but you're centuries behind us on theory. So don't make the mistake of thinking we're on anything like an even keel. Now that you gave up your hostages, you're all out of advantages."

"That's where you're wrong, Mister Collier. Because I always have a contingency plan. And that means I can offer you the key to accessing the Ware's root levels. A key I've already put into place."

U.S.S. *Pioneer*

Pioneer was all but out of the fight. Propulsion and weapons were barely functional and Liao was contending with more than a dozen casualties in sickbay, fortunately none fatal as yet. But *Flabbjellah* and *sh'Lavan* were crippled with several fatalities each, *Kinaph* was barely staying in the fight, *Thelasa-vei* had lost its portside engines and a quarter of its engineering crew, and the damn drones kept repairing their own shields and weapons. Grimly, Reed gave the order to the other captains: "At all costs, take out the control ship. It must be destroyed completely."

The two *Kumari*-class cruisers and *Kinaph* grouped for the attack on the command ship. Reed ordered Tallarico to join them in the attack and Williams to ready whatever remaining weapons she could muster, "even if it means opening an airlock and throwing spare parts at them."

But moments later, one of the drone ships strafed them again, and when the smoke and thunder cleared, *Pioneer* was down for good. "Propulsion is totally dead," Williams reported. "Only one cannon's functional and we can't maneuver to aim it."

"Even long-range comms are down," Ensign Grev added. "We're close enough to talk to the hub complex, but the battle group is already out of range."

As if Grev's words had been an invocation, a hail came in from the complex. *"Malcolm, it's Collier,"* came Tucker's voice. His old friend quickly filled him in on the events aboard the hub. *"We may have a way into the root command levels. Vabion says that when he plugged Travis into the data core, he modified the interface. He rigged it to give him access. Captain, he set up Travis as his back door into the root command level!"*

Reed traded a stunned look with Williams. "Do you believe he's telling the truth?"

"He's got a motive I trust, let's put it that way. But we need time to get it to work. You have to order your ships not to target the command drone."

"I'm afraid that's not possible," Reed told him grimly. "They're already attacking the command ship, and our long-range comms are down. We can't tell them to stop. Whatever you're going to do . . . you've got to do it fast."

24

June 3, 2165
U.S.S. Endeavour

ON THE BRIDGE'S MAIN VIEWER, Admiral Gardner looked as livid as any human Thanien ch'Revash had ever seen. He'd heard the slur "pink-skin" used against humans in the past, finding it rather inaccurate in the majority of cases, but now Gardner was shading past pink and toward bright red. *"A Starfleet admiral and captain taken hostage on a founding planet of the Federation! This is an outrage! You've got to do everything you can to find these terrorists before they kill Archer and T'Pol!"*

On the other side of the split-screen viewer image, First Minister Kuvak spoke with strained patience. *"My people are devoting all their resources to the search, Admiral. With all due respect, V'Las's revolutionaries pose an imminent threat to the lives of far more than two people. The brazenness of this strike suggests that they are prepared to commit far worse violence—perhaps even make good on the rhetoric of armed revolution they have propounded."*

"But I don't believe Admiral Archer and the captain are in imminent danger of execution, sir," Thanien said. "Had the intent been to kill them, they could have been struck with another missile. Instead, the purpose of the missile attack seems to have been to lure them into the open so they could be captured."

"That's even worse," Gardner cried. *"They could be torturing our people, mind-reading them for Starfleet secrets. Just how far do they plan to take this revolution anyway?"*

Lady T'Pau stepped forward to stand alongside Thanien. "Admiral. V'Las's first preoccupation appears to be Vulcan. As administrator of the High Command, he spent his career pushing the Vulcan people in a more militant direction. Now, he clearly seeks to resume that manipulation, to transform us back into what we were before Surak."

That doesn't rule out the possibility that he'll target other worlds, First Minister. He's certainly done it before.

"That is true."

"First Minister Kuvak," Gardner said after a moment, *"I'm ready to send a Starfleet task force to help contain this coup. All due respect to you, Commander Thanien, but* Endeavour *alone doesn't seem to be enough to handle a problem this large, certainly not with her captain missing and her security chief on the disabled list."*

"That would be most unwise, Admiral," T'Pau countered. Gardner goggled in shock that such a young woman would chastise him like a recalcitrant grandchild. "V'Las seeks to inflame our people's pride and resentment of outside imposition. A show of force from Starfleet at this stage would serve to provoke rebellion, not subdue it."

Gardner answered her through clenched teeth. *"Then what do you propose we do, First Minister?"*

T'Pau lifted an eyebrow. "Everything we can reasonably do is in the process of being done. The logical option at this point is to await results."

Frustrated, Gardner clenched a fist in midair, then half-heartedly let it thud against his desk. *"Sit and wait, while the galaxy may be falling around us. Thank you for the reminder of why I'm so eager to retire."* He met Thanien's eyes. *"Commander . . . please continue to do everything in your power to bring Jonathan Archer back safely—so that he can put up with this madness from now on instead of me."*

＊   ＊   ＊

"Any change . . . Skon?"

Of course, thought Hoshi Sato, taking Takashi Kimura's remaining hand as she sat beside his bed in sickbay, two partitions over from where the Vulcan professor lay in his healing trance. *Even now, his first thoughts are for others.* "There's no change. Phlox says that might be a good sign—but maybe he's just trying to be reassuring."

"Phlox . . . tells like it is." He sounded confident—though not without more complex feelings, for Phlox had been very blunt about the challenges Kimura would face in his recovery. In modern society, with technological assistance and the support of a caring community, Takashi would still be able to lead a rich, full life—but it would not be the life he wanted, and he would not be quite the man he was. He could focus on the here and now well enough, carry on conversations with his usual charm, but the words didn't come so easily. Sometimes he grew frustrated, and Sato didn't know whether it was because he struggled to find the words to convey his thoughts or because the thoughts themselves were more muddled. The grasp of strategy and planning that had made him such an effective armory officer, and such a keen poker player, was probably gone forever.

But his regard for others proved he was still the man she loved. "Vulcans . . . good at healing minds," he said. "Surel . . . proved with me. Skon just . . . need time in his head . . . put house back in order. T'Rama won't . . . be alone."

"I hope so," Sato said. "A boy deserves a father. Vulcans no less than anyone."

He squeezed her hand. "He's *alive.* Could be worse. Could always be worse." He shrugged. "Why I'm not bitter. Always . . . was always ready . . . make sacrifice for crew. But thought . . . it meant dying." He chuckled. "See? Could be worse."

She sniffled. "You don't have to play strong with me, Takashi. This is going to be hard. For both of us, but especially for you. We have to . . . we have to face that honestly, so we can deal with it."

"Be fine. I . . . have family. Sapporo . . . take good care. But you . . . here without me." He frowned. "Is . . . what you want?"

Her eyes widened. "No! I don't—I mean, the last thing I want is to end it. Certainly not now. But . . . what I do here, it's . . ."

"Important. I know." He met her eyes evenly. "Is a way. Be together. Actually easier now . . . not on the same ship."

"What do you mean?" she asked, hushed.

Kimura smiled. "Marry me."

The first coherent thought to enter Sato's mind after a long, stunned moment was, *So much for not being able to plan ahead.* He'd clearly been thinking this over during his long hours lying here with little else to do. But the proposal overwhelmed her with a flood of questions. Yes, not serving on the same ship would remove the greatest obstacle to marriage, but what about the other obstacles? The distance, the separation—and yes, admittedly, the burdens of caring for Takashi over the years ahead were a daunting prospect. Could she devote so much of herself to another person's needs, when her life was devoted to Starfleet now? Could she bear to give up Starfleet? Could she commit to raising children when her husband would be almost as dependent upon her? And what if his condition took a turn for the worse? She envisioned T'Rama, mere weeks from giving birth, unsure if her mate would survive to greet their son.

Before she could formulate any kind of reply, she realized that Phlox was shaking her shoulder. "Hoshi! The bridge is calling. You're needed there on an urgent matter."

Kimura nodded to her, encouraging her to go. She hoped he couldn't see how relieved she was to retreat from his bedside.

The signal from the Kel Province had been fragmentary, but once Thanien had caught a static-filled glimpse of Professor T'Nol speaking with unwonted urgency, he had considered it important to know why she was hailing *Endeavour*. He had little doubt that she had been associated with V'Las's radicals all along. But her signal had been rerouted somehow to make it more difficult to detect—and since the Anti-revisionist leader had clearly wanted to contact *Endeavour*, that suggested she was trying to conceal her transmission from someone else. Possibly even her own allies.

Once Commander Sato took over the communications station, she swiftly cleared up the signal, showing the gaunt professor seated at a console in a sparse room, a closed doorway the only visible feature behind her. "This is Commander Thanien of *Endeavour*," the first officer announced. "We read you now, Professor. Please repeat."

"I believe V'Las has gone mad," T'Nol said. *"The violence he plans is not logical and will harm Vulcan. That is why I tell you this—not for your own benefit, but for Vulcan's."*

"Yes, understood," Thanien replied, reining in his impatience. "Can you tell us where Admiral Archer and Captain T'Pol are being held?"

"First you must be aware that your vessel has been sabotaged," T'Nol told him. Thanien's antennae pulled back, and he saw shocked reactions among the rest of the bridge crew—immediately giving way to action as they began to run diagnostics and alert their respective departments to stand ready for instructions. *"V'Las intends your vessel's destruction to signal the commencement of an*

armed takeover of Vulcan, using military vessels and weaponry concealed in secret facilities."

"Can you describe the nature of the sabotage?"

T'Nol shook her head. *"I was not privy to that information. I recommend you evacuate T'Pau and all Vulcan nationals at once and remove your vessel from spacedock."*

Such great compassion for non-Vulcan life, Thanien thought. But his response was more calculated: "Professor, we have no reason to trust your word. As a show of good faith, I suggest you tell us where we can find Archer and T'Pol."

"Very well, if you insist. They are here, in this facility. We are located in Kel Province, on the—"

Her words broke off into a choking gasp as her rail-thin body convulsed. She fell forward onto the console, a smoking hole in her back. In the now-open doorway stood Commander Zadok, holding a particle weapon. He strode forward angrily and spoke into the pickup. *"It is too late for you—and your admiral!"* The transmission cut out.

"Hoshi, jam all incoming signals. Don't let any trigger pulse get through."

"On it, Commander."

"It may not be remotely triggered," Cutler said from the science station. "There may be a timer or a fail-safe."

"Any sign of an explosive device aboard?"

"Scanning now."

"Commander," Sato called. "I've backtraced T'Nol's transmission, using what she told me. They're in southern Kel Province, near the Burning Lake. That's a nuclear wasteland with electromagnetic anomalies that block sensors, like Vulcan's Forge on a smaller scale."

"Notify Vulcan security," Thanien ordered. "Mister Curry, prepare a rescue squad. Let's get the captain and the admiral back." He only hoped it was not too late to save their minds.

"No anomalous energy readings or excess masses," Cutler reported. "But a bomb could be masked somehow."

Thanien struck a control. "Bridge to Engineering. Are you monitoring, Commander?"

Tobin Dax wished he'd chosen a different time to confront his fears. He'd barely taken his first tentative steps into *Endeavour*'s primary engine room—mercifully not identical to *Pioneer*'s, for it was larger and located in a vaulted three-story chamber in the *Columbia*-class vessel's secondary hull—when the report of sabotage had come down from the bridge. Temporarily frozen in place, he'd ended up backing into the corner near the chief engineer's workstation on the upper level so he wouldn't get in the way. So he was able to listen in clearly on Michel Romaine's conversation with the bridge. "Yes, Mister Thanien," the stout, middle-aged chief replied in a light French accent. "Engine diagnostics read clean, but I can't rule out all forms of sabotage. We'll have to check every system."

"Simpler to shut down the warp reactor, surely," Thanien suggested.

Romaine shook his gray-templed head. "Depending on the nature of the sabotage, that could set it off. Interrupting a matter-antimatter reaction is as delicate an operation as maintaining one. If a key step goes wrong—"

"Understood, Michel. What about moving the ship? If we get far enough from spacedock, we could eject the core if necessary."

"Again, until we know what was sabotaged, even that would be risky. If it's some gradual, progressive damage, the thrust or a power surge could trigger it to fail sooner." He blinked. "Sir, the spacedock personnel could tow us into space."

"One of the spacedock personnel most likely sabotaged our ship. We

don't know who to trust. This is up to us, Commander. Find that sabotage quickly, so you can tell us how to respond to it. Have someone check the security feeds for any unauthorized personnel, anyone from spacedock doing anything suspicious."

Dax stepped forward, lowering the hand whose nails he'd been chewing on. "Um, I could do that." He looked at Romaine and the commander on the monitor sheepishly. "I, I want to help if I can."

"Appreciated, Doctor. Get to it."

Romaine stepped back and gestured to the console, indicating Dax was free to use it. But he looked at his fellow engineer in sympathy. "You can help a lot more than that, you know."

Dax threw him a brief, appreciative look, but then turned his focus to the monitors. "We'll see."

Kel Province, Vulcan

"My apologies, Administrator," Zadok reported. "It was necessary to terminate Professor T'Nol before she revealed our location."

"Not a problem, Commander," V'Las assured him as he watched Sokanis make his final preparations for his meld with Archer, adjusting the admiral's medications to promote a receptive state of mind. He had been amused by Archer's attempts to goad him into choosing him first, no doubt in the belief that he would be able to fight back in some way. V'Las had been happy to indulge the admiral's invitation, since Archer had not anticipated the use of psychoactive drugs in concert with telepathy. Left fully conscious, Archer would surely resist the meld and the implanted suggestions, and that could damage his brain and negate his usefulness. "Her part was effectively over anyway. Her followers will support me. And her inflexibility was starting to become an obstacle."

"Typical," T'Pol spat, her disgust unconcealed. "This is why people such as you will never triumph in the long run. You are so intolerant of even the slightest divergence from your views that you inevitably turn upon one another."

"Unless, my dear captain," V'Las answered, "I simply ensure that everyone agrees with me. Allow me to demonstrate on your precious human keeper."

"No!" T'Pol cried as Sokanis placed his hands on Archer's temples. "You will never succeed, V'Las. Other melding savants will be able to determine that our confessions have been coerced."

"By which point the government they support will have been soundly discredited. The people will believe me, not them."

"You cannot hide the truth forever!"

V'Las chuckled. "Where is your logic, T'Pol? Obviously I am convinced my plan will work, or I would not have reached this point. You cannot hope to change my mind with mere words, so why waste energy in the attempt?"

Her large eyes flashed at him. "Because sometimes the words themselves need to be said."

"What a very human sentiment."

"Yes," T'Pol told him, her conviction unwavering. "It is indeed."

25

June 5, 2165
Orion transport *Rimula-Bero*

DEVNA HAD SPENT most of the past few days in the company of Ronem-Kob, the engine tender. With her intelligence rank now restored, particularly in the wake of her success with the Deltans, it was her privilege to avail herself sexually of any male of her own slave tier or below, so long as Parrec-Sut did not demand her services for himself. Ronem-Kob was young and pretty, and spending time with him in the engine bay let Devna keep her distance from the cargo hold and the unwavering stares of its hairless occupants. She encouraged him to talk about his work, telling him that the sound of his voice aroused her; but she could tell he simply enjoyed being listened to (as most people did—indeed, her work depended on it), and so he went on chattering in considerable detail about the workings of ship systems that he assured her she could not and did not need to understand.

Thus, she was present when Parrec-Sut called from the command deck to alert Kob that a Starfleet vessel was closing on *Rimula-Bero*'s course from ahead. Convinced it must be a chance convergence, Sut had ordered the ship to slow and change course—but then the Starfleet ship had altered course to match, confirming that they had been spotted despite all their stealth measures. By this time, Devna had made her way to the command deck, where she was allowed so long as she did not distract the men from their duties. So she was present when the ship was identified as a *Daedalus*-class vessel, an older Earth model. Sut had been pleased and ordered maximum warp, hoping to outrun it. But the starship easily overtook their transport; as Devna could have told Sut if he'd asked, this class had undergone a major refit and engine upgrade in recent years. *"Orion vessel. This is Captain Bryce Shumar of the U.S.S. Essex,"* came a commanding voice over the comm. *"You have been identified as the vessel responsible for the abduction of thirty-three citizens of the Delta system and the murder of six others. On behalf of Delta Four, I demand that you stand down and release your captives at once."*

"It's a bluff, Master," said the pilot, Anoben-Lot. "We're in open space. Starfleet has no jurisdiction."

"We're in open space, so we're as open to raiding as anyone else," Sut countered.

"But they're Starfleet. They wouldn't dare."

"Do you want to take that chance? Look for a gas giant, a micronebula, anywhere we can hide."

Anoben-Lot checked the charts. "Nothing in range, Master. *Essex* still closing."

"Disperse warp, then," Sut ordered. "At impulse, we can outmaneuver them. Ready weapons!"

Indeed, Devna knew, past encounters had shown that an Orion slave ship's speed and maneuverability at sublight could be decisive advantages over Starfleet's capital ships. Sut should have been able to weave in and out, hurling potshots at the sphere-prowed human vessel to wear down its shields while handily eluding the arcs of its return fire. But somehow, less than a minute into the engagement, the vector Sut commanded Lot to follow took the transport straight into the path of a phase cannon blast, knocking Devna to the mercifully cushion-strewn deck. The damage hobbled the ship's further evasions and it soon took still more damage. Either *Essex*'s tactics were the work of a master, Devna thought . . . or Sut's left much to be desired.

By now, Ziraine had reached the command deck. As the senior female slave, she served as Parrec-Sut's chief adviser, and now she advised him: "Beam the cargo into space, Master. The humans will hasten to their rescue, allowing us time to slip away."

"And drop shields? Are you mad?" Sut roared at her.

"They will not destroy us while we have the cargo aboard!"

The ship rumbled from another blow. "All aft weapons now disabled," Anoben-Lot reported. "Shall we attack head-on?"

"And bring down more of their wrath?" Sut roared. "No . . . we have to . . . we have to survive this. Hail them. Give our surrender."

"Surrender?" Ziraine questioned. "Oh. I see—lure them in, then fire when their shields fall."

"No, they wouldn't fall for that. We have no choice."

The harem-mistress was aghast. "True surrender? While we can still fight?"

"Don't question me, Ziraine!" Sut backhanded her across the face. "Remember your place." Ziraine looked more surprised than hurt, but she subsided.

Devna, for her part, watched in silence as Sut allowed *Essex* to dock with *Rimula-Bero*, then meekly escorted its security team to the hold so they could retrieve the Deltans. The team was led by a tall, striking human woman with short hair and brown skin a shade darker than Pelia's. Introducing herself to the Deltans as Lieutenant Morgan Kelly, she looked dismayed to see their various states of undress and bruising, as well as the lack of four of the thirty-three she had come to find.

"Technically," she told them with compassion, "we don't have the authority to arrest these people under Federation law. But if you want to make an arrest on behalf of the Deltans, we'll escort them back to your system for trial."

The Deltans exchanged many looks and touches, and fewer words, before Pelia stepped forward and spoke for the group. "Let them go," she said. "Give them—and their people—the chance to learn from their mistakes. We wish only to return to our own."

"Are you sure?" Kelly asked. "Because there's nothing to stop them from trying this again."

"We can improve our own defenses. And punishing these few will not change their civilization." Pelia's eyes locked with Devna's, and there was understanding and gratitude in their depths. "Perhaps some among them will bring greater enlightenment to their kind."

Kelly clearly resented having to release Parrec-Sut, but she did her duty. Pelia and the other Deltans vanished through the lock, and *Essex* decoupled and vanished into warp. Only the fragrance of the Deltans lingered in the ship.

Along with the stink of Parrec-Sut's humiliation and rage. When he demanded an investigation and discovered the undetected engine misalignment that had caused the stray emission *Essex* had homed in on, he punished Ronem-Kob viciously for his incompetence. Devna found herself surprisingly uncomfortable with the engine tender's fate. True, the poor young slave was totally blameless—except in the sense that he had told Devna exactly what she had needed to know in order to create the malfunction. But he could not be blamed for that, because she was an expert at extracting information from her lovers; he'd never had a chance. So he certainly didn't deserve to suffer under Parrec-Sut's lash. But why should Devna feel bad about that? She should be grateful that she wasn't the one being punished. She had been conditioned to enjoy physical pain and humiliation, but there were always more creative tortures, and punishments that would permanently disfigure her and make her useless as a spy. Would she really have preferred to bring that suffering down on herself, just for the liberty of a few aliens? Madness.

But the feeling didn't go away. Devna gradually realized that the empathy the Deltans had awakened in her, the empathy that had driven her to set them free, was not limited to them. Seeing anyone suffer, even for the sake of her own goals, was now difficult to bear. And enduring punishment herself in order to spare others, as mad as it seemed, felt like it could have actually been the right thing to do.

How can I live like this now? she asked herself. Such tender sentiments might work on Delta, but they were no way to survive as a slave and spy in the Orion Syndicate. If she wished to endure under the Three Sisters, then she had to stay ruthless.

But the alternative was forming in her mind despite her fear of even considering it:

Maybe I don't have to remain their slave.

June 10, 2165
Ware hub complex

Tucker had to admit that Daskel Vabion knew what he was doing. For all the backwardness of the Vanotli's culture, he had a remarkable insight into computer science. It was a sobering reminder that genius existed in every era—that societies accustomed to letting technology do their heavy lifting complacently assumed they were smarter than their forebears when, if anything, they no longer needed to be. Vabion's intellect was clearly ahead of his time, even if the same could not be said for his ethics.

But then, ethics were a luxury in Tucker's line of work. His bosses in Section 31 would expect him to pursue much the same goal as Vabion—namely, to gain insight into the Ware and bring its technological secrets home for the Federation. The possibilities were immense: a solution to the transporter problem; instant cures for all manner of disease and injury; advanced matter replication; drone ships for defense so that lives would no longer have to be lost defending Federation worlds. With this kind of technology, the Federation would be securely protected, wealthy beyond measure, and able to attract countless new members with the benefits it offered.

"This is the key," Olivia Akomo told him. "We've been trying to access the root programming through just the data core, but the hardware's too deeply integrated with the organic processors. It's the living brains that give the system its dynamism, its adaptability." She shook her head. "I should've seen it—it's the same principle we're working on with the neural processors back home. If we want to reprogram the system, we need that kind of labile interface. We need the system to be aware of itself so it can redirect itself. We should've been directing our efforts toward tapping into the interface through the living processors, rather than simply removing them from the circuit!"

"Will you listen to yourself?" That was Zeheri, the Vanotli woman. "They're not 'processors,' they're people! I thought you wanted to get them out, to stop the Ware from taking more of them. Now you sound just like Vabion, wanting to use them to give yourselves control!"

"I'm just being practical," Akomo countered. "I was brought here for my expertise with neural circuitry, and that's my conclusion. I'm not insensitive to the humanitarian concerns here, but we have to think about the benefits to the greater number."

"At the expense of the individual? I've seen where that leads."

"Need I remind you," Vabion interposed, "that Mister Mayweather is about to be fired upon by his own people? We need to gain control of the system quickly, before the opportunity is taken from us. We do not have time for an ethical debate."

"He's right," said Akomo. "Vabion's way is our best option."

"And if you choose convenience over ethics now, what happens the next time? And the next?" Zeheri shifted her gaze to Tucker. "Please. I don't understand all this scientific business, but I understand that Travis is one of your own people. He's your friend, your crewmate. And . . ." She lowered her eyes briefly. "He's someone very special. I've never known anyone so full of life, and the thought of him lying there helpless, wasting away . . . If you're really his friends, you can't just reduce him to that. Not when it's his own life on the line. Give *him* a chance to fight for it."

Tucker's training told him to argue—or, better yet, to play along and then do the sensible thing anyway, knowing she couldn't tell the difference until it was too late. If he did what she suggested, there was no telling if it would work at all, let alone in time to prevent *Vol'Rala* and the others from destroying the command ship.

But he found he could not so easily deny her words. Seeing Olivia Akomo side with the likes of Vabion was startling. Commander ch'Gesrit had been right: The enticements the Ware offered were compelling. All this power and luxury could be yours, and all you had to do was value it above the occasional sapient life. It was only a few unimportant people, after all, surely outweighed by the good the Ware did for the majority of others. That had probably been the thinking of the Ware's creators, the reason they'd instituted this system in the first place. And it was so easy, he realized as he watched Akomo standing comfortably by Vabion's side, to succumb to the same temptation.

But those few individuals were not unimportant—certainly not to their friends and families. Travis Mayweather *had* been his friend once. They'd served together for four years, had each other's backs through the worst ordeals and most astonishing wonders that any human had ever experienced before. Their trust in each other had never wavered—until Tucker had renounced his crew and lied to his friends. He had used Travis, betrayed his trust, in the name of what he had believed was the greater good. But if it had been so good, if it had been the right thing to do, wouldn't Travis have agreed with it if he'd simply been consulted?

When it came right down to it, Charles Tucker realized, the people who had the most right to decide what to do about the Ware—and the ones in the best position to do something about it—were the ones who were not being given a say in the decision. But he also realized that Vabion's tap into Mayweather's mind was the key to changing that. Yes, it would give them access to the root levels of the Ware. But it could also give him access to Travis. To send his friend a wake-up call . . .

And put the power in his hands.

Pebru command ship

Is there such a thing as consciousness without awareness of the self?

No; he was aware of himself—just not in the way he was used to. Travis Mayweather had always perceived himself on a very somatic level, dedicating himself to physical development and achievement: weightlifting, wrestling, mountaineering, caving. His hobby of seeking out the gravitational sweet spot of every ship had been in pursuit of the physical sensation of free fall and the physical challenge of locating that one precise spot amid all the conduits and corridors of a vessel. Not to mention his more intimate physical endeavors over the years, from the early experiments with Stefania and Juan among *Horizon*'s cargo containers to the connection he'd shared with Urwen Zeheri. There had been more to them all than the purely physical, but his body was central to his engagement with the world around him. To be without awareness of that body was strange and disquieting. He should be panicking—but panic was a thing of the body, a rush of hormones and adrenaline. A mind in isolation could only panic in the abstract.

Which left him free to focus his attention on what he *was* feeling in lieu of physical sensation. For there was more here than just his mind. He was part of a larger pattern of activity. Strange, confusing sensory input, somehow unsophisticated and below a conscious level, even though it was on *his* level now, the whole of the input his conscious mind could sense. The pattern was unclear, but it was cold, repetitive, formulaic, like . . .

Like a machine.

He was back in the Ware.

Mayweather remembered now, the memory so physically linked that it had been hard to access: fighting against Vabion's effort to put him back into the data core, fighting the pear-shaped, armored creatures who were the root of all his problems, then failing as their drugs took hold. He had never thought to regain consciousness again. Certainly not like this. How could he be awake inside the Ware? He had no memory of such a thing from his first ordeal. Could he have simply forgotten once he was rescued?

But even as he examined his state of consciousness, he realized there was information there, awaiting his access. It was more an intuitive understanding than anything in words, like the internal senses that informed him whether he was hungry or cold or told him where his feet were when he wasn't looking. He realized he was aware of the command ship's status, and his own, on the same innate level. Yes—he was on a command ship, controlling a set of drones. Other beings, the armored aliens, were being sustained by its life support systems. So were several adjunct processors—live captives, including himself. And he, and only he, had been . . . activated. His mind had been restored to consciousness by an outside command, sent through a modification in his neural interface. Vabion's modification—he remembered that much. But why would Vabion want him awake?

No. He sensed further status information. The command had come from a separate Ware facility, a central complex. The complex was compromised by external interference, its biological processors removed, its core programming under attack. The attackers had come in vessels that were now closing in on his command ship, while its drone ships acted vigorously in its defense.

In other words . . . *Starfleet. The task force took the hub. One of my own people woke me up.* And who was the expert who'd been brought here specifically to decipher the Ware's control systems?

Trip. He woke me up.

It could have been someone else, he supposed. But somehow, he knew. Perhaps Tucker had transmitted some sort of identity code through the interface, something Mayweather's mind recognized on a subconscious level.

Or maybe he just knew that only a true friend would do this for him.

Sure, if they'd managed to hack in through his neural processor, it might have allowed them to control the Ware from the outside. That must have been what Vabion intended with his modifications, a plan to use Mayweather as a conduit for taking control. That interface could have been used to shut down the command ship and the drones before the attacking Starfleet vessels managed to blow them up, and Mayweather along with it. If not, it would at least have pointed the way toward how to do it the next time they managed to modify a neural interface.

But instead, whoever was on the other end of that transmission had chosen to wake him up. They had felt he was entitled to know his own plight—and trusted him to handle it.

It made no sense that he would take that as proof that Tucker was behind it. Not after all the years the man had lied to him, hidden from him. But here in this semiconscious space, this void with all nonessentials stripped away, all that remained to Mayweather were the fundamentals. And he knew that when it came right down to it, Charles Tucker would always have his back.

Even if it sometimes took Tucker a while to remember it.

So: He was awake and immobilized, trapped inside a robot ship that was about to be blown up by his fellow Starfleet officers to keep it from blowing them up first. He had been given the right and the ability to know his situation and to shape his own fate. So what the hell could he do about it?

Even as he asked, he knew. The longer he spent in this state, the more he came to understand the cybernetic mindspace he was in. And Mayweather recognized that he was not alone here. There were more than half a dozen other minds with him, all dormant, all existing in a state of repetitive, frantic activity somewhere between dream and seizure. There was no telling how long they'd been in place, how far gone their minds were from all that arduous use. But if it were possible, they deserved to wake up as much as he had. And now that it had been done for him, he knew how to do it for them.

It wasn't simple. It took a committed effort of will, like forcing a numbed limb to move, but he pushed relentlessly until, one by one, he felt them awaken. They communicated with him, some clearly, others weakly, but it came to him in thoughts rather than words. The common theme was confusion and fear; none of the others understood what had been done to them. Mayweather strove to inform them, and somehow the concept got across: They had been taken, they were being used, they were in danger, and now they had a chance to save themselves and many others as well.

We can free ourselves? Shut this down so we'll wake up? Stop the fighting so we won't be destroyed?

Yes, he told them. *But there's more at stake here than just us.* He shared the big picture with them: the interstellar network of Ware stations and planetary seedings, the preying on innocent lives, the disruption of entire worlds. *There are many more like us out there. Part of the same network.*

You woke us, the voices replied. *Can we do the same for them?*

All they could do was try. A caution came from a couple of the other minds: The command ship was taking damage, and they might not have long to work. *We could concentrate on shutting this ship down now,* he advised, *and then help the others later.*

But the suggestion provoked a fierce reaction, and he knew it came as much from within him as from the others. *They wouldn't want to be trapped this way a moment longer than they had to. We must help them.*

Subspace transceivers switched on. Signals probed out, seeking interface with other Ware facilities. Return signals pinged back, connections were made. Mayweather sent out the wake-up call, the others echoing it with him. Their signals could only reach so far, but as they shared their knowledge with the other minds they reached, they heard those minds' assurances that they would carry it forward as far as their own signals could reach.

Now Mayweather could feel something like pain and heat, the command ship's warnings that it was taking damage. *You have done enough*, the voices came from elsewhere. *You have begun our awakening. Now you must complete yours.*

Waking their bodies was not something the system had any protocols for. Normally it just kept them on life support until they wasted away. But the more time they spent with active minds, the more they understood their environment and the more control they gained over it. They were conscious within it, and a conscious mind was one able to affect its own state. They could wake themselves up—and they could shut the Ware down.

In the end, it was not unlike willing themselves awake from a nightmare.

Ware hub complex

Tucker saw Vabion look around in surprise when the lights and circulation fans in the data core faded out, leaving only the illumination from Tucker and Akomo's equipment to see by. "What has happened?" he demanded.

The channel from *Pioneer* was still open, though. *"The drone ships are powering down, sir,"* came Williams's voice. *"They're drifting out of formation!"*

Sangupta traded an uneasy look with Zeheri, aware they weren't out of the woods yet. "Let's just hope Captain sh'Prenni figures out what's going on."

The Vanotli woman frowned. "She wouldn't keep firing on a ship that's stopped shooting back, would she?"

The science officer hesitated. "Andorians can be . . . hard to calm down when they're in the heat of battle."

"Sh'Prenni's also a Starfleet captain, Lieutenant," came Reed's sharp voice. *"And Starfleet rules of engagement are clear."*

Still, Tucker heard a sigh of relief from Reed when Williams reported, *"Task force is breaking off, sir. It's over."* She gave a heartfelt sigh herself. *"Whatever you did over there, Collier, it worked."*

Tucker smiled. "It wasn't us. All I did was give Travis the chance to help himself. I figured, who was in a better position?"

"You realize what you've done, don't you?" Vabion asked. "All you've achieved is a simple shutdown. The processors are awakening, removing themselves from the network. This doesn't help us gain control of the Ware."

"No, it doesn't," Urwen Zeheri told him. "But it keeps it from having any more control of us."

Olivia Akomo was staring at Tucker, her surprise giving way to abashment, as though she'd just realized her oversight in thinking of the captives as circuit components rather than individuals with free will. *Maybe there's hope for her yet,* he thought, giving her a smile and a nod.

And maybe there's hope for me, too.

26

"There," Tobin Dax said after a good thirty-five minutes of searching. He froze an image on the security feed. "That face. I saw him at the debate house the other day. He was out for blood. Aliens are the enemy, that sort of thing."

"I'll track him," Romaine said. Further checking of the security feeds showed the burly young Vulcan accessing the deuterium command processors. Romaine was startled. "The deuterium? My teams have been focused on the anti-deuterium assembly."

"Misdirection again," Dax muttered. "Like with the *Kir'Shara*. That's how these people operate. The obvious is just a decoy. We need to think: How do you destroy a warp reactor in the most innocuous way possible? Something nobody would think to look for?"

Romaine stared. "You want us to think of what nobody would think of?"

"Come on."

Dax led him to the command processor bay alongside the starboard deuterium conditioning conduits. Romaine scanned the access panel and shook his head. The two then raced across the upper-level gangways to the port conditioner's processing bay. "Yes. There's a residual magnetic flux on the lock—it's been accessed recently."

"Open it." The human engineer nodded and removed the panel, and Dax brought his scanner to bear on the circuits inside. "If some of the chips are new . . ."

Romaine shook his head. "We had an upgrade two days ago. Dozens of the chips are new."

"And our man cleaned up after himself. No recent skin oils or epidermal cells on any of them." He pondered. "What does this processor control?"

Romaine thought about it. "Mostly monitoring and regulation systems—deuterium flow, containment pressure, reactant temperature, injector synchronization, field symmetry . . ."

Most of those were critical enough that any disruption would be obvious. Except . . . "Temperature," Dax muttered. "Could it be?"

"Could what be?"

"Sorry. Um, what's the most basic rule about warp reactions and temperature?"

"That you can't mix matter and antimatter cold." He frowned. "But it can't be that. We'd already have blown up."

"*Why* would we have blown up?"

"You know why."

"Bear with me. I need to think this out. Why are cold reactants bad?"

"Because the streams don't have enough kinetic energy to penetrate the dilithium matrix. They scatter in the reaction chamber, begin annihilating outside the crystal, eroding it and the articulation frame. Sooner or later, the frame gives way or the crystal shatters. Once the streams meet without mediation, you get an annihilation pulse triggering a cascade reaction that ruptures the core. Like I said, it would've happened already."

"If the matter stream were *cold*. What if it were just *cool?* A thousand degrees or so below optimum?"

Romaine pondered. "The deuterons would scatter more slowly. The crystals would erode gradually. It might take a few hours to build up to catastrophic failure."

"Plenty of time for Mister Debate Club to get away."

"But is it enough time to save the ship?" Romaine was already halfway down the ladder, rushing to the monitoring console beneath the portside deuterium injector conduit. After a moment, he shook his head. "The matter stream's reading nominal temperature."

"But the processor controls the sensors. He must have sabotaged *them,* otherwise we'd have gotten an alarm already. Them and the thermal regulation circuits. We need to bypass the sensors to make sure."

Romaine ordered one of his engineers to take a manual reading. By the time the two men made it up the ladder and along the gangway to the reactor's manual control console, she had the result ready. Romaine read her report on the core monitor screen and grimaced. "The deuterium going into the reactor is too cool. From these readings, it has been for hours."

"I was afraid of that," Dax said. "The crystals must already be compromised."

"But we can't just power down. The plasma could backflush into the chamber, trigger the cascade."

"How about a controlled implosion? Rely on pure magnetic containment to direct the reaction."

The human engineer stared. "Are you crazy? I wouldn't even know how to begin the calculations for that."

"Sorry, bad idea." He glanced up at the three pairs of plasma conduits that formed a tentlike arch above the reactor before him, channeling the luminous warp plasma from the reactor buffers toward the nacelles. "But that means we have to vent the plasma!"

"Into spacedock?"

"It's all we've got." Dax hit the intercom. "Engineering to bridge."

"Bridge. Thanien here."

"We need to vent the plasma from the warp reactor before we can safely shut it down, sir. And for that, we need to be clear of spacedock. *Fast.*"

"You said that would be dangerous."

"I'm afraid it's extremely dangerous, sir. But it's all we've got." He glanced at Romaine. "I already said that. Sorry."

"Don't apologize," the Frenchman said. "It *is* all we've got."

"Are you ready, Ensign?"

Pedro Ortega looked up from the helm station and nodded to Thanien. "Yes, Commander." The young flight controller had already spent the past half-hour simulating the most delicate spacedock exit he could devise, the one that would put the least strain on *Endeavour*'s systems, just in case the engineers concluded it was necessary—as they now had. "It's as good as I can get it."

"No time to refine it further. Disengage umbilicals and proceed on minimal thrusters."

"Aye, sir."

Thanien tried not to jump at the sound of the umbilicals uncoupling; if the reactor breached, his eardrums would no longer exist to hear it. He simply maintained his calm and monitored the bridge as though everything were normal, for that was what would help the crew do their jobs the most effectively. Ortega worked the controls with a careful hand to nudge the starship forward out of its spacedock berth. Sato at communications and Alonzo at tactical monitored the team that had been dispatched to rescue

Archer and T'Pol, while Cutler worked on a detailed scan of the Burning Lake area to alert the team to any threats they might face. To the rear of the bridge, T'Pau and Soval stood side by side with uncanny stoicism. Were they just that confident in the crew, Thanien wondered, or was this how Vulcans prepared themselves for death? He chose to pretend it was the former.

"Clear of spacedock," Ortega reported after twenty seconds. He kept the thrusters firing at minimal levels for another twenty before canceling the burn. "Proceeding on momentum. Safe venting distance in twenty-six seconds."

"Cutting it close," Romaine called, sounding urgent. *"We're reading a temperature and pressure surge within the reactor core. The cascade is starting."*

"Can we still vent the warp plasma?"

"The more contaminated it gets, the more the reactions will damage the conduits. If they fail—"

"Understood. Ortega, rotate the vents away from spacedock. Romaine, vent as soon as Ortega gives the word!"

"There's no more time!" Tobin Dax cried.

"Just a few more seconds!" Ortega called as he pitched the ship forward. After what seemed like forever, he cried, "Go, go!"

"Venting now!" Romaine called.

The ship trembled and rocked. Thanien knew the plasma roaring through the conduits had matter-antimatter annihilations going on within it even now, contained by magnetic fields that were not designed to withstand such reactions. In essence, they were expelling an explosion in progress, and they could only hope to disperse it quickly enough that the ship would be mostly intact afterward.

But the force of the superheated plasma bursting from the

ship was like a rocket's thrust. *Endeavour* jerked and began to tumble, knocking Thanien and the Vulcans to the deck. The inertial dampers must have been damaged—what else might fail? As he pushed himself up from the metal deck, the tremors of the ongoing eruption sent shocks through his fingers. It felt like the ship was being torn apart.

Yet a moment later, as T'Pau helped pull him to his feet, the rumbling quickly subsided. *"Plasma is vented, sir,"* a breathless Romaine called from engineering. *"Warp core shutdown in progress. It's over."*

Phlox picked himself up off the floor, brushing off his tunic. "Is everyone all right?" he asked, addressing his menagerie of creatures as much as sickbay's more humanoid occupants. Striding over to the recovery beds, he saw that Kimura had somehow managed to stay in place, but—

"Skon!" The cry came from T'Rama, who had come to be with her husband during the crisis, despite all her insistence about her proximity making no logical difference. Phlox hastened to her side, seeing that the comatose older Vulcan had been knocked from his bed, his head striking the adjacent wall on the way down. Kneeling over him, Phlox saw a trickle of blood running from his temple. *Further head injury on top of a concussion,* he thought, not encouraged by the development.

But then Phlox realized that Skon's eyes were fluttering open. After a moment, they focused on T'Rama. "My wife," he croaked. Feebly he raised two fingers, and she brushed them warmly with two of her own. "I am gratified that you and our son are safe."

"Not nearly so gratified as I am, my husband."

"Of course," Phlox said. "Vulcans often need a physical

shock to awaken from a healing trance. I suppose I should be grateful—I'm not fond of slapping my own patients."

Kel Province

T'Pol had been trying without success to contact Charles Tucker through their telepathic bond. She had hoped the strength of Trip's mind could help her resist the brainwashing once V'Las's melder began his assault on her. At the very least, she hoped his presence in her mind could help her endure another violation. But he was either too far away or too mentally distracted to join her in the link. She could get a vague sense of his presence, enough to bring her some reassurance, but was unable to draw his attention. This was not unprecedented; their ability to connect without direct contact had always been intermittent, occurring mainly in times of strong emotion and need. This occasion certainly qualified for her, but even that was no guarantee of success, especially if he were sufficiently preoccupied by his own assignment. She was on her own.

Archer moaned, his head shaking under the aged melder's grip. Despite the drugs and the influence of the meld, he was still resisting, and T'Pol could see that the melding adept was struggling. It was conceivable that the admiral might actually succeed at holding the melder at bay. The human will could be truly impressive at times. And Archer's determination was particularly unyielding, fueled by the ideals and hopes for the future to which he clung so tightly, and by his deep dedication to his friends and colleagues. T'Pol feared, though, that his resistance would result in damage to his brain. Invasive melding, as she knew from experience, was a violent assault on the central nervous system, creating chemical imbalances that could cause permanent harm. T'Pol had instructed him, as best she could in the brief time available, in the techniques of resistance, but applying them was entirely in his hands. It was intolerable that there was nothing she could do to assist her friend.

As intolerable as watching V'Las standing over Archer, gloating at the harm he was inflicting on the man who had brought about his own ruin. "Have patience, T'Pol," he told her, noting her eyes upon him. "Your turn will come soon."

Despite all her study of Surak's word, some part of her yearned to inflict violence upon him for that. So for a moment she thought it was her imagination when a distant explosion sounded from somewhere in the compound. But soon, Zadok burst into the room. "Administrator! Vulcan Security is here, with a Starfleet team."

"What? How did we not detect their approach?"

"They exploited the interference around the lake, as did we! Sir, we are compromised. We must get you safely to the fleet."

"No!" V'Las stared covetously at Archer and T'Pol. "Not when I'm so close to bringing them down."

"The coup will still work without them, sir. We cannot succeed without you!"

The appeal to his ego persuaded him, predictably enough. "Very well. But not without the original! We still need that!"

"I'll escort you, sir." A burst of Starfleet-issue particle rifle fire sounded. T'Pol had never imagined she would find that sound so agreeable. "But we must hurry! I'll get Sokanis."

"Leave him! It will take too long to break the meld." At Zadok's hesitation, V'Las roared, "You wanted me to go, so let us go!"

They fled, and T'Pol waited, staring tensely at the melder and hoping he had not done too much damage already.

Moments later, Subdirector T'Syra led a team into the room. Seeing Sokanis with Archer, she rushed over, took a breath, and put her own hands on the melder's head. Meanwhile, a subaltern came over to T'Pol and worked to free her restraints. Before long, Sokanis gasped, convulsed, and fell unconscious to the floor.

Now free, T'Pol rushed to Archer's side. "I had to pull him out rather forcibly," T'Syra said, nodding toward the man on the floor. "I may have damaged him."

"I care only about the damage to the admiral," T'Pol told her in a rough voice. "How is he?"

T'Syra laid a hand on Archer's brow, more delicately this time. After a few moments, she opened her eyes and withdrew her hand. "He is disoriented, and he has been under great strain. But I believe whatever this man was attempting was unsuccessful. The admiral has strong mental barriers."

"Excellent," T'Pol said, striding toward the door. "Try to bring him around. I'm going after V'Las." T'Syra was wise enough to make no attempt to stop her.

Heading swiftly down the corridor, still clad only in her black undershirt and shorts, T'Pol soon spotted an *Endeavour* tactical team led by Crewman Valmar. "Cover me," she ordered them; though they responded with admirable efficiency, they still needed to run to catch up with her. Valmar slapped a spare phase pistol into her hand once he caught up.

And not a moment too soon. They came upon V'Las and Zadok just as they were entering a chamber off a side corridor. Zadok and another guard opened fire, forcing the team to take cover around the corner. But T'Pol was not willing to wait through a prolonged firefight. Calling up her memory of the enemies' positions, she calculated her motion precisely, then dropped to the floor in clear view of the two assailants.

She had stunned them both before they could adjust their aim downward. She converted her remaining momentum into a tumble and came up to her bare feet, then hastened to the door. Peeking inside, she saw V'Las and another Vulcan closing an upright container some fifty centimeters high, evidently preparing to take it with them. V'Las spotted her and ducked behind the container and the platform on which it rested. The other man, evidently not a combatant, ducked for cover. Moments later, V'Las fired from his position, pinning T'Pol outside the door.

But Valmar's team had caught up by now, and more phase pistol fire poured into the room. She peered around the door frame again to see V'Las making one more grab for the container. She fired, grazing his left shoulder and causing his arm to fall limp. With a growl of frustration, V'Las activated a communicator. "Get me out of here now!"

T'Pol fired determinedly, but a transporter shimmer engulfed him and left only empty air behind.

While the guards poured in and secured the room, T'Pol made her way over to the container. Its size and shape were strikingly similar to . . . she didn't dare think it. She simply found the catch and slowly opened the shell.

Some moments passed before she realized T'Syra had reached them. "We are evacuating Archer for treatment," she said. "But I have a report from my people in the base's transporter facility. V'Las was beamed there, then off-planet. We believe he's beamed aboard his fleet. He will no doubt signal the attack at any moment."

But T'Pol could not draw her eyes away from the item within the container. "No doubt. But that may no longer be a problem."

*   *   *

Vulcan battleship *Karik-tor*

"But Administrator," Commander T'Faral insisted, "without Commander Zadok to lead the fleet, and with Space Central still intact, our odds of success fall to—"

"Never mind the odds!" V'Las insisted, cradling his limp left arm as he strode across the upper deck of the *Maymora*-class battleship's bridge. "*Endeavour* is crippled, at least, and it will take days for Starfleet reinforcements to arrive. We may lose more of our forces, but we can still prevail."

"I am more concerned with our ability to hold on to a victory. Our plan depended on the people's sympathy."

"The people will still support us," V'Las said. "I will speak to them, convince them our cause is logical and just. I will lead them as I did—"

"Commander!" The impertinence of the subaltern's interruption offended V'Las. But T'Faral heeded him anyway, and he resumed. "A transmission is coming in from the Burning Lake outpost!"

V'Las's eyes widened. "Jam it! Don't let it get out!"

"We are not in position to do so, sir."

"Then get into position! Break orbit and descend on Vulcan!"

"Without T'Khut's magnetic pole to shield us, we will be exposed," T'Faral countered.

By now, the subaltern had put the transmission on the viewer, and V'Las cursed inwardly in Romulan as Captain T'Pol appeared on the screen holding the one thing that he knew would ruin him. "*People of Vulcan,*" she said, "*I am speaking to you from a base just seized from Administrator V'Las's forces. And what you see before you is the* Kir'Shara. *The original item, stolen from the Science Academy Museum and replaced with a forged duplicate.*" She nodded offscreen, and a moment later, V'Las's forger moved into view, escorted by Subdirector T'Syra. *"This is Sudok, who has confessed to the creation of the forgery. Vulcan Security is now in the process of gathering evidence that will verify his story."* She turned to Sudok. *"Please explain why the Kir'Shara was not destroyed."*

Sudok made no attempt to conceal the truth. *"Administrator V'Las tasked me with altering the text of the original artifact to conform to his own ideology. This would take years of meticulous work to achieve undetectably, but his intention was to reveal the alleged discovery of the genuine Kir'Shara after some years of Starfleet occupation of Vulcan, in order to create the perception that V'Las's doctrines had been Surak's all along."*

"Which would have discredited the Starfleet occupiers and the government they supported," T'Pol interpreted. *"And tricked the public into throwing their allegiance behind V'Las."*

"I believe that was the intention, yes."

It frustrated V'Las that he had needed to select a forger based on skill rather than loyalty to the cause. If he'd had two good hands, he would have killed the man before beaming away.

T'Pol continued: *"Do you give your word that this is the original Kir'Shara and that the recently discovered forgery was your own handiwork on V'Las's behalf?"*

"I do so affirm."

T'Faral was staring at V'Las with open scorn now. "You knew when you evacuated that they had possession of the *Kir'Shara*. You knew they would discredit you."

"It does not matter! Once we have pacified the capital, we will control all communications. We can tell the people whatever we wish."

"They will not believe you now. Why did you not destroy the artifact?"

"I knew there would always be some who believed it had

been genuine. I needed to prove to them that they should stand with me!"

"So you have jeopardized our entire coup for the sake of your pride. And now you would have your own loyal followers throw their lives away in an ill-advised assault that has already failed."

"Mind your attitude, Commander! You grow insubordinate."

"I grow disillusioned," T'Faral riposted. "For decades, I believed your way was right for Vulcan. I believed you wished to make us strong. Now I see you wished only to make us dupes for your own power." She drew her sidearm. "Administrator V'Las, I am placing you under—"

V'Las coldly fired the sidearm he had hidden in the sleeve of his robe. The burned wreck of T'Faral's body flopped to the deck a moment later. Others in her bridge crew rose in shock, but V'Las was pleased to see several others drawing their own weapons and moving to his support. At least there were some who still obeyed him.

"Now," V'Las said, turning to the flight controller, who warily eyed the firearms pointed at her head. "Set a course out of the system. Head for the nearest border of Federation space."

The flight controller wordlessly, grudgingly complied. He would have to find a suitable replacement among his loyalists, to maximize their chances of dodging pursuit until they were beyond Federation control. It infuriated V'Las to have to leave Vulcan to the Syrannite and human weaklings, but now there was no choice. The Federation had a number of enemies; somewhere there must be one who would give him a haven.

But I have come back before, V'Las told himself. *Vulcan is my home—and one day it will bow to me.*

27

June 11, 2165
U.S.S. Pioneer

"As nearly as we can tell," Malcolm Reed reported to Admiral Shran over the bridge viewscreen, "the captives have been awakened and have deactivated the Ware across the entire territory of the Pebru, including all the pre-warp planets they'd seeded. All Ware technology within the Pebru network has shut down except for basic functions like life support— fortunately, continuing the existing environmental conditions rather than reverting to some other default. A lot of Pebru are stranded in space right now, but they'll survive until they can be rescued."

Even relayed through *Tashmaji* and the subspace amplifiers the task force had laid on their way into this space, the signal from Starfleet Headquarters was low-resolution and noisy. Still, Reed could clearly see the disgust in the Andorian chief of staff's face and antennae. *"A better fate than they deserve, if you ask me."*

"I sympathize, Admiral, but in a way, the Pebru are victims as much as anyone else. They've been completely dependent upon the Ware since it first descended on *their* homeworld centuries ago. We sent you Doctor Liao's medical scans of the Pebru we captured: Without the prosthetic hands on their Ware-manufactured armor, their forelimbs barely have the capacity to handle tools."

"But they made others pay the price for the gifts the Ware gave them. That makes them no better than parasites."

"Their leaders, yes. But from what we gather, most of the Pebru had no idea of any of that. We've gotten reports in the past few days of Pebru being astounded and horrified to discover there had been living beings trapped in their Ware cores."

"Or so they claimed." Shran settled in his chair. "Unfortunately, the Federation has no jurisdiction there. It'll have to be up to their neighbors and victims to decide how to deal with their crimes."

Next to Reed, Captain sh'Prenni crossed her arms. "And under Federation law, we have an obligation to rescue the Pebru stranded by our efforts—even if it's just to deliver them to trial. The rest of the task force is working on that now, sir."

"Then I'm sure it will be done efficiently, Thenar." Shran turned back to the other captain. "But I'm sure you realize, Malcolm, that there's a deeper problem."

"Yes, sir. We still haven't found the original source of the Ware. And there's no evidence that our awakening protocol spread any farther than Pebru space."

"I can confirm that," sh'Prenni said. "*Kinaph* got a report from our Balduk friends: There are still Ware stations active on the other side of their territory." She smiled. "On the positive side, thanks to Mister Mayweather and the unwitting Mister Vabion, we now have a way to shut down the Ware. Collier's team is already working on a way to convert it into a signal we can transmit, although it may be difficult to punch it through the data cores' shielding. Failing that, we can always board the stations and program it into the interfaces manually. Either way, we have an effective weapon now—albeit a weapon that will restore life rather than taking it."

"Then your mission is clear, Captains. Once your repairs are complete, *you're to continue seeking the Ware's creators and doing what you can to neutralize their threat."*

"Yes, sir," Reed replied. "Our engineers are doing a fine job repairing our ships, and without any Ware assistance, I might add." He tugged on his uniform collar. "Albeit with a few parts cannibalized from their drone ships here and there."

Shran leaned forward with interest. *"Any significant technological advances I should know about?"*

"Unfortunately, not much of their technology is compatible with our systems, and some is based on principles we don't understand yet. Much of it is advanced molecular-level technology that's virtually inert without an active data core . . . animating it, for want of a better word. The engineers believe that further study could pay off in years to come, but in the immediate term, our best advantage is the awakening protocol." He sighed. "It's frustrating that we still have no answers to the questions we were sent to find. Why was the Ware created? Why does it function the way it does? There's still so much that doesn't add up."

"You're closer than you were before, Malcolm," Shran reminded him. *"And you've liberated over half a dozen species with a single blow. That's no small accomplishment."*

"Thank you, sir." But any pride Reed took in that achievement was tempered by the knowledge that it would not be easy for the worlds dependent on the Ware to adapt to its sudden absence. He trusted that the Federation would send relief missions, but it would tax the young nation mightily unless the task force could gain the support of more local allies.

"So what do you intend to do with this Vabion?" the admiral queried. *"Try him for hijacking Zabathu and threatening your personnel, or remand him to the Vanotli for his crimes against their world?"*

Reed traded an uneasy look with sh'Prenni before

answering. "Regrettably, sir, none of us have the jurisdiction to arrest him for his crimes on Vanot. Even Miss Zeheri was stripped of that authority. And Vabion made a persuasive case that we still need his assistance in rescuing the stranded Pebru and helping to restore basic subsistence to their society. We may even need his help in dealing with the larger Ware threat. Like it or not, he's spent longer studying the technology than any of us, and he's remarkably intelligent. Given how little understanding the Pebru have of the Ware, he's the best expert we have."

"Very well," Shran said, not looking happy. *"But I trust you'll keep a close eye on him."*

"No question, sir."

"Speaking of Vanot, by the way . . . what do you suggest we do about them?"

Reed frowned in thought. "We'll assess that once we arrive at their world. We'll be relying heavily on Miss Zeheri's judgment."

June 13, 2165
Stone Valley Hold, Vanot

Urwen Zeheri clasped Travis Mayweather's arm as they stood at the window of Najola Rehen's apartment, watching the plume of smoke that rose from the smoldering ruins of Worldwide Automatics' brand-new fabrication center. "I never knew exposing the truth would lead to this," she said. "Yes, the captives are free, WWA is broken, Vabion is gone, the Hemracine government is collapsing, and we no longer have cameras and microphones monitoring our every move. But to see rank and file Vanotli erupting into such violence . . ."

"They're entitled to be angry," Travis said, caressing her

shoulder. It was a relief to see him back in Vanotli disguise, looking "normal" again, even though she knew it was a lie. "What Vabion and the Ware almost did to your world . . ."

Her own reaction to his appearance shamed her. "It's not just anger, Travis. It's fear. Our world was . . . invaded . . . by something more alien than we ever imagined. Not just Underlanders but machines from space. To know that there's a whole universe out there now . . ." She shook her head. "We're used to guarding against danger from the sky. But storms and lightning are one thing. Knowing there are creatures out there with malevolent intentions . . . we aren't taking it well."

"Maybe the Federation could help. Show your people that we aren't all like that."

She shook her head. "We thought the Ware was benevolent. We wouldn't trust that promise again." She sighed. "We're a proud people, Travis. We need to solve our own problems."

He lowered his head. "I understand."

She glanced back into the next room, where Rey Sangupta was regaling Ganler with some of his adventures, which Ganler had dreams of turning into movie serials. Now that the reality of people from space was known, the young apprentice wanted to get in on the inevitable boom of space adventure stories, and maybe sneak in some subversive messages of tolerance for the alien to balance out the paranoid fantasies that would surely dominate the screen. It was quite a challenge to take on, but Ganler was confident that the verisimilitude he could get from Rey would give his scripts the edge they needed to succeed. Although Zeheri suspected that the human was embellishing his tales for the boy's benefit. Sky whales swimming in the atmosphere of a gas planet? Who would ever believe that?

Still, it was a relief that Ganler was even alive. She had feared for the boy when they had returned without Vabion to deactivate his explosive collar, but the release code Vabion had provided had worked. The man was ruthless in pursuing his goals, but it seemed he wasn't vindictive or gratuitously dishonest. Not much of a virtue, but at least it meant Ganler was safe. And with his ambition, he might end up as wealthy as Vabion one day—though Zeheri had far more faith in Ganler to use it wisely and with compassion. Especially with the example of Starfleet to aspire to.

"Maybe in a generation or two," she told Travis, "we'll be ready for you to return. At least some of us have learned that there are good people out there." She stroked his cheek.

The gesture made him fidget. "Urwen . . . I don't deserve that. You were right—keeping you in the dark only got you and Ganler into trouble."

"No, I was wrong. You only wanted to keep us safe, and you did. If you'd told us the truth, we wouldn't have believed you, and then we wouldn't have let you help us." She kissed him. "Don't ever doubt your good intentions, Travis. You saved our world—and many more."

He returned the kiss, making it last much longer. "I wish I could stay. Or that you could come with me."

She shook her head. "I'm one of the only people who knows what really happened. They need me here. There's even talk of installing me in the new government. Hopefully not too close to the top. I couldn't handle that much paperwork." Stroking his cheek, she went on. "And you need to find the source of the Ware and stop it for good."

"I know." He took her hands. "Still . . . *Pioneer*'s repairs won't be finished for another couple of days. I don't have to leave just yet."

Grinning, she pulled him toward the bedroom. "Tell them to take as much time as they need."

June 15, 2165
U.S.S. Pioneer

Mayweather found Charles Tucker in engineering, supervising one last set of calibrations to the warp core before *Pioneer* set out on its mission once more. "Right where you belong," he said by way of greeting.

Tucker studied him cautiously before replying. "Not for a while now," he said, making his way down from the reactor control platform so they could speak more privately. "But it's nice to be reminded."

"There could still be a life for you here, you know."

"There are a lot of reason why there couldn't," the older man replied. "But I'm kinda surprised you want me here."

"Are you kidding, Trip?" He remembered to whisper the last word. "You saved me."

"You saved yourself."

"Only after you woke me up."

Tucker looked away uneasily. "I almost didn't. We could've learned a lot more about the technology if we'd left you in there. Kept it running, taken control."

"But in the end, you trusted me. And you proved I could trust you." He clasped Tucker's shoulder. "I'm sorry it took me so long to figure that out. I understand now that there can be good reasons for keeping a secret."

"Maybe not good enough—not with the people who really matter."

Mayweather studied him. "Does that mean you're finally going to tell Hoshi you're alive?"

"I don't know, Travis," Tucker replied. "I'm not sure I could face Hoshi's wrath. You're a pussycat next to her, you know." They shared a laugh. "But seriously . . . if I can find a way to do it safely, I'll read her in. There's more than one kind of need to know."

Mayweather studied him. *Read her in?* He even talked like a spy now. "We'll never really get the band back together, will we?"

Tucker thought it over for a while, pausing to take in the soothing rumble and dancing lights of the warp core. "Nothing lasts forever, Travis. But that doesn't mean it stops being a part of us."

"No," Mayweather said, recalling those last two days with Urwen Zeheri. "I guess it doesn't."

28

June 10, 2165
U.S.S. Essex

BRYCE SHUMAR WAS GRATEFUL that the Deltans had been able to send a ship to rendezvous with *Essex* and take the liberated captives aboard. The intervening five days had been something of a strain on the crew, and particularly on Caroline Paris. The Deltans had done their best to respect the humans' psychological fragility and keep their sensuality to themselves; but it hadn't helped that the ex-prisoners had been mostly nude, and blithely unconcerned about that fact, when they were brought aboard *Essex*. Lieutenant Kelly, showing remarkable self-discipline as one would expect from such an accomplished Romulan War veteran, had ordered her security team ahead to clear the corridors, as much to distract her own people from the Deltans' allure as to minimize the crew's exposure. Still, glimpses had been caught, pheromones had been sniffed, and it had been a challenge to keep the crew's minds on their duties ever since. Of course Shumar had restricted the rescued Deltans to their guest quarters for the safety of the crew—but in the wake of their ordeal, the lot of them had been engaged in frequent and vigorous, well, stress relief, and the air filtration system had only been able to do so much with the resultant surge of pheromones.

Shumar had been ready to confine Paris to sickbay under constant watch for the duration, but his exec had shown a degree of restraint that surpassed even Kelly's. She'd admitted to him in private how deeply aroused she had been since the Deltans' arrival, but she had nonetheless managed to stay focused on her duties. He'd always considered Paris somewhat . . . relaxed in the discipline department, so this was something of a revelation, and Shumar felt he had done her an injustice. "Don't worry about it," she assured him. "I never was that disciplined before. Never needed it this much." Still, she said, her yearning for the Deltans wasn't as intense as she had feared. "I think it's because I don't . . . know any of them from before. I think the bond is something very personal. If I were reunited with Serima . . . I might lose myself again. But this—this is just physical. I can handle that."

As a result, Shumar decided to let Paris join him in greeting the crew of the Deltan vessel that finally arrived to pick up the rescuees. He was surprised to see that Prime Minister Mod'hira had personally come to recover them—and to extend her formal thanks to Shumar. "You have done us a great service, Captain," Mod'hira told him. "The people of Dhei are now twice in your debt. Three times, in fact, for our first meeting came when your people rescued our own." She lowered her head, then looked toward Shumar through her long eyelashes. "It would be a shame, I feel, if we were unable to be friends after such acts of kindness."

Shumar stammered and tugged at his collar until Paris nudged him in the side. "If our *peoples* couldn't be friends, she means."

"Ah. Yes, of course. Understood." He cleared his throat. "I agree, Prime Minister, yes." Finally he was able to remember what he'd been meaning to say. "In light of recent events, I think some sort of relationship—err, alliance between the Federation and Delta is worth pursuing, as a matter of security. That is, your security, as news of your, err, distinctive appeal becomes more widely known in the galaxy."

Mod'hira nodded. "And the security of others," she conceded, "if anyone should succeed in corrupting our gifts as the Orions intended to."

"Yes. Indeed. I'm glad you understand."

She gave him an indulgent smile. "Still—there are clearly obstacles that must be surmounted. Perhaps that burden lies on us; we will need to learn to restrain our behavior and attire in our interactions with younger races, to ensure that relations remain safely celibate."

"It's not all on you," Paris told her, not easily. "We could stand to refine our own regulations. Make sure we learn more about other species before we . . . fraternize."

"A shame that such restraint should be necessary," Mod'hira lilted, "but since it is, we show wisdom in accepting it. With care and delicacy, Captain—Commander—I believe our peoples can build toward a true friendship." She tilted her head, pursing her luxuriant lips. "Indeed, the concept behind your Federation is a compelling one. Perhaps, in time, when we are both ready, we will join you."

Trusting in his British reserve as an anchor, Shumar dared to shake her hand, refusing to be distracted by how soft and delicate it was. "When that day comes," he managed to say, "you will be welcomed."

Once Mod'hira and her retinue had left and *Essex* was free of Deltans once more, Shumar sagged—then glared at Paris when she laughed at him. "Don't worry about it," she told him. "We've all been there. I recommend a long, cold shower."

Shumar tugged down on his tunic hem. "Yes, well. You have the conn, Commander. I'll be . . . in my quarters."

* * *

June 11, 2165
ShiKahr

Soreth wandered the streets of the residential district, uncertain where to go. He'd been reluctant to return to the debate house, for V'Las's actions and those of the Vulcans he'd duped had forced Soreth to struggle with an unwelcome emotion: embarrassment. V'Las had said so many of the right things that Soreth and many other reasonable Vulcans had allowed themselves to be tricked into supporting a cause whose true agenda had been far more selfish and destructive. The self-styled champion of Vulcan logic and purity had proven himself as erratic, dishonest, and aggressive as any Andorian or human.

Worse, the *Kir'Shara* had been proven genuine after all, calling Soreth's convictions about melders into question. Could it be that he had been wrong to see their practices as a harmful aberration? Had the medical studies been as fraudulent as was now claimed? He could not believe that. Melding was so emotional, so inimical to proper Vulcan restraint and propriety. How could it be in keeping with Surak's teachings?

As he wandered into a public square, Soreth heard a familiar voice emanating from a large news screen: the voice of Admiral Jonathan Archer. Soreth had little wish to listen to a human gloating about the Federation's victory. Particularly this human, who did not have a reputation as a great orator. But soon he heard Archer refer to a familiar notion, and despite his preferences, he found himself listening to the admiral's words:

"My friend Doctor Phlox recently passed along an idea he heard a young Vulcan woman put forth: that the origins of wise words don't matter as much as their content. It doesn't matter where wisdom comes from, or

who said it first—because true wisdom comes from within. It isn't something carved in stone that we follow blindly; it's something we think about and arrive at through our own judgment. And that means that wisdom evolves as we evolve—as our circumstances change, as our needs change. The lessons of the past inform the present, but they can't be allowed to constrain our choices about the future.

"Yes, the Kir'Shara is real. Its words were written by Surak himself. But that doesn't mean there's no room for debate. Surak's words were the beginning of the conversation—not the end. For eighteen hundred years, Vulcans have been discussing and debating Surak's lessons, deciding how to apply them to their own lives, their own needs. And so they've interpreted those lessons in their own ways, sometimes disagreeing with each other about exactly how to apply them.

"But most of those disagreements were sincere and honest—not deliberate corruptions like V'Las attempted. Vulcans are different from one another, so the wisdom they discover in Surak's words—and in their own insights—will be different too. But you're all starting from the same place, with the same goals as Surak: a peaceful, logical, united Vulcan. So instead of dwelling on the differences between your views, I think the people of Vulcan should focus on the common roots of your beliefs, and on your common hope for peace.

"Maybe that's what Surak meant by 'infinite diversity in infinite combinations.' It's by listening to each other's diversity, contemplating others' wisdom as well as our own, that lets us add to our own wisdom, to apply it more broadly, more adaptably. The universe changes over time, and wisdom has to change with it.

"Surak could not have imagined the Federation. He never wrote anything that spoke of it directly, because it was beyond the limits of his experience. So only we can decide what the Federation means to us. But I'm willing to venture a guess that Surak would have approved of the Federation. Because it's the ultimate expression of diversity in combination. And the insights that we all bring—that we share with one another—enable us to discover more wisdom than we could on our own.

"So we shouldn't look to any single text, written thousands of years ago, as our sole source of wisdom. Those words are important; they should be remembered and contemplated. But wisdom comes from many sources. And we should be willing to listen to one another to discover them. Even those—perhaps especially those—who see the world differently than we do."

Soreth was impressed despite himself. There was some wisdom in Archer's words—though by his own admission, he had borrowed them from a Vulcan. A Vulcan with whom Soreth had disagreed emphatically, true—but perhaps that did not mean her position was unworthy of contemplation.

Yes, Surak had acknowledged the fundamental role of melding in Vulcan life—but he had also warned explicitly of its abuses. It had a role to play, perhaps, but a narrow one. It should be regulated and disciplined as strictly as emotion itself, kept private and not flaunted freely. Melders' abilities might not be anomalous, but the indulgence of them was still reckless and uncouth. The fallout of recent events would give melders more license to promote their eccentricities as the true word of Surak—but they had no more monopoly on their interpretation than had V'Las.

Soreth strode out of the square, setting his course resolutely for the debate house so he could share these new insights. The public might be reluctant to listen in the wake of V'Las, but he would find a way to divorce the message from V'Las's corruptions. For one thing, he would no longer speak out against the Federation. It seemed he had misjudged that institution, for it had made no effort to crack down in the days since the abortive coup, allowing the Vulcan government—its Syrannite allies, true, but admittedly not the puppets V'Las had claimed—to handle the restoration of order internally. And if Archer, the Federation's chief spokesperson, could speak with such respect and openness toward Vulcan culture, maybe there was hope for the humans yet. They might genuinely amount to something one day—provided they had Vulcans guiding them in the right direction.

"An excellent speech, Admiral," T'Pol told Archer once he had stepped down from the podium in the council chamber. "Admirably free of references to mammalian birthing procedures."

Archer sighed. "Are people ever going to let me live the gazelle speech down?" But his annoyance was as good-natured and humorous as he knew her teasing was.

Her reply was more serious. "After today, I think they might."

He caught her subtext, but he did not shy away from it now. "You know, I've been thinking," he said as they made their way from the chamber. "Going over what I said back in that bunker . . . about my responsibility for my own wake."

"You did not fail in your responsibilities, Admiral," T'Pol told him with appreciation. "To me or to anyone else."

He smiled. "I'm not saying I did. But there are bigger responsibilities. I've been dancing around it for years, insisting I'm just an explorer, but I have to face it: whether I intended it or not, my decisions have ended up shaping the fate of worlds. My actions contributed to the rise of the Federation, and that means I bear some responsibility for the decisions the Federation makes, the battles it has to wage to keep on the right track, whether against criminals like Garos and the Orion Syndicate or aspiring dictators like V'Las and Maltuvis. All of that is part of my wake, part of the impact of my choices. So if I want to be effective at managing the consequences of those choices, then I have to stop retreating from the level of responsibility that goes with them."

T'Pol's brows quirked in approval. "Then should I offer

congratulations on your impending promotion to Starfleet chief of staff?"

He gave her a sidelong look. "I'm taking the promotion, all right. But maybe you'd better offer condolences instead. Something tells me I'm in for a rough ride."

Epilogue

June 25, 2165
ShiKahr Residential District

SKON AND T'RAMA'S CHILD was the most dignified-looking baby Hoshi Sato had ever seen.

The newest addition to the S'chn T'gai family line of Clan Hgrtcha had been born more than a week before, but between Skon and T'Rama's adjustment to parenthood, the rebuilding of their home, the repairs to *Endeavour*, and Takashi Kimura's ongoing recovery from his injuries, this was her and Kimura's first opportunity to come visit the newborn child. But they hadn't come alone. Captain T'Pol, Phlox, and Tobin Dax— who had stuck around to assist in *Endeavour*'s repairs—had shuttled down with them to pay their respects to the family who had contributed and risked so much in the recent crisis. Iloja of Prim could not be with them, though; he was currently on a tour through Vulcan's major cities and districts, observing the people's recovery from the crisis with an eye toward composing an epic serial poem on the subject, and taking advantage of his new popularity as a public philosopher to make his own opinions emphatically known. The Vulcans were unaccustomed to such a frank, rude public speaker as Iloja, but maybe they sensed it was what they needed in the wake of the polite deceptions of the past.

The baby, conversely, was startlingly well behaved for a week-old infant, and it seemed to Sato that there was already a keen intelligence in his eyes. Though that was no surprise, considering his pedigree. With a mathematician, computer expert, and linguist for a father and a detective and aspiring diplomat for a mother, the boy would grow up with a wealth of opportunities for achievement and all the skills he needed to take advantage of them. She expected impressive things in the child's future. And she was glad that he would grow up on a Vulcan where he would have the freedom to pursue whatever goals he chose.

"My diplomatic career will have to be deferred for at least several years," T'Rama told her guests, "until our son has grown enough to gain a degree of independence. But I am young, and I should have decades beyond that in which to pursue diplomacy—if I do not decide to seek another path in the interim."

"I shall be here to assist in the boy's upbringing as well, of course," Skon said. "But in the short term, it will be necessary to divide my attentions somewhat. Now that the *Kir'Shara* is back where it belongs, I consider it important to complete my translation of it as soon as I am able. I believe recent events have given me new insights into Surak's intentions."

Kimura spoke from his wheelchair, still struggling with the words but determined to retrain his speech center through practice. "You mean . . . his lessons . . . peace, unity? Bringing Vulcan together?"

Skon looked surprised. "Yes, I suppose that is a factor as well. But I was referring to the birth of my son." He gazed down at the quiet but alert child. "I believe I understand now why we call Surak the father of all we became. History attributes him with no known mate or children, but his siblings had heirs, and he was the head of his House, giving him responsibility for his family. Some contemporaries claimed that he abrogated that responsibility when he went into the desert to seek enlightenment . . . but I believe he was driven by a deeper sense of obligation to his heirs and descendants. He recognized that the actions we take do not merely affect our own immediate concerns or our conflicts with our rivals in the here and now . . . but that every decision we make shapes the world our descendants will be born into. Thus, we have an obligation to base our choices on their needs, not our own wishes or whatever ill fate we wish upon our rivals."

"That's a lovely sentiment," Sato said, "but I have to admit, it doesn't sound very logical to me."

Skon considered. "Perhaps it does not. Logic is the means by which we find peace and wisdom. That does not make it the end in itself. Knowing that, I believe, will help me interpret Surak's writings more authentically now." He placed his hand on his child's brow. "And it has also inspired us to choose a name for our son. A cognate of Surak's name in the language of the nation whose nuclear weapon caused Surak's lethal radiation sickness, but whom he forgave in his final days. Though Surak did not live to see it, these people came to embrace his teachings fully and did much to spread them to the rest of Vulcan, in penance for their crimes."

T'Rama handed Sato a ceremonial banner she had made for the child, inscribed with his name in traditional calligraphy. "Choosing this name expresses our hope that our son will continue the family tradition and become a diplomat and peacemaker."

Hoshi studied the calligraphy for a moment and smiled. "Sarek," she said. "It's a beautiful name. And a beautiful sentiment."

"A reminder of what matters most to us all," Skon said, absently stroking Sarek's head. "I trust it will motivate me to continue working to build a better Vulcan for my son . . . and for his children."

"As will we all," T'Pol assured him.

"There is no doubt of that in your case, Captain," T'Rama said. "V'Las called you a traitor to Vulcan. But you have brought Vulcan with you to the stars, and to the Federation. You give us a voice where it is needed, no less than Commissioner Soval or Councillor T'Maran does." She tilted her head. "Perhaps one day you will consider a diplomatic career yourself."

"I had never considered that as an option," T'Pol replied after a moment's thought. "But there are always possibilities."

"I think you'd be a terrific ambassador, Captain," Sato said.

"Thank you, Hoshi."

"Don't believe her," Kimura quipped. "Just . . . wants you out of the way . . . so she can get big chair."

Sato, Phlox, and Tobin laughed, and though T'Pol did not, she smoothly replied, "Then she will have a long wait. I will not be going anywhere soon—except aboard *Endeavour*."

"We wouldn't have it any other way, Captain," Hoshi assured her.

Kimura turned to Dax. "How about you . . . Tobin? Done good work . . . fixing ship. Stick around?"

The Trill blushed. "Thanks, Takashi. I'm glad I could help. But . . . I just don't think I'm cut out for starship duty. Not in this lifetime, anyway." Sato frowned at the odd turn of phrase, but he went on. "And before you say anything, Phlox, it's not that I'm backing away from a challenge. I'm actually feeling kind of confident now after, you know, saving your necks and all." The non-Vulcans laughed again. "I actually want to find a worthwhile challenge. But I want something new. Something more than just engines and starships, something that'll give me new experiences, new memories to add to my store. Who knows?" he said, reaching out a finger to little Sarek, letting his tiny digits reflexively close around it. "Starting a family could be one hell of a challenge. Almost as big a challenge as finding someone who'd put up with me as a husband."

"What a marvelous idea!" Phlox beamed, clapping Tobin on the back and making him jump. The sudden movement annoyed Sarek, and T'Rama held him closer to comfort him. "Family is one of the worthiest challenges anyone can face. If you need a sample, why, come to Vaneel's wedding on Denobula! I'd love to introduce you to my entire extended clan. It will either convince you conclusively of the joys and benefits of having a family . . . or frighten you off of the idea altogether." Phlox cackled in anticipation.

"I'll, uh, think it over," Tobin said, tugging on his collar.

The small talk went on, but Hoshi found her attention drifting away from it. She let herself wander off, and Kimura soon followed in his wheelchair. She didn't mind; it was what she'd wanted. He'd always been good at reading her moods. Even his loss of perceptual clarity and advance planning skills hadn't cost him that—which told her a great deal. "Penny for thoughts?"

Standing by the reglazed windows to the rear courtyard, she studied the ornate fountain and the soothing shimmer of the water that cascaded from its multiple arms. "I was thinking about how happy—well, how serene Skon and T'Rama look with their baby."

"Happy. Vulcan or not—happy."

"I think you're right." Taking a deep breath, she turned to him. "Takashi . . . there's a question you asked a while back that I never answered."

He was very still. "Noticed that."

"I'm . . . not ready to leave Starfleet. Not for a while yet. There's still so much I believe I can contribute."

"Understand." He lowered his eyes.

She knelt in front of him. "But if you and I have to live apart, Takashi . . . then I want it to be clear that our lives are still intertwined. Inseparable. Takashi Kimura . . . yes. I will marry you."

He pulled her into an embrace with his one arm, and she felt tears of joy and anticipation—and maybe one or two more complex feelings—fill her eyes. It wasn't long before the others gathered around them, for they had not reckoned on Vulcan hearing and Denobulan snooping. "This is wonderful!" Phlox beamed. "Then you can come to the wedding, too! You and Vaneel can get married together! Denobulans love multiple weddings, you know!"

Hoshi promised him they would think about it. But she knew the actual wedding itself would be the least of the things she'd have to start planning for, now that she had chosen to spend her life with Takashi. She'd just committed herself to many new challenges and obstacles. It was almost as frightening a decision as it had been to join *Enterprise*'s crew fourteen years ago.

But those years in Starfleet had changed her. This time, she knew, she would face her fears without doubt or complaint. That was the only way to cope with the challenges ahead.

June 29, 2165
Pebru command ship

"You will make us strong again?"

"Not so loud," Daskel Vabion cautioned the Pebru administrator who watched over his shoulder as he delicately reconfigured the dormant control pathways of the Ware data core. "As far as our Andorian keepers know, I'm simply restoring minimal propulsion capability to allow you to maintain commerce between your colony worlds." Administrator Garep had already been told that by the Starfleet captain, of course, but Vabion had little faith in the Pebru's ability to retain information.

"But you are doing more."

"I am attempting to. But these Starfleet people are intelligent. It isn't easy to conceal the exploits I'm installing in the system. So you must be patient. What I need you to do is continue your act of desperation. Convince Starfleet that you're helpless without my assistance. That shouldn't be too difficult."

"Just finish soon," Garep said. "Make us masters of the Ware again and you will be rewarded. Fail, and you will not fare so well."

The Pebru's threat was rather feeble without the Ware-made armor and prosthetic limbs to give it a sense of power. Stripped to mere clothes, it looked like nothing so much as an overweight, short-legged monotreme that his university roommate had once kept as a pet. But even if the administrator had been physically imposing, Vabion would have been unconcerned. Once the Pebru had served their purpose, they would no longer be needed. He would have a Ware battleship at his disposal and would have taken the first step toward gaining full control of the technology. He would need to recruit a few . . . volunteers . . . to serve as organic processors in order to reactivate the full capacity of the system and access its higher functions. But there were plenty of Pebru around, and surely they were good for something. If Vabion believed in justice, poetic or otherwise, he might think it served them right to take a turn at last.

But instead, Daskel Vabion believed in practicality. He had a purpose: to acquire more knowledge, wealth, and power than any of the lesser minds that surrounded him. And now that he was no longer limited to a single primitive world, he had unprecedented resources to aid him in achieving it.

Vabion smiled to himself as he registered a subtle feedback pulse within the circuit. He was now one step closer to bringing the weapons under his control.

STAR TREK: ENTERPRISE
RISE OF THE FEDERATION
will continue

Acknowledgments

ONCE AGAIN, I'LL TRY to avoid repeating acknowledgments given in earlier volumes, aside from thanking Margaret and Ed at Pocket Books for continuing to hire me to do these things, and to my readers for their enthusiasm about seeing the Federation's early years chronicled.

Thanks to Cousin Cynthia for her input on the San Francisco Bay Area and the environs of Starfleet Headquarters, and to her and Aunt Shirley for the family genealogy discussion that led me to swipe two names from my ancestor Zadok Alonzo Bennett. And thanks to Marco Palmieri for reminding me that good villains are defined by the choices they compel the heroes to make.

The story of the *Kir'Shara* and the Vulcan reformation was related in the *Star Trek: Enterprise* episodes "The Forge," written by Judith and Garfield Reeves-Stevens, "Awakening," written by André Bormanis, and "*Kir'Shara*," written by Mike Sussman. The characters of V'Las (Robert Foxworth) and Kuvak (John Rubinstein) debuted in those episodes, which also introduced the younger version of T'Pau (Kara Zediker), a character who appeared in the original series episode "Amok Time," written by Theodore Sturgeon. The intervening events on Vulcan and elsewhere, including the alleged fate of V'Las, were established in the *Star Trek: Enterprise* novels *The Good That Men Do* and *Kobayashi Maru* by Andy Mangels and Michael A. Martin and *The Romulan War: Beneath the Raptor's Wing* and *The Romulan War: To Brave the Storm* by Martin.

The hundred-year war between the Vulcans and Romulans

was alluded to in *Star Trek: Voyager*: "Death Wish," teleplay by Michael Piller and story by Shawn Piller, but otherwise left mysterious. *Beneath the Raptor's Wing* alludes to a mentor of Soval's recalling the closing phases of the war, allowing a rough estimate of its timing.

The description of Skon and T'Rama's (later Sarek's) home is based on its depiction in the *Star Trek: The Animated Series* episode "Yesteryear," written by D. C. Fontana. The term "reasoning force" for the Vulcan civil police, the place name Dycoon, and the Sas-a-shar Desert come from Alan Dean Foster's novelization of "Yesteryear" in *Star Trek Log One*. Various details of the portrayal of ShiKahr and Vulcan culture and history are drawn from *Star Trek: Unspoken Truth* by Margaret Wander Bonanno and *Star Trek: Myriad Universes—Shattered Light: The Tears of Eridanus* by Steve Mollmann and Michael Schuster.

Tobin Dax's acquaintance with Iloja of Prim on Vulcan was established in *Star Trek: Deep Space Nine*: "Destiny," written by David S. Cohen and Martin A. Winer. Iloja's background was fleshed out in *Star Trek: Titan—Taking Wing* by Mangels and Martin. For Cardassian backstory I drew on *Star Trek: Deep Space Nine—A Stitch in Time* by Andrew J. Robinson, *Star Trek: The Fall—The Crimson Shadow* by Una McCormack (who was kind enough to answer my questions), and *Star Trek: New Worlds, New Civilizations* by Michael Jan Friedman, as well as canonical references in various episodes. Tobin's acquaintance with Skon was established in *The Romulan War* as well as the now out-of-continuity story *Star Trek: The Lives of Dax*: "Dead Man's Hand" by Jeffrey Lang. Skon was established as Sarek's father in *Star Trek III: The Search for Spock* by Harve Bennett. Skon's age is implicit from *Star Trek: Enterprise*: "In a Mirror, Darkly," written by Sussman.

In that episode, the Mirror counterpart of the *Star Trek: First Contact* character usually identified as Skon's father Solkar is murdered in 2063, yet Mirror Spock still exists in "Mirror, Mirror," so Skon was presumably conceived before that date. Thanks to the Memory Beta wiki for pointing this out. T'Rama's age is suggested in her debut story "A Girl for Every Star" by John Takis in *Star Trek: Strange New Worlds V*, which describes her as Archer's contemporary, and by her description as a young woman in *Beneath the Raptor's Wing*.

For Vulcan linguistics, I drew on the Vulcan Language Dictionary at www.starbase-10.de/vld and the Vulcan Calligraphy fan site at korsaya.org/vulcan-calligraphy/. For details on warp reactor anatomy, I'm indebted to The Enterprise Project at www.waxingmoondesign.com (and to its supplemental page on Facebook for the specifics of *Endeavour's* engine room) as well as the *Star Trek: The Next Generation Technical Manual* by Rick Sternbach and Michael Okuda. The concept that matter and antimatter cannot be mixed cold is from TOS: "The Naked Time" by John D. F. Black.

President Haroun al-Rashid was established in *Star Trek: Articles of the Federation* by Keith R.A. DeCandido; the remainder of his name and his appearance are my own extrapolation. Soreth is from my debut novel *Star Trek: Ex Machina*.

The Ware is my own name for the technology behind the automated repair station introduced in *Star Trek: Enterprise*: "Dead Stop," written by Sussman and Phyllis Strong. Thanks to Mike for answering my questions about the episode, and to the repair station's designer Doug Drexler for providing design artwork and insights. The Ware battleships are inspired in part by an unused design for the episode by John Eaves.

The movie Trip plays for Malcolm is the 1966 20th Century Fox parody *Our Man Flint*, directed by Daniel Mann and written by Hal Fimberg and Ben Starr. The described scene features James Coburn and Lee J. Cobb as well as Shelby Grant, Sigrid Valdis, Gianna Serra, and Helen Funai. The music was by future *Star Trek* composer Jerry Goldsmith, which might possibly cause the universe to implode in a paradox.

Abramson (with an "ah" sound) is one of the historical aliases of Flint in *Star Trek* "Requiem for Methuselah," written by Jerome Bixby. His Wilson Evergreen alias was established in *Star Trek: The Eugenics Wars—The Rise and Fall of Khan Noonien Singh, Volume One* by Greg Cox, and Jerome Drexel was from "The Immortality Blues" by Marc Carlson, published in *Star Trek Strange New Worlds 09*.

The Carreon and their history with the Deltans were created by Robert Greenberger in *Star Trek: The Next Generation—Gateways: Doors Into Chaos*. The *E.C.S. Horizon*'s encounter with the Deltans was established in *Star Trek: Enterprise*: "Bound," written by Manny Coto, and established as Earth's first contact with the race in my own *Star Trek: Department of Temporal Investigations—Watching the Clock*.

Alert readers may note that, in contrast to the first two volumes of *Rise of the Federation*, I have now begun incorporating some tidbits from *Federation: The First 150 Years* by David A. Goodman, such as Earth Cargo Services founder Davida Rossi and certain elements of V'Las's backstory (though I've interpreted it in my own way). Although Goodman's version of Federation history differs substantially from the Pocket novel continuity in certain key areas (mainly the major wars and the *Rise of the Federation* era), most of the rest is, in my opinion, compatible with the novels and offers the only currently available insights on certain aspects of Trek history. So I feel it's worthwhile to draw on the book's precedents where they're reconcilable and useful.

About the Author

CHRISTOPHER L. BENNETT is a lifelong resident of Cincinnati, Ohio, with bachelor's degrees in physics and history from the University of Cincinnati. He has written such critically acclaimed *Star Trek* novels as *Ex Machina* and *The Buried Age*; the *Star Trek: Titan* novels *Orion's Hounds* and *Over a Torrent Sea*; the *Department of Temporal Investigations* series including the novels *Watching the Clock* and *Forgotten History* and the novella *The Collectors*; and the *Enterprise—Rise of the Federation* series, so far including *A Choice of Futures* and *Tower of Babel*. His shorter works include stories in the anniversary anthologies *Constellations*, *The Sky's the Limit*, *Prophecy and Change*, and *Distant Shores*. Beyond *Star Trek*, he has penned the novels *X-Men: Watchers on the Walls* and *Spider-Man: Drowned in Thunder*. His original work includes the hard science fiction superhero novel *Only Superhuman*, as well as several novelettes in *Analog* and other science fiction magazines. More information and annotations can be found at home .fuse.net/ChristopherLBennett, and the author's blog can be found at christopherlbennett.wordpress.com.